JAMES W. NICHOL has been a prominent playwright in
Canada since 1970. *Midnight Cab* was inspired by his immensely
popular radio drama of the same name, broadcast on CBC,
Canada's national radio station. His adaptation of Margaret
Laurence's *Stone Angel* is currently revived in productions
across Canada. James W. Nichol lives in rural Stratford,
Ontario. *Midnight Cab* is his first novel. He is currently work-
ing on a second.

JAMES W. NICHOL

MIDNIGHT CAB

CANONGATE

First published in Great Britain in 2004 by
Canongate Books Ltd
14 High Street
Edinburgh EH1 1TE

Originally published in Canada in 2002 by Alfred A. Knopf,
a division of Random House of Canada Limited, Toronto

10 9 8 7 6 5 4 3 2 1

British Library Cataloguing-in-Publication Data
A catalogue record for this book is available on
request from the British Library

ISBN 1 84195 448 9

Text design: CS Richardson

Printed and bound by Creative Print and Design,
Ebbw Vale, Wales

www.canongate.net

FOR JUDI

Midnight Cab

CHAPTER ONE

• •

1995

Three-year-old Walker Devereaux is standing near a road, though he's too short to see it. Tall grass surrounds him, grass the tawny colour of a lion's mane in the late afternoon sun. Occasionally, cars swish by.

He holds onto a square of wire fence with all his might and stares through it towards more grass angling sharply up a hill, and silvery moss further up, and towering shelves of black rock.

"Hold on," she had whispered, "hold on tight." Her shadow over him, her dark hair descending, covering his face, her warm breath against his ear.

But he already was holding on, so tight the wire was cutting into his hands, so afraid of something or someone that he didn't dare shift his eyes from that square of wire, or the grass. And then she was gone.

The rusty wire turns his hands orange, the afternoon sun gets colder. He begins to sway. The hill bends over him, the tall grass marches by him like an army on the move, chattering, banners flying against the sky. Still he struggles to listen to the sound of the approaching cars, each one bringing his mother back, each one passing by.

And then one stops.

He hears the slam of a car door. His heart leaps but he can't turn to see, he's stuck to the fence by now. All he can do is cling there in the dusk and stare up the hill and wait.

A man's voice rings out. "I told you. Come on up here. Look at this."

He can hear the man rustling through the grass. A puffy red face bobs out of the gloom, suspends itself beside his ear.

"Let go of the fence, son," the red face says.

But he can't, even though he tries, so the man has to reach out and pry his fingers off the wire, one at a time.

"Jesus God," the man says.

• •

THAT WAS THE BEGINNING of everything, nineteen-year-old Walker Devereaux's first memory. He had been abandoned; not left in the care of a friend, or with the Children's Aid, or even in some bleak motel room, but dropped off at the side of a road like an unwanted puppy. And always the question, the aching question, *why?*

The bus lurched. Traffic began to slow down, an unbroken line of cars and campers and boat trailers, as weekenders tried to shoehorn themselves back into Toronto on a Sunday night.

Walker stared out his window. So many people, big-city people. He was already beginning to feel like a small-town dork.

He looked down at his worn jeans. He had a tear in the right knee, but in his case it wasn't a matter of fashion, it was just a tear.

He tried to stretch out his legs without touching the middle-aged woman crammed into the seat beside him. They'd sat there together for the better part of sixteen hours, unavoidably rubbing elbows from time to time but saying almost nothing. Once, she'd got out a Kleenex to dab at some tears. Walker hadn't known what to say, so he hadn't said anything. He'd assumed she was lonely, because he was lonely, for his adoptive family, for his friends. And for Cathy.

One thing about his family, they all stuck together. They'd thrown him a big party the night before, and there they were early the next morning—everyone but his mother and his three younger sisters hungover, heads pounding—standing bravely in the bright morning sun on the main street of Big River, waiting for the bus to pull in from Thunder Bay.

And when it did, all six of his sisters began advising him on how to survive in the big city, as if they knew, his three brothers-in-law shook his hand, and Gerard Devereaux, a forester all his life, a drinker all his life, stayed silent as usual amidst the female cacophony, but he looked straight into Walker's eyes as if he didn't expect to see him any time soon. Mary Louise Devereaux's arms were suddenly around his neck, and her lips were fiercely on his cheek and lips; his best friend Stewey helped him stow his duffel bag in the belly of the bus, and all his friends and family gathered around and said, good luck, Walker. Good luck!

But Cathy stayed away. He had known she would. One night, parked in his old truck, she'd said, "Walker, this doesn't have anything to do with me."

"You could come along," Walker had said, not really meaning it. "See the world."

"You stupid ass," she had replied, turning her face away.

He could have kissed her. He could have whispered, "I don't want to lose you." He could have smelled her delicious smell, mixed in with that perfume she was always dabbing behind her ears that drove him crazy, he could have drawn her to him one more time and cupped her breasts in his hands and murmured, "We can go, we can stay. As long as we're together, Cath, that's all I care about," and they would have steamed up the truck one more time. But he didn't. Because there was more to it than just his desire to see the world. He'd discovered something. Something he didn't want to tell anyone.

"I'm going, Cath," he'd said.

CHAPTER TWO

1 9 6 1

BOBBY RUBBED HIS NOSE on the screen in the window. It felt good. Comforting. Up and down. Up and down.

He could see his father sitting in the gazebo in the backyard. He couldn't see all of him, just his legs, the linen slacks so white they made Bobby's eyes ache. And then his father moved, crossing one enormous two-toned shoe over the other, the laces tied in looping bows, the white leather not quite as white as his slacks, the tan leather exactly the colour of his socks.

Far below him, Bobby could see his mother crossing the yard and climbing the fan-shaped steps towards his father. She was carrying a tray. Glasses shimmered, ice tinkled.

She stood there for a moment, her head cut off by the line of the roof, her body covered in flowers rippling on some diaphanous material that Bobby could see right through.

His father was working. He was always working. Most of the time he was somewhere far away, but sometimes he would work in the room downstairs that smelt like cigars, and Bobby would have to be quiet. Sometimes his father would sit outside.

Bobby could hear his mother's voice chattering away. Chatter, chatter. Finally she sat on the steps, her face looking smudged in the late summer light. She wasn't talking any more, she was just looking off somewhere. She started to rub her hand across her mouth, back and forth.

And Bobby continued to rub his nose gently against the screen, too. Back and forth. Back and forth.

His mother got up suddenly and, crossing the lawn again, she disappeared.

His father's legs remained white and motionless, the creases in his slacks sharp as knives.

Bobby pressed his face harder against the warm screen. It slit wide open with the softest of sounds. He climbed out onto the windowsill and sat there, wreathed in green leaves of ivy, his pudgy little legs in their bright yellow pyjamas suspended over the edge.

His father's long white legs still didn't move.

Bobby let go and fell through a long green ivy tunnel, hurtling towards the rock garden and the shrubs below. He walked across the grass towards the gazebo. And now his father got up and came to the top of the steps to greet him, and his tanned face broke into his famous smile, teeth as white as any movie star's, and he was amazed at his son, at his bravery, his indestructibility. Any moment now, he would pick Bobby up, and Bobby would be pressed against his rough cheek, the scent of his cologne and his body filling Bobby's head, sending him spinning off into safety, into drowsiness, into bliss.

Bobby was rubbing his nose raw on the screen. His father's legs hadn't moved.

Bobby touched the end of his nose with his finger. It hurt.

CHAPTER THREE

• •

WALKER HAD THE ADDRESS of a student hostel on Church Street. His plan was to stay there for a night or two while he found a permanent place; then, settled in somewhere, he'd look for work. He had two hundred dollars in cash in his wallet and two thousand dollars in traveller's cheques.

His mother had nearly fainted when he'd said he was going to clean out his bank account.

"For godsakes, don't take all that money. Open a bank account in Toronto and get them to transfer your balance. You'll be robbed and killed before you're even there a day!"

But Walker had insisted. He didn't want to wait for any banking rigamarole, he'd need eight or nine hundred dollars right away for first and last month's rent, and though he could sleep on the floor in his bedroll and eat in a restaurant for a few days, he'd need to buy some kind of bed soon, and a pot and a kettle and a spoon and a knife and....

"It's okay, Mom," he'd said, reaching out and putting his hand over hers.

An ancient Chinese couple, arm in arm, were walking across the intersection near the bus station. They didn't look at Walker. They didn't look at anybody. Walker was to learn over the next few days that city people rarely did, with the exception of hookers, panhandlers and lunatics.

"Could you tell me where Church Street is?" Walker asked.

The old lady pulled her bowlegged husband close and kept walking. The man looked up and, with a sudden toothless smile, jerked his thumb back over his shoulder.

"Thanks," Walker said.

He crossed and started walking in that direction, east, though he didn't know it. He strode along in a loose-limbed way, glad to feel the stretch of his muscles. The warm city air filled his lungs, smelling faintly, curiously, like fresh-baked bread. It hadn't occurred to him to ask whether Church Street was two blocks or twenty. He had just assumed that, wherever it was, it would be within walking distance. He'd tramped miles on ice-encrusted snowshoes, through alder thickets and over frozen marshes, doggedly following the trapline Gerard Devereaux liked to run for extra income. Walking through a city, no matter how far, had to be a cinch.

When Walker's final adoption papers had come through, the June before he'd turned thirteen, the Devereaux family had thrown a party. His little sisters had given him funny presents, like a can of split-pea soup because he was now half French Canadian (his father's side) and a box of tea because he was now half English Canadian (his mother's side). His oldest sister had presented him with a large blue knitted baby's bonnet; Walker had thanked her and pulled it down over his head. Everyone had given speeches, including, surprisingly, Gerard.

Now, passing the lighted store windows, Walker felt guilty. He'd been lying for weeks about why he wanted to go to Toronto, talking vaguely of getting away, seeing the larger picture, tasting independence.

The truth was, he'd come to Toronto to look for his real mother—the one who'd bent over him sixteen years before, the dark shadowy one, the undecipherable ghost who had whispered in his ear, "Hold on, hold on tight."

The summer before—the day after Walker had turned eighteen and gained the legal right to examine his file at the Children's Aid office in Sudbury—he and Stewey had climbed into Walker's rusty pickup truck and made the long trip down. It had seemed the thing to do. A kind of coming-of-age ritual.

The Children's Aid office was an old three-storey building of yellow brick with rows of small windows. A child's drawing of a cock-eyed house with puffs of smoke coming out of its chimney was taped to the glass front doors. Walker didn't recognize the building, though he knew he had been there at least once before, when he was three years old.

He recognized Heather Duncan, though, and she recognized him. He'd called the week before and she knew he was coming, but just the same she said she'd have recognized him anywhere. She was near retirement now—her hair had turned from brown to steely grey—but the sharp eyes behind her tortoiseshell glasses were the same, as was her vigorous hug.

He knew that they probably looked a little ridiculous to Stewey, since Walker, at six foot two, was a foot taller than she was, so her face was squished up against his chest. But Walker didn't care what Stewey thought; he hugged her back. She had been his worker all the years he was in care in Sudbury. He had climbed up on her lap, clung to her hand as she introduced him to new foster parents, and then other new foster parents—five foster homes in eight years.

"Why can't I stay with you?" he had asked, more than once.

"Against the rules," she'd said. "But don't worry, I won't let anything happen to you."

Which didn't turn out to be exactly true, because he got his head pushed down the toilet by some kids in the first place he went, and he got a belt buckle across the back from the foster dad in another, and he got pencils stuck up his bum by some girl going through a difficult puberty in a third. But he never told anyone, never. He just became incorrigible, and that was why Heather Duncan had to keep putting him in her car and moving him.

She did her best. She kissed him on the cheek. She gave him chewing gum. She was his best friend.

She even cried, when the Graziano family decided to move two hundred miles further north to Thunder Bay and, since they were the best foster parents he'd ever had, and since he hadn't gotten into any fights in school for most of that year, the Children's Aid decided that he should move up there with them. He was eleven years old and a ward of the Crown by that time.

Heather Duncan asked him if he really wanted to go and Walker thought about it for a minute, his young face pinched in deliberation. He thought of all the tiny bedrooms in all the different houses, all the cots and bunk beds, all the fear and fighting, the secret threats that he'd better be good or else, the drunken parties, the maudlin, blubbery kisses, the inscrutable adult comings and goings. He thought about not knowing what was going to happen to him from one moment to the next. He said yes.

Unfortunately, Mr. Graziano lost his job almost as soon as they arrived in Thunder Bay. One night he pushed his wife, who'd made the mistake of getting pregnant for the fourth time, right through the glass in the front door. There was blood all over. Walker was removed once again by the Children's Aid, sent this time to Gerard and Mary Louise Devereaux's home in Big River, a small town just south of Thunder Bay. It was the middle of winter, and the snowdrifts were higher than the roof of Heather Duncan's car.

Walker looked out the frosted window towards his next new home. It was a tall old clapboard house, painted white, and in front of it was a circle of three snowmen of diminishing sizes, with a fedora, a baseball cap and a cabbage stuck on top of their respective heads. They looked for all the world as if they were engrossed in some very important conversation. Walker, clinging to an old cardboard suitcase full of his clothes, toothbrush and comic books, allowed himself to risk a smile.

Now Heather Duncan was on the phone, calling someone to come downstairs. She was saying that Walker Devereaux and friend—and here she paused to give Stewey a professional onceover, as if deciding whether he was a good influence or not—had just arrived from Big River.

She gave Walker a pat on the cheek and told him it would be worth his life not to drop by her office before he left, because she was going to take them both out for dinner that night. Walker said that sounded good to him, Stewey agreed and, with that, Heather Duncan turned and disappeared down the hall.

"She's friendly," Stewey allowed.

Walker fished cigarette papers out of his pocket. He was feeling more anxious than he'd thought he would.

Stewey knew all about Walker, all Walker could tell him, anyway. They had become best friends not long after Walker arrived at the Devereaux's, when Stewey and his gang jumped him after school and Stewey sat on his back stuffing snow down his collar, cheerfully announcing that he was going to knock his brains out.

Suddenly, and Stewey could never figure out quite how, he was no longer on top of this skinny raven-haired kid, but on the bottom, and a small, hard-knuckled fist was descending at the speed of light towards his face.

As blood started to gush from Stewey's nose, Walker was up and running, breaking through the ring of astonished kids, racing down the snow-packed road like a jewel thief, heading back towards the Devereaux's place.

For two weeks Stewey issued dire threats. What he wasn't going to do to Walker wasn't even worth thinking about. He was going to smash his head with a baseball bat, he was going to break both his arms, he was going to cut off his pecker and feed it to Harvey

Chester's dog. But there was something about the way Walker just walked on, his slight body both loose and taut as a steel spring all at the same time, and the way that, when Stewey and his gang got in front of him so he couldn't walk by, he wouldn't look away either, but held his gaze steady into Stewey's bright blue eyes, that both frightened and attracted Stewey. But mostly it was the silence that attracted him, the profound stillness that seemed to wrap itself around Walker, as if he were walking in some other place, existing somewhere else, even when he was standing right in front of you.

So one day, instead of threatening him or giving him a tough-guy look, Stewey just said hi, and Walker said hi back. And a day or two later they found themselves beside each other leaning up against the old board fence at recess. They didn't say anything but they didn't move away either. And then one day they walked home together and Stewey told Walker how much he hated his father, because his father had a girlfriend in Terrace Bay and everybody knew it except his mother. Walker nodded and said, "That stinks." And they became friends.

The person Heather Duncan had called, who was now coming quickly down the staircase, turned out to be the guardian of the inactive client files in the Sudbury district. She also turned out to be only a few years older than Walker and Stewey, and the possessor of long reddish hair, wonderfully round brown eyes and a pert body residing quite splendidly, at that moment, in a soft yellow pantsuit.

Stewey's freckled face and bright red hair went one shade brighter as he introduced himself to Carolyn McEwan as L.H. Stewart, test pilot and well-known philanthropist from Big River. She smiled warmly, almost laughed, and asked if they would like to follow her.

"I would," Stewey said.

They followed her up to the third floor, while she turned back every two or three steps to ask how their trip had been, and what Big

River was like, and whether they were getting any rain up there this summer, because the bush around Sudbury was so dry.

Walker knew she was turning around because she realized that, between turns, two pairs of eyes were fixed like laser guns on her rear end, which was making her self-conscious. He liked her for that. He winked at Stewey and his heart lightened a little, his legs felt less wooden, the rolled smoke in his damp hands—which he knew he couldn't smoke in there—felt a little less desirable.

There couldn't be anything of much significance in his file. The police had searched for his parents or anyone who knew him for months. No, for years, or so he'd been told by Heather Duncan.

His picture and description had been sent to every police organization and every likely agency across Canada. It had been sent to the FBI and circulated by them through the United States. For all he knew, it had even been given to Interpol. But nothing had come back. No one frantically searching for, or even mildly interested in, this three-year-old kid who referred to himself by the improbable name of Walker, and who said his mommy had left him.

Carolyn ushered them into a long, narrow office filled almost to overflowing with a boardroom table, eight wooden chairs and five rows of metal filing cabinets.

"Sit down, guys," she said. She picked up two file folders, one new and thin, the other old, thick and dog-eared. She put both files in front of Walker and sat down opposite him.

Walker's heart started to pound. There's nothing in there, he reminded himself. He'd only come to confirm that there was nothing in there.

"How are you feeling, Walker?" Carolyn asked.

"Fine. Why?"

"Just wondering. Sometimes people feel a little anxious when they learn the specifics about their birth parents and what kind of environment they came from. But"—she looked genuinely sympathetic, and started to roll a pencil nervously in her hand—"this is the most unusual file I've ever encountered."

"Why's that?" Walker said.

She glanced at Stewey.

"Flash and I are buds," Stewey assured her. "Right, Flash?" Stewey had been calling Walker "Flash" ever since Walker had gotten a breakaway in a peewee tournament in Schreiber six years before and had tripped over the other team's blue line.

Walker nodded.

Carolyn smiled at Stewey, and he began to glow again.

"This file"—Carolyn tapped the bulging old file with her pencil—"I don't think it's going to interest you too much, but you can certainly look through it. It's full of our standard client reports on how you were getting along at your various foster homes and at school, and a lot of notes back and forth from teachers. And a few encounters with the police. For fights. You did seem to get into a few of those, didn't you?" She glanced up at Walker's face, high-cheekboned and handsome except for his nose, which was flattened and pushed off to the side.

Walker grinned at her. "Not a fight. A hockey stick."

Flushing a little, she hurried on. "There's all the paperwork around the wardship with the Crown. And the transfer up to Thunder Bay. But the personal items and the items that have to do with how you first came into care, I thought you'd be mainly interested in seeing those, so I transferred them into a smaller file." She tapped the brand-new file with her pencil.

"Personal items," Walker repeated, feeling his throat tighten. He wasn't sure he wanted anything to change. He'd gotten used to things as they were. There were certain advantages to having a past as strikingly desolate as a blank piece of paper. You could write anything on it you wanted, and through the years he had. Maybe he was the child of some mafiosa woman from New Jersey who wanted her child to grow up safely away from a family vendetta. Or maybe he was the kidnapped heir to some European fortune. Or maybe—taunted for years for being the bastard son of a drunken squaw because of his crow-black hair and dusky complexion—he was part native, scion of proud warriors. Or maybe, like Superman, he had been sent here by his loving parents from some doomed planet, except that he hadn't discovered any special powers. Or maybe....

Carolyn was looking at him in that caring, worried way again, a way that seemed to have more to do with her temperament than her profession. "Maybe I shouldn't have said personal items," she explained. "There are only two things here that I guess you could call personal. It's mainly information about how you were found and the efforts the police made to determine who you were. There's a summary in here that the Ontario Provincial Police submitted to our director. After they, um...."

"Gave up?" Walker offered.

"Yes. Walker, you understand that there's no way I can help you locate your birth parents. I'd like to but I have no information at all. I've had two cases where a newborn was left somewhere and the mother was never located. What makes your case so unusual is the fact that you were three years old."

"More or less. Heather told me, when I was older, that I didn't know my birthday. So they picked one out for me. July first."

For the first time, Stewey seemed uncomfortable being there. He started examining his well-chewed fingernails.

Carolyn opened the new file, picked up a folded letter sitting on top of the other papers and handed it to Walker. As she did, a small colour photograph fell out of the letter.

"Oops," she said.

Walker looked at her. She shook her head. "The police had both these things. They didn't lead anywhere."

He picked up the photograph. Two little girls were floating on a lake, one holding onto an inner tube, the other riding on an air mattress. They looked not much more than three years old themselves.

An attractive woman was standing waist-deep between the girls, one hand resting on the inner tube, the other on the shoulder of the little girl straddling the air mattress. The woman's hair was tucked under a white bathing cap and she was dressed in a black one-piece swimsuit. She was smiling at the person standing in deeper water, taking the picture. Behind them—quite a distance behind, because they seemed to be standing far out in the lake—small muddy waves rolled up on a sandy beach.

Above the beach and to one side of the picture, a steep sand cliff fringed with pine trees threw a shadow across the water. On the other side, a low-slung, reddish log cabin with a screened-in porch clung to some parched grass. There was a flagless flagpole standing in front of it, and closer to the water a huge round boulder, painted bright white, protruded from the sand.

"There's something on the back," Carolyn said.

Walker turned it over and read, written in pencil, "Mary's Point. June 2, 1964."

"Flash," Stewey whispered, peering over Walker's shoulder, "maybe that's your mom."

Walker's eyes stung. He turned the photo over again. The smiling woman's face was blurry now.

Walker did the math. He had been born sometime around 1976, so this was twelve years before. The woman looked, at his best guess, in her mid-thirties, so she would have been about forty-seven when he was born. Was that possible, to have a child at forty-seven?

"I don't think she's your mother," Carolyn said gently. "If you read the letter."

Walker's fingers felt as though they belonged to someone else. He unfolded the paper. The letter was written, not too neatly, with a blue ballpoint pen.

Sept. 15/79

Dear Lennie,

Fab news! I can't wait!!

Guess what I found? Aren't we cute? Do you think he looks like you? Only prettier? I'm kidding. But I bet he's sooo sweet. Like his father, right? And I'm still a virgin! I can't believe it! And I tried really hard this summer, too!! But anyway, you'll be here soon, with your two men. I've already bought him a present, the little one, I mean. I guess you look after the big one, right??? I hate keeping a secret, but I swear to god I've kept my mouth shut, I really have. For three years!!! Some kind of record!

This is going to be really short, 'cause I'm just on my way to the Bridge and I'm already late. Call as soon as you get in, or if you can't call, send me a message by passenger pigeon, something! Dying to see you! Dying to see *everybody*! The big bird, toto. Fab!

Your best and forever friend,
Love, love, love, love,
Kim

Walker looked up at Carolyn. "Where did they get this?"

"It was in your pocket when they found you. The letter and that photograph, according to the police notes. But unfortunately, that was all there was."

"Let me see," Stewey said, tugging on one corner of the letter.

Walker let it go and turned back to the photograph. He wasn't interested in the woman now, but in the two little girls. The one clinging to the tube was half turned away, her dark wet hair sticking in strands to her face and her bare shoulders. The other one, wearing a yellow polka-dot swim cap and a frilly yellow swimsuit, was smiling straight at the camera.

"These little kids look about three, I guess. So if one of them is my—my mother"—Walker was figuring out dates again—"and this picture was taken in 1964...."

"She would have been about fifteen when you were born," Carolyn said.

"Jesus."

Stewey leaned over to look at the picture again. "Which one do you figure?"

Walker felt ridiculous looking at the two little girls as if they could give him any satisfactory answer, let alone heal the black hole opening up inside him. It had been a big mistake to come here. He felt worse than he had in years. He felt lost all over again.

He looked at Stewey. "I don't know," he said.

•   •

WITHIN A FEW MINUTES, Walker arrived at the street he was looking for. He checked the street numbers, determining which way he should turn, and headed south on Church towards the student hostel. It wouldn't be long now, he was thinking. It would feel good to stretch out on a cot and get some sleep. He'd look for a place to live tomorrow, and he'd have to find a job.

Church Street turned out to be deserted at this hour on a Sunday night. He walked past a row of pawnshops, bars across their windows, a store advertising that it bought and sold jewellery, and another that had a huge pile of used computers for sale behind its dusty windows.

Between two of the stores, in a dark doorway, he noticed a cardboard sign that announced, in large red letters, "Apartment For Rent"; in the white space below, someone had scribbled, "Apply Within."

He looked above the pawnshop to the second floor of the old building, where two windows were almost hidden under ornate and rotting wooden eaves. He could hear pigeons cooing somewhere up there, but it was so inky black that he couldn't see them. Both the windows were dark.

He looked around. Almost directly across the street, a massive church loomed up over the trees.

I'll tell Mom I'm living near a church, he thought, smiling to himself. She was the church-goer in the family.

Mary Louise had known about his trip to Sudbury the summer before, of course. She'd encouraged him to go, because he needed to see that there really was nothing to see, nothing new to learn—to put all that behind him, finish high school, go to college, focus on the future. And her expressive grey eyes had shone on Walker with absolute certainty of his great future, as if, by the force of her own will, she could cause the gods of fate to submit to anything.

When he'd returned home, he'd sat at the kitchen table and told her and the whole family about his and Stewey's adventures, about going through his file with Carolyn McEwan and going out to supper that night with Heather Duncan.

He had told them about the police reports—that when he was found beside a secondary road off Highway 69, ten miles south of the French River, he was wearing brand-new clothes, all with U.S. labels; that he referred to himself as Walker all the time, so they had to assume that Walker was his first name; that, though he didn't say much else, he did keep repeating that his mommy was coming back for him, and he kept asking where his daddy was, and at night he cried out once or twice for what sounded like "Anna" or "Nana."

As to the letter and photograph found in his pocket, the reports said that though a concentrated effort had been made to identify these people and locate Mary's Point, the two items had not proved helpful, and that though they'd circulated Walker's picture and description both nationally and internationally, they'd received no inquiries or leads.

"We will continue to keep this file open, but regretfully, I have to report that no new information has come to light on this individual since the day he was found." This last from Inspector John Hayes of the Ontario Provincial Police, in his report to the director of the Sudbury Children's Aid Society in 1983.

The Devereaux family had sat at the kitchen table, passing around the letter and the photograph and, it seemed to Walker, sending awkward little glances his way. He knew they felt both pity and concern for him, so he joked that maybe he had been conceived by divine intervention, because his mother had been only fifteen years old. But to be teased by such elusive echoes of the past—who could smile at that?

Walker walked along Church Street, and once again thought to himself (for this statistic had become very important to him, and he kept turning it over in his mind, as if there might be some way to get around it) that there were almost three million people living in Metropolitan Toronto.

Three million people. And amongst them he had to find a woman called Kim, a woman who would be thirty-four years old by now. Because one night, sprawled across his bed and reading that letter for the umpteenth time, something that had always puzzled him had jumped out of hiding and stared him straight in the face.

"The big bird, toto." He had never been able to make any sense of that, so naturally it was the passage he'd puzzled over the most.

Lennie, who must be his mother (was her name Lenore? he wondered), had clearly hoped that the letter and the photograph would help the police identify him. But if that was her intention, why such vague clues? The police, according to their reports, hadn't found them helpful.

They did mention finding a Mary's Cove near Parry Sound, even dispatched a policeman to look for the cottage in the photograph, but it turned out, after a long boat ride, that Mary's Cove was an isolated, unpopulated and rock-choked bay.

They also noted that there were all kinds of unofficial names local people gave to beaches and coves and, yes, points of land, thousands of place names all through the north. They simply didn't have the manpower to cover them all.

But nowhere did the police mention puzzling over "The big bird, toto."

So was Kim literally referring to a big bird named Toto? Was his mother, this ghost (whose face he could not remember, no matter how hard he tried; only her dark hair, the feel of her breath, the words she'd spoken), supposed to arrive with not only her two men in tow but a parrot perched on her shoulder? Not likely.

Did Kim, the letter writer, mean *in toto*, which was Latin for "altogether," not that Walker had ever taken Latin in school but somehow that phrase had popped into his mind one night and he'd looked it up. "The big bird, altogether." Was that his mother's nickname, the big bird, and was Kim just saying she was glad they'd be united again? Certainly that seemed in keeping with the tone of the rest of the letter. But it also seemed a stretch. If she'd meant *in toto*, why hadn't she written *in toto*? Part of the problem was Kim's writing. Penmanship had obviously not been her strong point.

Walker had stared hard at the word *toto* until, like a small miracle, he'd actually seen it.

It wasn't one word at all. The first "o" and the second "t" didn't really join, they just kind of bumped into each other. It was two words, "to" and "to." And once he looked at them separately, he could also see that the cross on the second "t" was slightly higher than the one on the first, and the second "o" a little larger than the first. They were meant to be capitalized. "The big bird, to TO." That was what she had written. Torontonians habitually referred to their city by its first two letters. Even Walker knew that.

His mother and father had been planning to fly to Toronto some-time soon after Kim wrote that letter. He'd been found nineteen days later, on October fourth.

Walker looked once more at the two little girls in the photograph. The one continued to smile back at him. The other, her dark, wet hair obscuring her face, continued to turn away. Suddenly, Toronto was where Walker had to go.

• •

FADED GOLD LETTERS ACROSS a pebbled glass door on Church Street announced: International Student Hostel Association, Canadian Branch.

Walker lay on a cot in a dank-smelling room, his wallet and a bank envelope containing two thousand dollars' worth of traveller's cheques under his pillow, his old hockey duffel bag of clothes on the floor beside him. He tried to make out the colour of the ceiling. He tried to follow all the cracks that cobwebbed the plaster above him. He listened to the laboured breathing of his fellow travellers, three dark shapes under light blankets on either side of him. He tried to think of nothing at all.

He closed his eyes. His body felt as if it were still riding on the bus, as if it were rocking a little this way and that. The room began to spin slowly.

He strained to hear his mother's voice. Did she sound frightened? Angry? Or sad? Or resigned? Or relieved to be getting rid of him?

He could still see her—not her face but her shadow, her hair brushing against his face—feel the warmth of her breath on his ear. But the tone, the inflection of her words, would not come clear. It was as if, on that day, he knew what she was saying but refused to listen, refused to accept what was happening to him, and so lost her tone of voice. Lost her and lost her voice at the same time.

Walker was on the edge of sleep now, just drifting, yet still asking the same old question, *why?* If his mother had loved him, as the letter seemed to indicate and as the police reports suggested too—"well-kept child, new clothes, perfect health"—and if she had stuffed the letter and photograph in his pocket in a desperate hope that someone would identify him, then it had to mean she did not want to leave him there, had not planned to leave him there. And since she was there with him (he knew she had been there, he knew that woman had been his mother, he had not doubted this from the day he was found), why hadn't she returned? What mother separated from her child, a child she loved, wouldn't scream and bite and cry out to the world to recover him?

So now another question, more frightening than the first. Not only "Why?" but also "Who stopped you from coming back, what happened to you?"

And Walker drifted down, reaching out for a ghost, two ghosts: a dark-haired child clinging to an inner tube, and a woman with words but without a voice.

CHAPTER FOUR

1968

BOBBY REACHED UP AND FLICKED the middle switch, turning the lights on in the cellar. He had been waiting to do this all day, watching the hour hand of the clock in his grade-five classroom inch excruciatingly along a 180-degree arc from nine to three. But now he was back home, alone in the house. He had made himself a peanut butter sandwich, spread it slowly and eaten it even more slowly, to build up the anticipation. He was in control now.

Father was in his counting-house, counting out his money. Mother was out somewhere too, spending it. Or visiting her friends. Or doing good works of one kind or another. She didn't like to stay home during the day, rattling around in that huge house, as she put it. And it was the maid's day off.

Bobby walked down the warped, uncarpeted wooden stairs into the dingy cellar. His father had not finished the basement, as a lot of other kids' families had, with TV rooms and games rooms, fireplaces and bars. He didn't even call it a basement, but referred to it as "below." And he thought the fourteen rooms situated above ground should be adequate for anyone. So all there was down there was the laundry room, the pickle room, though there were no pickles or other preserves in sight, an enormous old coal bin sitting beside a large and relatively new oil furnace, and a series of storage rooms. A few of these rooms were crammed with cardboard boxes and discarded furniture; the one nearest the back set of stairs had the extra fridge and freezer in it.

Bobby walked along the narrow hallway that ran the length of the cellar, flicking on lights as he went, until he reached the last door.

He could hear them already. What were they saying? He pressed his ear against the peeling paint and listened. Who could tell? It was a foreign language. But they must be discussing him. Who else did they have to discuss? Did they make fun of him? Did they snicker behind his back? Hate him?

Bobby opened the door and flicked on the light.

The mice seemed to blink in the sudden glare, caught on their wire wheels and wire ladders and in the water trough and in their food trough, upstairs and downstairs and, yes, even in the basement of the elaborate coop that Bobby had built with his own hands.

They spun around to face the open door, all their pink noses and black diamond eyes pointed at Bobby.

This was Bobby's counting-house, his City of Mice. Bobby was the boss here, just as his father was the boss at The Plant, as he called the series of Dickensian brick buildings he owned down by the lake. No matter what the mice thought as they scurried through the sawdust and tumbled over each other, Bobby had all the power here. Bobby was in charge.

He closed the door and sat down on a folding bridge chair he had salvaged from one of the other storage rooms. He'd have to fetch them water soon. And feed them. Maybe change their sawdust. He could see it was soaked through in places and covered with little flecks of black shit. But for now, Bobby just sat there and stared at them.

When he had first built the coop out of odds and ends, and populated it with a dozen white mice and shown it to his father, his father had smiled.

"What is it?" his father asked.

"A city of mice," Bobby replied.

His father reached out and pulled Bobby into his body, so that Bobby's face pressed painfully against his belt buckle. He rubbed Bobby's head as if he'd just scored a goal.

"A clever boy, to build this by yourself," he said. And then, almost as an afterthought, he said, "You're a mouse, too."

Bobby looked up at his father, hoping to see another smile, but only the familiar shadow of disapproval passed over his father's face.

"Don't spend too much time down here," he said. And he went away.

But Bobby did spend a lot of time down there. He watched the mice fuck. He watched them have babies. The frantic mothers always buried their pink clusters of children deep in the sawdust. And often, an excited mob pressed in and snatched the children away. They tore at the tiny bodies, they dragged them around, they ate them.

Bobby began to study the mice more closely. Soon he could see that they were all different. He began to call them by name.

Some were more timid than others. Some tried to stay off by themselves. Some were wildly promiscuous. And some were bullies, stronger than the others, bowling them over and biting their tails, sitting in the food trough, growing fat, shitting wherever they pleased.

Over the past several days, one mouse in particular had begun to think he was the king of the City of Mice. He swaggered about, going anywhere he wanted in the house, upstairs, downstairs, pushing the others off the wheels and ladders, as if he had all the power. Bobby had been thinking about him all week. And each day the excitement inside him built, and the tightening anticipation. And now it was time.

He had done this before. He would always have to do it. Being master of the City of Mice, there was nothing else he could do.

Bobby got up and opened the upstairs door of the coop, and with a quick reach in he snatched up the offending mouse. He held him firmly in one hand and stroked the pink belly with the middle finger of his other hand. He pressed more firmly and he could feel the mouse's pulse beating under his finger, its blood ticking, ticking.

Arnold looked up at him—that was the name Bobby had given him—his black bead eyes staring into Bobby's.

Breathless with excitement, Bobby stood on his chair, reached up and flipped a piece of string off the rafter where he had hidden it. It dangled above the City of Mice, one end tied to a nail, the other end with a loop in it, swinging free.

Bobby slipped Arnold's head through the noose he'd used several times before, and tightened it around Arnold's neck. And then he let Arnold go.

Arnold jerked and squealed and twisted, trying to climb up the string, falling back, choking, swinging in the air.

And Bobby stood there, transfixed, watching him.

CHAPTER FIVE

• •

A T NINE-THIRTY THE NEXT MORNING, Walker was standing in front of the heavy wooden door beside the pawnshop. The Apartment For Rent sign was still taped to it.

He tried the door but it was locked. He stepped back to look up at the building again. It didn't look quite as promising as it had in the dark. He could see that a rusty piece of eavestrough dangled down and streaks of pigeon dung, like random brush strokes, decorated the red brick and festooned the two windowsills. The culprits dozed by the dozens up on the edge of the tin roof. Cracks in the glass had been repaired with jagged lines of white hockey tape, and one pane had been replaced by what looked like the side of a cereal box.

"What's the problem?"

A tiny, unshaven man wearing a beige windbreaker two sizes too big for him, his glasses perched on the end of his nose, was opening the pawnshop door and peering over his glasses at Walker.

Church Street was much busier now. Cars and delivery trucks and cabs were bumper to bumper, fighting for room to manoeuvre on the narrow street. Horns honked, exhaust fumes filled the air, a gust of wind blew old newspapers and discarded cigarette packs along the sidewalk.

"Nothing. Just interested in that apartment, but they say apply within and the door's locked."

"If that door was left open, you know what would happen?"

"No."

"You don't want to know. I don't want to know. Drunks, drugs, hookers, bums. You want to rent an apartment?"

"Yeah."

"Come in here. Come in," the man said, disappearing into the store, switching off the beeping alarm system and switching on the lights in three different locations.

The store was piled to the ceiling with everything anyone might be inspired to hock, from stereo equipment to ornate brass lamps, from microwaves to swords and muskets, and electric guitars hanging from the ceiling.

The man walked behind a long counter with a glass top that covered coin sets and watches and jewellery and knives of all kinds. He took off his windbreaker slowly, hung it up on a wooden halltree and turned back to Walker.

"Apply Within means in here," he said. "I've got two nice apartments, as it happens, available right this minute."

"That's great," Walker said.

The man took off his glasses, pulled out a clean white hanky and polished the lenses. In all his life, Walker hadn't actually seen anyone do that, except for characters in old black-and-white movies.

"I've got a one-bedroom, I've got a bachelor."

"Well, I guess all I need is a bachelor."

"You're all alone then?"

"Yeah."

"Employed?"

"I just got in last night. I'll be looking for work today," Walker said, looking steadily at the man.

The man put his glasses back on. Walker guessed his age to be somewhere close to sixty; his hair was grey and thinning. Sorrow lines, that was what his mother called them, cut deeply into his face.

"You're an ambitious boy?" he asked.

"I'll work at anything."

"Can you afford five hundred and fifty a month, eleven hundred up front for first and last month's rent?"

"Sure."

"When?"

"Right now. And I'll have a job in a week."

The man looked at Walker for another long moment, looked him up and down, the worn old hockey bag over his shoulder, his black hair falling carelessly over his forehead and over the collar of his jacket.

"If I can't find work, you'll still have the last month's rent," Walker added hopefully.

The man smiled just a little, and nodded.

After signing over eleven hundred dollars' worth of traveller's cheques, Walker had nine hundred left, plus about another eighty in his wallet. In return, he was the proud owner of two brass keys, one for the street door, the other for his bachelor apartment, which turned out to be the room at the front of the building with the two high, narrow windows under the eaves.

This front room was quite spacious, with a high ceiling, old water-stained wallpaper, and hot-water radiators painted metallic silver. There was a small bathroom down a narrow hall, no tub but a shower, and a windowless kitchen at the back that was big enough for a small table, if he'd had one, and was supplied with a stove and fridge that looked like the kind people hauled out to their camps all through the north—old, yellowing and ready to expire.

But it was Walker's first place of his own, and he thought it had to be the greatest apartment in Toronto.

He pushed up one of the windows, to a chorus of pigeon fluttering and squawking. He stuck his head out and surveyed Church Street, and the church across the street, and the park that surrounded it.

A few men and women—homeless, he was to discover later—were beginning to gather on the benches in the morning sun under the leafy trees. He could see high office buildings beyond. The sounds of honking and gear-shifting and engines roaring and streetcars dinging and clacking along their tracks filled the air. Street vendors yelled, couriers streaked by on their bikes and people hurried this way and that, jaywalking with hardly a look at the traffic because, Walker figured, they were so used to all the noise and confusion.

A black-and-white cat landed on the windowsill. Its nose was criss-crossed with old battle scars and one of its ears was hardly there at all. After a moment of bold calculation, it rubbed its blunt head against Walker's arm, stepped past him and jumped down inside the room. Tail held high, it sauntered across the floor and down the hall, looking for the kitchen.

Walker sat on the floor beside the window. The cat, having found the kitchen empty, came back and lay down beside him. Walker scratched its bumpy head and it began to purr, as loud as an outboard motor.

For a long time Walker sat there, watching and listening to the world outside. Then he spread the letter on the worn hardwood floor and put the photograph of the woman and the two little kids down beside it. He studied the dark-haired little girl again, the one half turning away.

"I'm here, Mom," he said.

• •

THAT AFTERNOON, Walker went shopping for used furniture at the Goodwill Store on Jarvis Street. He bought a cream imitation-leather pullout couch with a mattress that wasn't too badly stained, a small wooden table and two wooden chairs painted a thick glossy black, a small chest of drawers with the original veneer still hanging on in some places and a tiny portable colour TV with rabbit ears. It all came to five hundred and sixteen dollars with tax, and they promised to deliver it the very next day.

Now Walker had four hundred and sixty-some dollars left. Just the day before, he'd had more than two thousand. This was more or less as he'd expected but, just the same, the suddenness of it took his breath away.

He bought himself a newspaper and a city map in a corner store, rolled himself a smoke and started off down Adelaide Street.

Finding a job proved more difficult than he had thought. By the time six o'clock rolled around, he'd been to over a dozen factories and restaurants and stores, only to be met by long lines of fellow applicants. Apparently there was a recession going on. Or a depression. Depending on whether you were still clinging to your job by your fingernails, or you'd already been shaken loose.

He'd bought a frying pan and kettle, a can opener, a knife, fork and spoon earlier that day, and now he bought himself some groceries and a six-pack of beer. He made wieners and beans for supper and ate them right out of the frying pan; he figured he could buy a couple of plates when he found a job. He realized that there were all kinds of other things he'd need—a cereal bowl, glasses, salt and pepper shakers, the list seemed to go on forever. And when the sun went down he realized that he also needed a couple of lamps. There were only two overhead lights in his apartment, and neither one was in his living room.

He sat on the floor in the dark, smoked and drank his beer and watched the shadows and street lights play a game of chase against his two windows.

And again he thought about that lake the two little girls had been floating on, at Mary's Point, on June 2, 1964.

It was hard to keep your hand in the water long enough to catch a minnow in a minnow pail on June 2 in the north, let alone splash in a lake like those two little girls. But there they were, soaked, hair wringing wet, fooling around on an inner tube and an air mattress— which meant Mary's Point couldn't be near Parry Sound or the French River or anywhere around where he'd been found, so he didn't know what those cops had been thinking about. Mary's Point couldn't be up north at all.

It was past one by the time he crawled into his bedroll and fell asleep.

The next morning, the cat was back, he called his mother from a phone booth to give her his address and promised to get a phone immediately, and his furniture arrived. Things were beginning to shape up.

He fed the cat some milk in the frying pan, hauled the imitation-leather couch and chest of drawers to just the right spots in the living room, putting the colour TV on top of the chest, and carried the shiny black table and the two chairs into the kitchen. To celebrate, he named the cat Kerouac, in honour of his favourite writer and the inspiration behind his "see the world" excuse for coming to Toronto.

By mid-afternoon, Walker was having another long and fruitless day in the Toronto job market. As he crossed Parliament Street, steam seemed to lift right off the road, and he wouldn't have been surprised if the leather soles on his boots had begun to smoke. His eyes were full of dancing sun spots. His head ached. There wasn't a whisper of a breeze anywhere. He had never been in a place so hot in his life.

He glanced idly at a garage sitting near the back of a large lot. It was a two-storey brick building with rounded corners, painted a pale and flaking yellow, with two bays for cars and a wooden sign hanging lopsided over the front door announcing A.P. Cabs and, below that, in smaller letters, Owner Operated A. Piattelli.

As if to prove it, two cabs, painted blue and white with A.P. Cabs 752-8641 written all over them, were pulled up in front, and a few other cars were parked along the side.

Off by itself, at the other end of the building, an immaculate 1958 pink Cadillac Eldorado shone in the sun like a dream of California.

Walker was strolling by, staring at the Cadillac and wondering where the furry dice were that should be hanging from its rear-view mirror, when he noticed a sign in the dirty plate-glass window at the front of the garage. It was handwritten, printed in large, urgent letters with a broad red marking pen. It said HELP!

Walker stopped. He wasn't sure what he should do. Call the police? Apply for a job?

He looked at the building more closely. Both bay doors were open and he could see the shadowy figure of a man moving around in one of the bays. The man walked underneath a car suspended on a hoist. Walker could hear the bang of the air hose on a grease gun. Everything seemed normal. No robbery, arson or mayhem in progress. He decided to go in.

As he pushed open the front door, he was hit by a blast of cold air from a groaning air conditioner. He could see a woman sitting on the other side of a high wooden counter in the far corner of the room, her broad back towards him. Her wiry grey hair was standing up on her head as if waiting in vain for someone to brush it. She was talking on a two-way radio.

"Romeo? Where art thou, Romeo?" she said. An undecipherable squawk answered her. She took a last long drag on a smoke and stuffed it into an overflowing ashtray.

"What happened to that last call?" she wanted to know. More squawking.

"You took too long is what happened. I can't hog-tie people, you know, Romeo. I can't keep them waiting forever. They called back twice." More squawking.

Walker stepped into the room. The wooden floor was warped and worn. Several decades' worth of faded calendars, advertising everything from car polish to a funeral parlour on King Street, were nailed up on the painted walls. The area behind the counter was jammed with the dispatch desk and two other desks and several filing cabinets, every available space covered by a layer of files and business papers, as if the air conditioner had blown everything around.

"Give me one good reason why I should give you another ride," the dispatcher wanted to know, lighting up another smoke.

Walker moved past the counter, through an open doorway, down a wooden ramp. Another open door on his right led to the garage bays, and he could see the man greasing the car more clearly now. He was short and wiry, with a grey ponytail sticking out below his greasy ball cap. He didn't wear coveralls or boots, just battered running shoes, a filthy pair of jeans and a black T-shirt with a slurping red tongue emblazoned on it. He had about a five-day growth of grizzled beard, and looked to have no teeth as he forced the gun onto another nipple, black oil gleaming on his face, his mouth sunken in, and then a flash of pink gums as he cursed up into the underbelly of the car, "Oh, you fuckin' motherfucker!"

Walker continued down the dimly lit hall and came to a half-opened door with frosted glass. Inside the room, a very large man behind a very large desk, his feet propped up on an open drawer, was talking on the telephone.

"Twenty thou. I'm not kiddin' ya. If I'm lyin', I'm dyin'. Tony dropped in. You know, Tony the Thumb? Yeah. And that little weasel, what's his name? Herman? Those two are travelling together now. Yeah. Five o'clock in the fuckin' mornin'. I'm dead here, I'm fuckin' dead. They take me for granted."

The man glanced up and saw Walker peering at him through the doorway. His eyebrows went up a little but he kept talking on the phone. "That's what I'm sayin'. That's exactly what I'm sayin'."

He looked to Walker like a retired football player, his head huge and fringed with tight curly hair. A collection of gold chains glittered around his neck and a mass of grey chest hairs bushed out from his peach-coloured shirt.

"Yeah. Yeah. Look, there's some kid here to see me. I'll call you later." He hung up the phone, rocked back in his wooden swivel chair and nodded towards Walker. Walker pushed the door open and came in.

"Hi. Sorry to bother you. I saw the sign so I thought I'd apply."

The man's eyebrows went up again. "What sign?"

"The one that says HELP!"

The man sat there for a moment, thinking, his brow furrowing a little. He was somewhere between forty and fifty, Walker guessed, and despite his size there was something about him that wasn't so formidable at all. Some hint of amusement in his dark hound-dog eyes.

"HELP?" the man asked. Walker nodded.

The man got up from behind his desk—about three hundred pounds of him, dressed in khaki shorts, his legs almost devoid of hair, in sharp contrast to his chest, and several shades whiter than his swarthy face. He flopped around his desk in sandals, flopped past Walker and said, "Show me."

Walker followed him back to the front office. "In the window," he said.

The man walked around the counter and pushed his huge bulk between two filing cabinets. They both moved. "Jesus H. Christ," he said. He reached down and plucked up the sign leaning against the glass.

"Look at this, Donna," he said. "Did you see this?"

"I saw it when I came in."

"Why didn't you say somethin'?"

The woman shrugged. "Why should I?"

The phone rang. She picked it up. "A.P. Cabs," she said.

The man started back down the hall, scrunching up the cardboard sign as he went.

Walker thought to himself, well, so much for that. He was about to leave when the man yelled at him, "What do you think?"

"About what?" Walker replied.

"Women!"

"Well, um"—Walker smiled slowly—"actually, quite a lot."

"Yeah? They drive me crazy!" The man turned down the hall again. "Come here!" he yelled at Walker.

By the time Walker reached the office, the man was sitting behind his desk, peeling the wrapper off a cigar.

"Krista Papadopoulos."

"Pardon?" Walker said.

"Krista Papadopoulos! That's who put that sign in the window. She drives me crazy. She thinks she owns the place. She thinks she runs everything." He ran the cigar under his nose, smelling it, and proceeded to lick it from one end to the other. "Makes a cooler smoke," he said, by way of explanation.

Walker nodded.

"Sit down."

Walker sat on an old leather chair full of holes and creases.

"She thinks we're goin' to lose our licence if we don't hire a licensed mechanic. She's been buggin' me for weeks, yap yap yap. It's my stinkin' place, it's my stinkin' licence." He cut the end off the cigar with a pocket knife and lit it. "Besides, I've been gettin' away with it for years." A great cloud of smoke filled the office. "So she gets sarcastic. That's a sarcastic sign. Do you understand?" He pointed to the garbage can where he'd thrown it.

"Yeah," Walker said.

The man puffed on his cigar for a moment and, as if coming to a conclusion that he'd come to many times before, he said, "She's a pistol. What's your name?"

"Walker. Walker Devereaux."

The man extended a large, meaty hand across the desk. "Alphonso Piattelli. Nice to meet you, Walker."

"Nice to meet you, Mr. Piattelli," Walker said, as they shook hands.

"Ya drive, do ya?"

"Yeah."

"I got a beautiful little cab out there, just waitin' for you. Seventy bucks for the night shift. That's a great rate. Try to beat it."

"Um," Walker said. "You mean, like, drive a cab?"

Alphonso's eyebrows went up again. "This ain't the opera."

"You mean you'd pay me seventy bucks to drive a cab?"

"No. *You* pay *me* seventy bucks and you get to keep everything you make over." He looked at Walker with some pity. "You've never driven a cab, have you?"

"No."

"You don't have a licence to drive a cab, do you?"

"No."

"Then what the hell are you doin' here?"

"I wasn't sure what the job was."

"There ain't no job! That's just Krista Papadopoulos!"

"Yeah, well, I get that now." Walker started to get up.

"Sit down."

He sat down.

"Look, would you like to drive cab?"

"Sure."

"Hmmm," Alphonso said, puffing on his cigar. "It's a great job. It's a great job." He leaned towards Walker, taking him into his confidence: "You know your way around, though?"

"Not really. I just got here two days ago."

"That's not necessarily a problem. Where you from?"

"Big River."

"Where's that?"

"It's a small town just south of Thunder Bay."

"Where's that?"

"Up north."

"I want to show you somethin'," Alphonso said, getting up and flopping around the desk again.

He led Walker towards the back of the building and out a steel door into brilliant sunshine. A wave of heat washed over them. He pointed to a cab pulled up in the weeds beside a pile of rusty oil drums. "Number nineteen!" he exclaimed, stroking the car's fender. "She's a little beauty."

Walker looked at the blue-and-white cab, a very old and sad-looking Ford Ventura with bald tires and a back bumper held on by what looked like duct tape. Alphonso opened the driver's door. The hinges creaked.

"Joe's just given it a complete overhaul."

"Uh-huh."

"Now here's the deal. I'll pay you five bucks an hour to drive the night shift. Four-thirty to four-thirty tomorrow morning, twelve hours, got it? Sixty bucks in your pocket. What else are you gonna do?"

"Nothing much."

"Sit around, watch TV, some damn thing, right? This way, you're learning the business. Meanwhile, Krista enrols you in cabbie school. Do it now, it takes four days, costs you two hundred bucks. The commission's talkin' about upgrading the business or some fuckin' thing. Gonna be sixteen days and eight hundred bucks if you don't do it now, get it?"

"Yeah."

"Good boy. Now go away, get a nap, come back at four-thirty, Joe'll set you up."

"How will I know what to charge?"

"You got a meter. Joe'll show you. Just don't touch the radio. No matter who calls on that radio, you ignore them, all right? Don't answer nobody. Don't say nothin'. Got it?"

Walker looked down at his worn workboots for a moment. He hadn't thought about driving a cab, it hadn't occurred to him, but the more he thought about it, the more it appealed to him. Kerouac would do it.

"This is a special deal. Just till you get your licence. Then you pay me, like everybody else." Alphonso leaned up against the cab. It creaked ominously. He watched Walker through a cloud of cigar smoke. "It's 'cause I trust you to try your best. Otherwise you'll come back with just a few dollars and collect your sixty bucks, right? But I figure, a kid like you, you're goin' to try your guts out. You're goin' to come back with maybe two, three hundred bucks. I'm goin' to make money. You're goin' to make money. It's a temporary partner-ship kind of deal."

Walker looked at Alphonso wreathed in smoke. Alphonso grinned at him. Walker smiled back. It was a deal.

To celebrate, Walker went into the pawnshop to buy himself a tape deck and a lamp for his living room.

His landlord peered over his glasses. "You were lucky," he said.

"Why?"

"Someone came in today, wanting to rent your apartment. I said sorry, it was taken yesterday."

"Oh," Walker said, looking over a row of tape decks. "How'd he know it was for rent? You took the sign down yesterday."

The man shrugged. "Must have noticed it before. He asked me who'd rented the place. I said, some hockey player."

Walker picked out a tape deck and put it down carefully on the glass-topped counter. "Wonder why he'd care who'd rented it."

His landlord shrugged again.

"I'll take this one," Walker said.

* *

BY FIVE O'CLOCK THAT NIGHT, Walker was driving cab number nineteen, with his map of the city spread out on the seat beside him. He cruised up Parliament Street, and for no particular reason turned right on Gerrard. He crossed a bridge and in a few minutes found himself driving through Chinatown.

He glanced once again at the expanse of blue on the bottom of his map. Lake Ontario. He decided to drive south. He had known all along he'd drive south. It wouldn't take that long, he just wanted to get a glimpse of the lake, a warmer lake than any lake up north, it had to be. That done, he'd look for someone wanting a cab. Someone standing on a street corner, waving or something.

"New Boy!" The radio jumped to life. Walker jumped a little too. "New Boy, where are you? Speak up, New Boy."

Walker hesitated for a moment, deciding to follow Alphonso's instructions and ignore this female voice drilling through his head like a steel-tipped bullet.

"New Boy!"

Somehow, Walker didn't think this was Donna, smoking her smokes, wrapped in an old wool sweater against the blast of the air conditioner. It must be someone else.

"I know you're out there. Pick up or I'll call the cops, because you're in an unplated cab with no cabbie ID, if you'd like to know, and they'll throw you in the back of their cruiser and take you somewhere private and kick your ass right up over your ears, so PICK UP!"

Walker figured he had two choices: abandon the cab to avoid driving into a Hydro pole, or pick up. He picked up, pushed a button and said, "Hi," then let the button go again, just as Joe, the dubious mechanic, had shown him.

There was a moment of silence, then "That's better. Where are you?"

"I'm on Gerrard."

"What's your crossroad?"

"I don't know. I could stop and check my map. Oh, wait—I just went by Brian Crescent."

Another silence. Then "What's your name, New Boy?"

"Walker. Walker Devereaux."

"You're a virgin, aren't you, Walker?"

Walker hesitated.

"In the sense that you've never driven a cab before, have you, Walker?"

"No," he admitted.

"And you talked to Alphonso Piattelli, didn't you?"

"Yeah."

"Alphonso Piattelli is not someone you should be talking to. Alphonso Piattelli is a menace to everyone, including himself. If there was a prize for 'walking disaster,' Alphonso would have won it years ago, do you read me, New Boy?"

"Walker," he reminded her. "But he's the boss, the owner, isn't he?"

A longer silence.

"Well, that's what the sign out front says, anyway," he added, rather lamely, he thought.

"How much money have you made so far?"

"Well, I just started."

"Do you know who I am?"

"No," Walker said, and he thought, I don't want to know, either, will you just shut up?

"I'm the night dispatcher. Do you know what that means to you? You don't, do you? Well, it means everything to you. I control who gets what and when. I control all the traffic. You don't get squat, you don't make a cent, your radio is dead, if that's the way I want it. Do you read me, New Boy? Now bring that piece of junk back in, as carefully as possible, so you don't get arrested and we don't have our licence suspended just because Alphonso thought he could scam a few extra bucks, and so I don't lose my job!"

"Mr. Piattelli said I should just drive around and pick up people off the street."

An eerie silence percolated from the radio. It went on for a very long time. Walker broke first.

"Well, I guess I could come in."

"Right."

"So, um, who will I look for?"

"Krista Papadopoulos."

Walker pulled number nineteen up in front of the garage very carefully, climbed out of the cab and pushed through the heavy front door.

The air conditioner was still groaning and blasting out cold air but there didn't seem to be anybody in the front office. Then he noticed the top of someone's blonde head on the other side of the counter.

"Hi," he said.

The head came up and Walker found himself looking at the most startlingly bright blue eyes he'd ever seen. There was something doll-like about her face, as if she were time-travelling from the twenties, except that she didn't have that much makeup on, and her blonde, almost white hair wasn't cut short and permed in tight waves but fell around her face in damp spirals, as if she'd just gotten out of a shower.

Walker figured she was twenty-five, maybe thirty—older than him, anyway—and very unusual looking, very attractive, sexy almost. Not almost; with her red cupid lips, she was definitely sexy.

"Are you Krista? I'm the new boy." He smiled.

She fixed him with those astonishing eyes. The phone rang. Pushing off from the workspace below the counter, she magically floated away.

Walker came up to the counter. Now he could see that she was sitting in a wheelchair as she did a neat whirl in the middle of the cluttered room and coasted to the phone.

"A.P. Cabs," she said. "Okay." She scribbled something on a piece of paper. "Ten minutes. Thanks for calling." She turned to the radio. "Nick, where are you now?" Squawking. "Got a pickup, 1225 Yonge, they'll be standing out in front. Right. Listen, when you get a chance, can you drop around? I've got a rookie here, maybe you could take him out?" More squawking.

Walker studied her while she was talking, trying hard not to stare but taking her all in. She was wearing a silvery shirt with long sleeves that shimmered in the light coming through the window. And grey slacks with business-like creases, and patent leather boots with square heels. Small silver earrings dangled from her ears; a thin silver chain lay against the white skin of her neck.

She looked perfectly normal from the waist up—soft, a little plump, snug-looking. But her left hip angled out cruelly, pulling the other hip in and twisting her legs so that she seemed to be sitting almost sideways in her wheelchair. And she was small, maybe five feet at the most. A broken doll, Walker thought.

"Ten-four." She switched off the two-way, turned to face Walker and, with a little push, came cruising back.

"This is the worst-run, most pathetic cab company in the city. We have a fleet of eight cabs, three of which should be condemned. Our licence to operate is dangling by a thread. We've already had two cautions this year. Alphonso is a dangerous lunatic. Never speak to him again."

"Uh-huh," Walker said. "I saw your sign earlier today. That's why I came in."

Krista looked up at him and her eyes sparkled; she even smiled a little. God, she's really pretty, Walker thought.

"What do you want to be a cabbie for?"

"Well, I need the money, for one thing."

"What's your deal with Alphonso?"

"He was going to pay me five bucks an hour."

"Oh, for chrissake." Krista spun her wheelchair around, came to a stop and said, "He left me a note. A certain Walker Devereaux needed to be enrolled in cabbie school ASAP."

"I don't think I can afford the two hundred bucks."

"Sure you can."

Krista asked him to come around the counter. Walker strolled around and leaned against one of the desks. She rolled her chair up close to him, so that one wheel nudged his boot.

"Tell you what we'll do. Alphonso was going to pay you five for twelve hours, right? Sixty bucks."

Walker nodded.

"So he has to go through with that deal. We'll cover the first sixty, that takes it down to a hundred and forty."

"Can you do that?"

She set her chin a little. "I can do anything I want. I'll charge you ten dollars extra on your nightly rental fee until you've paid back the one forty, so fourteen nights and we're square. Right? How's that sound?"

"Good," Walker said.

She put out her small hand and they shook on it.

"Nick's a great guy. From Ethiopia. You'll like him. He'll drop by and take you out, show you stuff."

"Okay."

"Okay." She smiled up at him, letting go of his hand. "Now get lost, will you? I've got the books to do. Alphonso refuses to hire a bookkeeper, so I have to do them."

She swung away from him, wheeled around the other desk and opened a large ledger with a bang. There were no computers in sight. The phone rang.

"Shit," she said, spinning back to the phone. "A.P. Cabs."

• •

WALKER HAD TO DELAY HIS TRIP along the shore of Lake Ontario. He was on the run for the next two weeks, learning the practical side of the business at night from Nick and the official side during the day at cabbie school.

But the highlight of his day, the main thing, was breakfast. Breakfast at five o'clock in the morning, just as the first grey hint of dawn started to creep across the city. Breakfast at Ruby's Canadian-Chinese Cuisine 24-Hour Fine Dining Family Restaurant, because that was where Krista went, with a few of the night-shift guys.

Walker had hung back the first few mornings, watching Krista wheel over to her car, a 1979 Toyota Tercel with hand controls, and unlock its hatchback. She'd struggle out of her chair, support most of her weight on her left leg, collapse the chair and flip it into the back with almost scary dexterity. Then she'd haul out two aluminum crutches, one a bit shorter than the other, and, swinging between them, cross the street to the group of cabbies waiting on the other side.

One morning, as she manoeuvred out the open bay door, she glanced up at Walker, who was trying to look disinterested, leaning against the wall and rolling a smoke. She said, "Okay. Come on."

"Come on where?" He tried to play dumb.

"You know where. You're hungry, aren't you?"

"Sort of," he said, trailing casually behind her.

He tried to help her flip her chair into the hatchback, but she gave him such a dark look that he stopped.

He walked across the street beside her, trying hard to walk slowly without seeming to walk slowly on purpose, which was tricky because he was not a naturally slow walker, so he kept getting a little ahead of her. He was feeling ridiculously pleased that he was now part of the A.P. Cab breakfast club.

After a few mornings, they consistently found themselves sitting alone at the table as the others left for home to get some sleep. Walker wasn't sure whether Krista was stalling over breakfast or whether the others were leaving a bit earlier than usual, but it did seem to him that she was taking more time.

He liked looking at her, and it occurred to him that his first impression, the doll-like impression, had been shallow and wrong. She was a considerable person, as almost everyone, Walker had discovered in his short life, was a considerable person once you got to know them. And maybe Krista more than most, because one morning, sitting there carefully shredding a paper napkin into long strips, she told him about all the surgery she'd endured as a little kid to try to strip and relax the muscles in her back and legs, muscles that the palsy in her brain kept signalling to remain flexed and rigid. And how she'd clumped around in steel braces, looking like a miniature Boris Karloff, and how she'd fought to go to regular schools and be a regular kid, and how she was still fighting with her father, who was Greek and therefore ridiculously overprotective.

The thing was, she was perfectly capable of doing everything herself, she wanted to live on her own, but she couldn't bring herself to fight with her father and leave because it would probably kill him. Over the years he'd spent thousands of dollars renovating so that she could have her own special bathroom, and she could go upstairs and even down to the basement riding on electric lifts.

Walker nodded and thought of Mary Louise Devereaux.

And one morning, amid the coffee cups and dirty dishes and ketchup bottles and jugs of genuine artificial maple syrup that Ruby's sleepy grandson hadn't gotten around to clearing away yet, Walker told Krista his life story, too.

Once in a while Krista would look away, as if something in Walker's face was just too uncomfortable to watch. But mostly she locked onto him, onto every word. He told her everything.

"Can I see them?" she asked, meaning the letter and the photograph.

"Now?"

"I've got time," she said.

His apartment was only a few blocks away, but Krista drove there, as Walker was to discover she drove everywhere, as though she were fighting for first place in the Indy 500. In no time at all, the car slid to a stop in front of the pawnshop. They got out and she allowed him to hand her her crutches, in a kind of silent acknowledgement that something special was going on.

Walker unlocked the outside door that led up to his apartment, but as he pushed it open he realized that he had a problem. Krista swung up on her crutches. They stood there together, looking up the long flight of stairs to the second floor. The stairs didn't even have a handrail, which seemed to Walker, as he frantically searched for something tactful to say, to be definitely against some bylaw.

Krista didn't seem flustered. She just said, "You'll have to carry me."

Jesus Christ, Walker thought. "Do you trust me?" he asked.

"I guess I'll have to."

Walker bent down and picked her up in his arms. He thought she might feel really light, but she didn't. She felt solid. And soft. And warm.

She smiled at him, her face close to his. "Giddy-up," she said.

He carried her up the long flight of stairs, concentrating on each step, afraid he might stumble and drop her.

"Are you embarrassed?" she asked.

"No. Why?"

"Just wondered. Do you do this often?"

"Well, not lately."

He put her down carefully in the upstairs hallway, and unlocked his door.

The apartment, which had always given him a real sense of pleasure, now seemed pathetically empty to his eyes. All there was to see was a high-ceilinged, water-stained room with a forlorn little island of furniture in the middle. It looked as if a squatter had broken in with some furniture. Kerouac, lying derelict across the back of the couch with one eye swollen shut from a fight the night before, didn't help much.

Swinging on her crutches to the middle of the room, Krista looked around and said, "It'll be nice once you move in. Are you going to put up curtains?"

"Why?"

"I just wondered. It might warm things up."

"It's still summer. It's hot enough up here as it is."

She turned and smiled at him. "Yeah well, okay," she said. "Is this your cat?"

"No. He just showed up."

"What's his name?"

"Kerouac."

"Oh yeah?" She looked at the cat skeptically. "I wouldn't believe a word that cat said."

Walker showed her through the rest of the apartment, which didn't take long, and put the kettle on for coffee. They went back to the living room and she sat on the couch while he crouched in front of the chest of drawers. He felt under his worn leather jacket in the bottom drawer for the letter and photograph, pulled them out and sat down beside her.

Once again he felt stupid, caught in some misrepresentation. The letter and photograph seemed like such a paltry inheritance now, and he'd made them out to be so important.

Krista read the letter, then read it again. She stared at the photograph for a long time.

"It's not much to go on, I know," he said.

"Which one do you think's your mom?"

He hesitated.

"I think it's this one," she said, putting her finger on the dark-haired little girl.

"Why?"

"She's darker, for one thing. And it's her attitude—she's like you, or you're like her."

"What do you mean?"

"I just think she's your mother," Krista said.

"So do I."

They sat there in silence for a moment. Krista put her hand out and slipped her fingers between his. Walker was surprised.

"I'm going to find her," he said. Treacherous tears stung his eyes. The whistle on the kettle blew and he escaped into the kitchen.

When he came back carrying two coffees, Krista was still looking at the photograph. He'd already explained to her his theory about the cold water in northern lakes in early June. Now he said, "I think it might be Lake Ontario. If you live here, that's the logical place to go to the lake, right?"

"No," Krista replied, sipping at her coffee, the fourth one that morning. "No one has cottages on Lake Ontario. It's too cold. They have humungous houses all the way from here to Burlington, and maybe there's the odd cottage here and there, but it's not that kind of lake. In all my life I've never heard anyone say they were going to a cottage on Lake Ontario."

Walker sat down glumly beside her. "I guess it could be anywhere," he said. "It could be in the States. The labels on my clothes, they all came from the States."

"Do you know what it looks like?" she said, holding the photograph up closer to the lamp. "It looks like Camp Pokawaka."

"Oh?" Walker could feel his heart quickening a little.

"I used to go there all the time, it's a crippled kids' camp."

"Whereabouts?"

"Lake Erie."

"Lake Erie?"

"See how far out they are in the water? And how shallow it still is? And look at those high sand cliffs, and the pines. It looks just like Lake Erie."

"Is the water warm?"

"Like soup! That's because it's so shallow and sandy on the bottom. If it's hot in May, you can easily fool around in the water. We used to go there for wiener roasts every Victoria Day weekend, and most years we could swim. Well, we couldn't swim, really, except for one or two of us, but we could splash around. And one year, on May 24, the water was just like the middle of summer!"

"Where's Lake Erie?"

"Where's Lake Erie?" Suddenly she sounded like his mother, she almost threw her arms up, "It's a Great Lake, Walker. It's next to Lake Ontario. It's south-west from here. It's separated from Lake Ontario by Niagara Falls. Don't they teach you anything up north?"

"I knew that. I just didn't know exactly where it was. How far?"

"It took us about two and a half hours on the bus to get to Camp Pokawaka, but they always went too slowly. There's a map in my car."

She gave Walker her keys, and he ran back downstairs and found a map of the province in her glove compartment, under a hairbrush, assorted lipstick tubes, gas receipts and a sonic whistle to repel rapists. He ran back up the stairs, two steps at a time.

"That's Lake Erie," she said, pointing to a long, narrow patch of blue on the bottom of the map spread across their laps.

"Look at all these points." Walker's pulse was racing now. "Point Albino, Mohawk Point, Peacock Point, Turkey Point, Long Point. It's full of points!"

"Yeah. But I don't see any Mary's Point."

"That doesn't matter. Maybe it's not an official name. Maybe it's just what the locals call it. And look, once you get as far as Long Point there are no more points of land all the way to Detroit. It's almost a straight shoreline."

"Yeah, well, Long Point's a long drive from Toronto," Krista said. "I mean, if you lived in Toronto and had a cottage on Lake Erie, you'd want it to be closer. Camp Pokawaka was near Peacock Point, I think."

"So from the beginning of the lake, starting at Fort Erie and going to Long Point, how far is that? About"—Walker checked the scale on the map—"eighty miles. How many townships is that?"

"Why?"

"Because all I need to do is call each township office, talk to the clerks. They know all the local names. They know everything. If there's a Mary's Point, they'll know about it." He looked at the map again. "I bet there's eight, ten miles of shoreline in each township. So only eight or so townships. We could call them."

Krista's head came up. "We?"

"I mean, I could call them. I could go to the library and look them up."

"Just look on the map."

"I don't think they're on the map. Are they?"

"What are these names?"

"Counties."

"So what county is it?"

"Hard to tell, everything's scrunched up. Looks like Haldimand-Norfolk."

"So just call information for the county office, Walker. And they'll be able to give you phone numbers for all the township offices in their county, right?"

"Yeah," Walker agreed.

"Have you got a phone?"

"Not yet. They want a two-hundred-dollar deposit."

Krista sighed. "I'll call them. I'll do it from home."

"I'll pay you whatever it costs."

"You bet you will."

They talked for a while longer, until Krista realized that it was almost rush hour and some bastard tow truck would be pulling her car to the pound. Walker quickly put the letter and photograph back under his leather jacket. He locked his door and, picking her up with more confidence and holding her a little closer, carried her back down the stairs.

After she drove away, he decided to walk to a tiny basement variety store he'd discovered. He was low on milk and almost out of tobacco. That was another reason to like Krista: she didn't complain about his smoking. There seemed to be a lot of reasons, suddenly, why he liked her.

Carrying milk, tobacco and three magazines, he returned from the variety store and let himself in the street door. As he climbed the long wooden stairs, he could still feel the snug weight of Krista in his arms. He reached the hallway and was about to unlock his apartment door when he noticed that he didn't have to. The door jamb was splintered, and when he gave the door a push it swung wide open.

Walker ran for the kitchen, not even thinking that the thief or thieves might still be there, that he might get into some bloody, maybe even fatal fight. The kitchen was empty. Just the two wooden chairs and the table greeted him. He opened the fridge and the tiny freezer door. His bankroll, such as it was, was still safely hidden inside a frozen fish carton.

Walker hurried back to his apartment door and looked down the hallway. There was no one in sight.

He closed the door and looked around. Nothing seemed to be missing except Kerouac, who had obviously taken a powder out the open window again. The tape deck was still sitting there, big as life, on the windowsill.

Walker stared at it. Why didn't they steal my tape deck? he wondered.

He walked across the room and pulled out the bottom drawer of the chest. His leather jacket was still there, just as he'd left it, except that it had been pushed a little to the side.

Suddenly Walker felt as though he were coming down with the world's worst flu. He felt under the jacket, then pulled it out of the drawer. He pulled out his two sweaters, and his extra jeans.

The empty drawer stared up at him.

CHAPTER SIX

1972

ON HIS FIRST DAY AT Southam Military Academy in Tennessee, Bobby vomited in the toilet he shared with nine other boys. On his second day, he didn't feel anything. He had gone away to a special place inside himself. He was good at going away.

It had been his father's idea to send him to Southam. To toughen him up, make him self-reliant, a leader of men, capable of one day taking over the family business. The Plant.

He'd stood behind Bobby and squeezed his shoulders hard the day he'd announced to his wife that he'd already enrolled Bobby at Southam, and that Bobby needed to be on the parade ground, present and accounted for, a week that Monday.

Bobby was thirteen years old now. Sometimes he did very well at school—excelled, in fact—when he felt that a teacher had slighted him and needed to be reminded just who the most brilliant student in the class was. But once the teacher had made the mistake of praising him, Bobby would slack off again, drift away. If the schools he attended had believed in failure, he would have failed, but since they didn't (it sent the wrong message to fragile egos), he didn't.

Through the years, his mother had enrolled him in extra classes for gifted children and, at other times, remedial classes. She had had him tested by several experts who all agreed that her son had an IQ in the high normal range, but beyond that they all saw a different child.

Some thought he had one of a variety of neurological problems; others, specific emotional or behavioural problems; and still others, any combination of the above. Various drugs were recommended, behavioural modification techniques were recommended, alternative schools and school programs were recommended.

It pleased Bobby to be at the centre of all this attention, to sit in strange offices with his mother and listen to serious-looking men and women blabbing away. Sometimes he would do well on their tests, to surprise them. Other times he would decide to fuck up completely, to disappoint them. He'd watch them and he'd listen to what they said, but his face would be a wall. No one could see in. No one could tell what he was thinking.

Bobby's mother took him to museums, the theatre and the symphony. She cuddled him and stroked his hair and kissed his ears. She called him her brilliant boy. She worried about him all the time.

The decision to send Bobby away was made without her knowledge. Her husband had looked after it himself, feeling that all his son needed was the discipline of a military school. Although Bobby had never failed a grade, it was clear that he didn't take hold as he should, and there was something amorphous and, frankly, off-putting about him. Where were the sparkle and the charm, where was the self-confidence, where was the emerging powerhouse personality that his father so longed to see?

He had had his secretary send away for brochures and calendars. He had talked to families who had sent their sons to similar schools in the States. He had talked to the schools themselves, and had chosen Southam. It was the oldest, the most expensive, and had the finest tradition, going back all the way to the Civil War, turning out young men by the hundreds who, or so their calendar proclaimed, went on to be leaders in the military, politics, business, education, every field you could imagine.

And so, with anguish and a vague sense of foreboding that both surprised and frightened her, and knowing that she really had no choice, she'd said yes.

His father was always reminding Bobby that one day he'd have big shoes to fill. But Bobby already knew that, because when he was younger he had liked to sneak into his parents' bedroom and hide in the closet.

He'd always chosen his father's closet. He'd sit amongst rows of shining shoes and his face would brush against all the upside-down trousers. He'd feel comforted, the air full of the smell of shoe polish and aftershave and expensive wool tweed and, underneath it all, a faint, masculine smell.

His head would become heavy, and a drone would fill the air like a swarm of far-away bees. He'd curl up amongst his father's shoes, and soon he'd fall asleep.

When his parents had left him at Southam Military Academy, his mother had cried, though she'd tried hard not to. Bobby had looked at her tears as if they were trickling down the face of a stranger. There had always been some unreality, some distance between them. Even when she was holding him and stroking his hair, she might as well have been in another room. He couldn't feel her.

His father had turned him away from his mother and had crouched down to look him in the eye, man to man. He'd said, in his slightly accented voice, "No phone calls. No letters. Tough as whale-bone, captain."

Bobby had nodded.

He'd watched his parents leave from his window high up in the dormitory, south room twelve. As they walked out the gates, his mother had looked back, but his father hadn't turned around at all.

Now a double line of boys marched across the parade ground. They were half as tall as their commander. They were all dressed in grey uniforms, grey caps. Something familiar struck Bobby as he watched the long grey line quick-march around the yard.

One of his roommates walked in the door. Bobby looked at him.

"We're in a City of Mice," Bobby said.

CHAPTER SEVEN

· ·

WHEN WALKER TOLD KRISTA that his apartment had been broken into and the letter and photograph stolen, her blue eyes widened by half a size.

"That doesn't make any sense," she said. "Why would anyone do that?"

"I don't know."

"Maybe they were stoned on crack or something. Maybe they stole them by accident," she suggested.

"Yeah," Walker said.

They were sitting in Ruby's Canadian-Chinese Cuisine 24-Hour Fine Dining Family Restaurant. It was four o'clock in the afternoon, the same day Krista had visited Walker's apartment; she had later made phone calls to almost all the township offices in Haldimand-Norfolk County. She'd had six hours' sleep. Walker hadn't had any.

"Except they were under my leather jacket. So why didn't they steal the jacket, if they were looking for things to sell? That letter and photograph weren't worth anything."

The restaurant was empty except for Ruby herself, sitting at a back table by the kitchen door, doing her books.

"It was sixteen years ago. Nobody around here knows who I am," he continued, as if to reassure himself.

Krista nodded and sat in silence for a moment, watching him fish cigarette papers and tobacco from his shirt pocket.

"Why do you roll your own cigarettes?" she'd asked him one night while he was standing around watching Joe, the magic mechanic, try to stem an oil leak in cab number nineteen.

Echoing Gerard Devereaux, Walker had answered, "If I drop a smoke by accident, it goes out on its own. Not like ready-mades. Less chance of setting the bush on fire."

Krista had looked around at the midnight traffic on Parliament Street, and the two hookers standing on the corner. "Do you think that's a problem here?"

"Besides," he had added, giving her a warm smile, "it gives me something to do with my hands."

Now she watched his hands as he deftly rolled himself two smokes.

She'd had some startling news to report, too. She'd found out where Mary's Point was.

It was in McKormack Township, along the north shore of Lake Erie, or at least that was what the municipal clerk had told her, the fifth one she'd called that day. It wasn't an official name, it wasn't a community or anything like that, just a cluster of cottages a few miles off County Road 11, on a point of land named by a forgotten some-one in the distant past.

When Krista had reported this to Walker, he'd lifted her right up out of her wheelchair and spun her around.

"How come, if I did that, she'd slap me with a sexual harass-ment suit?" Alphonso had yelled.

"You've never thought of doing it," Krista had replied, perched in Walker's arms, her arms around his neck, her lips close to his ear. "And now it's too late."

Just a few minutes before, she'd felt triumphant and needed. Now, sitting in Ruby's, all she felt was some kind of shapeless apprehension.

"Some goof grabbed the letter and the photograph, just for the hell of it. For no reason at all," she suggested.

Walker nodded. He lit up one of his smokes. "If someone did something to my mother, they wouldn't want me to find out."

Krista felt her heart tighten. "You're making something out of nothing," she said. She took a deep breath and decided that she was going to ignore all this break-and-enter stuff. "So, do you still want to go out to Mary's Point?"

• •

IT WAS A SUNNY END-OF-AUGUST DAY, the first day they had off work together, when they drove west out of Toronto towards Lake Erie.

Krista had packed a picnic lunch. Walker had bought a bottle of red wine; when he'd asked her, she'd suggested red since it wouldn't need to be chilled.

"I could bring white and we could put it in the lake to chill," he had said.

"Just bring red," she had replied. "And not sparkling red, okay?"

This remark had made Walker worry about his choice. Finally, he'd decided on a French Merlot costing an exorbitant eighteen dollars. If she's not happy with this, he had thought to himself, she won't be happy with anything.

And now the sun was shining, and now that they'd cleared the city traffic and were safely out on the highway, Krista wasn't driving like a kamikaze pilot any more but was actually going along at the same speed as everybody else. And now they were smiling at each other, and laughing for no good reason except that they were together, and the windows were wide open and their hair was blowing crazily around.

Walker cranked the volume up. He'd brought along his old-time Delta Blues tapes and he was giving Krista a concert.

He glanced at her from time to time. She turned to smile at him now and then too, quickly turning back to watch the road. She was just tall enough to see out the windshield.

Her breasts looked deliciously full and heavy beneath her white cotton shirt with its stitched red and gold embroidery. The scoop neck offered him a tantalizing glimpse of soft, curving flesh. He felt his stomach tighten, and he shifted his legs.

"This is fun," she said.

"Uh-huh," he replied.

The clerk at the McKormack Township municipal office turned out to be large, motherly and helpful. She carefully drew a map to Mary's Point on the back of a dog-tag notice, telling them that they would see a sign just past a rural schoolhouse now converted into a very nice home owned by a lovely retired couple from Simcoe who raised the most beautiful orchids in a greenhouse out back.

Walker and Krista thanked her, and Walker, having waited for Krista to struggle down the three steps of the municipal office (just as he'd waited for her to struggle up them, trying not to look as if he was waiting but rather gazing with intense interest at the municipal works garage next door), opened the driver's door for her, took her crutches, threw them in the back and got in on the passenger side. They were getting good at this. It was almost feeling comfortable.

Krista pulled off County Road 11 at the Mary's Point sign and headed down a dusty track through tall grass and scraggly bushes. The Tercel bumped up over a sharp rise, and then down the other side into a large swale spanned, at one particularly swampy and pungent point, by a rattling wooden bridge.

Past the swale, the car climbed slowly over another more gentle rise. About a mile away, across a rippling stretch of cattails and wild grass and beyond a row of sand dunes, they could see the slate-grey waters of Lake Erie glinting under the sun.

They followed the dusty track until they reached a split-rail fence just at the spot where Mary's Point thrust itself out into the lake. The point was only lightly covered by sand and grass and scattered groves of walnut and scrub oak. A sign tacked up on a post proclaimed it to be private property.

The track led through an opening in the fence and split off in two directions. They could see the back of a large, chocolate-brown, cedar-shake cottage under some trees to the right. They could also see that someone had stretched a chain across the opening in the fence and secured it to a post with a padlock.

An old, weather-beaten barn dozed in the sun on their side of the fence. A narrower track led past the barn to the sandy beach below.

Krista turned her car to the right, bumped slowly by the barn and pulled up behind a sand dune. She turned off the engine.

"Now what?" she asked.

"We walk around the point, looking for a log cabin with a flag-pole and a big white rock out in front of it," he replied, getting out of the car.

"That's what I thought." Of course, she had known what they were going to do, but now she looked with some foreboding towards the wide stretch of soft sandy beach, and the muddy waves rolling in.

At first it was fun. Walker carried their lunch and the beach towel Krista had brought and the bottle of wine. Krista struggled across the sand on her crutches until she reached the hard-packed sand by the water's edge.

The warm wind flapped at their clothes and took their breath away. The waves curled over themselves, foaming and swooshing towards them, then sliding away in a bubbly retreat. A squadron of seagulls suspended themselves over their heads on outstretched wings.

The two of them stood there for a long moment, looking across the water and up at the sky. Then they turned and walked past another sign that said Private Beach Ahead.

It didn't take long for Walker to see that things weren't going to work out. When Krista swung along close enough to the water's edge to be on the hard, wet sand, extra-large waves would rush in and soak her leather shoes and white slacks and undermine the sand beneath her crutches. When she walked beyond the reach of the largest waves, the sand was soft and gave way under her. But she kept grimly on, still smiling whenever he turned to her. Sweat began to bead on her forehead and gleam on her cheeks. He didn't know what to say or do, so he just kept walking.

After what felt to him like ten minutes, they were still passing in front of the first cottage, the dark cedar-shake they'd seen from the road. It sat back from the lake, on a grassy rise, surrounded by tall oaks. An old rowboat was turned upside down in front of it, and all the shutters were closed on the porch windows. He could hear Krista breathing hard beside him, although he was just dawdling along.

He glanced at her again. This time she didn't look up and smile. Her face was set, sweat was running down her nose, her eyes were fixed on the treacherous, churned-up sand in front of her. She was breathing in soft little whines now, like a long-distance runner. Her breasts shone with sweat above her scoop-necked blouse. At this rate, Walker figured, it would take them the rest of the day to circle the point. At this rate, they'd never make it.

Her right crutch suddenly slid away from her. She nearly fell, but she recovered and kept on.

"Maybe we should have lunch now," Walker said.

"We've just started," she said.

"I'm hungry."

"No you're not."

She kept moving. Walker started to feel a bit panicky. How was he going to stop her?

Her mascara was beginning to smudge around her eyes, which made her white skin look even paler. Strands of blonde hair clung damply to her forehead. She kept her eyes on the sand in front of her, doggedly swinging, landing, swinging, landing, breath coming in painful little gulps.

Walker stopped and spread the beach towel on the sand. Krista kept going, so he sat on the towel. Finally she stopped too, about twenty feet away, and turned back to him.

"What are you doing?" she said.

"You should take your shoes off. Your feet are soaked."

"I'm not tired."

Walker nodded and began to roll a smoke.

Seagulls soared above their heads.

Finally Krista came back, throwing one of her crutches across the sand. She used the other to help herself sit on the towel. Then she threw that one away too.

Walker knew better than to say anything.

Krista just sat there, breathing hard, looking out over the lake. Her eyes were either full of sweat or full of tears, Walker couldn't tell which.

"Let's get drunk," he said finally.

She looked at him, looked away.

"Let's make love," he said.

"You wish," she replied, but without her usual spirit. "I hate this."

"Hate what?" he asked, though he already knew the answer.

She just shook her head. She lay down on her side of the beach towel, and pulled her knees up and hugged them. She was facing Walker, which he took to be a good sign, even though her eyes were closed. He lay down too, with his face close to hers.

He reached out and gently pushed wet strands of hair away from her forehead, trailed his hand down her cheek. She opened her eyes. Their faces were so close together that they could feel each other's warm breath. Her eyes looked as if they were made of a thousand pieces of broken glass.

I'm going to kiss her, Walker thought to himself.

"I can't do it."

"What?"

"Walk on this piss-fucking sand!" she said. She sat up abruptly. "What the hell is that?"

Walker twisted around to see what she was looking at. A great plume of smoke was rising, oily and black, billowing into the air back down the beach where they'd just come from.

"Somebody's burning something," Walker said.

"What?" Krista almost yelled, turning back to him, her eyes bright and full of alarm.

"Oh, Jesus Christ," Walker said. He jumped up and gathered her crutches.

"Just go on," she yelled, so he handed the crutches to her and, picking up his bottle of wine for some reason, started to walk, then run, back down the beach.

With his long legs flying, he was back at the Toyota in about one-twentieth the time it had taken them to walk that far. But he was too late. The car was engulfed in flames, the fire boiling and raging inside the locked doors and outside too, peeling the paint, melting the steering wheel and the hand controls, roaring and hissing, sending up clouds of black, toxic smoke. A tire exploded, then another, and finally the last two. The car settled onto the ground as if it were dying.

Walker couldn't get anywhere near it. All he could do was dance around it, feeling helpless, wondering whether the whole damn thing might explode and send shrapnel flying.

He could see Krista labouring down the beach towards him, trying to carry the beach towel and the lunch. She was still only halfway there.

He ran back up the beach to her. Though she couldn't see the car over the sand dune, she knew before he told her what was burning. She'd known as soon as she'd seen the smoke. What else was there to burn, except the barn, which she could see sitting undisturbed by the road?

"Krista, I'm sorry."

Krista dropped the towel and the picnic basket on the sand. Tears were running down her cheeks.

"Alphonso had a cab catch fire once," she said. "He didn't have any insurance."

"Do you?"

She grabbed Walker's arm. "I want to see it."

Walker picked her up and half walked, half ran back down the beach with her.

Her car looked like a piece of dull coal. Flames were still licking the roof and burning up the last of the upholstery. Blue flames shot out the intake hole of the gas tank.

They watched for a long time in silence, Krista in Walker's arms, clinging to his neck.

"How does a car catch on fire when it's not even running?" she finally asked.

"Electrical short," he said.

She didn't believe him. She was cold. Walker could feel her begin to shiver in his arms.

Soon afterwards the first curious cottager drove out the laneway to see what was going on. Then four people followed, one on foot, two in a car and one in a dune buggy. Somebody called the volunteer fire department, and a garage for a tow truck. They all seemed mostly concerned that such a stinking mess was fouling their beach and air.

However, when they saw that Krista used crutches, that she was crippled—or handicapped or physically challenged, depending on their degree of enlightenment—the little crowd suddenly became more solicitous. A tall, stylish-looking woman in white shorts and halter top, her skin burned a deep, rich coffee colour, came forward and offered them a ride into the nearest town. But after the local firemen had arrived and had dosed the fire with foam, and the pitiful remains of her beloved Tercel had been hoisted up behind the tow truck, Krista decided that she'd rather drive into town in the truck.

On the way, she asked Walker to pull the cork on his wine bottle. The three of them—Carl, the truck driver, Krista and Walker— passed it around. The bottle was empty by the time they pulled up in front of Carl's establishment in the village of Schuler, and Krista was feeling a little more philosophical.

"Lucky thing I decided not to bring my wheelchair along," she said.

"Look on the bright side," Carl advised. "Your car's a total write-off, so you can buy another one."

"But that was my first car. That's the only car I've ever owned."

"I'm sorry," Walker said.

Walker and Krista sat at a picnic table that squatted on a piece of parched grass beside Carl's garage and variety store. Krista was concerned that the mayonnaise might go bad if they didn't eat the sandwiches soon, so they ate their lunch, though neither one of them was feeling particularly hungry now. Walker ate all the pickles, too, and both pieces of peach pie that Krista's mom had tucked inside the basket.

After they were finished, they just sat there silently, watching the occasional car go by.

Carl had said that, around six that night, a bus would pass through Schuler heading for Toronto. They could stand on the road and wave it down. Krista had quickly said that that sounded like a good idea to her, which had made Walker feel even more depressed.

Now he studied her again. She was looking tired. She pushed a strand of hair away from her forehead, sipped on a pop. It was only four o'clock, two hours to wait, and the sun was still hot.

He didn't know whether to tell her or not, but he figured she deserved to know everything he knew. After all, it was, or had been, her car.

"I saw someone," he said.

She turned to look at him. "What do you mean, you saw someone?"

"When I ran up to the car, there was someone driving back out the lane towards the road."

She stared at him. "It could have been someone from one of the cottages, just going into town or something," she said.

"Then why didn't he stop?"

"Because he didn't notice anything."

"But he had to notice. He went right by. The car was already covered in flames. The smoke was blowing away from the lake, right across the road. He'd have to be blind not to see it."

"Maybe he was old. Old people get nervous; they don't like to stop when weird things happen."

Walker took a sip of his pop. "It was a black Audi, it looked new."

"But it doesn't make any sense." Her voice seemed on the edge of tears now.

"That's twice something hasn't made any sense," he reminded her. "And there's something else. Did you notice the gas cover was open?"

"So?"

"The gas cap was missing. I thought at first it had been blown off. I looked all around for it."

"Maybe it landed in the lake," she said. "Why don't you just try to scare me, Walker?"

She picked up her crutches, got up and swung away.

"Where are you going?"

"To look at my car."

Carl had pulled it around to the side of the garage. There wasn't much left to see.

At six-fifteen, the bus finally rolled through Schuler. Walker and Krista both waved at it. The bus pulled off onto the shoulder with an angry hiss of air brakes, and the door swung open.

Krista hurried after it. Walker walked beside her, carrying the basket and the beach towel.

When they reached the open door of the bus, she turned to him. She looked worried again. "You're sure you want to stay?"

Walker nodded. He wasn't going to give up on Mary's Point that easily.

"Keep the beach towel," she said.

He bent down and kissed her, though he hadn't planned on it. She kissed him back, pressing her mouth up against his, covering his mouth with hers. Then she turned away and he helped her up the high steps into the bus, and handed her the basket.

"Hell of a day, Walker," she said, as the door closed.

The bus began to move away. He couldn't see her through the dark windows, couldn't see her struggling down the swaying aisle to the first empty seat she could find, but he could imagine it.

He watched the bus disappear, then began to walk the opposite way, past the last house in Schuler, past a little clapboard church and the Schuler cemetery. He turned onto the same gravel road Carl had used driving into Schuler five hours before, and headed back towards Mary's Point.

He could still taste Krista on his lips.

Krista Papadopoulos. Floating in front of him as he walked along, dancing in front of him. Except that she couldn't float, only in her wheelchair. Except she couldn't dance, only in her imagination.

Walker broke into a run. He figured he had something like four miles to go.

By the time he walked up to the rail fence and circled around the barn, passing the blackened spot where Krista's car had been, it was almost eight o'clock. The sky had progressed from palest blue to royal blue, and now a pink flush crept across its darkening face.

Mary's Point was deep in shadow, except for the last red glow lighting up the tops of the trees.

Walker walked a little way down the beach, away from the point. The breeze had died, and little waves murmured over the cold sand.

He climbed between two sand dunes, up where the tall grass began to grow, knelt down and dug his hands into the sand. He could feel, very faintly, the last of the day's heat radiating against his skin. He looked over the plain of grass, almost invisible in the fading light, and the silhouettes of the cattails further on.

The moon had been joined by the evening star in the west. Not a star, really, Walker mused, but Venus. Mysterious Venus, shrouded in gossamer mist.

He spread out the beach towel, sat down and rolled himself a smoke. He'd wait until early morning, and then follow the shore all around the point.

A heron flew lazily over his head, down the shoreline to some dark haven for the night.

Walker turned his back against a sudden gust of wind, struck a match and drew the sharp smoke in deeply. All he had on was a light cotton shirt, his jeans and boots. Suddenly the air was cold. He figured that, once he grew sleepy, he'd roll up in the beach towel. If he needed more warmth, he could always pile up a mound of the wild grass that surrounded him and crawl underneath it.

"Walker is resourceful," Mary Louise had said, standing defiantly in her kitchen one day, announcing this news to one of her friends. But now Walker couldn't remember why she'd said it, why she'd felt it necessary at that very moment to defend him.

He wasn't sure what he was going to do the next morning. He had planned to find the cottage, show the photograph to people and see if they could identify the woman or the kids. But he no longer had the photograph, or the letter. And Krista no longer had her car.

He tried to picture the man driving the Audi, but his face remained a vague pink blob. No matter how hard he strained to remember, the features wouldn't come clear.

• •

AT FIRST LIGHT WALKER WOKE UP, wrapped in the towel, shivering. A mist hung over the grass and made the rise of land beyond invisible, but for some reason the air over the lake was perfectly clear. The water was as still and pale as the early morning sky. He could see far out, but there wasn't a line to show where the water and the sky met. There were no boats to help him gauge the distance. No birds flying. No sound.

Walker looked at his watch. It was five forty-five. He thought briefly of trying to make himself a fire, but settled for rolling and lighting a smoke instead. Then he washed his hands and face at the edge of the lake. He was hungry. He was thirsty as hell.

He eyed the water rippling around his workboots. You could drink Lake Superior water if you had to, and your stomach would survive. But Lake Erie? Walker had always heard that the lower Great Lakes were no better than open sewers, receptacles for everything Chicago, Detroit and Sarnia felt like dumping into them. He eyed the water again, scooped up one handful and drank it fast. Not able to stop himself, he drank some more.

Satisfied, he stood up and began to walk along the shore towards Mary's Point.

A dozen sandpipers met him going the other way, scurrying over the wet sand and through an inch of water, looking for all the world as though they were late for work.

Walker smiled at this thought. He was beginning to warm up and feel better.

He began to rehearse what he'd say once he found the cottage in the photograph. He still had the two first names from the letter, Kim, the writer, and Lennie, his mother. But over thirty years later, who would remember them?

The sun began to glow faintly through the fog to the east, like a far-off lighthouse, as Walker passed the Private Beach Ahead sign. In a moment he was standing in front of the same cedar-shake cottage he and Krista had seen the day before. The shutters were still closed. It looked as though no one was there.

He continued walking along the edge of the water. It was easier today, so much easier, without Krista. He thought that and immediately felt guilty. He tried to put her out of his mind.

He passed another cottage, this one larger than the first, a worn grey clapboard two storeys high—not a cottage but a summer house, really, with a gracious old-fashioned porch on two sides. But the lay of the land was nothing like what he was looking for. He needed a high sand cliff, with a row of pines running along the top and a wide, flat strip of beach below, but there was no hill in sight. The mist was drifting up through the top of the trees, thinning out, and as far as he could see along the shore, out towards the end of the point, the land sloped gently to the beach.

It was past six-thirty by the time he reached a flat shelf of rock that marked the furthest point of land. There was nothing but water in front of him.

Walker sat on a rocky ledge. He'd passed at least eight cottages. Mostly old, big and gracious-looking; and mostly empty. A few had cars or vans pulled up to them, but it seemed that everybody was still asleep.

He looked east. The rock shelf wrapped around the point as far as he could see. If there was no beach on the east side, and no sand hill, then, incredibly, he was on the wrong Mary's Point.

A tall, elderly man was approaching, walking across the flat rock, a slouch hat on and a fishing pole in his hand.

Walker got up quickly.

"Nice morning," he said to the man, passing him with plenty of rock between them.

"You visiting someone?" the man asked.

"You bet," Walker said. He started walking again, and didn't look back. He didn't have to, to know that the man was standing there watching after him.

The land began to rise, and rise sharply, on the east side of the point. Walker forgot about the man and broke into a trot, dropping off the rock shelf onto a pebbled beach that soon turned into a narrow swath of sand. He could see a cliff. He could see pine trees against the sky. He passed two cottages, but neither looked anything like the one in the photograph.

A woman was sitting on a chair far out in the water, an aluminum lawn chair whose legs seemed to perch and drift on the mirror-like surface. She was facing the sun. Suspended just above the water, it sent streaks of light racing towards her. She was dressed in some kind of flowery beach robe, her eyes protected behind dark glasses, her grey hair spilling out from under a scarf wrapped like a turban around her head. He stood on the shore and watched her for a moment.

A monster A-frame with huge glass windows sat on a knoll beside the sand cliff. Water lapped at the cliff's base. There was no beach in front of it. Something looked right, and something looked wrong. He thought to himself that maybe there were several other sand cliffs further along. Maybe this was just the wrong one.

He needed to wade out into the water, to see things from the perspective of the photograph.

He looked at the woman again. She was still floating there, about forty feet from shore.

Walker pulled off his boots and waded out. He didn't go directly towards the woman, he didn't want to startle her. He headed straight out, about fifteen feet off her starboard side, and when he got even with her he stood there in thigh-deep water, casually looking out over the lake and rolling himself a smoke.

He cleared his throat. Nothing. He struck a match, lit his smoke. Nothing.

"I think it's going to be another hot one today," he said loudly, trying to look as harmless as possible.

The woman jumped a little, turned to look at him. He smiled at her. "Morning."

He couldn't see her eyes behind her dark glasses. Her face was brown, her skin looked wrinkled and thin.

"Good morning," she said, in a voice light and clear.

"That's quite a trick, a floating chair," he said. "How do you manage that?"

The woman stared at him a moment. She said, "Anyone can do it. Why don't you come here?"

Walker waded over and, when he'd almost reached her, he stubbed his foot on what felt like a slippery stone wall. He found a foothold, and stepped up onto the flat top of a huge boulder sitting two inches under water.

"Not such a trick, is it?" the woman said. "It's easier to get up on the other side. I come here every morning, if the lake's quiet and the weather's clear. This is my rock."

Walker nodded. "It's a great spot."

"I intend to die sitting here."

He looked down at her.

"Not just yet, dear. Who do you belong to?"

"No one," he said. No one, he thought. He'd been working on his cover story, though.

"I was just driving by and I saw the sign to Mary's Point. My mother used to visit her grandmother here. She was always telling me about it, so I thought I'd turn in and try to find her grandmother's cottage. Just to say I saw it, you know?"

"Have you seen it?" the old woman asked.

"Not so far. I know what it looks like. I've seen photographs. Maybe I haven't gone far enough?"

"Hmm." She studied him for another moment. "What was her name? Your mother's grandmother?"

Walker was ready with a made-up name. "Davidson."

"Davidson," the old woman repeated. "When was the last time your mother was here?"

"Oh," Walker said, "I think maybe about 1964."

"Well then you're wrong. There's never been a Davidson. I've been coming here with my family since I was born, which was some time prior to 1964, as you might well guess. I know everybody and everybody knows me, which has not always been a blessing. Maybe you've confused your points, dear. God knows there are more than enough."

"I'm sure it was Mary's Point," Walker said. "A log cabin with a screened-in porch. It looked like it was painted kind of dark red. It was beside a sand cliff like this one, but there was a beach, there was a flagpole, and a huge stone painted white in front."

"In front of what?"

"Well, sort of on the beach. Out front."

"Do you know Long Point?" she asked. "If you go there, you'll see this large swamp behind a beach. Do you know what you'll find half submerged in that swamp?"

"No."

"Cottages, dear. Over the last years, the water has risen in Lake Erie by almost two feet. Winter storms have dragged cottages into the lake, or, at Long Point, pushed them off a spit of land right back into that swamp. It's frightful. Because it's so shallow here, we've lost twenty feet of beach."

Walker stared at her. "Meaning?"

"Meaning you have the wrong name, dear. If you're talking about the sixties, your mother's grandmother's name wasn't Davidson, it was Miller. The Miller family, from Toronto. I knew them all. They had the only log cabin on the point. It used to be where that monstrosity behind us is sitting right now. And," she said, for the first time pulling her dark glasses down a little, so that she could peer over them with cloudy hazel eyes, "do you know where that huge boulder painted white is?"

Walker nodded. He knew now.

He was close to his mother, close to where that little kid had clung to her inner tube thirty-one years before.

"I'm standing on it," he said.

CHAPTER EIGHT

• •

BOBBY LOVED HIS UNIFORM: the heavy black boots he polished every night that added an inch and a half to his height, the thick wool socks pulled snugly up to just below his knobby knees, the grey pants with the black pleat stripes and the wide black belt, the dull brown-green undershirt just like the Marines wore, the tight blue shirt and collar stiff with starch, the dark blue tie, the grey jacket with silver-buttoned epaulettes, and particularly the grey beret with the black trim and the "Glorious Southam" silver pin fixed square to the centre, the beret itself worn at just the precise tilt to the right. And he hated everything else.

He hated learning to march, couldn't get the moves down with any kind of precision, no matter how hard he tried (and he did try, for the first week). He hated being shouted at by his drill sergeant all the time. He hated being hazed by the seniors. He hated showering together in slippery gleaming groups, with all the shouting, laughter, wet-towel slapping; hated having to pee in long lines because he couldn't pee when anyone was around; everybody else seemed to be able to pee at will and there he stood as if he were playing with himself, straining to go, and nothing would come out; hated sleeping six to a room, hated all the accents from deep south to midwest to northeastern; hated their damn Yankee know-it-all brashness, their overflowing confidence, their profound stupidity. Hated all his teachers, all his courses, the buildings, the cold damp weather, rain sliding down his neck, the stupid little town that sat in a mine-scarred valley three miles to the west and sent plumes of grey-black smoke up into the low cloud cover all day and all night, except Sundays. He hated the minister who led the boys in prayer at general assembly, hated Major J.K. Kellum, who seemed to be the boss of the place, hated the American flag, hated the food, hated not sleeping at night, hated feeling for himself in the dark, the only one in the whole place abusing himself night after night after night, wanker, pale as the moon, soft as a girl, no one home, no one inside, just a shadow riding the night air, invisible, Bobby all gone, Bobby not here. He hated six o'clock reveille.

He felt he was just one small push, one sharp remark away from crying all the time. Toronto seemed like only the vaguest of memories, it seemed an infinitely long time ago. He didn't miss his mother at all but, with his wet little noodle of a penis cradled in his hand, he dreamt about his father every night.

Late one afternoon, four boys were waiting in the hallway for Bobby when he got out of his science class. Two of them were roommates and two were senior boys.

"We're putting a hit on faggot Dimarco," they informed him.

A trap, Bobby immediately thought, they're not after Dimarco, they're after me. He eased over to one wall, leaned against it as casually as he could. At least his back was covered.

"Oh?" he said.

"You know Dimarco. The little shit from town? His old man's the mayor or something? Walks like a fuckin' girl?"

They all started to talk at once.

"Fuckin' faggot."

"Why's he here, anyway?"

"Because his old man's the mayor."

"Looks like a fuckin' cocker spaniel. No, really. I got a cocker spaniel at home, big fuckin' brown eyes on him, curly hair, just like that little fag Dimarco.'

"So you want to come along?" one of the older boys said.

"To do what?" Bobby asked.

"Jump him, on his way to town."

"Pull his fuckin' pants down."

"Grease 'im."

"Grease him?" Bobby said.

All the boys laughed. One of them, a roommate of Bobby's, pulled a large tube of toothpaste out of his pocket.

"Look, Mom. No cavities."

Again all the boys laughed. Bobby ventured a fleeting smile.

"So why don't you come?"

"Come on!"

Bobby couldn't figure out why they were asking him to join in. Nobody liked him. He didn't have any friends. He didn't want any friends.

He eyed the tube of toothpaste. They were trying to lure him out of the grounds, along the path that ambled down the valley into the town below. They were going to pretend to wait for Dimarco, but they were going to jump him. Do him. Bobby could feel his sphincter muscles pull tight. A little charge of electricity ran through his balls.

Bobby said, "I have an extra lab with Brainless Baines. A makeup. He just told me. I'm supposed to get my other notebook and come right back here."

"Oh." The boys shrugged, nodded. At least they were convinced.

Bobby was good at lying. He was good at anything he wanted to be good at.

He watched the boys shuffle out the door and head across the compound towards the east gate.

Bobby knew Dimarco. Carlo Dimarco. Wop. Fag. One of a few

town kids, kids of the well-to-do who sent their boys to Southam. Townies. Day students. Maybe Dimarco was a fag. He was pretty enough to be a girl.

Bobby thought of Dimarco, his long dark eyelashes, curly black hair, soft pink cheeks, his sensitive eager face. He walked slightly flat-footed and he was almost as hopeless as Bobby on the parade ground. He had a plump ass just like a girl's.

Bobby's heart started to pound a little as he thought about Dimarco. What a pussy. What a fuckin' little fruit. If the other guys held him down, he thought, I'd kick the bastard right in the face.

He peered out the small narrow window in the door. The four boys were just disappearing through an opening in the high stone wall, heading in the direction of the road that led to town. Maybe they were telling the truth. Maybe, for some reason Bobby couldn't fathom, they did want him to come along, be part of it. Part of the gang.

Bobby pushed the door open. A gust of cold November air met him, took his breath away. He shivered, stepped outside. There was a kind of mist in the air, an invisible drizzle that immediately started to bead like tiny diamonds on his grey wool jacket. He stood there for a moment, deciding what to do. He could run up to his room, get rid of his books, put on his overcoat. Or he could follow them, dressed as he was; the other boys didn't have their overcoats on. Or he could forget it altogether.

But he couldn't forget it altogether. He couldn't stop thinking of those four boys all over Dimarco, punching him, kicking him, dragging him around. He could see it, see Dimarco on the ground now, struggling, whimpering, crying. Somebody was reaching down, undoing his belt.

Bobby looked around. Everything gleamed, wet with rain. He could see his breath in the air. His heart was racing and his stomach felt as if there was something squeezing it. The courtyard was empty except for a gaggle of junior boys in their shorts and cleats, heading for the sports field.

Bobby walked quickly across the compound and slipped out the east gate.

He crossed the road and headed along the path that was a short-cut down the hillside into town. The ground was soaked and he hardly made a sound. Every time he brushed against a branch, a splash of cold water hit his face. He strained to hear the other boys but they were silent, waiting somewhere in ambush. For who? For him? Did they know he would follow them? Suddenly he thought to himself, of course they did!

But he couldn't stop himself. He crept on, stepping slowly, listening, taking another step.

He came to a clearing, a natural lookout over the valley on a clear day, but now just a vantage point into clouds of mist floating through the tops of the nearest trees.

He didn't dare go any further. As a soldier, as a strategist, he had screwed up. He didn't know where the four boys were. He didn't know where Dimarco was. He didn't even really know the terrain, though he had walked alone into town and slowly, wearily, back up the winding path a couple of times. Dimarco and the other town kids did this twice a day. How soft could Dimarco be?

Bobby was sweating, cold and sweating all at the same time.

Where are those bastards? It is a trap! They're after me!

He looked wildly around. Nothing. Just a muffled, heavy silence. Then he heard some shouting up on the road. He had it figured out almost immediately.

Dimarco hadn't taken the path, he'd walked along the road, because he knew those guys were after him. But they'd outsmarted him, because they knew he knew, so that was where they'd ambushed him—up on the road. Bobby could hear them dragging him down through the trees, down the hill towards Bobby. Whoops and shouts and laughter. Even a rebel yell.

They stopped. There was some thrashing around in the trees above him. Grunting. Soft cries.

Bobby started to climb up the slippery hill. He was soaked through in a moment, shivering, breaths coming in sharp little bites.

He could see two of the boys, just in part, through some of the branches. One of the older boys, one of the seniors, had the tube of toothpaste in his hand. He was smiling down at something.

"Open 'im up," he said.

Bobby couldn't go any closer or they'd see him. He lay on the ground, trembling, his breath caught in his throat, his heart pounding.

And then he was ambushed himself, surprised by a rising tide of feeling, an inner storm.

Oh, he moaned softly, oh, and rocked his head back and forth, and his body jerked and spasmed deliciously against the ground.

CHAPTER NINE

• •

"How many Millers do you figure live in Toronto?" Krista asked Walker, her eyebrows arching ironically, her eyes a little cold.

She was sitting at her dispatch desk inside the office, but she might as well have been sitting down the hall. Some distance had come between them, though Walker wasn't sure why.

"One thousand, eight hundred and thirty-three," he replied.

"You've counted them?" she said. "If you phoned ten a day, it would take you half a year."

She gave her wheelchair a push, sped backwards across the room, did a one-eighty and came to a stop facing the counter. She ripped open an account book. "And maybe they have an unlisted number, anyway. Or maybe they've moved."

Walker continued to sit on the edge of a desk and watch the back of her blonde head. She started punching numbers on a calculator.

She'd been like this ever since he'd returned from Mary's Point two days before. He didn't know why and he couldn't see how to find out. When his mother would suddenly, inexplicably "go off," as his father put it, there was no way of figuring her out either.

"What the hell's biting your ass?" Gerard would ask her, which only made her jaw set more firmly and her grey eyes flash as though, if she had a gun, she'd kill him. His father would go silent too, so they'd both be silent for a week or two and then, just as mysteriously, she wouldn't be "off" any more; something ridiculous would happen and she'd laugh her wonderful throaty laugh, and suddenly the house would feel full of sunlight.

Walker stole another glance at Krista. She was going to punch the numbers right off her calculator in a minute.

He knew she was angry about her car. And he knew she was frightened. The break and enter, the burning car—maybe it was as simple as that. She was distancing herself from him, choosing self-preservation.

She turned another page in the account book, looked up at him and said, "It's obvious, isn't it? We're following your mother's trail, and somebody's following ours."

The phone rang. She said, "Shit," pushed off from the counter, glided backwards to the dispatch desk, did a turn and picked up the phone.

"A.P. Cabs. Uh-huh. Okay, you've got it. Side door."

It was only four o'clock. Krista didn't start her shift for another half-hour, but Donna was busy in the john.

Krista turned to the radio. "Simon, where are you, Simon? Okay, parcel pickup, 684 Sherbourne, side door...how the hell would I know?"

Alphonso came bursting through the front door, followed by a gaggle of adolescent girls dressed in identical green plaid skirts, green knee socks, white blouses and green blazers. They were all carrying notepads at the ready, like secretaries in training.

"This is what you don't allow," Alphonso said to the girls. "Fraternizing between a driver and a dispatcher. It causes jealousy among the rank and file. How do the other drivers know that this punk here ain't gettin' twice as many rides?"

"Believe me, he ain't," Krista said, giving Alphonso a very dark look.

Walker retreated to the other side of the counter. "Hi," he said to the girls. They all smiled back at him, giggled and said, "Hi."

"Don't talk to him. He's trouble," Alphonso said.

Walker did look a little like trouble to the girls, with his handsome face and glamorously crooked nose. Of course, they were only twelve and thirteen years old.

"He took her out on a date and burned her car," Alphonso said, his eyes crinkling a little.

"Alphonso," Krista said, "put a sock in it." She came drifting across the office in her wheelchair. "So which of these young ladies is your niece?"

Alphonso put a huge hand on a pretty dark-haired girl's shoulder.

"This here's Rebecca Applebaum. She's half Jewish but she's all Italian, right, Beck?"

"He's been saying that since I can remember. He thinks it's funny," Rebecca sighed, but with a smile. Humouring Uncle Alphonso. "Hi."

"Hi. I'm Krista Papadopoulos. Swedish and Greek."

"And I'm gone," Alphonso announced, backing away. "Got a lot of things to do, girls. Otherwise I'd explain everything my personal self." He disappeared down the hall towards his office.

"Okay," Krista said, "if you'll just come around the counter this way, I'll show you how a business should never be run. Because A.P. Cabs is a disaster."

All five girls smiled at Walker as they brushed past him.

"Don't you have anything to do, Walker?" Krista asked.

As Walker was about to slide into cab nineteen and start the graveyard shift, Alphonso came out of the building. "Stick around," he said. "I need you."

"What for?"

"I got an engagement."

Walker had discovered, on starting work at A.P. Cabs, that "engagement" always meant "a very promising poker game."

Alphonso played high-stakes poker in a continuous game that floated around the city. Sometimes they played at A.P. Cabs, in a room upstairs, with Joe, the mechanic, posted outside to keep an eye out for cops. Since the government received no cut, it seemed that the government took a dim view of floating games of chance, even though they were up to their ears in revenues from lotteries and casinos. Alphonso had pointed this irony out to Walker on several occasions.

"You gotta take the girls home for me," he said. "And I mean home, right to their front doors. Don't let them talk you into anything. Don't drop them off on Yonge Street or anywhere else, for chrissake."

Walker could see that he took his responsibilities as an uncle very seriously.

"They won't all fit," he said, indicating the tight and shabby confines of number nineteen. "How'd you get them down here?" he asked, as if he didn't know the answer.

Alphonso grimaced, shuffled around, reluctantly reached into his pocket and handed Walker a set of keys. "Okay, but you put one scratch on it, I'll bronze your cojones and hang 'em over the front door for good luck. And don't set fire to it."

The girls all fitted into Alphonso's immaculate pink 1958 Eldorado with no problem. Two in the front. Three in the back. Released from taking notes on how not to run a business, they were bouncing off the ceiling. Walker pulled out of the parking lot. He'd always wanted to drive a vintage, classic Caddy.

"Turn on the radio, Walker! No, sing to us, Walker! No, put on a tape, put on a tape, put on a tape!" God, they were noisy, but Walker hadn't been raised with six sisters for nothing.

Alphonso had had a tape deck installed, his only concession to modern times; everything else was original. The huge glove compartment was full of tapes, all Tina Turner. The girls screamed with laughter. Soon the car was jumping to the beat of "What's Love Got to Do with It?"

"I've got an idea, girls," Walker said. "Why don't we drive to California?"

Pandemonium! A great idea! They could live on the beach, they could surf, they could get their breasts enhanced and be Pamela Anderson. This last remark from Rebecca Applebaum. Things were really getting silly. The girls were laughing so hard, Walker thought they might get hysterical.

What if one of them gets sick? he thought. I'd better calm things down.

"Don't kick the back of the seat, okay?" he said. "Alphonso will fire me."

They didn't even hear him.

"We have to stop at the Bridge first," one of the girls was shouting. "Tell Anders we're going to California with Walker!"

"She'll say, can I come too?" another one shouted.

"You're steaming up the windows," Walker said. Then his heart stopped.

He twisted around. "What did you say?" he asked a flush-faced girl in the back.

"What about?" the girl said. "Miss Anders?"

"She's the headmistress," another one said.

"The head bat," said a third one.

"No," Walker said, "it was something about going to the Bridge."

"Oh, that."

"The Bridge, Walker. That's what we call it."

"Our school."

"St. Bridget's."

"You know Saint Bridget, don't you, Walker?" Rebecca Applebaum asked. "She's one of the patron saints of Ireland."

"You call your school the Bridge?" Walker asked.

"Sure. Everybody does," Rebecca said.

●　●

WALKER LEANED OVER THE TABLE at Ruby's and asked Krista to stay on a little after breakfast. She was already half up on her feet and about to leave with the rest of the breakfast gang. She hadn't spoken one word to him, except "Pass the maple syrup."

She sat back down reluctantly, looking as if she'd just been asked to stay after school. Walker waited until the others had left.

"What's wrong?"

"Nothing," Krista said. "Do I look like something's wrong?"

"Yes." And then he knew what it was.

"I'm sorry I didn't come back on the bus, and go out there with you another day. We could have found that cottage together," he said.

She stared at him. "You'd never have found it with a gimp on your arm."

It was like a silent thunderclap. It was as if all the air had gone out of Ruby's. As if the same knife had stabbed them both. So that was what it had been, all along. Not fear but humiliation, about floundering through the sand. And about his success, as he'd so thoughtlessly described it to her, running off the rocky point, down the pebbled beach to the sand cliff and the woman in her chair. Free and unburdened.

Krista looked at him, not helplessly or pitiably but with enough fierce energy to burn a hole in a wall.

He couldn't stand it any longer. He leaned across the table, took her face in his hands and kissed her. Her lips opened, her mouth opened, her tongue was on his lips, his mouth, his tongue.

"Hey you, stop that," Ruby said, banging a pot against the counter.

Four streetsweepers on a coffee break and a couple of sleepy hookers laughed and hooted. Someone even clapped.

Walker and Krista ignored them.

They walked across the street in a daze. He asked her if she wanted to go over to his place—the words just came out, as easy as that.

"How?" she asked.

Since her car had burned up, given that her insurance hadn't provided for a rental, she'd been getting one of the other cabbies to drive her back and forth from home.

"One of the guys?" Walker suggested.

"Are you out of your mind? Then they'd really have something to talk about, wouldn't they? Do you want Alphonso on your case?"

"Okay," he said. "We could catch a streetcar."

Krista stood there in the early morning sun as if she were trying to figure out a puzzle. He felt her hand brush against his thigh. He almost fell down.

"Not just yet," Krista said, "okay? Let's wait a while."

"Why?" Walker almost yelled.

"Because. Don't make a big deal out of it."

Big deal? What the hell does that mean? he thought.

"So what was it you wanted to tell me?" Krista asked.

He stood there for a long moment, then said, "Remember what Kim said in the letter? She said, 'This is going to be really short, 'cause I'm on my way to the Bridge and I'm already late.' I know where the Bridge is."

A shadow that looked a lot like dread passed over Krista's face. "Where?"

"Where Alphonso's niece and all those kids go to school. St. Bridget's. The kids call it the Bridge. I thought maybe it was the name of some restaurant, or some place to hang out. But it's the school Kim was going to. She went to St. Bridget's!"

"So?"

"The chances are good that Lennie went there too. At some time, anyway. The school should have a record of a Miller girl attending classes in the early seventies. They should have an address on file for a Kim or a Lennie Miller."

"That's over twenty years ago. Would they still have it? And even if they do, what makes you think they'd give it to you? That's private information."

Walker had been driving his cab and thinking about that all night. It was all he had been thinking about. "I'm going to tell them I'm working on a family tree."

"Oh, for godsakes," Krista said. "They'll never believe you."

Walker looked a little lost.

"Walker?"

"What?"

"Maybe if I went in and asked, if I said I was doing a family tree, it might work. For one thing, I'm a girl, right? And what's even better, I'm really sweet and I'm on crutches. I could even look like I'm in pain."

Walker brightened. "Good idea," he said.

That afternoon, he watched Krista struggle up three wide flagstone steps towards a large stone building with stained-glass windows and a discreet sign that read, St. Bridget's Academy. She wrestled with a massive wooden door and disappeared inside.

Walker, sitting across the street in Nick's old Chrysler LeBaron that he'd let them borrow for a couple of hours, glanced in the rearview mirror. A couple of kids in St. Bridget uniforms were walking away from him, down the sidewalk. A woman pushing a baby carriage and walking a silky-looking wolfhound was approaching the car.

The houses surrounding the school were three storeys high, of red or brown brick, with sweeping verandas and second-storey sunrooms, shadowed by thick bushes and trees. All the houses on that street, and in that whole district, were equally large.

Wealthy, Walker thought. You'd have to be rich to live in Forest Hill. And to send your kid to this school.

•   •

"FAMILY TREE OR NO, MISS MILLER, it's out of the question," a middle-aged woman said to Krista, her grey hair swept back in a bun, her smug expression unblemished by any trace of makeup. She was dressed in a brown suit and sensible shoes and had a pencil stuck in her hair, as though she'd just been shot with an arrow. And no wonder, Krista thought.

Krista was standing in front of the registrar's desk in a mahogany-panelled room. Two other women—one looking at least as old as the building, and the other younger and plump and more fashionably dressed—were sitting at two other desks. All three had lifted their heads when Krista came in, and all three were still staring at her. Only the plump one looked even remotely sympathetic.

"That's really disappointing," Krista said.

"It's a matter of confidentiality. You understand. We couldn't possibly give out information about our girls or their families without prior authorization."

"Willy-nilly," the ancient one chimed in.

"It's just a family tree, though. I only need an address so I can write them a letter myself."

"Do you have a famous ancestor?" the one with the pencil sticking out of her hair wanted to know.

"Not really," Krista replied.

"Then why bother?" the old one countered.

Krista could see that this was going nowhere. "I noticed your library across the hall. Would it be all right for me to browse in there for a few minutes? Do you have yearbooks?"

"I'm sure that would be fine," the plump one said, then—

realizing she'd spoken out of rank—blanched a little. "Wouldn't it?"

The ancient one didn't move a muscle.

"Why don't you go with her, Mary?" the smug, pencilled one said, turning back to her work. "You're not that busy."

Mary, looking upset, got up from her desk and walked stiffly across the gleaming hardwood hallway into the library. Krista followed her.

It was a narrow room. A row of arched stained-glass windows shone in vibrant blues and yellows, and old-looking books crammed the wooden bookshelves on all four walls. Two heavy oak tables and assorted chairs were arranged strategically around the room, and a marble fireplace sat in one corner, a wavy mirror over its mantel reflecting the room in a slightly hallucinatory way.

Krista looked up at her reflection, and found it difficult to imagine why any young girl would want to come into that room to do anything.

As if she'd read Krista's mind, the woman said, "This is the old library, actually. We have a nice new one, with videos and computers and microfiche, in the new wing. This is more of a historical room, all the old natural science and history and geography textbooks. They're a real hoot to read, and of course families give us old books from time to time, we don't like to throw them out. And we do keep the yearbooks in here, as well." She pointed to a low shelf on the far side of the room. "You'll find a complete set all along there. The old ones are quite rare. We don't lend them out, of course."

"Of course," Krista replied, swinging slowly over to that side of the room.

"You just take all the time you need, and if you want anything, you know where I am."

• •

WALKER HAD JUST FINISHED ROLLING his second smoke when he saw Krista squeeze out the huge front door, struggle down the stairs and swing along the flagstones towards him. He got out, opened the passenger door and took her crutches, putting them in the back seat.

"Did you find out anything?" he asked her.

"Let's go," she said.

"How did you do?" he persisted.

She pulled up her sweater. Three shiny red yearbooks were stuck down the top of her slacks.

Walker stared at them for a moment, clenched his cigarette between his teeth and grinned. Bonnie and Clyde. They pulled away from the school with a squeal of tires.

Nobody had seen Alphonso since yesterday, when he'd told Walker he had an urgent meeting to attend. Walker and Krista hurried by a suspicious Joe Smart, went into Alphonso's empty office and closed the door.

Krista had lifted the yearbooks 1973–74, 74–75 and 75–76, because the letter from Kim to Lennie had been written in September of 1979, when Walker was already three years old. St. Bridget didn't seem like a school that would tolerate a pregnant student, so if Lennie had gone there, it would have been at least three years before.

She spread the yearbooks out on Alphonso's desk. "I'll mail them back when we're done. I'll just make sure there's no return address," she said.

Walker picked up one of the yearbooks and sat down on the old leather chair. Krista sat behind the desk and began to look through a second one. The room was silent for several minutes, with just the crisp sound of glossy pages being turned.

"I found her!" Krista said.

Walker hurried around the desk.

Krista had the 1974–75 yearbook opened at class 9-B's picture, with a list of the kids' names underneath. Her finger was under the words "Kimberly Miller, second row, third from right."

Walker looked at the picture. All the girls were dressed in exactly the same uniforms as Alphonso's niece and her friends. A pretty blonde girl with short curly hair in the second row smiled back at him.

"I think that's the one sitting on the air mattress," he said.

"So we were right," Krista said. "The dark one must be your mother."

With Walker looking over her shoulder, she turned the pages until she'd almost reached the end of the book. There were two facing pages of candid photographs with funny captions near the back. Girls of St. Bridget playing field hockey, girls of St. Bridget at a formal dance, girls of St. Bridget at a track meet. And in the hallowed halls of the school itself.

At exactly the same time, their eyes fell on a small photograph at the bottom of the right-hand page. Two girls were clinging to the sides of what looked like a large waste-bin on wheels, having a free ride down a hall, being pushed along by a bemused-looking janitor. The girls were facing each other and laughing. The caption read, "Kim Miller and Lennie Nuremborski help Mr. Taylor."

"Oh Jesus," Walker said.

Krista turned back to the class 9-B picture. Standing one row behind and to the left of Kimberly Miller was the same tall, dark-haired girl. She was looking off to the side somewhere, as if she'd just seen someone. She was the only girl who wasn't looking directly at the camera. She was the only girl who wasn't smiling.

Walker looked at the list of the girls' names. It said, Lenore Nuremborski.

"She's so pretty," Krista said.

Walker tried it out. "Lenore Nuremborski." Then, feeling slightly light-headed, he said, "I wonder if she's already pregnant?"

CHAPTER TEN

· ·

BOBBY WATCHED CARLO DIMARCO. He had a scrape across one soft cheek but he hadn't told anyone how he'd gotten it. He'd probably made up some story about slipping and falling, for the benefit of his mother and his father, the mayor.

He was gaining points for his silence. And some respect. He'd had toothpaste squeezed up his bum and he hadn't ratted on anyone. Someone might tell him a joke soon. Someone might even become his friend. Then Bobby would be the only soldier at Southam without a friend. This thought made Bobby smile a secret smile. He felt a kind of triumph.

Bobby watched him every chance he got. In class. On the sports field, where they both tried to get away with doing as little as possible. On parade for Major Kellum, who inspected his little soldiers closely, moving up and down their ranks with excruciating slowness, pulling on someone's loose tie, someone's soiled collar, someone's not-quite-at-the-perfect-angle beret.

"What a flaming asshole," all the kids said about Major Kellum, after lights out. "What a fuckin' nutcase."

Bobby followed Carlo Dimarco around. He liked to stand or sit as close as possible to him. He liked to look at his long eyelashes, his soft curls, his pudgy girl's hands. Dimarco was smaller than Bobby by half a head, he was a year younger, and he made Bobby's heart race.

Because the wop had said not a word. The wop knew how to keep his mouth shut.

Bobby walked down the steep path to the town one day, feeling as if he were having an out-of-body experience. He went into a drugstore and bought a tube of toothpaste. He looked carefully for the smallest one. He didn't just want to squeeze some toothpaste up Dimarco's ass, he wanted to shove the tube up there too.

At the cash register, he wondered if the woman could see his hands tremble as he paid for it. He wondered if she knew what it was for.

He ran back down the street and halfway up the path, until he couldn't run any more, until he couldn't breathe. He sat on the side of the hill. He could see in his mind Dimarco thrashing underneath him. He could see the tube of toothpaste going in. Could imagine squeezing the damn thing, wrenching it around until Dimarco screamed. Until he just screamed. And yet, afterwards, Dimarco would keep quiet. It couldn't be more perfect. Dimarco wouldn't tell a soul.

Bobby hid the toothpaste in a sock in his drawer. At night, Dimarco would blubber and cry in Bobby's dreams. At night, Dimarco would beg for mercy.

And each day Bobby followed him around. The anticipation was almost unbearable.

Late one afternoon, Bobby watched Dimarco leave the field house, his schoolbooks in a bag over his shoulder. Little Carlo hadn't bothered showering after the soccer game out on the cold muddy pitch. Maybe because he was shy. Maybe because he was still wary. Bobby could tell he hadn't showered because his hair was dry. His curls rubbed against his coat collar.

Bobby leaned against the wall outside the door as Dimarco passed. "Good game?" he asked.

Dimarco shrugged his shoulders, glanced at Bobby, seemed to blush a little and hurried on. Bobby fell into step beside him.

"We play Blue on Thursday," he said.

Dimarco nodded.

Bobby thought maybe Dimarco had noticed him watching, always hanging around. He'd been cautious enough, but there was something in the way the boy was hurrying across the lawn that made him wonder. Maybe he's scared of me already, he thought, and the thought made his heart beat even faster.

"I'm going into town. I'll walk with you," Bobby said.

Dimarco was silent.

They crossed the road together and walked along the side of it.

"Do you want to take the road or the path?" Bobby asked.

Again Dimarco looked at him, seemed to flush a little. He said, "The path."

It was the end of November. The sky was cold and grey, trying to make up its mind whether to rain or snow. The wind made Bobby shiver even though he was wearing his new tweed overcoat, one of a mountain of things his mother had bought in preparation for his first year in a Tennessee military school.

He wondered if Dimarco felt cold too. He didn't look cold, but then he'd been playing soccer for an hour.

As soon as they dropped off the ridge, skidding down the steep part of the path into the sheltering trees below, Bobby felt warmer. It was darker, too. The sun had disappeared behind the far hills about a half-hour before. Shadows crept through the woods on both sides of the path. Gloom hung in the branches.

Bobby couldn't think of anything else to say. Dimarco was walking quickly beside him, his shorter legs moving fast. And down they went, down through the trees, winding towards the valley below.

There was no one in sight, but Bobby could hear something calling in the distance.

"What's that?"

"Just a crow," Dimarco replied.

Bobby grabbed him by the head and swung him off the path.

They went rolling down the steep incline together, Bobby holding onto the other boy's coat, bumping against trees, rolling through bushes.

Bobby tried to get a grip on Dimarco's neck but Dimarco kicked wildly and shoved his hands into Bobby's face. He was stronger than he looked, punching and kicking for all he was worth as they tumbled over logs and stones and landed in a heap in a hollow below.

Bobby tried to hold him with one hand and feel around in his coat pocket for the rope and the toothpaste with the other, because he'd planned to tie a rope around Dimarco's neck and to sit on his back half-strangling him—he could control him that way, and get his pants down too. But the rope was hopelessly tangled in his pocket and he couldn't find the tube of toothpaste. Meanwhile Dimarco, in his army boots, was kicking at him with all his might.

Bobby swarmed on top of him, exerting his larger size, his marginally greater strength, and pressed Dimarco's face into the mossy wet ground, pummelling him with his other hand. It was all he could do to keep him down. He pulled out the ball of rope, and the toothpaste went flying somewhere down the hill. This wasn't what he had planned, this wasn't what he had imagined at all.

He went back to pummelling Dimarco on his back. Exhausted, he wrapped his arms tightly around the boy's head and tried to catch his breath, pressing his head down against Dimarco's.

He remained there, lying on top of Dimarco and breathing hard against the back of his neck. He let his whole weight rest on the boy, who for some reason was now lying quietly beneath him. Bobby felt a rush of blood shudder through his whole body. Dimarco's eyes were open. He was just staring at the ground. He smelled warm.

The goddamn freak, Bobby thought. He got up quickly and sat on Dimarco's back, looking around for the toothpaste, but it was lost somewhere in the underbrush below.

Bobby could hardly breathe now. He reached under Dimarco and felt for his belt, wrenching it this way and that. It came loose.

He grabbed Dimarco's trousers in both hands and pulled hard. Like some devastating secret, like some shattering, life-changing sight, the snow-white flesh appeared beneath him. The plump, curving, dreamt-of flesh. The planned-for flesh.

Bobby felt sick. He didn't know what to do.

Dimarco lay still but his eyes were open wide. There was a streak of mud on his face. Bobby lay down on him again, with a kind of groan. He could feel Dimarco shifting under him, raising himself a little.

A rush of blood flooded into Bobby's groin. He started to thrust himself at Dimarco, wildly fumbled under his coat for his own belt, his fly, pulled out his swollen cock and with a cry spurted his almost clear juvenile jism over Dimarco's bum.

He stumbled back up on his feet. Fucking faggot, fucking faggot, a deep voice was yelling in his head, like a roar, like an explosion in his ears.

Dimarco turned a little to look up at him. He smiled. Bobby was sure of it.

He staggered backwards, scrambled back up the hill and fell over a rotting log. He picked it up and came back down the hill to where the boy was still lying, almost lost in the shadows now, resting on one hip.

Bobby could hardly see him; he almost tripped, and there were tears in his eyes.

"Fucking faggot!" he screamed, and he swung the log at Dimarco's head.

CHAPTER ELEVEN

. .

WALKER CHECKED THE TORONTO phone directory in Alphonso's office. Unlike the prolific Millers, there were only three Nuremborskis listed. One address was in Forest Hill, on a street just five blocks from the school.

"I'll go to each one, anyway," he said.

"And do what?" Krista replied.

"Knock on their doors and ask if they know a Lenore Nuremborski who attended St. Bridget's around 1974."

"And if they say yes?"

"I'll say I'm her son."

"Someone knows everything you're doing. If they did something awful to your mother, what makes you think they won't do something awful to you? You can't just wander around knocking on doors!"

"This is my mother!" Walker yelled.

Krista jumped. She didn't say anything more. She just stared hard at Walker as he shoved aside the phone book. They'd found three more pictures of Lenore Nuremborski. And whether it was a class portrait or an informal snapshot, there was not one where she was looking at the camera. She was always turned a little away, always looking off.

Krista could see that Walker had his mother's strong mouth. His hair seemed darker than hers, though, pitch-black and shiny, falling over his forehead as he looked once again at her pictures in the book.

"Her family could have moved away, you know?" Krista finally said.

"I know."

"And they're probably, they're almost certainly not going to say anything to you, even if they do know something. Are they?" she asked.

Walker looked up at her. "I'm hoping they will," he said.

Fifteen minutes later, at the beginning of his night shift, Walker took off in cab nineteen to visit all three Nuremborskis.

The address on Eastern Avenue turned out to be a frame house trapped between a police auto pound and an abandoned railway wheelhouse with rusty tracks disappearing into weeds. Graffiti was spray-painted all over the walls. A sad-looking Doberman, chained to the door frame and resigned to boredom, lay on the small cement porch.

As Walker pulled up, he could see a large man working on a motorbike around the back. He got out of the cab. The Doberman rose to attention, bristling and barking, looking pleased to have something to do. The man screamed at it to shut up, but with no effect whatsoever.

Walker strolled up to the man and asked him if he was G. Nuremborski. The man's eyes slid towards the road and Walker's cab, then back to Walker.

"Who wants to know?"

"There's no problem. My mother's name is Nuremborski, that's all. I'm looking for information about her. I thought you might be a relative. Her first name was Lenore. She went to St. Bridget's school for girls, in Forest Hill, around 1974."

"No shit," the man said. "Do they wear those tiny little skirts, them girls? Jesus Christ, there ought to be a law." He grabbed at his balls and jiggled them.

"I think there is," Walker said.

The man smiled. "Fucked if I know any Lenore," he said.

Walker nodded. He looked at the house again. His mother could be tied up in there, for all he knew. He thanked the man, walked back to his battered cab and drove away.

Sixteen years. Whatever had happened, had happened sixteen years ago. Then why was he feeling such a growing panic, feeling that if he just drove fast enough right now, if he was just smart enough right now, he could still rescue her?

His mother was a child floating on an inner tube, she was fourteen years old, tall and pretty, in a green blazer and plaid skirt, she was a woman, whispering. His mother was a ghost.

Walker drove quickly through traffic and in twenty minutes he was pulling into a driveway off Bayview Avenue, the second Nuremborski address. He was not all that far from Forest Hill now. He coasted alongside an expensive-looking, relatively new split-level house, and came to a stop in front of a three-car garage.

He was about to get out when he caught sight of a young girl, a teenager, standing in the backyard. She was playing with a dog, a half-grown golden Lab. The big pup was bounding all around her. She was tall and slim, and her hair was dark.

Walker stepped out of the cab. Apparently the girl hadn't heard him. She threw a ball the length of the yard and the pup tore after it, straight through a flower garden.

Walker came up to the waist-high fence.

"Hi," he called.

The girl turned towards him. He was half expecting to see his mother, but the girl's skin was pale and her face was round. She was wearing jeans and a baggy hockey sweater.

"Hi," she said, seeing the cab and walking over to him. "You must have the wrong address. There's no one home."

Walker could see a flicker of tension cross her face as she realized she'd said the wrong thing.

Walker tried to look harmless. He smiled and said, "I'm not on a call, I'm trying to locate my mother, as stupid as that sounds."

The girl's expression changed; she was instantly interested.

"What do you mean?"

"This is Carl Nuremborski's residence, isn't it?"

"My dad," she replied. She looked at him closely now, as if anticipating some shock, as if he were about to say, guess what, I'm your brother.

"When I was a kid, I was separated from my parents. I know my mother's name was Lenore Nuremborski, I know she went to St. Bridget's school about twenty years ago, but that's all I know. I'm trying to trace her."

"Really?" she said. "That's so weird. Not weird, but you know what I mean."

"Yeah," Walker said. "So I was just wondering if your dad might know if—"

"He doesn't know anything," she interrupted. "Not about that kind of thing. I had to visit my grandmother and call my aunt in Victoria to do this genealogy chart for school, like when I was like ten years old? He didn't even know his grandfathers' first names or where they came from or anything."

"You did a chart?"

"Uh-huh."

"Do you remember if there was a Lenore?"

"I don't think there was. I'm sorry."

"That's okay."

"No one in our family ever went to St. Bridget's, I'm almost positive. I've heard of it, though."

"You wouldn't happen to still have that chart, would you?" Walker asked. "Not that I don't trust your memory or anything, but...."

"Sure. My mother keeps everything. Do you want to see it?"

"Yeah, thanks. I'll hang out here."

"Okay," the girl said, pale green eyes dancing. She turned and ran quickly across the patio, slid open a glass door and disappeared inside.

Walker amused himself by trying to persuade her dog to drop the ball, held firmly in its mouth now and gleaming with saliva. The gangly pup dashed around in circles, shaking its head furiously this way and that. Walker leaned over the fence and made a grab for the ball but the pup dodged. There was no way it was giving up that ball.

The girl came back out, carrying a notebook with bright blue covers. She walked through the gate and handed it to Walker. The cover announced, in neat block letters, "Angela Nuremborski's Family Tree."

"I was just ten," she said defensively.

Walker grinned and looked through it in the fading light. She was right. No Lenore Nuremborski. He handed the notebook back to her.

She stood beside him, looking through the pages. "My branch of the family came from Russia," she was saying, "from the Ukraine. There was some kind of religious persecution or something. I have notes in here somewhere. So they left. They went to Saskatchewan first, because it reminded them of home."

Her head was bent over her notebook. Walker could see the nape of her white, slender neck. She trusted him now. She was vulnerable. He thought of Lenore.

"Thanks for everything," he said.

Cab nineteen drifted under a long canopy of leafy branches as it moved through Forest Hill and pulled up in front of a hulking brown-brick three-storey house. As if on cue, the street lights went on.

The house was set back further from the road than the others around it, and perhaps it had been sitting there longer, too. It was a dreary, flat-faced house. He could see three rows of windows, twelve in all. They were dark.

Walker got out of the cab and walked up the sloping lawn. The grass hadn't been cut for some time, and along one side of the property a high board fence was drooping against overgrown ever-greens and bushes.

Walker climbed the narrow steps up under a pillared and flat-roofed portico that protected the front door. For some reason he stood there in the deepening shadows, hesitating. He looked up.

A tiny red light stared back down at him. A camera, attached to the brick wall just below the ceiling, fixed him with its round lens.

Walker rang the bell, looked up at the camera again and smiled. He rang again. Waited. Rang again.

A row of dark cypress trees marked the property line on the other side. A narrow driveway covered with crushed red tile ran beside the tall trees and disappeared past the corner of the house.

Walker was thinking of having a look down the driveway when a faint yellow light bloomed in the fanlight above the door. He could hear the laborious turning of locks, sliding of bolts, and a chain being slipped out of its metal clasp. The heavy door opened. An old man with a sallow face and two plastic tubes stuck up his nose peered out.

"Mr. Nuremborski?" Walker said. "Have I got the right address?"

He could hear the old man's breathing, a deep, bubbling sound. He was wearing a sweater coat pulled over a yellowing undershirt, trousers shiny and wrinkled, slippers a faded plaid. The man slowly raised his bloodshot, rheumy eyes and stared straight into Walker's with such intensity that Walker could feel his throat tighten.

"Are you J. Nuremborski?" he persisted. "I'm trying to trace a relative of mine, a Lenore Nuremborski, she went to St. Bridget school for girls about 1974, you know St. Bridget's, it's just a few blocks from here."

The old man didn't answer. He continued to look at Walker as if he were searching for something, as if he saw something in Walker's face that amazed him. His jaw went slack. His mouth opened a little but no sound, other than the faint gurgling of his lungs, came out.

"I'm her son," Walker said.

The old man waved a bony hand in front of his own face, as if trying to shake off a pestering fly.

A middle-aged man peered around the door at Walker. He was big, dressed in a dark blue business suit and tie.

"Hello," he said.

The old man turned and shuffled back down the long hallway, dragging a shiny green canister on a little trolley behind him. Walker watched him disappear around a corner.

"Can I help you with something?" the big man asked, stepping in front of Walker. Round wire-rimmed glasses perched on his fleshy nose. Small sly eyes sized Walker up.

"I'm trying to trace my mother. Her name was Lenore Nuremborski. She was called Lennie by her friends. She disappeared sixteen years ago." He was surprised at how aggressive his voice sounded. He felt desperate all of a sudden.

"Mr. Nuremborski certainly can't help you there," the man said, in a voice soft as butter. "He's a bachelor. He came to this country all by himself many years ago. He has only one living relative, a sister, back in Poland. He's all alone, I'm afraid. Always has been. Sorry."

The man nodded sadly, as if in commiseration, and slowly closed the door. The locks were turned, the bolts slid back into place, the chain rattled against the door.

•   •

AT 9:30 THE NEXT MORNING, back from his poker game with a two-day growth of salt-and-pepper beard wreathing his swarthy face, Alphonso stepped wearily out of a rival cab and pushed through the grimy front door of A.P. Cabs, one thousand, six hundred and twenty-two dollars lighter.

At 9:31, Joe Smart informed him that cab nineteen was missing.

"What do you mean, missin'?"

"Missin', okay, missin'!" Joe spluttered. He'd had false teeth once, but he'd put them down somewhere and damned if he could ever find them again. "Son of a bitch never came back!"

Joe didn't like Walker. He thought he was a goddamn smart aleck. He didn't like the way Walker had become part of the breakfast club so soon, while Joe was still waiting for his first invitation. He didn't like the way he was taking advantage of poor crippled Krista, screwing her probably from here to Sunday. Walker had burned her car up, too. And he particularly didn't like the way Alphonso would kid around with Walker, give him a poke on the shoulder the way he used to do with Joe.

"He stole my cab?"

"Nobody knows, okay? Krista says he just fucked off with it for a while. He can't do that! What if there was another cabbie waiting for it?"

Of course, they both knew there wasn't. There wasn't another cabbie stupid enough or desperate enough to drive number nineteen.

"He didn't come back?" Alphonso mused, scratching his beard.

"The fuckin' kid's a pain in the fuckin' ass!" Joe sent an involuntary stream of spittle in almost a perfect arc past Alphonso's left shoulder.

At 9:35 the phone rang at the residence of George Papadopoulos.

"Hey, Georgie," Alphonso said. "How you been, where's that gorgeous daughter of yours?"

"Asleep," George said. George was a substantial man, but of few words and of dour temperament. He'd been a successful player for years in the stock market, and he was a private banker for half the Greek-owned businesses on the Danforth. He was respected, loved, even feared a little. No one was a truer friend, no one a more implacable enemy. The word on the street was, do not fuck with Georgie Papadopoulos.

"I gotta speak to her," Alphonso said.

"She's asleep," George repeated. "Call back at three-thirty."

"Who's that? Is that for me?" Krista yelled at her father, wheeling out of the kitchen. She had her pyjamas on but she hadn't been able to get to sleep. All she could think of was Walker. She'd just come down on her lift and poured herself another coffee, one more thing guaranteed to drive her father nuts.

George thought she drank way too much coffee and slept way too little. Not unrelated phenomena, he had pointed out. And she shouldn't be working through the night and sleeping during the day, anyway. She should get a day job, not work at that dump of Piattelli's. She was too smart. She damn near ran the place. She should be working for him, her father, like a good girl, but every time he suggested that she stuck her finger down her throat and made gagging noises.

"No, it's not for you," George said to Krista, and to Alphonso, "Call back," and hung up the phone.

"Who was that?"

"The useless bum you work for. Go and get some sleep. You're pale. You'll be sick. I got to go to work. He'll phone you back at three-thirty."

"Jesus Christ, you've got your nerve," Krista said, wheeling by him, picking up the phone and dialling.

"When you say Jesus Christ, your hands should be together and your eyes closed," George reminded her. "You don't sleep, you'll make yourself sick. Die young or die old," he added for good measure, as he walked out the front door.

Krista set Alphonso straight. Walker had not stolen number nineteen. Who in his right mind would?

"Where is he, then? 'Cause I'm on the verge of calling the cops."

"You wouldn't call the cops if you were being murdered, you'd be afraid they'd look at your books," Krista countered. "He just borrowed it for the day. He's gone back to Lake Erie."

"He's gone where to what?" Alphonso said.

"Well, it's kind of...." Krista thought for a moment. It was difficult to explain, particularly since Walker's search for his mother was supposed to be just between the two of them. "It's kind of about my car, but I can't tell you why," she said, and hung up.

Walker had pulled up in front of the McKormack Township municipal office just after six that morning. It had actually been someone's house in another life, but had now been converted into several offices and a council chamber. He hadn't expected anyone to be there, and no one was. A diffuse light was just beginning to creep up over the horizon.

He'd backed in along the side of the municipal works garage, turned off the engine, closed his eyes and, after a few minutes, fallen into a fitful sleep.

By the time a late-model car pulled up in front of the municipal office, he was awake again. He watched a large woman struggle out of the car, pull herself heavily up the steps, unlock the front door and go inside. He recognized her as the township clerk who'd directed them to Mary's Point the week before. She hadn't noticed the cab.

The sun was up now. Walker got wearily out of the cab. The trees were just beginning to turn gold and red on a distant hill. There was a bite to the country air that woke him up, made him feel better.

"I need your help," he said to the clerk.

She was busy putting her makeup on in the washroom, and looked surprised to see a customer standing at her counter so early, watching her through the open bathroom door.

"Do you remember me?" he said.

"Yes, I think so." The woman came into the office but her freshly made up face looked slightly perplexed.

"I was here a few days ago with a friend. We asked directions to Mary's Point?"

"Oh, that girl! Yes!" she said, then added quickly, "I remember you both."

"We found Mary's Point all right, but we didn't find what I was looking for."

"What do you mean?"

"That I really need your help," Walker said.

Catching the edge of desperation in his voice, the woman came closer to the counter. Walker hesitated for a moment, then told her that he'd been abandoned when he was three years old, and that he was looking for his mother.

The clerk's mouth made a little O.

The only information he had about her, Walker went on, was that on June 2, 1964, when she was just a little kid, she'd had her photograph taken at the cottage of a Miller family on Mary's Point.

Walker recounted his childhood in Big River, and told her about coming to Toronto, learning to drive cab and beginning the search. As he spoke, the woman kept shaking her head in sad wonder.

Finally, he asked her the question he'd been leading up to. "Do the people who own cottages on Mary's Point pay township taxes?"

She looked more sharply at him, and let a second or two go by. "Of course."

"How do they get their tax bills? Do you mail them?"

"Twice a year," she replied.

"A woman I met on the beach remembered the Miller family. They sold their cottage years ago. But if, say, they'd lived in Toronto, would you have sent their taxes to their home address?"

The woman was smart, he could see that. He wouldn't have to say anything more. In fact, he sensed that it would be better if he didn't.

"All the information in this office is confidential," she finally said.

Walker remained silent.

"Tax rolls and assessments are confidential," she said.

Walker didn't respond.

"All our current information is in computer files. Anything prior to 1985 is on card files. We had a student here this summer, transferring our old files onto the computer. Janis Turcott, Wilma Turcott's oldest. You wouldn't know her, of course. She goes to McMaster, she's a lovely girl, she's in her first year."

Walker didn't move.

The big woman glanced out the front windows. There was no one around. She turned and walked towards a door in the back wall.

"We like to save as much of the old information as we can," she went on, "but we're running out of room. What we need is a historical society around here, with its own building and its own archives. People have been saying to me for years, 'What a good idea, Marilyn,' but no one does anything about it."

She opened the door, switched on a light in the back and disappeared inside.

When she came back out empty-handed, Walker's heart sank. She walked over to a desk and sat down, blew her nose and began shuffling some papers around.

After a while, and without looking up at Walker, she said, "I can't tell you the Miller family's address, but if you were to look for them at 1628 Rosewood Avenue in Toronto you probably wouldn't miss them by much."

"Thank you," Walker said.

She didn't reply. She didn't look up at him. She started to sort the papers on her desk into three piles, as if she were sitting in her office by herself, as if he weren't there, as if he'd never been there at all.

CHAPTER TWELVE

• •

OBBY'S FATHER TOOK THE TIME TO FLY down and talk to Major J.K. Kellum personally. He sat with him in his office for over an hour, but nevertheless he could not dissuade the major from his decision. Bobby was to be expelled, drummed out of the regiment, for his vicious assault on Carlo Dimarco.

Bobby was surprised. Even though Dimarco was bleeding from a cut on his forehead where the edge of the log had whumped down on his skull, even though his right eye immediately began to disappear under a swelling that grew as big and blue as an Easter egg, Bobby had expected him to keep the code of silence. Dimarco, the little fag, had let him down.

Bobby had left him bleeding and half-blind in the hollow. He had stumbled back to his dormitory, crawled into bed with his clothes on and told one of his roommates that he was sick with the flu. He had lain there motionless until lights out, had lain sleepless all night.

It was all Dimarco's fault. He should kill him. That was what he should do. What had Dimarco been smiling about? What had he thought he knew? Bobby's body shook with rage, then felt cold and exhausted, then grew treacherously aroused by the memory of Dimarco lying there. Then the rage returned.

He would tie Dimarco up with ropes. He would strangle him. He could see Dimarco suspended high between two trees, his tongue swollen, hanging out; could see him dead.

Bobby resisted as long as he could, then touched himself. Dimarco was spinning on his ropes in front of him, he could feel himself swelling in his hand, Dimarco was *dead*....

At roll call the next morning Bobby looked all around, but Dimarco wasn't there. Later that morning, in the middle of a civics class, two senior boys showed up and asked for Bobby. They took him firmly by his arms and marched him across the square to Major J.K. Kellum's office.

The major was waiting for him in full uniform. He paced back and forth as Bobby sat on a very straight, hard wooden chair. He informed Bobby that the mayor of Harristown had driven up to see him and had told him that his son, Carlo, was in the hospital that very moment with a concussion and a hemorrhaging right eye. Did Bobby know anything about that?

Bobby said very loudly, as he had been instructed, "No, sir!"

The major said, "Out of all the students in this school, why do you suppose I picked you, if you had nothing to do with it? Did I just pull a name out of a hat? Is it just your bad luck? Or do you suppose Carlo Dimarco has made an accusation?"

Bobby thought about this for a moment. What had Dimarco said? Had he told his father everything? Not everything! Had the mayor of Harristown roared up the hill in his car that morning, burst into the major's office and accused Bobby of playing bad doggy with his boy?

Bobby's brain took off and flew around the room like a bird.

The major was leaning in towards him now, holding his enormous, flat red face only inches away. His eyes were bloodshot. Bobby could see purple veins in his nose.

Did you pull out your wee-wee? Did you go all wet? Did you try to bum-fuck that boy? Bobby could almost hear those terrible words—did hear them—was that what the major had said?

The major's grim mouth hadn't moved.

Bobby heard a growl, a low rumble from somewhere. His head felt as if it were being squeezed by two huge hands, his eyes were going to pop. The room was full of cotton. The air was full of the drone of bees.

Bobby went inside. He didn't say one more word. His body remained sitting at attention in front of Major J.K. Kellum, but Bobby wasn't there.

And he didn't talk to anyone—not the major, not the school nurse, not the Harristown chief of police, who, on the insistence of Dimarco's father, made the long trip up to the top of the hill to interrogate him, not any of his roommates (though he did listen; he listened very closely to everyone, and learned that Dimarco hadn't talked about his pants being pulled down, only about Bobby inexplicably attacking him and hitting him on the head), for the two days it took his father to arrive.

Fight on your natural battleground, he had learned that much from the school, and so he did. Bobby's natural battleground was subterranean or, better still, he thought to himself as he sat wordless in his room for two days, aquatic. You have to swim deep down to engage me in battle, he thought, for I am a creature, rarely seen. No one knows my language.

It was only after his father's fruitless interview with the major, and after he had packed all the new clothes his mother had bought him at the Eaton's College Street store and was sitting safely beside his father in the back of a cab, and after the cab had cleared the stone gates of Southam and headed downhill, that Bobby spoke.

"Dimarco can't breathe under water," he said.

His father did not reply. His father turned slowly away from him and stared out the window.

A week after he arrived back in Toronto—a week filled with arguments between his mother and his father, which she won— they agreed that Bobby would not be sent to another boarding school ever again. It was obviously too great a strain on his sensitive disposition.

Two days after their arguments ceased, his father, like a man trying to will the impossible, gave Bobby an official tour of the company he'd inherit one day.

He led him through a maze of turn-of-the-century factory buildings, refurbished and brightly lit, and introduced him to endless rows of machinists and millwrights, polishers and welders, shippers and receivers, and showed him a labyrinth of offices full of engineers and managers and junior staff and secretaries. He took him up the wide stairs to the executive floor and introduced him to the comptroller and the secretary-treasurer, and the VP of sales and the VP of marketing, and all their secretaries; he took him into the boardroom with its impossibly long table and fourteen leather chairs, its portraits of his father and his father's father and his father's father's father, looking like a Prussian soldier—looking not unlike Major J.K. Kellum himself.

His mother had dressed him carefully in his best suit, his shiniest shoes, his most conservative tie, and had combed his hair; she would have shaved his thirteen-year-old face, if he'd had any whiskers.

He tried to shake everyone's hand with a firm grip, look them straight in the eye, as his father had told him to do. He tried to stand as erect as he could, shoulders back, chin out a little. He tried to smile with just the right touch of irony, of distance, even of condescension, as his father did.

They were all jockeying for power, all these greasy, grinning, bright-eyed men. Bobby could see that. He could see right through them.

He would be their boss one day. He would have all the power.

His heart raced a little as he imagined himself sitting in the chair at the head of this long table. It would be his job to teach each man how to behave. They would all be frightened of him.

Alone now in the broadloomed and wood-panelled boardroom, Bobby's father took him in his arms. "This business does not go out of the family," he whispered in the boy's ear. He kissed his cheek, hugged him tight. "You know that your mother can have no more children, no more sons."

Bobby hadn't known that. He had a younger sister but he never paid any attention to her. His father did—he fussed over her, called her his princess, bounced her on his knee—but it was a son, a son he wanted. A daughter was not part of his business plan.

He held Bobby at arm's length, smiled a hopeless kind of smile at him. His hands began to dig into Bobby's shoulders. Bobby's mouth popped open and he almost screamed.

His father's eyes were becoming fierce, set in some grim struggle both with Bobby and with his own thoughts. He squeezed and, just as abruptly, he let him go. He walked through a side door and into his private office. The door closed with a click.

Bobby stood there, crying a little, rubbing his shoulders. He sat down in one of the chairs and stayed there for half an hour. He could smell his father's aftershave. It was thick in the air, it was comforting. He kept on waiting, but the door to the private office remained closed.

It started to get dark. The light in the boardroom was fading, the air was turning grey.

Bobby got off the chair, walked back down the wide stairs and went home.

CHAPTER THIRTEEN

• •

"Y OU'RE WHO?" MRS. MILLER ASKED, peering out from behind her door.

Walker, looking a little bedraggled and sleep-deprived, was standing on a front porch on Rosewood Avenue.

"Mrs. Miller, I'm Lenore Nuremborski's son," he repeated. "My name's Walker. And I'm looking for Kim."

"Oh?" Mrs. Miller said, still looking surprised. "Lenore. Yes. And how is she?"

"Fine," he said. "She's fine."

"Good." Mrs. Miller opened the front door a little more. "Kim hasn't seen her in years, of course. Not since Lenore moved to England."

"Uh-huh," Walker replied. England, he thought. "I guess that's right. That's why she wanted me to say hi. Because she hadn't seen her for so long."

Mrs. Miller still looked a little puzzled. "Well, come in, Walker," she said.

Handsome in her early sixties, well dressed and well tanned and still colouring her hair a streaky blonde, Mrs. Miller led Walker down a carpeted hallway, through twin glass doors and into a large, plushly furnished living room.

"I suppose you've visited your grandfather already?"

"Yes," he said.

"Please sit down." She indicated a flowered couch. Walker sank into the puffy cushions about a foot.

"Would you like something to drink? I have sherry."

"That would be great."

Mrs. Miller opened a door on a large china cabinet and very carefully filled two small wineglasses half full.

"How is your grandfather? He hasn't been well for years, I understand. Not that I ever knew him. I knew of him, more than I knew him. My late husband was a business associate of his."

"I don't know that much about him either," Walker replied. "Mother never talked much about him. I just dropped in quickly and said hi."

She crossed the room and handed him a glass of sherry. "So how is he?" She sat down opposite Walker, watching him closely.

Walker decided he might as well gamble. "He's sick. There's something wrong with his breathing. I don't think living in that big house in Forest Hill is good for him. It feels sort of damp to me."

Mrs. Miller stared at him. "That's too bad," she said. "Living in England, I would have thought you'd be used to the damp."

"You never get that used to it." Feeling like an idiot, Walker quickly took a large sip of his sherry. It burned going down.

"You know, Walker," she said, smiling pleasantly—but her eyes were troubled, perhaps even slightly nervous—"maybe it's just me, maybe I have a tin ear, but you don't have a trace of an English accent."

"That's because I've spent a lot of time in New Brunswick," Walker said, thinking fast. "Mother sent me to school there. She didn't like the English school system. But this is my first trip to Toronto." Changing the subject, he said, "I think I saw a picture of you once."

"Oh?"

"It was a photograph of Kim and my mom floating in a lake.

They were about three years old and I think you were with them. Standing out in the water at Mary's Point. You had a cottage there, right?"

"Yes, that's right," she replied. "Years ago. Your mother would visit Kim one summer and Kim would visit Lennie the next summer. It was a sort of ritual. They were inseparable, ever since they fought over the same toy at Windover. That was a daycare centre. I was on the board. All my kids went to it. And I adored your grandmother. She was a wonderful woman."

Walker nodded. "Where's Kim living now? My mother would really like it if I dropped in to say hello."

"I don't think she's heard from your mother in years. I remember her telling me that Lennie and her husband had moved to England. And I think I remember that she went over to Jake's to ask for Lennie's address. But for some reason, Jake wouldn't give it to her. He was like that, if you don't mind me saying. He was difficult. At least, that's the impression I got from your grandmother. Anyway, I do remember Kim fuming about it for quite a while. It bothered her. But life goes on."

"Mom was never one for writing letters. But she made me promise, if I ever got to Toronto, to drop in on Kim," Walker insisted gently.

"Kim has three children of her own now. How many did Lenore have?"

"Just me."

"What does your father do?"

"He's an accountant."

"Oh?"

"Yes. He's done quite well for himself," Walker said, hoping that might sound a little English. "They have a nice place on the outskirts of London. Mom's never worked."

"She was a great kid. She and Kim were always having these

giggling fits. Big secrets between them. They were so cute together. Kim lives in Paris."

"Oh," Walker said, his breath going out of him. Oh no, he thought.

"Paris, Ontario. It's not far, only sixty miles or so. When Norman was alive, we used to drive there every three or four weeks. Her husband's an orthodontic surgeon. Kim teaches grade four. Well, she used to, she's taking a little break. Their lives are so busy, and with three kids—it exhausts me just to think about it. It's just go, go, go. Well, I don't get to see them so much now. I don't like to drive."

"I'd love to go there, see the countryside. I could call first and drop in for just a second. Say hello."

Mrs. Miller thought for a long time, looking as if something was troubling her. "You know, I think Kim would be thrilled to see you, Walker," she said, "I'm sure she still misses your mother."

"My mother misses her."

As soon as she had written down Kim's phone number and address, Walker said he'd better leave, he was supposed to meet a couple of friends from his school.

"So how did you get here?" Mrs. Miller asked, as she let him out the front door and looked up and down the street. Walker had parked number nineteen around the corner.

"I took the bus along Eglinton," he lied, "then walked. Thanks a lot."

He strode quickly away. When he turned, she was still standing on her porch, watching him.

●   ●

"WELCOME BACK," Alphonso said, standing in one of the open bay doors of the garage and puffing on a cigar as Walker got out of his cab.

Krista had just arrived too, in time to start her night shift. Nick had given her a ride downtown and he was lifting her wheelchair out of the trunk of his old Chrysler.

Alphonso yelled over to her, "Your boyfriend's decided to give himself up!"

Krista came swinging over to Walker, ignoring her wheelchair for the moment. "Hi," she said.

Joe came out of the gloom of the garage, looking as if he'd just rolled in a pile of grease. He was brandishing a large rubber hammer.

"You want I knock some fuckin' sense into his head?" he asked Alphonso.

"You want I punch your lights out?" Krista hissed back at him.

"He stole the fuckin' cab!" Joe spluttered, although the cab was standing there in plain sight. He turned to Alphonso, hoping he'd back him up. Alphonso stood there grinning.

"How's Lake Erie?" Alphonso asked.

"I'm sorry," Walker said. "I had to go and see a relative." He glanced at Krista. "It was kind of an emergency. I'm real sorry."

"You're sorry, I'm sorry," Alphonso replied, "'cause I gotta charge you rent for the day shift too. You tied the cab up all day."

"Nobody drives that stupid cab but Walker. Don't be such a certified jerk," Krista said. "Come on, Walker."

"I'll pay if you want me to," Walker said to Alphonso.

"I want," Alphonso said, "but your boss there don't want, so I guess I'll have to absorb the loss." He blew a stream of blue smoke up into the air. He was enjoying himself. "Looks like she's got you wrapped around her little finger."

"Yeah, looks like." Walker grinned.

"Wanker," Joe said.

Krista got into her wheelchair, wheeled herself through the bay door and pushed herself up one of several ramps Alphonso had installed for her. Walker followed. Once they were alone in the hallway, she stopped, half turning her wheelchair, and whispered, "What happened?"

Walker knelt down beside her, kissed her. "I know where Kim lives," he said.

• •

ABOUT SIXTY MILES WEST OF TORONTO, the attractive houses of Paris, Ontario glinted in the sun, covering the high hills surrounding the forks of the Nith and Grand Rivers. According to her mother's directions, Kim Miller—now Kim Miller-Best, married with three children—lived a few miles north of the town, on the east side of the Grand River valley.

It was about eleven o'clock Wednesday morning when Walker and Krista, driving Nick's beat-up Chrysler, pulled into Kim's driveway. They had taken the previous night off to rest up, and they had to return Nick's car by four-thirty that afternoon, the end of his shift and the beginning of theirs.

Earlier that morning, Walker had left a bowl of milk out for Kerouac, and a window open just enough to accommodate his random comings and goings. Then he'd walked over to A.P. Cabs, picked up Nick's car and driven up to meet Krista. She was already standing at the end of her driveway, waiting for him. George Papadopoulos was not amused that once again his daughter was going off with this young stranger, considering what had happened the last time.

The torched car was still burning in Krista's mind, too; that was one of the reasons she was with Walker now. She was afraid for him. Maybe, if someone was following him around, planning to hurt him, her presence would change his mind.

And she was also sitting beside him in Nick's car because she couldn't stand not being with him. It was as simple, and as complicated, as that.

Kim Miller-Best's house was built long and low. Its subdued grey stone and glass, its rough pine boards and series of cedar-shake roofs on three levels, seemed to blend in with the groves of tall pines and massive cedars that surrounded it. It was unobtrusive and impressive, all at the same time.

A red minivan shone in the driveway, and what looked like a small sports car was parked on the grass, hidden under a tight brown raincover.

Krista looked at the house. "It's gorgeous," she said—the first thing she'd said for quite a while.

The atmosphere in the car had been tense. Krista wanted Walker to call from Toronto first; it was the civilized thing to do. No one just dropped in, it was ignorant. But Walker was afraid that if he called and forewarned Kim, she might say, "I don't want to see you, I don't know anything about your mother."

Krista had begun to wonder just how much this Kim Miller-Best could know, anyway. Probably not much. Surely Kim would have done something about Lennie's abandoned baby at the time, if she'd known. She wouldn't have stayed silent.

Krista had tried to put this to Walker as diplomatically as possible on the drive up. "This could be a real loser," she'd said.

"What do you mean?"

"Don't be surprised if she doesn't know anything more about what happened to your mother, or where she is now, than you do. If she'd known you were abandoned, she would have gone to the police. Or done something. Wouldn't she?"

"I don't know," Walker replied. "That's the point. I don't know anything. And she knows something. What was the big secret she was talking about in her letter?"

"We've already decided what that secret was—that your mother was pregnant. She was only fourteen, for godsakes."

"We can't be sure that's the secret," he countered. "Anyway, her mother's probably called her by now. Kim will know I'm around."

"What if she's not home? What if they're on holiday?"

"We'll wait."

"I'm just trying to say that the trail might stop here, that's all. This might be where it ends, so don't get upset."

"It won't," Walker replied.

He got out of the car, walked up to the front door and rang the bell. Krista waited in the car. There was no way she was going to get out until she saw somebody. Until they were invited to come in.

Walker peered through a window in the front door. The room beyond had a high vaulted ceiling with open wooden beams. Sunlight flooded in from a skylight above.

He rang again. He could hear the sound of chimes ascending, then descending. He looked back at Krista. She was still sitting in the car, watching him. Saying to herself, I told you so.

Walker rang again. The chimes chimed. Still no one came. He shrugged at Krista and had to smile, almost laugh. He knew what she was thinking: that he was an idiot.

The wind through the tops of the pines sounded like rushing water. The air was cool but somehow the sun still felt warm. He could smell the tang of the cedars.

He decided to walk around to the back of the house. If Kim was on a lower level, maybe she couldn't hear the chimes. Or maybe she was working outside in a garden.

Walker walked down a flight of wooden steps dug into the side of the hill beside the house. As he did, he noticed that the flower gardens built on wooden tiers beside him contained more weeds than flowers, dry and brown and delicate as lace.

The wind was strong here, unbroken by the house. The river valley stretched out below him to the north and south, a great mass of hardwoods flaming into colour, with swaths of pine for contrast and, deeper down in the valley, the darker green of cedars and the silver of willows, massive and overhanging the river.

The scene looked domestic and wild, all at the same time. Comfortable and foreboding. Though the cedars smelled like the north, this didn't look like the north at all.

Walker looked across the back of the house but couldn't see anyone. Faintly, intermittently in the wind, he began to hear music. It was classical—or it seemed classical to Walker. A cello, maybe. A flock of violins, a sweet long line of horns. As he moved across the patio towards the music, a full orchestra met him, in a great wave of sound.

Two glass doors had been pushed open as wide as they could go. The wind billowed heavy yellow drapes on either side, swinging them back and forth on their tracks. Walker looked in through the doors and saw the weak glow of a lamp at the far end of the room, a cluster of plaid-covered chairs and couches, a long, low, rough-hewn table. He called, "Mrs. Miller-Best? Hello? Anyone home?" His voice sounded small and uncertain against the crescendo of the orchestra.

Someone must be here, he thought. People didn't lock their doors in Big River, but they didn't leave them wide open, either.

"Hello?" Walker yelled, louder this time. But no one called back, and no one appeared on the stairs at the far end of the room.

A human hand, white, dazzling in the shadows of the room, was draped over the end of a couch. The more Walker stared at it, to make sure he was seeing what he was seeing, the whiter it seemed to become.

"Mrs. Miller-Best?"

The hand remained motionless.

He stepped through the open doors and moved towards the couch.

"Mrs. Miller-Best, excuse me? Hello?"

The hand didn't move. Walker stood there for a moment, not sure what to do. He circled around the hand.

A woman dressed in pyjamas and a housecoat was lying face down, sprawled on the couch. Her brownish-blonde hair obscured her face. Her feet were bare and as white as her hand. Her other arm was hidden somewhere underneath her.

Walker didn't know what to do—whether to touch her or yell as loud as he could. He leaned forward to see if there was a pulse beating in her neck, if her back was moving gently up and down, but he couldn't tell. The music was becoming louder—kettledrums, cymbals.

He looked around to see where the music was coming from and spotted a stereo deck, its green numbers glowing from inside an old pine cabinet. He turned towards it. The room filled with a scream.

Kim Miller-Best was up on her knees, holding her dressing gown closed tightly in front of her, her eyes wide and frightened.

"Hi," Walker said.

"Who the hell are you?" Her voice was thick and heavy-sounding, and she seemed to be having a hard time focusing on him.

"I'm sorry I scared you. I'm Walker. You know, your friend Lennie Nuremborski's son?"

She continued to stare at him.

"I rang at the front, then I came around to the back," he continued. "Can we turn this down a bit, do you think?" He nodded hopefully towards the stereo.

Kim looked him up and down, as though the information was seeping in a bit at a time. Walker. Lennie's son. Her mouth dropped open a little. She rubbed it with the back of her hand.

"Really?"

"Uh-huh," Walker replied.

She got off the couch and, using it for support, stood there for a moment. She smiled weakly at him.

"I was dead asleep."

"I'm really sorry," Walker said. "I shouldn't have come in like that."

He could smell the sweetness of liquor on her breath, although he was standing ten feet away.

Kim nodded, squeezed her face in her hands as if trying to wake herself up, walked unsteadily to the stereo and turned it off.

The silence was profound.

"You are Kim?" Walker asked.

"I think so," she said, walking back to the couch. She bent over and picked something up off the floor, keeping her back to Walker. He caught a glimpse of a glass and a half-empty bottle.

"This place is a bit of a mess, we had a party last night," she said over her shoulder, as she walked behind a bar in the corner, bent down and came back up empty-handed. "I wasn't expecting company."

She smiled. She was pretty, in a strained, pinched way. She staggered a little.

"Are you okay?"

"Sure," she said, catching her balance. "I was fast asleep, I got up too fast, I'm dizzy." She navigated carefully around the bar and sat down on a chair.

"My God, Lennie's son!" she said suddenly. "I haven't seen her, I haven't heard from her or heard anything about her, or anything at all, for years and years!"

"Did your mother call you? I dropped in to see her."

"Yes, she did. God, how old are you, Walker?"

"Nineteen."

"That's what I thought you'd be. I've got three kids, six, eight and ten. Two boys and a girl. Isn't that hard to believe?"

"Uh-huh. That's nice, though. Um, I have a friend out in the car, actually. I wonder if I could bring her in. I know I should have called you first, but I was...I really wanted to see you!" For the first time, Walker let a little of his feelings out.

Kim's face softened immediately. She was pretty. Walker felt suddenly proud that this woman had been his mother's best friend.

"I wanted to see you, too. God, look at you. You're so dark and everything. Lennie was dark, but not as dark as you. But I can see her in you, you know. I can. The way you hold your head. Something is definitely there. I missed her so much. I still miss her! I miss those old days!" She looked as if she might start crying. "Bring your friend in, of course. Give me five minutes to get myself together, will you, Walker?"

Walker circled the house again and ran up the steps to the car. Krista was where he'd left her.

"I was just about to honk the horn, or drive away, maybe," she said to him as he got back in.

"She's here," he said. "She's invited us inside. We just have to wait five minutes, until she gets dressed."

"It's almost noon."

"She seems real nice," Walker went on. "We've talked a little already. Nothing important, just her saying how much she misses my mom and stuff. She's pissed."

"She's what?"

"Pissed...a bit."

"Jesus Christ, she's pissed?"

"Just a bit."

"What on?"

"She had a bottle of something. Vodka, maybe."

"That figures," Krista said, looking the house over again. "Too much money, so she's unhappy. She should work nights for next to nothing. Then she'd feel great."

"Yeah," he agreed, grinning. He started to roll a smoke. "Do you feel great?" he asked her.

"Ha, ha. Is this one of your stupid jokes?"

"No," he replied, his spirits soaring for some reason. "I was just inquiring."

Five minutes later, Kim Miller-Best reappeared. She had brushed her hair back with a certain dramatic flair, and she'd pulled on tan slacks and a bulky, multicoloured turtleneck. A flush of discreet makeup gave her anxious face a blush of colour. She'd even slipped on a pair of small gold earrings. Walker felt flattered.

She ushered them into the sun-filled front room. Off-white, roughly plastered walls towered up some fourteen feet, accented by large, vibrantly coloured abstract paintings. Off-white furniture and wrought-iron and glass tables were strategically placed about the room. Hand-woven rugs in muted colours lay on the glossy broad-planked floors.

"What a beautiful room," Krista said, as she swung in on her crutches.

"It gets lots of light," Kim replied. "Sit down, anywhere."

Walker took Krista's crutches from her as she eased herself down on one of the sofas. He sat beside her.

"Can I get anyone a drink?" Kim asked hopefully.

"Not for me," Krista said.

"I'm okay too," Walker said.

Kim picked up a drink sitting on a glass table, and sat down.

"I usually don't, myself, this early. But the house seems cold. There's a chill in the air." She took a discreet sip.

Maybe that's because you've got a hurricane blowing in through the back, Walker thought to himself. But he said, "It's really kind of you to see us. I've got lots of questions."

Kim looked a little surprised. "I thought I had the questions," she said. "I want to know all about Lennie. All I know is that she's been living in England forever, and Mom says you've been at school in New Brunswick. That's all I know."

Walker could feel Krista's eyes on him.

"That big house in Forest Hill," Krista asked, "is that where Lennie lived with her family?"

"Well, yes," Kim said. She looked back at Walker. "You were over at your grandfather's, weren't you?"

"To tell you the truth, I wasn't exactly sure where I was," he replied. "I'd never seen him. I didn't know where he lived. I didn't even know I had a grandfather until a couple of days ago."

"Lennie didn't tell you about him?" Kim asked.

Walker hesitated for a moment. "The thing is," he said, "I don't know Lennie either. I mean, I can hardly remember her."

Kim fell silent. She just sat there staring at him, her drink suspended in mid-air.

Walker struggled on. "Do you remember a letter you sent my mother? You wrote it on September 15, 1979. It was about Lennie and my dad and me flying into Toronto."

"But Walker, you never arrived," she said. "I waited for days for a call. I hardly left home. I even sent a telegram. I never heard from Lennie again."

"I wonder, could you tell me what the secret was? You said in your letter that you'd managed to keep some secret between the two of you for over three years."

"That Lennie was pregnant, of course," Kim replied.

"Of course," Walker said. He could feel Krista's eyes on him again.

"Where did you send the telegram? The one you sent when they didn't arrive?" Krista asked.

"Jamaica," Kim said, and then, "What do you mean, you don't know your mother?" She was sitting on the edge of her chair now, her drink forgotten in her hand. "What do you mean?"

Walker told Kim his story, all he knew of it, anyway. He moved back through time, from telling his made-up New Brunswick story to her mother, to coming to Toronto in August, to growing up in Big River, to the years before, in foster homes in Sudbury. When he got to the part about being abandoned on the side of the road, Kim put her hand to her mouth and tears started to run down her cheeks. When he said he had been found a few miles south of the French River, she spilled her drink. Or a little of it, anyway.

"The Nuremborskis had a cottage on the French River," she said. "Well, it was more like a house. I used to go up there. Lennie would stay one summer at my cottage and I'd stay the next with her."

Kim looked around the room as if she half expected to see Lennie. "What the hell happened?" she whispered.

"I don't know," Walker said.

"I should have insisted," Kim cried. "I should have told Jake I wanted to see Lennie. I shouldn't have taken any of his bullshit for an answer. I knew something was wrong!"

"What did he say?" Walker asked.

"That Lennie had met someone recently, while she was in Jamaica. Fallen in love. She was supposed to be down there to attend some private school, but really she was there because she was pregnant. I wasn't supposed to know that. Jake didn't know I knew. That was the secret between Lennie and me. Jake said that Lennie and this man were flying to England, back to her fiancé's home, to get married. He said that Lennie would get in touch with me if she wanted to, but that he wasn't free to give out her address. It was up to Lennie to decide which of her friends she wanted to keep in touch with. But you see, I couldn't even tell him what I knew, because I had promised! I couldn't say that I'd had a letter from Lennie and she'd said she was flying back to Toronto. I wasn't supposed to know anything about you or your dad or anything!"

Kim downed the rest of her drink. "I went back to Jake one other time and asked him if he'd heard anything from her, and could I please have her new address in England? He said yes, of course he'd heard from her. She was happy. She wanted to start a new life. He closed the door in my face."

Walker was sitting on the edge of his seat now. "What had she told you about my dad and me?" he asked.

"Everything. I didn't go up to Lennie's place that summer, because I'd gotten my first summer job. But she called me late one night. She said she'd met this guy, he was working at the new marina on the river, he was seventeen, I think. She was only fourteen, you know."

"I know," Walker said.

"So anyway, she was pregnant and she loved him like crazy and she didn't know what to do. I didn't know what to do either. The whole thing blew my mind. So we'd just talk to each other, real late at night. Talk and talk. One night, she said she'd told her mother she was pregnant. And her mother had told her father. They had this big meeting with her and her boyfriend. Jake went crazy. You can imagine. He wanted to arrest her boyfriend. He wanted Lennie to have an abortion. But there was no way. Lennie, when she got stubborn, you could just forget about talking to her. Besides, she and your dad really loved each other, that's what she told me. They wanted to live together. They wanted to get married. This made Jake even crazier. Lennie thought she'd have to run away somewhere. This went on for days. Lennie was calling me every night; she'd reverse the charges, so all my summer job money was going to my father to pay long distance. But I didn't care, she was my best friend. It was Lennie's mom who came up with the idea. She was the one who got Jake to go along with it. They had this place in Jamaica. On some island off the south coast. Lennie's mom loved it down there, she spent every winter there. Lennie used to go down to visit her at Christmas and Easter. I don't think Mrs. Nuremborski was very happy living with Jake. Who would be? He was domineering, and condescending as hell. And kind of scary. So you see, this was Mrs. Nuremborski's chance to spend more time away. Lennie called me to say that her father had agreed, she could go to their place in Jamaica for a while, and they'd tell everyone she was going to some fancy school down there. Her boyfriend was going too, of course. That was the deal. Otherwise Lennie wouldn't go. She'd have her baby in Jamaica, her mother would look after her, and in a year or so, if her boyfriend and Lennie were still in love, they could get married. Jake finally agreed to go along with the deal, since there was no alternative and Lennie was getting more pregnant every day, but on one condition. She could not correspond with any of her friends or get in contact with them in any way. She was to be perfectly discreet about everything. Lennie promised, and then, of course, she called me. I was sworn to secrecy."

"No wonder no one knew who you were or where you came from," Krista said to Walker.

"I'm Jamaican," Walker said, looking a little stunned.

"So when you were lost, you were a long way from home," Kim added helpfully.

"Do you have her letters?" Walker asked.

"I cleaned out all my stuff when I went away to university," Kim replied. "I started throwing out a little bit, and then I just kept going. I don't know why. The beginning of one part of my life and the end of another, I guess. Or maybe I was having a nervous breakdown. I don't know. I can't remember."

Kim looked away from Walker, towards the front window. She seemed to be thinking of another time, another place. "Well, I got married, had kids, taught school for a while. I mean, it's wonderful, I have a wonderful life, but it feels...." She glanced at her glass but it was empty.

"I've been thinking of Lennie more lately, for some reason," she said. "But I assumed Jake had told me the truth. Or a half-truth, anyway. That the three of you had moved to England. That she did want to start a new life with new friends. That's what I've thought all these years!" She was starting to get teary-eyed again.

"Did she write about me?" Walker asked.

"Of course she did! Of course. All about you! All about your dad! She was crazy in love with you both. Kyle and Little Kyle."

"What?" Walker said.

"That's what she called you. That's what I remember. Your dad was Kyle, and you were Little Kyle."

"Not Walker?" Krista asked.

"Well, I don't know. I was surprised when Mom said your name was Walker. I guess I'd forgotten. She must have told me your real name. She must have. All I can remember, because I thought it was so cute, you know, is Little Kyle. And she said your dad was really good-looking, he was an artist, he wrote his own songs and played the guitar. But, Walker, the thing that really threw your grandfather off was that Kyle was half Indian."

"Half Indian?" Walker echoed.

"From out west somewhere. I remember her saying that he'd run away from home when he was just a kid, and he'd been looking after himself ever since. When they went to Jamaica, he hired on as part of a crew. You know, those companies that lease yachts and provide the crew and a chef and everything? He loved it. He was a born sailor, your mom said, but she was worried about the storms. She'd write about this storm and that storm and Kyle away at sea, I remember that. I remember when you were born, I remember that. And she was my best friend, and something's happened to her! And you were left on the side of the road, and I didn't know anything was wrong, and I didn't do anything!" A fresh stream of tears started down her cheeks. She tried to catch them with the backs of her hands.

"We did everything together," she went on. "I got really sick and had to have my tonsils out, and then I got some kind of infection and I had to stay in bed forever, and she came over every day with my schoolwork and helped me. And when she broke her leg, I carried her books for weeks."

Kim was fast becoming a mess. Her hands were dripping. Krista searched in her small leather shoulderbag and handed Walker some Kleenex, and Walker passed it to Kim.

"I have some somewhere," Kim said, looking around helplessly, pressing the Kleenex to her eyes.

"What about my grandmother?" Walker asked. "Lennie's mother? Haven't you spoken to her?"

Kim looked up at him. Her eyes were red and puffy. "She died, Walker. About the same time you were born."

"What do you think happened to my mom and dad?" he asked, crouching beside her.

She touched his face. Her fingers felt cold and wet. "I honestly don't know," she said. "But Lennie would not abandon her baby!"

"I know," Walker replied, "I know she wouldn't. But I can't even prove I'm her son. If I go to the police without anything, they'll think I'm a nutcase."

"You have that letter I wrote."

Walker and Krista glanced at each other.

"It was stolen," Walker said. "I don't have anything."

"Oh," Kim said. "Well, you look like her...." And then, rallying once again to his side, she declared, "I know you're her son because you described my letter."

As Kim and Walker headed back towards Nick's car, Walker felt dazed. The sun seemed to be dancing a crazy dance in the high blue sky. Krista got to the car ahead of him and opened the passenger door.

"Oh Jesus Christ!" she cried, lurching back a little.

A cat was lying in the sun on the passenger seat. It had a network of old scars across its nose and head. It was black and white.

Walker reached in and felt under the cat's neck. It was cool to the touch. He could see that its eyes were open just a slit, and a bluish film glinted between the lids.

"Kerouac," Krista said.

CHAPTER FOURTEEN

1974

BOBBY WALKED DOWN THE PATH through flickering shadow and sunlight. It was past noon. His mother had just made him some soup and an omelette with a lot of funny-looking green things in it. Onions and spinach and herbs and stuff. It was supposed to be healthy. She was constantly telling him that he'd have a growth spurt soon. He'd wake up one day and his legs would be six inches longer. His hands would suddenly look like mitts. He'd have to start to shave. Bobby had always been more or less the same size as other boys his age. Now, at fifteen, other boys had passed him by.

He had spent the previous year at a special school where each student, in classrooms with only four or five other students, received all the attention he or she required, or so the school brochure said. The school even announced optimistically, on a sign over the front door, Every Student Is An Exceptional Student.

Bobby felt exceptional. He knew he would do great things with his life. He would speak in front of masses of people, and they would cheer and reach out their hands to him. They would love him with a love unreserved and unconditional. Sometimes he closed his eyes and he could hear them cheer, like static on the radio, like a roar, like one long-held note of panic and delight.

He kept secret how special he was, and how important he was going to be, from everyone. It made him smile that no one knew. Not even his father. What a surprise his father had in store. How proud he would be, and how sorry, too. He would enfold Bobby in his arms and hold him gently, he would beg Bobby's forgiveness. And Bobby would forgive him.

But right now, his father was as blind as ever to the glories the future held. He was lying across the stern of the *Chestnut Alley*, his head invisible, hidden below the hatch that gave access to the inboard motor. He was tinkering. Bobby could hear the *tink tink tink* of a wrench or a hammer tapping gingerly against the motor.

Bobby stepped off the path onto the dock and into full sunlight. Despite the wide expanse of black water sparkling in front of him, it was hot here, hotter than beneath the trees, certainly hotter than inside the tall clapboard summer house that sat across the road and up the hill behind him.

Bobby wanted to walk along the dock, step into the *Chestnut Alley* and help his father, but he couldn't. His father would give him The Look. The Look frightened him. It wasn't an angry look, or dismissive or disgusted. Not exactly. It was as if his father could look right through him, as easily as through empty air; as if his father could will him into nothingness, so that all that was left was a faintly bad smell. The Look chilled him to his core.

Bobby sat on the edge of the dock and gazed across the water. The distant shore wasn't the other side of a lake, it was a line of pine-covered islands. There was more water beyond them. And it wasn't a lake. It was a river.

Bobby hated the river. It was too cold, for one thing, and it was powerful. When he waded into the black water, which wasn't very often, the current pulled at his legs relentlessly, hypnotically.

The *Chestnut Alley* shone in the sun, polished to a deep red and bronze glow. Bobby could hear the water lapping the length of the sleek, low-slung hull. It nuzzled and purred a little against the protective edging on the dock. The *Chestnut Alley* was old, genteel, painstakingly constructed during the winter of 1926 at the local boatworks.

Bobby's father had a sailboat and another powerboat, but this was the only boat he really cared about. It was made of teak and rosewood and mahogany. It had plush velvet seats. Its large, gleaming Chrysler engine pushed it quietly across the water on an exquisitely flat line, with the deep bubbling thrust of twin props. When it came in to dock the engine burbled, so that Bobby could feel the boat vibrating gently in every bone in his body.

His father always talked about the *Chestnut Alley* and the Roaring Twenties in the same breath. Bobby had no idea what he was talking about, but driving the boat made his father happy, so being in the boat when his father was driving made Bobby happy too.

Lately, for some reason, though his father still worked on the boat whenever he could get up here from Toronto, he didn't take it out for a spin much any more. And when he did, he always went alone.

His father had laid his tools out carefully on a leather and cloth apron beside him. Now he raised his head and reached for something with a greasy hand. Bobby looked but couldn't see which tool he needed. His father caught sight of him sitting at the edge of the dock, just beyond the nodding nose of the boat. He looked at Bobby for a moment, and then through him, stuck his head back down beside the engine and continued to work.

Bobby didn't feel so warm any more. His legs felt cold under his jeans. He wished he had the courage to sit nearer. His father might call out the name of a tool he needed, and Bobby would know exactly which one to give him. His father would smile, a smile that was warm and happily surprised all at the same time. He'd say, "Thank you, Robert."

Bobby stayed where he was. He couldn't risk moving closer. He thought maybe he'd go swimming instead. Maybe he'd slip down beneath the river. His father would have to look for him then. He'd be frightened. He'd run up and down. Where has Bobby gone? Where has my son gone?

A boy from two families down the lake was hopping from rock

to rock, coming along the shore. His name was Alex Johnson. Even though he was only ten years old, Bobby knew his name. Everyone knew his name. He was just that kind of kid. He disappeared behind the boathouse and reappeared, jumping down on the dock.

"Hi," he said.

Bobby looked at him. His blond hair was matted to his forehead and neck, sticky with sweat. His face was always eager, he was always up to something. His slim, tanned slip of a body was partially covered by a red, sun-faded T-shirt and a silver bathing suit. He was wearing black sandals. His knees looked red and dirty from crawling around somewhere, doing something.

"Hi," Bobby replied.

"We went fishin' this morning. My dad caught two pickerel. I didn't catch anythin'." He knelt beside the stern of the boat.

"Hi!" he called out to Bobby's father.

Bobby's father raised his head, saw that it was Alex and smiled.

"Hello there, Alex. Do me a favour, will you? Hand me that screwdriver right there."

Alex nimbly crawled onto the stern of the boat and handed him the screwdriver he'd pointed out. Bobby knew that his father could have reached for it just as easily as asking Alex. And besides, Alex had crawled across the polished deck. He'd left scuff marks. How many times in the past had Bobby caught holy shit for doing that?

"Thanks," his father said, not making anything special out of it, as if he were speaking to another man. He leaned down into the engine hold again.

"Wanna build a raft?" Alex said to Bobby, walking over to him. "I'm looking for driftwood. I'm gonna build a raft."

"Why don't you just use a boat?" Bobby asked, looking up at him. The sun was shining right behind the little boy's head. It looked as if he had a halo. Bobby had to squint to see him.

"Not as much fun. Besides, Dad won't let me, by myself."

"Do you think he'll let you go out on some stupid raft, then?" Bobby asked, with an older boy's dismissive smirk.

"I won't tell him. He won't know. You want to?" Alex asked, mischief in his eyes.

"Maybe."

With that encouragement, Alex sat down close beside the bigger boy.

He smelled like warm grass to Bobby. He smelled like water. He smelled like the sun. The fine little hairs on his arms and legs were bleached white. He'd been staying up on the river most of that summer with his mother, just as Bobby had. Even though Bobby was fifteen, he didn't have any friends. He didn't fit in anywhere. He didn't want to.

"We're havin' a barbecue," Alex said. He stretched and tried to dip his toe in the water but he couldn't reach. He took off his sandals, turned onto his stomach and slid down off the dock until his feet sank slowly into the water.

Bobby looked towards his father. He was still busy, decapitated, lying on his boat.

Bobby reached out and took Alex's small wrist in his hand. It felt bony and frail. His skin felt warm. "Don't fall in," Bobby said.

Alex looked up at him and smiled.

"You wanna go swimmin?" Alex said.

Bobby held onto his wrist. He could feel the muscles across his own stomach tighten. A little shudder travelled through him. He wondered if Alex had noticed, but he hadn't seemed to.

Something familiar flooded through Bobby's body, something delicious stirred in his blood. He thought of Carlo Dimarco, and he tightened his grip on Alex's wrist.

The boy didn't seem to notice. He was looking back at his feet now, and kicking lazily in the water.

CHAPTER FIFTEEN

. .

W ALKER PLACED THE ROCKS he'd lifted from a pile at
the end of a field on the body of Kerouac, the vagabond cat.
Soon they formed a little stone crypt.

He was crouching under the scarred limbs of an oak tree
that must have been clinging to the edge of the river valley for over a
hundred years. Krista had refused to get out of the car. Her face
looked pale.

They drove back to Toronto in silence. Krista stared out at the
passing countryside for almost the entire trip. Walker reached out and
brushed his hand against her cheek, he pulled on her ear gently, but
she didn't smile.

"I'm an Indian," he whispered at her, but she didn't even turn to
look at him.

Walker's past and his present had just met, and it had killed a
cat. Whatever else Krista was thinking, she was keeping to herself.

They pulled into A.P. Cabs about twenty minutes after four that
afternoon, in time to give Nick back his car when he came off the day
shift, get two coffees-to-go over at Ruby's and, without any sleep,
start their twelve-hour shifts.

Krista didn't think Walker should drive that night. Walker said
he was okay. Walker didn't think Krista should dispatch that night.
Krista said, then who the hell would?

She made Walker promise that he wouldn't go back to the Nuremborski house. He promised, climbed into number nineteen, pulled out of the lot and disappeared into the rush-hour traffic. Forest Hill drew him like a magnet.

The days were getting shorter now. A cool evening breeze had come down from the north, and the leaves were falling in Forest Hill. Walker could hardly hear the sound of his tires as he drifted through the leaf-filled streets.

He turned into the lane that led by the Nuremborski house. The grass was still too long, the shrubbery still wild and overgrown. The green paint around the sagging eaves of the building was worn and flaking. Moss and grass and sprigs of maple trees grew out of the eaves. The bricks on the chimneys were cracked and breaking off.

Walker came to a stop and looked down the length of the driveway. Now he could see that the side wall extended beyond the original back corner, and that in the recent past a two-storey addition of yellow brick had been built.

The driveway led to a large wooden garage that might have been a stable in the old days. It was unpainted and looked just as neglected as the main house; one door was open and swinging a little in the wind.

No lights glowed inside any of the rooms in the front of the house. The place might have been abandoned, emptied of all its furnishings except for some stained drapes and blinds. But Walker knew better.

With a considerable exercise of willpower, he took his foot off the brake and drove on.

Walker was certain that the old man in that house, his grandfather, knew what had happened to his mother. But what would be the use of ringing the bell? He'd wave off any inquiry about Lennie, wave it off with his bony hand, just as he had before.

Walker drove around the city streets, half-heartedly looking for people waving for a cab. He hoped he wouldn't see anyone. Krista kept radioing him, giving him new business, keeping him busy, staying in touch, her voice betraying her fear for him.

By seven o'clock he'd made almost as much money as Alphonso would charge him for renting the cab that night, and he knew he needed a plan. He had to have a plan. His lost mother, his half-Indian father, his own blood pumping through his veins demanded that he have a plan.

He drove down the narrow lane in Forest Hill again, but this time, instead of parking out front, he pulled right into the driveway. He was Lennie's son. He was a Nuremborski. He belonged there.

This feeling lasted for as long as it took him to open the door and get out of the cab. Standing there, he began to feel the same tightness in his chest as three nights before. And he began to be aware of something else—some kind of fluttering in the air, some presence in the dark. He leaned against the cab. What felt like a child's fear, formless and intense, flooded through him. He closed his eyes and waited for it to pass.

Walker looked at the house again. It was just the same as before. He started towards it, walking through the long grass. He climbed the steps and rang the bell.

There was already a faint glow in the fanlight. As he stared up at the red light in the camera, he was feeling better. He thought he'd give them a full-face, no-nonsense view, although he still had no idea what he was going to say or do. Just demand the truth. The truth!

He rang again. Waited. Rang again. And again. No one came, no one was going to come. He knew that, no matter how many times he rang, no one would come.

He crossed purposefully to the edge of the driveway and walked along the side of the house. Bits of the broken red tile crunched under his workboots, but he didn't care.

Someone had killed Kerouac to scare him, but the move had had the opposite effect. The more Walker thought about it, the more he was convinced that it had been an act of weakness. After all, if someone had been watching Kerouac come and go through his window long enough to know that Walker was feeding the cat and cared for it, he'd been watching Walker come and go too. Walker was just as available to meet an untimely end as the cat.

Here I am, Walker thought as he walked down the dark driveway, I'm here now, if you've got the guts.

He'd almost reached the yellow brick of the addition when he heard a groan. He stopped. A far-off banging. The same groan again.

Walker stared through the murky dark. Another hollow bang, a groan. The swinging door he'd seen on the old garage came into his mind. As the wind gusted around the house, he listened. Bang, groan.

He moved along the driveway again, but more cautiously now, until he reached the far corner of the addition. He could see the garage, a darker shape against the surrounding gloom. He stepped out a few feet beyond the corner of the house.

Three lighted windows shone in the dark: two in the addition, both filled with a hazy blue light that hung in the air like clouds, and a smaller window just below the eaves on the third floor. A back door had been left half open and a soft band of yellow light streamed out.

Walker could make out a few stone steps leading from the driveway to the lower level of the backyard. The yard itself seemed crowded with the black shapes of trees and bushes, and in the middle loomed a more substantial domed shape.

He moved towards the shape. It seemed a dull mustard colour now, but he still couldn't make out what it was. He looked back at the house. No one appeared at the lighted door.

He took another step and the structure, a large gazebo, drifted into focus. It had wide, sweeping stairs with a long wooden ramp suspended over them, rising on a gentle slope.

Two more steps and a glint of metal flashed from inside the gazebo.

Walker stopped. He could see a wheelchair now, and a dark form wrapped in a blanket. A blotch of white skin, an uncertain face.

Walker crept closer. The person was not looking at him but was turned slightly away: a man perhaps in his thirties, his head hanging to one side, resting loosely against his shoulder as if he were sleeping—or as if someone had just broken his neck.

"How dare you?" a voice hissed in Walker's ear; a hand spun him around.

Walker was face to face with the same man who'd come to the door three nights before, the man in the business suit, with the wire-rimmed glasses.

Walker was over six feet. The man in front of him was at least half a head taller, with a firm hold on the collar of Walker's leather jacket.

"Get off this property," the man said, seizing Walker's sleeve with his other hand.

"The man in that house," Walker said, surprised that he could find any words at all, "is my grandfather!"

"Wrong," the man replied, jerking Walker away from the gazebo and spinning him around but keeping a firm grip on his jacket. "And you're trespassing."

Walker, quick as an uncoiling snake, threw up both his arms and knocked the big man's hands away.

"I want to talk to Jake Nuremborski," he said.

The man gave him a push on the chest that jolted his teeth and sent him backwards about two feet.

"Get off this property," he repeated.

Walker looked past him towards the gazebo. It was receding into darkness again, but he could still see it clearly enough to know that the man in the wheelchair had disappeared.

"Move it!" Another jolt to the chest.

As Walker stumbled towards the steps that led up to the driveway, he took a good look at the big man. Though he clearly knew how to use his height and weight for leverage, Walker sensed some fear in his strained, fleshy face. He'd already seen how quick Walker was, how easily he'd broken his grip. Sweat was gleaming on the man's forehead and there was a slight tremor in his voice. And he was all of fifty years old.

"Mr. Nuremborski has powerful friends," the man was hissing now. "How would you like to be arrested, psychologically tested? How would you like to be put away? There's nothing here for you. No one wants you, you are not part of this. Stay away from now on or Mr. Nuremborski will go to the police."

"*I'll* go to the police!" Walker said.

The man considered Walker for a moment. "Do that, and you'll end up in a mental hospital, eating Pablum." And he added—more gently, trying a new tack—"Son, you're wrong. For godsakes, this is not your family."

Walker stumbled up the stone steps, walked back to his cab and got in. When he turned on the engine and the headlights, the man was standing right in front of him.

A wave of frustration washed over Walker; it made him want to cry out, to drive into the man and run him over.

Instead, he threw the cab into reverse and, with the wheels spitting crushed tiles, backed out with a roar, braked and squealed away.

••

"YOU REALLY ARE GOING to get yourself killed," Krista said at Ruby's the next morning, after Walker told her what had happened. Then she shrugged. If he wasn't going to keep his word, do what he promised—like stay away from that place—there was nothing she could do about it. The hell with him.

They sat at the table by the front window for a long time, Krista sipping coffee and Walker smoking. They'd been awake for almost twenty-four hours.

"Who do you think that man in the wheelchair was?" she finally asked.

Walker didn't answer for a moment, and then he said, "He could be my father."

"Maybe," Krista replied cautiously. She could see that Walker was close to the brink, and she didn't want to push him over.

He got up from the table.

"Where're you going?" she asked.

"Home to sleep."

They crossed back over the road together. Walker kissed her, a tired kiss, and headed down the sidewalk towards Church Street. Krista stood there watching him go. She thought he might turn around and wave back to her, but he didn't.

His apartment was only fifteen minutes away. He climbed the long wooden steps, unlocked his door—now secured with a shiny new deadbolt—and walked across the mostly empty room, empty now even of Kerouac. He flopped down on top of the pullout couch, still pulled out from twenty-four hours before, and lay there, on top of his rumpled sheets, as still as death.

He woke up six hours later, straight out of a dream. He'd been sailing but he was alone and he'd never been sailing before. He didn't know how to steer properly, and the wind was pushing him somewhere he didn't want to go. He looked out over the water and it shone like burnished bronze, it curled up all around him, impossibly high, towering, as if he were sailing across the bottom of a bronze bowl. The sails cracked in the wind.

When he opened his eyes, he was already sitting up in the middle of his bed, his clothes still on except for his shabby old workboots. He couldn't remember pulling them off. He glanced at his alarm clock. It was just past noon.

He got out of bed, felt around in his jeans pockets and pulled out a folded piece of paper. It had Kim Miller-Best's address and phone number on it.

He picked up the phone he'd finally been able to afford, and dialled the number. The phone at the other end rang, and rang again. He wondered if she'd be awake. He could see her pale white hand hanging over the end of the couch in the room downstairs. The phone was picked up on the eighth ring.

"Hello," Kim said. Her voice sounded a little thick.

"Hi. It's me. Walker."

"Walker?" she said.

"You know, Lennie's son."

"Oh, yes. Lennie's son. Poor Lennie!" There was a rustling at the other end of the line. Walker could almost see her rubbing the back of her hand against her mouth.

"Kim?" he finally said.

She came back on the line. "Hi." She was drunk, about twice what she had been the other day, it seemed to him.

"I was just wondering," Walker said. "You know the summer place you said they had on the French River?"

"Uh-huh," she said. "It was a big thing with turrets and everything. Our cottage was just made out of logs." This thought seemed to dismay her for some reason. There was another fumbling rustle at her end.

"Kim?"

"Uh-huh?"

"Do you remember where Lennie's cottage was, exactly? How to get there?"

Silence. He carried on. "Remember how I told you that I was found about ten miles south of the French River? And we all agreed that the only reason I'd be way up there was because of the Nuremborskis' summer house?" He waited.

Finally Kim said, "Uh-huh. I remember."

"I'm going up there," he said.

CHAPTER SIXTEEN

• •

BOBBY WATCHED ALEX STRUGGLE with a piece of driftwood almost as big around as he was. It was wedged between two rocks, half in, half out of the water. Alex was standing waist-deep in the river with his arms around the log, trying to pry it loose.

"Help me!" he called to Bobby.

Bobby was sitting on the edge of a flat rock, somewhat above and a little distance down the shore from Alex, watching him. Alex had been trying to build a raft for the last half-hour.

They had left Bobby's father with his head buried in the engine compartment of *Chestnut Alley*, and had slipped off the west end of the dock together, walking along a trail at the water's edge.

The trail led through The Tract, as it was locally called—ten square miles of crown land, undeveloped and unspoiled, that sat just west of his father's property. The Tract was important to his father because it meant that no one could build next to him on that side. And since they had two acres of waterfront, the first cottage up the river to the east couldn't even be seen, except for an annoying flagpole.

His father liked his privacy, as had his father before him, who'd originally established the family company in Canada in 1914, at the beginning of the Great War, and who'd had the summer house built in 1924, the year Bobby's father had been born.

Bobby and Alex, walking single file with Alex in the lead, had continued along the pine-needled path, through shadowed stands of pines and spruce, through the sweet-smelling, sleep-inducing summer air, until they'd reached a grassy opening in the forest. Just below the path, over a high bank, a small, white-pebbled cove nestled beside the river. It was here that Alex had been trying to construct his raft, dragging pieces of driftwood up onto the beach.

"Come on, Bobby. Help!" He was still wrestling with the log.

"It's waterlogged anyway," Bobby said.

"No it isn't!" Alex cried, thrashing around in the water. It looked as though the log had him, rather than the other way around.

Bobby slipped off his rocky perch and wandered down to the edge of the water.

"I almost got it," groaned Alex.

There was no way Bobby was going to step into the water, but he walked along the shore to Alex and, kneeling at the wedged end of the log, pulled one of the rocks back an inch or so. The log came loose; Alex fell backwards, regained his feet. His red T-shirt was completely soaked now but he didn't care.

"Got it," he yelped exultantly, floating the log back towards his other pieces. "Told you it'd float," he said.

Alex busied himself laying the pieces of driftwood beside each other up on the dry beach, but they were all different lengths and sizes.

"I know where there's a patch of blueberries," Bobby said.

"Where?" Alex replied, not that interested, still busy arranging his sticks and logs.

"Higher up," Bobby said. "Anyway, that won't work."

"Why not?"

"How're you going to make it stay together? You need rope and nails. You need a saw. You need to cut yourself crosspieces."

"I know," Alex said. "I was just finding the wood first. My dad has all that stuff. We can sneak it out. We can come back after supper." Alex looked up at Bobby, his eyes expectant. He loved action, particularly if it appeared dangerous to him. "Okay?"

"Let's go up to the blueberry patch first," Bobby said.

"Okay." Alex thought he'd just made a deal with an older boy. He was pleased with himself.

With Bobby leading the way this time, they crossed the opening in the forest and, walking away from the path, entered the dark line of trees beyond. They had to pick their way around rotting logs sinking into the ground, over fallen branches and under sweeping boughs. After a few minutes, they came to a series of rocky ledges that led upwards to the highest point of land in that whole area. They climbed over a shelf of rock, and up another one. Bobby had to reach back and haul Alex up. He seemed so light to Bobby, as if there were nothing to him at all.

The two boys stood on this second shelf and looked back where they'd come from. They were at about the same height as the trees now, and they could see the river sparkling beyond.

Bobby sat down on a patch of dry grass and looked puzzled. "I don't know where it is now. I'm not sure," he said.

Alex squatted beside him. "I don't know either," he said.

Bobby was on fire. He wanted to hold Alex so badly that he could hardly stand it. He wanted to snuggle his nose in the boy's neck and smell him all over. He wanted to wrap his arms around him.

Bobby's cock—tender and aching sweetly before, as the two of them had moved deeper into the forest—sprang against his jeans now, pounding with blood, taking his breath away. But he couldn't do anything about it. Because he wasn't a fag. He wasn't. His eyes filled with tears. *Goddamn Alex!*

"You need a haircut," Bobby said. His voice sounded to him as though it were someone else's. He reached out and touched Alex's hair. A jolt of electricity passed through his arm.

"There's no blueberries here, anyways," Alex said, getting up and moving a little away. "You want to come to my place? We're havin' a barbecue."

"It's too early." Bobby leaned back on his elbows. He wondered if Alex could see the bulge in his jeans.

"I know. I mean later. Let's go."

"In a minute." Alex was bossy, Alex was a take-charge man, Bobby thought to himself. And he wasn't even looking at Bobby's swollen jeans. He wasn't paying any attention to Bobby at all. He'd sat down on a rock with his back to Bobby, and now he was taking off his sandals, trying to dry them off. Bobby was beneath his notice.

Alex will run a factory one day, Bobby thought to himself, he'll have the power. Bobby could tell this, just the way Alex was sitting and the way he went about everything. He had handed his father that tool as casually as his father had thanked him for it. Two men. A little man and a big man.

And what about Bobby? Bobby with his cock? What should he do? Pull it out and whack off in front of Alex? Alex would just walk away. Bobby would be beneath contempt then, wouldn't he? Alex would have all the power.

Bobby felt waves of desire radiate around his thighs and up his stomach. He turned a little on his elbow and stared more directly at Alex, who was picking a scab on his leg now. And the more Bobby watched him—drank in his blond, tousled hair, his skinny, tanned and scraped legs, his arms, thin and fragile-looking—the more he wanted to press that little body hard against his own. And then Bobby would explode. He knew he'd totally explode, his cock, his eyes, his hands, his everything.

Bobby whimpered.

Alex looked at him.

Bobby stood up quickly. His whole body felt like a flame. He looked across the trees towards the river. It seemed a thousand miles away.

"We could play a game," Bobby said.

"What kind of game?" Alex was instantly interested.

"We could play like we were soldiers," Bobby said. "We could be enemies. This could be a fort and you have to climb up the hill under cover, you know?" He looked at Alex. The boy was following every word he said now, with rapt attention. "You could surprise me and take me prisoner. Tie me up. And then we can take turns. Then I'll tie you up."

"We don't have any rope," Alex said.

"Did you ever want to be a girl?" Bobby asked him.

Alex made a face. "Why don't you make me sick!"

"Me neither." Bobby could feel his whole body trembling. "I know where there's some rope," he said.

CHAPTER SEVENTEEN

· ·

KRISTA HAD FINALLY SETTLED with her insurance company over her Toyota. They'd given her a cheque for eight hundred and twenty-four dollars.

"What the hell am I supposed to do with this, buy a scooter?" she'd exclaimed at the time. She'd been told that she should regard herself as very lucky, since her car, in reality, wasn't worth spit. They'd given her a break.

"Some break," she complained to Walker.

"Yeah," he replied, even more distracted than usual, leaning on the counter at A.P. Cabs and watching her work. "I know where the Nuremborski summer house is."

She looked up. "How'd you manage that?"

"I phoned Kim. She's given me directions."

"Why do you want to go up there? It's probably sold, or maybe it's torn down like that cottage at Mary's Point."

"Maybe I'll remember something."

"Like what? That was sixteen years ago."

"I don't know!" Walker almost cried out. "I have to do something. Maybe that was my father sitting in that wheelchair."

"Walker, you're going to make yourself sick! There's only one person who knows, Jake Nuremborski, and he's not talking. So go to the police, tell them what you know. If they can't help, then...."

Krista hesitated. She couldn't think of a then.

The phone rang. She pushed herself over to it. "A.P. Cabs. Yeah. Yeah. Okay. Cowboy hats. No kidding. Welcome to Toronto, you'll be easy to spot. Ten minutes."

She put the phone down. "Want to pick up three cowboys rootin' it up, corner of Victoria and Dundas?"

"Canadian or American?"

She smiled. "Shut up. Are you going to work or aren't you? Your shift's started, you know?"

"I'm going up to the French River."

"Walker, someone killed your cat," she said, somewhat hopelessly. He didn't reply.

Krista knew she couldn't stop him. And she couldn't be with him all the time, either. She couldn't protect him. "Number nineteen will never make it up there," she said. "Besides, Joe will shoot you."

The cigar in Alphonso Piattelli's mouth drooped but didn't fall out when Krista asked him if Walker could borrow his Caddy for a couple of days. His brown eyes widened, his brow furrowed; he leaned back in his chair behind his desk and scratched his head vigorously; he even whistled once, as Krista told him Walker's real story, his true story, but he never said no. He just listened. And when Krista was finished, he opened the middle drawer of his desk and fished out the keys to his car. He dangled them in the air.

"Your idea about goin' to the cops is stupid," he said.

"I thought you might say that."

"He ain't got no incriminating evidence on anybody. They couldn't do nothin'. They hear crazy stories every day."

"I know."

"And that probably wasn't his old man in that wheelchair," Alphonso added for good measure.

"Maybe it wasn't. Maybe it was," Krista said, feeling exhausted for some reason.

"So are you two like a couple, or what?"

"What's that got to do with anything?"

"I don't know. He's some crazy kid, that's all, with all this lost parent stuff. One thing's for sure, he's not going to stay around here for long, a young kid like him." Alphonso looked at Krista. She didn't seem to be getting his point. "So just don't get too bent out of shape about him, you know?"

Her eyes narrowed. "You mean he's not going to stick around for someone like me? Is that what you mean?"

"No!"

She took the keys and, holding onto her crutches, pulled herself out of the chair. Her hips looked even more twisted than usual to Alphonso. Her shoulders hunched up like a bird's as she supported her weight and swung towards the door.

"I just mean your old man would put a contract out on me if somethin' went wrong," Alphonso blurted.

Krista turned back to him. Her eyes were shiny with tears. "Go to hell," she said.

"Oh, Jesus Christ," Alphonso moaned, as she disappeared down the hall. All he was trying to do was make her think a little, whoa up a bit. He'd seen the two of them kissy-facing around. Just so she wouldn't get herself hurt. Because she was so, well, small or something. And he loved her, like a daughter or something. And he'd given her the goddamn keys, what more did she want? Alphonso felt terrible.

"He says, if you put a scratch on it, you have to work for him ten years for free," Krista said, dropping the keys into Walker's hand.

Walker was standing outside the bay, beside number nineteen. He could feel Joe Smart's eyes on him from somewhere inside the gloom of the garage, but he couldn't see him. "I still say I should have asked him myself."

"Never send a man to do a woman's job."

He looked at her more closely. She looked funny, as if she'd been walking into a stiff wind—her eyes shiny, her face blotched a little red. "Everything all right?" he asked.

"Sure."

"Thanks for this."

"Okay." She turned abruptly away from him, and swung back through the open bay towards the side door.

● | ●

WALKER STOPPED OFF AT HIS PLACE just long enough to pick up his toothbrush and toothpaste and a change of underwear and socks, sticking them all in a plastic shopping bag. He ran back downstairs, tossed the bag onto the plush back seat of the Cadillac and headed north out of town.

On another day, at another time, in another life, it would have been fun driving this car in stop-and-go traffic. Everybody looked to see who the driver was. Alphonso liked driving his pink Caddy wearing Hawaiian-style shirts in the summer, and a black tailored overcoat with a beaver collar that he thought made him look like a Chicago don in the winter. Alphonso looked good in the Caddy, but Walker, with his leather jacket, his long black hair and his brooding face, looked even better.

But today the Cadillac could have been Walker's old Dodge truck, or even the carbon-monoxide special, number nineteen, as far as Walker was concerned. He was hardly aware of what he was driving, or of the other cars around him or anyone looking his way. He was too busy thinking about Krista.

He put on a Tina Turner tape and smoked one of the five smokes he'd rolled beforehand, in anticipation of the four-hour drive. Now, since the Caddy was standing still half the time, it seemed it might be closer to five hours.

He couldn't get Krista out of his mind. Something had definitely been wrong. She'd turned her back on him, hadn't even wished him good luck, let alone kissed him. Maybe she'd given up on him. Maybe she believed that he'd already driven himself nuts, that he was already beyond hope.

A sudden depression threatened to engulf him. He could hardly move his arms. His head felt sick.

It was about eight o'clock in the evening, dark and raining hard, by the time Walker reached the town of Parry Sound along Highway 69. He was less than an hour from the French River. He decided to get something to eat. Afterwards he'd look for a roadside park with a washroom. There was no sense pushing on to the French River at this time of night. Kim hadn't been exactly sure where the summer house was, through the haze of the intervening years and the alcohol fumes. She was positive that the house was just outside a little village called Weirtown, on a sharp turn in the road as it came up to the river. Somewhere.

It would be better to wait for light.

Walker ate a double hamburger and fries, and drank a pop and two coffees, in an almost empty fast-food franchise.

He looked at his reflection in the window. Walker Devereaux. Walker Nuremborski. Lost.

It was just past nine when he left the restaurant. He'd dawdled for as long as he could, but it was still too soon to go to sleep.

The rain was falling even harder, pounding down on the thick steel roof of the Caddy, as he ducked into the car and slammed the door. He drove back to the highway and turned north again, looking for a roadside park because he couldn't afford a motel room. He wasn't exactly broke, but he wasn't exactly not broke, either. He'd used up all the money he'd brought from Big River quite a while ago. He had exactly forty-eight dollars and twenty-two cents on him, after he'd paid for his meal, and five hundred and thirty dollars towards his next month's rent hidden in the empty fish carton in the freezer of his refrigerator.

He drove the big car off the highway into a picnic area and passed a sign stating that no overnight parking or camping was allowed.

Walker steered onto the soggy lawn, eased between two picnic tables and stopped behind a small rest-room building. With any luck, particularly in late October on a rainy night, the cops wouldn't bother checking the parks.

He turned off the car's lights and the engine. It was pitch-black. He couldn't even see the steering wheel. He'd had the heater on just a touch, to keep off the dampness. He could feel the cold and wet creep back in now. He was wide awake.

As his eyes adjusted, the deep amber of the steering wheel came into focus. Through the passenger-side window, he noticed a faint glow of light near the highway. A phone booth.

He stared at it for a long time. He thought about Krista, and stared at it some more. He started the car again, switched on the headlights and drove up tight to the phone booth. He turned off the engine again and sat there, thinking.

If he did call her, it would only be to say hi and that he was okay, and that Alphonso's precious car was unscathed. That was all.

He got out and, splashing around the car, stepped into the phone booth. The only number he could remember for work was the A.P. Cab call number. He reversed the charges.

"A.P. Cabs," he heard Krista say. She seemed very far away.

The automated operator's voice announced, "You have a collect call from...," and there was a pause where Walker could insert his name. He thought of saying Walker Devereaux, then Walker Nuremborski. Finally he just said, "Walker."

The recording continued, "If you choose to accept these charges, please indicate by pressing one now. Or by saying yes or no clearly after the tone. Do you accept these charges?"

Walker heard the tone and then silence. His heart sank. The operator clicked on again, one last chance. "We did not hear a response, please indicate by saying either yes or no after the tone, do you accept these charges?" Walker heard the tone again.

"Yes," Krista said faintly.

"Thank you," the automated operator replied. "Please go ahead."

"Hi," Walker said.

"Hi," Krista said. "Where are you?"

"About twenty miles or so from the river. I've stopped for the night. I didn't think you were going to accept the call."

"I didn't hear the beep the first time."

"Oh," he said, not convinced. "I just thought I'd call to say you can tell Mr. Piattelli his car is still okay."

"And you're not dead yet."

"No."

"Have you seen anyone following you?"

"No."

"Do you have any reason to believe that someone isn't following you?"

"No."

Krista sighed. "Just thought I'd check. What's that noise?"

"Rain. It's raining hard here. I'm in a phone booth."

"So are you at a motel?"

"There's no phone in my room," Walker replied, obscurely.

"A cheap one, eh?"

"Yeah. Anyway, I just thought I'd call."

"So it's raining."

"Yeah."

A long silence ensued. "What are you hoping to do up there, exactly?" Krista finally asked.

"I'm hoping to find someone who's known something for all

these years but didn't think it was important. Or maybe someone who was afraid to say anything."

A gust of wind shook the phone booth. Rain washed down the windows.

Walker could see a car approaching. It slowed down, almost stopped and then moved on into the dark, leaving a small wake on the flooded roadway behind it.

"Walker?" Krista said. Her voice sounded soft now.

"Yeah?"

"I've got three lines ringing. I've got to go."

"Okay."

"Walker?"

"Yeah?"

"Nothing." A small silence. "See you," she said, and hung up.

Walker got back into the car, turned it around and parked again behind the rest-room building. He turned off the lights and engine, got out again, opened the back door and climbed in. His hair was soaked.

He rolled a window down a quarter of an inch for air, locked the doors, pulled off his boots and lay across the soft back seat. Even though he bent his knees, the top of his head was still pushing against the padded armrest on the other door. He could feel the cold already. He held his leather jacket tightly around him and closed his eyes. He lay there for a long time, listening to the rain drumming down, and thinking about Krista.

He thought he'd never get to sleep. He tried to distract himself by picturing the French River; he'd glimpsed it from the bus window in August, deep and black in its canyon, moving powerfully towards the open waters of Georgian Bay. His mind wandered back to the car that had almost stopped on the highway in front of the telephone booth. He had hardly been able to see it in the dark, just a smear of lights. But he knew that he would have been clearly visible under the booth's overhead light. He decided to put that thought out of his mind.

He tried to picture the Nuremborski summer house as Kim had described it to him, way bigger than her log cabin, with turrets and everything. He tried to picture a little boy sitting on the steps of that summer house. He tried to picture the little boy's parents sitting there too. He could see the familiar shadow of his mother, but her face was hidden. As always.

His father's face looked just like the face of the man in the wheelchair.

CHAPTER EIGHTEEN

· ·

1995

DETECTIVE SERGEANT WILFRED KISS, Homicide, Metro Toronto Police, opened up another can of beer. He was neither drunk nor sober, just cruising in that rosy in-between place.

It had become a ritual. Once a month he would drive over to his friend's house on the east edge of Toronto, sit in the large screened-in porch at the back and drink a few beers. Summer or winter, it didn't matter, his friend always wanted to sit outside. It just seemed right, somehow. Whatever he was carrying around inside him, in his heart and in his soul, it was too big for inside the house. Kiss could remember lots of times when the snow was blowing right through the screens, and the two of them still sat out there on summer loungers, drinking cold beer.

The trees in the backyard were ablaze with all kinds of colours. There was a sharp tang, almost a bonfire smell in the cool air, though no one was allowed to burn leaves any more.

Kiss glanced at his friend, whose face looked as if it had been washed too many times, or maybe held underwater too long. Soft. Puffy. Almost luminescent. With what? Grief? Pain? Thoughts of the unspeakable?

Kiss had seen so much death that its horror hardly registered any more. Cadavers by the ton.

He glanced at his friend again. They hadn't said anything to each other for the past half-hour. A new record. The truth was, they'd run out of words of any importance years before. For the last long while, all they'd thought of to talk about had been the Blue Jays and politics, or the Argonauts and politics, or the Leafs and politics, depending on the season. They hadn't talked about the man's son or his wife for years. Not for years.

"Those leaves are pretty," Kiss said.

"Yeah. Real pretty."

"Too bad you can't burn them any more. Remember how at night you could look down the streets and there'd be these glowing piles of leaves as far as you could see? You could ride your bike right through. Send sparks all over the fucking place. Catch your ass on fire."

"Yeah, I remember." But he didn't laugh.

Kiss poured himself a little more beer out of the can, watched it slide down the side of his glass.

His friend knew a lot more about death than Kiss did. Kiss was kind of a voyeur in that department. An outsider, a guest. But he feared not for long. Something, he knew, was moving deep inside his gut. Some bulbous white membrane. Part of him, like his liver or his spleen. Kiss guessed cancer, but he hadn't gone to a doctor, hadn't been to one in years. And he hadn't told anybody else about it. There was no one else to tell.

He glanced over at his friend again, who had settled back down inside himself. Collapsed into some deep thought.

Kiss often wondered whether his coming over and sitting there gave the man any comfort at all. Maybe that wasn't why he came over, anyway. Not the whole reason. Maybe it was to keep close to the heart of the cop business, to remember why he forced himself out of bed every morning, why it was important to keep doing what he did. Because sometimes, he swore to God, he had no idea why he got up at all. Or why he should look another corpse in its glassy-eyed fucked-up face.

"Getting colder, you can almost smell snow in the air," Kiss said.

His friend didn't reply. He was truly off somewhere. Happy thoughts, Kiss hoped, happy memories of his son and his wife. The beautiful young wife and the little son he had lost so many years before.

Kiss knew he would keep coming over once a month with his carton of beer, for whatever reason, offering whatever comfort he could. There was nothing else he could do. He would sit there in windstorms and rain and blizzards, he'd sit there with his friend until the end of time.

CHAPTER NINETEEN

. .

THE FRENCH RIVER WAS INVISIBLE, covered by a mist as plumy as smoke and as white as snow. The sky was perfectly blue. The sun sent long black shadows across the highway. The rain of the night before remained in large puddles and streams of water running everywhere. The weather had turned cold.

Walker was standing on a high bridge, shivering, looking upriver—the direction he had to go.

The mist extended as far as he could see, washing gently against the pines clinging to the canyon face and spilling over the top. Frost coated the metal guardrail. Walker's bare hand melted right through it.

He got back in Alphonso's Caddy, cozy with heat, and drove a mile past the bridge, turning east onto a secondary road. According to Kim's directions, Road 528, the main road along the North Channel of the French River, went right through the small village of Weirtown.

"We called it Weirdtown," Kim had said, "because we were from Toronto and everybody looked so weird. All there was to do was sit on the steps of the general store or go bowling. They had this really bizarre bowling alley, it only had two lanes."

"So how far away was their summer house?" Walker had asked her.

"Not far. Just a walk. Lennie and I walked into town all the time. There were boys there."

"Is that where she met my dad?"

"Must have. There was this big marina complex somebody had built. It was almost new. I think he worked there."

On his drive up the day before, Walker had bought an Ontario road map at a gas station. He'd found Weirtown on the map, more or less as Kim had remembered, on the edge of a sheltered bay where for some distance the land must have flattened out to meet the river, and the river, in response, had widened into what looked like a large lake. It was twelve miles from Highway 69.

At just past seven o'clock in the morning, Walker drove into the town of Ouellette and pulled up to what seemed to be the only restaurant and gas bar open for miles. He gassed up the Caddy and tried to fill himself up on the cheap as well, with two orders of toast and two coffees.

After Ouellette, the road swung closer to the river. The mist became so thick that he had to slow almost to a crawl in the dips and valleys. It was like driving through milk.

A large green sign floated by. Walker was entering Crown Forest, Lot Number 189.

The land seemed to rise now, not in swoops and dives but in a slow, determined climb. Walker drove blind until the big car broke out into sunlight.

Down in the valley, the mist was rising off the river, spiralling up and evaporating into the warming air. Patches of water glinted through for the first time, like brushed steel.

Walker passed a lookout area. Kim had told him that the Nuremborski house was the first place past the lookout. He was getting close.

Another green sign announced that he was now leaving Crown Forest, Lot Number 189. A smaller sign, tacked up on a nearby telephone pole, said Weirtown—2 Miles. But it pointed down a narrow sideroad to the right.

Walker pulled up. The road he was on seemed to be running parallel with the river now, maybe even angling a little away from it. But the sideroad headed straight down into the valley.

He decided that though Kim had remembered the lookout, maybe she'd forgotten the turn. He spun the wheel and eased the Cadillac between two walls of trees. The big car tipped steadily down for a few moments, and then came up over a slight rise. The river was right in front of him.

Walker spun the wheel, following the road sharply left. And immediately, as if someone had raised a curtain and revealed it, he saw the Nuremborski summer house.

The vision was so sudden, the effect so powerful, that he nearly drove over the bank and into the water. The Cadillac skidded a little, came to a stop.

A narrow house sat on top of a hill to his left. Three storeys high, it had one large, square turret that commanded a view of the river, not the two or three that Kim remembered. Its creamy yellow paint was curled with age. A wide and graceful porch, the most welcoming aspect of the house, surrounded it on at least three sides. The windows were boarded up; so was the front door.

A silver maple, bereft of most of its leaves, sat in the front yard. A thick rope hung from one of its lower branches, the frayed end stirring aimlessly against the ground.

Walker turned off the road, pulling the car up the leaf-strewn driveway, and stopped. He got out.

A sign nailed to the tree said Private Property—Trespassers Will Be Prosecuted. There was another sign, saying exactly the same thing, nailed to a post on the veranda. But the sparse grass, brown now, had been cut, and the shrubs below the boarded-up windows were trimmed. It looked neater than the Nuremborski house in Forest Hill.

Walker looked around. There were no other houses or cottages anywhere in sight. He looked down towards the river. He could see that the sandy path that led from the house to the road appeared again on the other side, and then disappeared over a rocky ledge. He decided to follow it.

Across the road, a short flight of wooden steps led down off the rock ledge. He could see the path again, leading towards the river.

He followed it to the water's edge. A long wooden dock—the worse for winter wear, knocked off its pilings by ice and spring floods—was sitting half in and half out of the water. A boathouse at one end of the dock, the size of a small barn, leaned precariously headfirst towards the river. Its roof ridge had snapped and cracked open, revealing weathered, mossy beams underneath.

Walker walked over to the boathouse and peered through a dusty side window. At first he couldn't see anything, but then, in the shaft of light coming through the split in the roof, he could just make out some old sails and tackle hanging from the opposite wall, and the shine of the water below. The nose of a half-submerged boat was pointing up in the air. Water lapped gently around the driver's seat. Half the wooden wheel was under water.

It seemed like an old-fashioned powerboat to Walker. He'd seen pictures of them, with their sleek wooden hulls, their long graceful bows. But in this case, all the wax and oils and stain had peeled and bubbled and flaked. The wood underneath looked mottled and sick. And Walker could see that it was spotted with shit, too; splattered with years of bird shit.

He backed off the perilous board he was standing on, suspended over the water beside the boathouse, and got back on solid ground. He looked up at the house again.

From where he was standing, he could see only its faded shingled roof and its square turret. The windows in the turret were boarded up too.

Walker began to feel the child's panic flooding back again, as it had in Forest Hill, his breath unable to escape his throat, his heart beating wildly. He walked quickly back to the house and got into the car. Sweat as cold as ice water started to run down his ribs, his nose began to run, his eyes began to run, everything was running.

He backed out of the driveway and drove half-blind down the road, passing a few cottages, some big, some small. Within a few minutes he was in Weirtown. He pulled up and parked, wiped his eyes, blew his nose. What the hell was happening to him?

He looked around. Weirtown came slowly into focus.

He was parked across from a hardware store, a long wooden building that also housed the local post office. A hair stylist, on his side of the street, was next door to a pet grooming service. Two real estate offices, their windows covered by photographs, faced off against each other on opposite sides of the street, and a general store dominated the only intersection in town.

Walker thought, those are the steps that Kim and Lennie sat on, looking for boys.

A woman in an apartment over the general store stepped out on a small balcony and began hanging wet clothes on a line, even though it was still early in the morning. An old man with a stiff back came out of the hardware store, a pile of mail in his arms. He climbed painfully into a truck, drove by Walker and turned down a narrow side street, towards the river. Walker could see the bright metal roofs of a large development some way off in the direction the old man was driving.

The marina, he thought to himself. The place where his father, his guitar-playing, song-writing father, had worked nineteen years before.

Had he worn his hair long? Had it been braided? Would they have liked each other if they'd met? If he drove over to the marina right now and somehow, through some wormhole in time and space, his father was standing there on the dock, would they recognize each other?

He's in a wheelchair, Walker thought. Pale of face now. His black hair shorn. Or is he?

Walker closed his eyes. His head was beginning to throb.

And then he thought, why was the summer house boarded up? Because, obviously, it wasn't being used. Probably hadn't been used in years, given the look of Jake Nuremborski with those tubes up his nose. Why hadn't he sold it? Because he didn't want to. But why?

Walker soldiered on, pursuing his line of thought. His mother had abandoned him beside a road about eighteen miles away. How had his grandfather responded? By boarding up the summer house? His grandson was lost and his response was to board up the house?

Walker looked towards the real estate office across the street. A sign above the picture window said Nietzsche and Son, Real Estate Brokers. The real estate office right beside him looked to be open too, but he thought he'd go with Nietzsche and Son. He'd read his way through *Thus Spake Zarathustra* just the previous year. He took it as an omen.

Walker opened the office door. An enormous man in a beige suit, standing near a desk and thumbing through some papers, looked around. Walker could hear his laboured breathing from across the room. He was bigger by far than Alphonso. He seemed to fill up the whole office.

"Hi there," he breathed.

"Hi," Walker said. "I'm Walker Nuremborski."

The man's huge face became more attentive by several degrees.

"Nuremborski?" he repeated, and stuck out a large, meaty hand. "I'm Herman Nietzsche."

Walker shook his hand.

"The only Nuremborskis I know of, they own a property on the river here. Any relation?"

"Yes," Walker said, "I'm one of them."

"Well, well," the man said. He smiled. "We never thought we'd see 'one of them' again." He sank into an extra-large swivel chair, his legs grateful, Walker imagined. He sighed as he sank, and then his body came to a stop. The chair creaked loudly but it didn't break. He caught his breath. "So what can I do for you?" he finally said, gesturing for Walker to sit in a small wooden chair by the desk.

"My grandfather's very sick. My mother wasn't sure just what was going on with the summer house, she's been away for years, so I told her I'd come up and check."

"I'm not sure I understand what you mean," the man said.

"Grandfather can't talk any more. His papers are in a mess. We weren't even sure whether he still owned the place. But I guess he does."

Walker was good at lying when he had to be. And he'd had to be lots of times, growing up tough in multiple households in Sudbury. One foster mother had reported to Heather Duncan that Walker could lie with a smooth face. He'd taken it as a compliment.

"Ah," the man said, "I get it. You want to know if your grandfather still owns it."

"It's the big frame house with three storeys and a turret," Walker added helpfully.

"I know the house, everybody knows that house. I have dozens of people coming in here every summer wanting to buy it. Which means I have to say, over and over again, that it's not for sale and probably never will be. I could get a hundred and a half for that property, easily. As a real estate professional," he added, with a look that invited Walker to share in his concern, "you have to understand, that makes me kind of sad."

"I bet," Walker said.

"Your grandfather still does own it," the man continued in his somewhat ponderous way. "But it sounds, sadly, like it might be coming on the market now. I would recommend, and I'm sure everyone around here would concur, that your good mother list with us. We've been serving this community now, father and son, for over fifty years. I have a desk drawer of customers ready-made for that place." He reached down and opened a drawer in his desk, by way of demonstration.

"I can guarantee a hundred and a half—no, I can get two hundred thousand for it. I think I know where I can get two twenty, though I'm not promising that." He closed the drawer.

"Do you know about what year it was boarded up?" Walker asked.

"Well, let's see." The man leaned back a little, his chair complaining ominously. "I'd say about—"

"Nineteen-eighty," a disembodied voice floated up over the half-partition behind the agent's back.

"That's right," he agreed. "Nineteen-eighty would be the year."

"Do you know why?" Walker asked, looking expectantly towards the wall. There was silence from the man in front of him, and from the wall.

Walker added, "You said that, as far as you knew, it would never be up for sale. I'm wondering how you knew that."

"How did we know that, Daddy?" the man called Herman Nietzsche said.

"Fred Evans told us," the voice from behind the wall came back.

"Oh, that's right. Fred's a lawyer in town, he looks after the place, sees that somebody cuts the lawn, that kind of thing. When it was first boarded up, we thought it might be for sale, so we inquired of Mr. Evans and he told us."

"Told you what?" Walker asked pleasantly.

"That Mr. Nuremborski wasn't interested in selling it, I suppose."

"I wonder why not," Walker ventured. "It seems a bit strange to leave the house boarded up for fifteen years."

"Jake Nuremborski was a strange man," the disembodied voice came back. "No offence."

"Of course not," Walker said, in the direction of the wall. He waited for more but, when nothing else was said, he continued, "Why do you say that? That he was strange?"

"I didn't know him much myself," Herman Nietzsche broke in. "I knew his boat by sight, though. We'd be sitting there fishing, and once or twice a year one of the boys would look up and say, here comes Old Man Nuremborski. He'd cruise by in this vintage mahogany launch, you could hardly hear it, it was as smooth as silk."

"But you don't know why he boarded the place up?"

"We don't like to talk about it," the agent replied, with a pained look. He puffed out his flabby cheeks.

"Talk about what?"

"Some little kid was murdered down there. A boy."

"Oh?"

"The Nuremborski place was the closest to where it happened, maybe it bothered him."

"That wasn't it," the voice said.

"I'm not saying it was, Daddy. I'm just speculating. That's what people say."

"Well, they're wrong. That happened years before they boarded the place up. You should know that."

"Well, maybe I should." The man looked at Walker and shook his huge head as if to say, Jesus Christ, there he goes again.

Walker could hear a scrape of a chair and then a tiny man appeared from behind the partition. He was as small as his son was large, but nevertheless there was a definite resemblance. They even wore the same kind of beige suits with yellow ties, except that the father could have fitted into a sleeve of his son's suit.

"That was a good four, five years before Mr. Nuremborski closed up his place. Don't confuse things, Herm. Besides, it won't affect our ability to sell that property. Hardly anyone remembers that incident around here, and of course no one from outside does. It's not a factor."

Nietzsche Senior walked across the office and peered out the window. "Is that your car over there?" he asked.

"Yes, it is," Walker said.

"You haven't been in to see Myerscroft, have you?"

Myerscroft, Walker remembered, was the name on the other real estate office.

"No," Walker said, "I came here first."

"Good. The truth is, Ralph is in the early stages of Alzheimer's, but nobody has the guts to tell him."

"We don't know that for sure," his son said, wincing a little.

"It's obvious," the old man replied. "So you're the grandson? I'm sorry to hear Mr. Nuremborski is failing. Here's a word of advice. It will be well worth repainting that place and sprucing it up. A little money invested before it goes on the market will come back to you threefold."

"Thank you," Walker said. "What exactly happened to that boy?" Walker looked back at the man behind the desk.

The man glanced at his father. "As Daddy says, it's a long time ago. And not exactly what the Board of Commerce would consider a selling point. But I personally do remember it. I was a volunteer fireman at the time. I saw it."

"Herman couldn't sleep for a week," said Nietzsche Senior. "His mother thought he'd have to be put on pills. But that was a good four or five years before the Nuremborskis left. Give him one of your cards, Herm."

The old man came back from the door and shook Walker's hand. "As soon as your grandfather passes, we'll be more than pleased to help you and your mother out." For a little man, he had a surprisingly strong handshake.

"Thank you," Walker said. "Just curious, but why did you say Grandfather was strange?"

The tiny man smiled as warm a smile as he could muster. "I just meant he was a man who kept to himself. His wife and their children were here most of the summer. She'd come in to town all the time, just to look for somebody to talk to, at least that's what I used to think. Real friendly. But not him. He wasn't around much anyway, and when he was, he was the type who let you know he had a little more money than you did. So closing up the place, just walking away and leaving it sit there, never seemed like such an unlikely thing for a man like that to do. Just proving to everybody around here that he didn't need the money. That's all."

"So you knew my grandmother?"

"Friendly, lovely woman."

"And my mom, Lenore?"

The man seemed to be searching his memory. "Lenore. That's right."

"And there were other kids?" Walker asked.

The little man looked surprised. "One. Your uncle, isn't he? Don't you know your own family?"

"Of course," Walker said. "I wasn't sure my uncle was born by then."

"He's older than your mother."

"Oh, that's right, of course he is. I've just got it mixed up."

The little man looked at Walker closely, then stuck his hand out again.

Walker shook it again.

"You came to the right place," he announced. "We'll treat you right." He turned briskly and walked behind the wall. Walker could hear the chair scrape against the wooden floor as he sat down.

"Here's my card." Herman Nietzsche handed Walker a gold-lettered business card.

"Thanks," Walker replied. Leaning a little towards the man, he asked, "What did happen to that boy? If you don't mind."

The man didn't say anything at first. Then his great head started to nod slowly back and forth, in a kind of self-comforting motion. "Somebody got him," he finally said. "Tied him up in a tree. He was slit open."

Walker flinched. His throat tightened again.

"The coroner figured it was while he was still alive. Some of his guts slid out, you know. Oh well, a long time ago. Better forgotten." He tried to smile, his massive cheeks struggling upwards.

"Where was he found?" Walker asked.

"There's crown land past your grandfather's place. We found him the next morning, not that far off a trail. He was only ten years old or so, a summer kid, a cottage kid. He'd been missing all night."

"Was anyone caught?"

The man looked at Walker and shook his head. He looked away.

"I'll never forget it," he said.

CHAPTER TWENTY

• •

I T WAS DUSK BY THE TIME Alex Johnson's father knocked at their door. Lennie, Bobby's thirteen-year-old sister, came down the back hall and opened the screen door. Though she was two years younger, she was almost as tall as Bobby, her face long and delicate, her hair dark.

"Hello, Mr. Johnson," she said.

She knew most of their summer neighbours, but it was unusual for anyone to come to their place when her father was there. He'd made it known to everyone, and not indirectly, either, that on the rare occasions when he did manage to get up to the river, it was to rest and enjoy his solitude, not to entertain the neighbours.

Mr. Johnson from two cottages down, a tall, slight man with thinning blond hair, looked worried. "You haven't seen Alex, have you? He didn't come home for supper, we've been looking for him."

"No," she said, "I haven't seen him all day."

Mr. Johnson nodded distractedly. "I cooked hot dogs on the barbecue, his favourite. It's almost nine o'clock."

She invited him to come in, told him she'd get her mother and she'd also go and ask her brother whether he'd seen Alex. He thanked her and stepped into the lighted hall.

Bobby had said that he wasn't feeling very well, that he had the flu or something. He'd gone to bed before supper. When Lennie came into his room, she could see his shape in the bed, despite the darkness.

"Bobby," she said, "are you awake?"

"What?" he murmured weakly.

"Have you seen that kid Alex Johnson? His dad's looking for him."

Bobby raised his head a little. "No," he said. He sank down again.

"Okay."

She closed the door. Bobby could hear her go back down the stairs. He could hear voices in the hallway below, too, but didn't have the energy or the interest to sneak over to his door to listen. He felt as if something was pressing down on him. He felt as if he weighed two hundred pounds.

He hid his face under his pillow again. He could feel his breath hot and moist, as though he were in a cave.

He thought of Alex for the hundredth time, a rag in his mouth, his arms over his head, strung up by some frayed old rope Bobby had found in the shed behind the house.

The boy had spun around and around, about three feet off the ground, until Bobby had tied two pieces of rope around his ankles too, and tied those ropes to the tree. Then he was still.

To start with, Bobby had taken him prisoner and commanded him to take off his shirt. Alex had played the game and pulled the faded red T-shirt over his head. Then Bobby had tied his wrists in front of him and thrown the rope over a branch. Alex had looked up, trying to figure out what Bobby had in mind. He had already had his turn, he'd tied Bobby up, but not like that.

"I have to question you," Bobby had said to him by way of explanation, but his voice had sounded raspy, as if he had a sore throat.

And Bobby had said, "You passed the screwdriver to my father. You're quite the man."

Before Alex could answer, Bobby had wrapped his arm around the little boy's head, jammed an oily rag deep into his mouth and pulled hard on the rope. Alex had jerked right up off the ground.

Now Bobby lay in his bed and began to tremble. All he'd really wanted to do was pull down Alex's silver bathing suit and see his little white bum. All he'd wanted to do was sip and suck on his tender little dink. But he couldn't. He couldn't, because he wasn't a fag. He'd wanted to, Alex had been making him want to—he'd felt sick, he wanted to so much—but he couldn't.

He had felt for his pocket knife then, the knife he'd purchased in the town below Southam Military Academy as protection against the senior boys. As it happened, he'd never had to use it.

He'd stood in front of Alex, his knife open. He'd known what he had to do. He had to make Alex a girl.

There was some kind of explosion in the air. There was blood up to his wrist and his fist gleamed like the head of a dream penis, pushing into the girl-slit he had made. He ejaculated out of every pore in his body. He fell, almost fainted.

Bobby squirmed in the bed, buried his head further under the pillow. He had to stop thinking about Alex. He had to go to sleep. But he was wide awake.

He could hear people going out the back screen door. The door slapped shut.

He got out of bed and looked out his window.

Below him, hurrying down the driveway, he could see his mother pulling on a jacket, and his sister walking along beside Mr. Johnson too. They were going to help Mr. Johnson look for Alex.

Bobby stood in front of the mirror for a moment. He could just make out his face in the dark. He had crossed over to some other place, some other way of being in the world. But he didn't look like a monster. Suddenly he could see light all around his head. He looked magical, he looked like some kind of angel.

His father had gone out for a ride in the *Chestnut Alley* after working on the boat for most of the day. It was late now but he still hadn't returned. But that wasn't unusual. His father liked to ride at night, swinging a shiny chrome searchlight slowly back and forth, picking out the buoys in the channel. And when he'd finally had enough and he pointed the nose of the *Chestnut Alley* towards home, he'd transfix the boathouse with his beam of light and the *Chestnut Alley* would come bubbling, burbling back to shore.

Bobby pulled on his running shoes and a jacket and a baseball cap, and ran down the stairs to wait on the dock for his father's return.

His father had seen him with Alex, or at least he had seen Alex and him at the same time. Whatever his father might say or do when asked about Alex, Bobby only knew that he wanted to be as close to his father as possible when it happened. He wanted his father to feel the power that was in his son now. Bobby had finally done something. He had done an extraordinary thing.

As he walked down to the dock, a light seemed to surround his whole body. It radiated from his arms and shoulders, shone from his hands and his legs. Surely other people could see it. They'd be afraid at first, Bobby thought to himself, but then they'd cluster around. They'd tremble and fall on their knees. He wouldn't hurt them, he'd lift them up. His father would be standing there watching him. His eyes would be full of wonder and love.

When Bobby reached the dock, he could see several boats with their lights on, searching up and down the shore, and some people walking along the road behind him carrying flashlights. A police cruiser turned the sharp corner on the road and stopped beside them. There was conversation—Bobby strained to hear but couldn't make out what they were saying—and the cruiser pulled slowly away. The people crossed the road and cut down to the river, in the direction of the trail that led into The Tract beyond.

No one had noticed Bobby standing there. No one had seen the light shining off his body. And now Bobby couldn't see it either.

A cold mist was beginning to rise off the river. Bobby began to shiver and his teeth began to chatter, as if he were a small, angry animal. His legs were shaking and he wanted to lie down, but instead he crawled up the bank behind the dock. The air was full of voices. Everyone was talking about Alex. In the boats. On the dark paths. In all the cottages.

Bobby lay there for a while with his hands over his ears. When he felt better, he sat up and looked out on the river, past the line of boats searching along the shore. He was looking for a beacon of light sweeping across the water. He was looking for his father.

An OPP officer was standing on the dock, cap tipped back, having a smoke, by the time his father did return. Bobby was still sitting on the bank but he was calmer now, quiet inside. And though the mist was still rising from the water, he could hardly feel it.

His first sight of the cop, struggling down the wooden steps with his flushed face and fat ass, hadn't terrified Bobby at all. The man had only reminded him how much smarter he was than everybody else in the world. He was the chosen one. He'd almost laughed out loud.

"Everybody's looking for the Johnson kid," the cop had said as he passed Bobby.

"I know," Bobby had replied. "My mother's over at the Johnson place now. So's my sister."

The cop had fished out a cigarette pack from the inside pocket of his jacket. Interpreting Bobby's position, sitting with his arms around his knees and looking mournfully over the water, as an attitude of sadness, he'd said, "Don't you worry, son. We'll find him."

"I know," Bobby had replied.

It was just then that his father's beam of light had appeared, as he manoeuvred the *Chestnut Alley* carefully in off the river.

The cop bent down awkwardly to catch the prow of the boat. As he did, Bobby could see his father, eyes intense, glance all around. The heat of his father's eyes landed on him. His father looked back at the cop.

Without a word, he cut the engine and stepped nimbly out, tying off the stern and bow. That job finished, he straightened up and, smiling his gleaming smile, said, "Thank you, officer. Is there some trouble?"

"There's a kid lost. Everybody's out looking for him."

"Who?" his father asked, his dangerously sharp eyes stabbing towards Bobby again. Bobby just sat there on the ground under the faint yellow dock light, his face half hidden by the peak of his cap.

"A kid called Alex Johnson," the cop said.

His father's face didn't betray anything. It remained exactly the same as a second before, just as handsome and just as attentive. "Alex?" his father said. "He's a nice kid. I hope they find him." He headed for the boathouse to get the tarp he used to cover the boat at night.

"You didn't happen to see him today, did you?" the cop asked.

"No," he said, not looking around, picking up the tarp.

The cop turned to Bobby, as if he'd suddenly remembered him. "You didn't see Alex today, son?" Before Bobby had a chance to answer, the cop turned back to his father. "Is this your boy?"

Bobby's father was already spreading the tarp painstakingly over the *Chestnut Alley*, working from the bow towards the stern. "Yes," he said, without looking up.

The cop turned back to Bobby. "Did you see Alex today?"

"No. No, I didn't," Bobby said. He looked past the cop. His father had stopped pulling on the tarp. He was on his knees on the slick wooden deck and he was staring directly at Bobby.

Now the cold came back, and Bobby started to shiver again. He clamped his jaws tight so his teeth wouldn't chatter.

The cop flicked his cigarette out over the water. It arced through the dark like a miniature flare. He said, to no one in particular, "Well, back to work."

The cop walked past Bobby.

Bobby could hear him climbing slowly up the stairs. After a moment, he dared to look back at the boat.

His father was in the same position, crouched on the deck. He hadn't moved at all. He was still staring at Bobby.

CHAPTER TWENTY-ONE

• ○

WALKER DROVE OUT OF WEIRTOWN and headed back towards the Nuremborski summer house. Nietzsche Senior had said that the house had been boarded up in 1980. He'd sounded sure, and to Walker he seemed like a man who would remember his dates.

I was found October 4, 1979, Walker thought to himself, and the old man closes down the house the next year. His boat sits in the boathouse year after year, until it springs a leak and sinks. He never comes back. Why? Because he has a big head and he wants to show off?

The murdered boy surfaced in Walker's mind, entrails fanning out, floating in water, for some reason. He pushed the image back down. It had nothing to do with him.

Two children. That had come as a surprise, though it shouldn't have. People did have more than one child. It had never occurred to him that there could be any other child than Lenore, though.

Walker was getting close to the house. He could tell by the escalating beat of his heart. When it came in sight, he slowed the Caddy and then stopped in the middle of the road.

He turned into the driveway, drove up the slope again and turned off the engine. After his heart quieted down, he pushed the door open and got out.

The breeze was more persistent now, coming off the river and shooshing through the branches of the pines at the sides and back of the narrow house.

He decided to walk towards the back. The wooden veranda that surrounded the house on three sides stopped at the back corner. A broad boardwalk had been built close to the ground, running the width of the house, with steps at each end leading back up to the veranda. There were two doors off the boardwalk, near the centre of the back wall, covered with sheets of weathered plywood.

An old shed sat back in the trees. The door was half open.

Walker climbed up a sloping rock shelf towards the shed. Its cedar-shake sides bulged with rot. He opened the door the rest of the way and looked inside.

Two workbenches, the wooden floor and the rafters were all strewn with the collected debris of many years.

He stepped inside. It was perfectly silent in the shed. He couldn't even hear the wind in the pines that towered right above him.

Walker felt very tired, as though he wanted to go to sleep. There was no answer here. No answer anywhere he looked. Despair opened up inside him.

Then he stepped on something. Crouching down, he picked up a hammer lying half-hidden under some oily rags on the floor. Its head was covered with a rusty red stain and its handle was stained almost black with oil.

Walker held it in his hand, began to squeeze it so tightly he thought his fingers would crack. He turned and walked out of the shed. Running back down the slope to the house, he stepped up on the boardwalk and threw himself against the plywood sheeting on one of the doors. He bounced back, but nevertheless, it made him feel better.

Using the claw of the hammer, he attacked the board again, working the claw under its edge. The plywood soon split around a nail driven into the frame of the door.

Encouraged, he worked along the edge of the plywood; wood split, nails pulled out. The thick sheet of plywood started to give way.

Dropping the hammer, Walker grabbed the edge of the board with both hands, wrenching back and forth. The board, still attached by bent nails on the one side, swung open with a sharp squeal, and hung there cockeyed.

A sturdy-looking, windowless wooden door confronted Walker. A large padlock and a rusty latch held it closed.

He looked around. A circle of mismatched stones and boulders marked the border of what had once been a raised garden. He chose the largest stone he could carry, cradled it in his arms and, running at the door, flung it at the lock.

The door gave a satisfying shudder but the lock held. Walker picked up the boulder again and, this time hoisting it up in shotput style, took another run at the door. As the boulder crashed into the lock, screws hidden under the latch tore loose. The door swung inward, hitting the wall with a satisfying bang.

It was dark inside the house. A patch of sunlight fell across a faded mat by the open door. A windbreaker and a straw hat hung from a row of coathooks on the wall.

Walker stepped inside. He was looking down a narrow hallway that seemed to open into a wider hall near the front of the house. Light slanted in through the transom above the boarded-up front door.

He listened. The house creaked in the wind. He peered into a room on his right.

The room captured more light than the hall. Sunlight slipped around and between boards nailed over its windows. A large cast-iron stove stood directly across the room beside a newer, smaller, white electric one. A long wooden table and chairs filled up the centre. A teapot and coffee carafe were sitting on the table and two glasses, washed and turned upside down, had been left to dry on a tea towel by the sink.

Everything in the room—and the room itself, because of the greyness of the light—looked to Walker like something out of an old black-and-white movie.

He flipped on a light switch. Nothing happened. He walked across the kitchen and touched the tea towel, just to make sure it wasn't damp. It felt dry and stiff under his hand.

The room directly across the hall from the kitchen was smaller and had a fireplace. There were piles of magazines on end tables, and books in bookshelves. Watercolours of towns and lakes and wild-flowers hung on the walls. And all this too looked like an old black-and-white movie. Without much effort, Walker could see fourteen-year-old Lennie coming into the room. She flopped down on the wicker sofa, picked up one of the magazines, started looking through it.

He turned away and moved down the hall towards the front of the house.

A formal dining table was set for eight in one of the two front rooms, with empty serving dishes and bowls and tarnished silver plat-ters and plates and cutlery all arranged. Clean linen napkins were neatly folded in each place, yellowing with age.

The other front room, seemed the kind his Grandmother Devereaux would have called a front parlour. Although it had more formal furnishings than the room without the fireplace, it seemed pleasantly casual too, even summery, as if the woman of the house, with an eye to the Victorian era but wanting the room to be warm and welcoming, had managed an unlikely alchemy of the two.

This was his real grandmother's room, Walker thought, his grandmother Nuremborski.

He walked the length of the room and all around it, around the dusty tables and high-backed chairs and settees, around the wicker plant stands with long-dead plants. Cobwebs hung in dirty strings from the high ceiling, cobwebs covered mirrors and lampshades like delicate lace.

Walker felt inexpressibly sad.

His eyes fell on a telephone sitting on an end table. He lifted the receiver and put it to his ear. Silence. A torn-off piece of newspaper was lying beside the phone. Someone had scribbled a phone number in the margin, as if writing in a great hurry. Walker picked it up and stuck it in his shirt pocket.

He stood in the front hallway and looked up the stairs that led to the second floor. If his parents had stayed overnight in October of 1979—if the three of them had stayed overnight—then wouldn't the most likely place to find proof of their visit be where they had unpacked their bags, and laid out their personal belongings? In a bedroom?

The second floor was darker than the first, but a thin band of light came in around the boards nailed to the upstairs hall window. Walker groped his way along the wall and looked into one of the bedrooms. The blind was pulled down but its edges glowed faintly with sunlight.

He felt his way into the room and pulled up the blind. Dust motes spiralled upwards in bands of light. Through the cracks, he could see the bare branches of the maple tree just outside the window. The pink Caddy was still sitting below him. But another car was sitting there too.

Walker stared at its sleek black shape. It looked familiar, somehow. Mary's Point...the car driving out of the lane after Krista's car caught fire. The new Audi.

Walker turned quickly, listened. The house was still creaking in the wind. He strained to sort out the creaks, listening for footsteps coming towards him up the stairs. If there was only one way into the house, there was only one way out.

His first impulse, a child's impulse, was to hide somewhere. But why? Why should he hide? Anger overwhelmed his fear. It was a relief to feel anger.

He crossed the bedroom without any attempt to soften his

footsteps, and walked back the length of the hall. He stood at the top of the stairs and listened again. There was still nothing to be heard other than the sound of the wind and the creak of the house. He started down the stairs.

By the time he'd gone halfway down, he could see in the dim light of the front hall a pair of highly polished dress shoes and sharply creased pants. The further he went, the more he could see. The suit coat. The tie. The round wire-rimmed glasses. The man who'd pushed him and told him that he wasn't and never would be a Nuremborski, was standing below him.

The big man remained motionless, staring up at Walker. Walker stopped on the stairs, keeping a few steps between them.

"You were at Mary's Point," Walker said, his voice echoing a little in the house. "You torched my friend's car."

The man didn't change expression, didn't move.

Walker tensed, adrenalin pounding through his body. Fight or flight. Which would it be?

The seconds ticked off. It was the other man who broke eye contact first. He started to brush some dust off his suit. Suddenly he looked a little nervous. "I stole the letter and the photograph, too," he said. "Not exactly my line of work."

"You killed my cat," Walker said.

"I wasn't aware he was yours." He looked up at Walker and smiled a thin smile. "I thought he had adopted you."

Walker stayed where he was. "What exactly is your line of work?"

"That's a good question," the man replied. "It seems, more and more, almost anything." He stared up intensely at Walker. Walker stayed silent.

"I'm Mr. Nuremborski's private secretary, and have been for many years. My name is Chester Simmons. Why don't you come down here so we can talk?"

"About what?" Walker replied. For the first time, he noticed that the man was carrying a thin leather portfolio.

"About your inheritance," the man said. "We need more light."

He turned and began to walk down the hall towards the back of the house. "Let's get this over with," he said.

Walker came down the rest of the stairs and watched Simmons disappear into the kitchen. He reappeared in a moment, carrying two wooden chairs, and set them down in the hallway in a patch of sun near the open back door.

"This is better," he said.

Walker walked slowly towards him. The man sat down on one of the chairs. Walker stopped.

"If you'll sit down, I'll explain everything."

Walker picked up the other chair, turned it backwards and sat down. That way, he could get up fast with the chair in his hands, ready to inflict mayhem on the man's head, if he needed to. "Go ahead," he said.

"First off, I do what Mr. Nuremborski orders me to do, not because I think it's the right thing but, frankly, because I can't afford not to. I am not a young man any more."

"You killed my cat," Walker repeated, feeling very little fear of the man now. Mr. Nuremborski's secretary closed his eyes for a moment, as if he were hoping everything might just go away.

"What happened to Lennie?" Walker said. "What happened to my mother?"

The man opened his eyes and shook his head. "No," he said, "that's the thing. You've got that all wrong, even though it ends up the same."

"What do you mean?"

"I mean Lenore Nuremborski is not your mother. You're Robert Nuremborski's son."

Walker sat there for a moment. "What?" he said.

"You're Robert Nuremborski's son," the big man repeated.

Walker got up.

"I'm Lennie's son," he said, his mind racing through all the reasons why he must be her son, trying to sort them out, but he couldn't remember what they were. "I saw the photograph. I saw the letter. I've talked to her best friend. I've talked to Kim Miller-Best!" he shouted, his voice racing through the house.

"I know," the man said.

Walker had a sudden impulse to smash his head with the chair. But instead he struggled on, as if he were trying to run through water. "Lenore had a son, I read the letter."

"Yes, she did. His name is Edward William Jenkins. He's a student at Edinburgh University."

"She got pregnant when she was just a kid," Walker went on, a bit crazily, as if she could only have had him, and not some other baby.

"That's right." The man began to open the leather ties on the portfolio. "She and her husband moved to Jamaica to have the baby, and subsequently they emigrated to England." He glanced up at Walker through his round wire-rimmed glasses. "You've been barking up the wrong tree."

Walker sat down again. He had to slow things down, he had to think.

"How did you know where I lived? And where's my photograph? And where's my letter?"

"As per Mr. Nuremborski's instructions, I destroyed them both." Suddenly the man looked almost apologetic.

"How did you know the letter and photograph were there to steal in the first place? How'd you know I'd moved to Toronto? And if this guy is my father, how come I was in care? A crown ward? And if I'm this guy's son, how come I was abandoned twenty miles from here when I was three years old?"

Walker was fighting back tears now, like some stupid little kid. His voice was too loud. He could feel his body beginning to shiver. It infuriated him, because he didn't want to show the man what he was feeling. Besides, he wanted to keep his mind clear.

"A woman showed up at this summer house one day, with a little boy," the man said, in a softer voice now. "She claimed that he was Robert's son and that Robert had to take responsibility for him, she couldn't look after him any longer, she was going to leave him with Robert. Unfortunately for her, Jake Nuremborski was here too. You'd have to know Jake, particularly before he'd sold off his company. He was a very formidable man. Robert, his only son, on the other hand, was not. He was, well, troubled—that's how the company people, such as myself, referred to him. Which meant, among other things, that he was a drunk. Sorry, but you did ask. Anyway, this woman was no catch either. Some local Indian he'd met in a bar."

The man hesitated but Walker didn't move a muscle.

"She'd had his child and he'd given her some money, but now she was sick of the kid and sick of him and she had a new boyfriend. She was moving on. And that's all there was to it. Of course, it wasn't going to be that simple. Jake asked Robert if what this woman was claiming was true. Robert said she was lying, he hardly knew her; he was afraid of his father, absolutely terrified of him. So the old man kicked the woman and her kid off the property. He said if she ever showed her face again, he'd have her arrested."

Walker got up from his chair and leaned his back against the wall. The house was tilting, listing like a ship in a storm. He closed his eyes.

"But of course, as you well know, Walker, she didn't just go away. That afternoon, she called Robert and said she'd left his kid beside a road. She told him where, and that he'd better do something about it, because she and her boyfriend were on their way to parts unknown."

Walker moved down the hall to the front of the house and stood leaning against the wall there, his back to Simmons.

The man had to raise his voice a little for Walker to hear, but he stayed sitting where he was. "Jake asked Robert what the call was about, Robert told him and Jake asked him again if it was true what he'd said, that the little boy wasn't his son. Robert swore it was true. Jake said, 'Forget she was ever here. Don't get involved. Someone will find the kid.' He's a very hard man when he wants to be, our Mr. Nuremborski."

"Yeah," Walker said.

"Robert started to drink, drank all that day, finally drove off to find you. But he never did. Either you'd already been picked up by somebody else or he was too confused and drunk to know exactly where to look. According to Jake, he came back half out of his mind. He started to scream at his old man, for the first time in his life, probably, and staggered off along the edge of the lake. When it got dark, Jake started to worry. He took a light and went to look for him."

Walker could hear the man getting up from his chair now.

"He found Robert lying at the bottom of a cliff beside the river. He'd either jumped or fallen."

Walker turned. Simmons was standing by his chair, still near the open door, half in sunlight, half in the gloom of the hallway.

"He's the man in the wheelchair," Walker said.

"Yes, he's the man in the wheelchair. Paralyzed except for some movement in his hands. The damage to his brain was massive. A nurse lives with him, takes care of him. He's with us but he's not with us, if you know what I mean."

He opened the portfolio and pulled out a few pages of neatly typed paper. They seemed to shine in the sunlight.

Walker didn't move. "If my grandfather ordered you to break into my apartment, he had to know who I was before I showed up at his place. How did he manage that?"

"Yes, how indeed?" Simmons replied. "Years ago, your grand-father called me into his office, told me he needed a personal favour. He wanted me to pose as a newspaperman who'd had a tip that an abandoned kid had been picked up beside a highway near Sudbury. I contacted the police there and they told me they'd turned you over to Sudbury Children's Aid. Over the years, I became a friend of a friend of yours."

"Who?" Walker asked.

"Heather Duncan."

Simmons sat back down on his chair, adjusting the portfolio and papers on his lap. "Come and sit down now, please. Social workers don't make a lot of money, Walker. They have to think of retirement."

Walker remained where he was. "Heather Duncan?"

"She gave us yearly reports. I had explained everything, without giving her any names, of course. I was posing as a lawyer; I'm a man of many trades. I told her how my client felt a certain responsibility towards you, since there was a chance that you might actually be his grandson, given how his son had acted that day. But he wasn't inter-ested in another grandson. A bastard grandson. Nevertheless, he did want to be in a position to help you financially if you ever needed it. Heather Duncan was doing you a favour."

Walker walked back up the hall. He felt dizzy. "What did she tell you?"

"Everything. Where you were living in Sudbury, the move to Thunder Bay, all about the Devereaux family in Big River. She kept in touch with you all those years, didn't she?"

Walker nodded. He felt sick.

"She told me that you'd visited Sudbury last year to look through your file, the one with the letter and photograph in it. And she found out your address in Toronto from your family in Big River and gave it to me, the same day you moved in. That was the end of it. If it makes you feel any better, she's off the payroll now."

It didn't. Heather Duncan, who'd held him tight and who'd even got teary-eyed at times. Tears of guilt, Walker thought. She'd known who he was all along.

"Don't blame her."

"No," Walker said. He rubbed his face in his hands. He just wanted to wake up.

Simmons held the pages out to Walker.

"Mr. Nuremborski was not and is still not interested in acquiring a new grandson. He's in poor health. And he doesn't want any complications concerning his estate. He wants to be left alone."

Walker took the papers and sat down once again. He looked at the top page. Lots of words and numbered clauses.

The man continued, "We tried to discourage you, but obviously we failed. And we soon realized that it was becoming increasingly messy, because you were confused, in an understandable way, I suppose, about who your parents were."

Walker looked at the other pages. More words, more numbered clauses. He couldn't make himself read them. The papers were shaking in his hand.

"Believe it or not, the old man has taken a shine to you. Probably because you're as determined as he is." The secretary paused, smiled. "I'm glad you're sitting down. Mr. Nuremborski is prepared to give you a gift of four hundred thousand dollars."

Walker looked up at him.

"Why? Because he wants you to be a success in life and, quite frankly, because he doesn't want his estate to become involved in a paternity suit. All you have to do is sign this document. It certifies that Walker Devereaux is simply a talented young man who Mr. Nuremborski has met, admires and is helping out, and that you have no further expectations or claims whatsoever, and forever, period. And then he wants you to go away."

"I see," Walker said.

"I have a certified cheque with me for four hundred thousand dollars, made out in your name. All you have to do is initial each page, here, and sign the last page here." He leaned over a little and pointed out the places for Walker to sign. "Thank God I won't have to follow you around any more."

He pulled a pen out of a leather loop on the side of the portfolio and offered it to Walker.

"Tell my grandfather that my mother is Lenore Nuremborski," Walker said.

Blood drained from the man's face. "Are you making a joke?" he asked.

"No."

Simmons reached into his portfolio, fumbled for a moment and held a cheque in front of Walker's face. It was certified, all right. And it had Walker's name on it, and it was for four hundred thousand dollars.

"This is an incredibly generous offer. You don't have a legal leg to stand on. Robert can't testify to anything, he's a vegetable. You can't even force a blood test. Get it?" The man's eyes were starting to bug out behind his glasses. "Are you a complete fool? Sign the documents, take the money and run!" He held out his pen again.

"No."

The man lurched out of his chair.

Walker stood up too, and held the man's papers out to him.

Simmons glared at him but he looked frightened, close to despair. "You're nineteen years old. When you're thirty-nine, you're going to hate yourself," he said.

Walker continued to hold out the papers. The man took them and stuffed them inside his portfolio. He held the cheque up in front of Walker's face again. One last try.

Walker shook his head.

The man stuffed the cheque back into his portfolio.

"How do you suppose that letter and photograph got in my pocket?" Walker asked, trying to keep his voice as calm as possible. "Since the letter wasn't addressed to Jake Nuremborski, or Robert either. Since it was sent to Lenore Nuremborski in Jamaica!"

The secretary stepped out on the wooden boardwalk into full sunlight. He turned back to Walker. With the light reflecting off his glasses, he looked blind.

"You know your problem?" he said, "You're a lot dumber than you think you are. Lenore and her husband had already left Jamaica when that letter arrived. So the housekeeper sent it back to Canada, care of Mr. Nuremborski. It was here, the photograph too, on a table in the front room. Your mother stole them when she was here, and stuck them in your pocket so that, when she left you beside the road, you'd be identified as a Nuremborski. You'd be brought back here! Get it?" He looked around hopelessly. "But it just didn't work out that way."

He turned back to Walker, desperate. "Look in the mirror," he said. "What do you see? You see a half-breed. You see your mother's son. For chrissake, sign the papers! Take your money!"

Walker shook his head again. He's scared pissless, he thought, scared of Jake Nuremborski.

"Robert Nuremborski is your father," the secretary insisted. "You've just made the most expensive mistake of your life." With one last look at Walker, he turned and walked away.

Walker listened until he heard Simmons back out of the driveway. The noise of the car receded in the distance. There was just the sound of the wind again. The creak of the house. Walker was about to leave too when he heard something else. Footsteps, he was absolutely sure. Someone was crossing the floor right above him.

He moved back down the hall as silently as he could, and looked up the stairs. He didn't see anything at first. And then, at the top of the stairs, an almost featureless face, like a full moon, materialized out of the dark. It was staring down at him. Walker stared back up, and it disappeared.

Walker began to move up the steps. "Who's there?" he said.

He certainly didn't know who was there. Someone who was in the house before he broke in? Someone who knew another way in?

Walker stopped halfway up the stairs. It wasn't Robert. Robert was his father. Robert was in a wheelchair. It wasn't the man who had been following him. The man who had been following him had just left.

"Who's there?" Walker said again.

An empty house was an inviting place for anyone. A stranger passing along the road. A squatter.

"This is private property," Walker said, somewhat ludicrously.

No response from the darkness above. The man might leave. The man might stay. Walker didn't really care.

He turned away and walked back down the stairs. Climbing back into Alphonso's cadillac, he felt more tired than he'd ever felt in his life. He backed out of the driveway, and drove towards Toronto.

He'd been offered four hundred thousand dollars to get lost. His mother had dumped him on the side of the road because she had a new boyfriend and he was an inconvenience. His father was a weakling, a drunk. And a vegetable.

Walker almost started to laugh. He could feel a kind of hysteria building up in his throat. He tried to cut it off, for fear that, if he ever let it out, he might never stop.

"The question is," he addressed himself, his voice sounding thin and strained in the car, "the question is, do I believe him?" He struggled with that question, gave up. He couldn't think any more.

Four long hours later, he turned down the narrow lane in Forest Hill, heading for Jake Nuremborski's house. He needed to fall into bed. He needed to sleep for a year. But he couldn't help himself.

It had been a sunny late October day, but now the sun was edging down behind the trees, throwing a cold red glow against the walls and windows of the houses.

At first the Nuremborski house looked just the same as before. Shabby and overgrown, desolate. And then he saw—far up the driveway, wrapped in a yellow plaid blanket, sitting in his wheelchair and turned to face the glow of the setting sun—Robert Nuremborski.

Walker stopped and got out of the Caddy.

Robert was sitting there looking like the subject of some religious painting, his hair lit by the glowing sun, his face staring blindly heavenward, red light turning all the colours of his blanket to fire. Walker came up to him but he didn't move, he didn't seem aware that his son was there.

His son? Walker looked down at the man's face. His head resting on one shoulder, tilted up at an odd angle. His eyes were closed.

Walker bent down in front of him to see him more closely. His face was finer than Walker's, more delicate, but the high cheekbones were there and something familiar, too, in the long line of the jaw. His hair was black but not so pitch-black as to be almost blue, like Walker's. But then, the woman in question was native, wasn't she?

Walker wanted to say something, but he didn't know what. He suddenly realized that he was feeling at peace beside this man. All his terrible tension, his hurt, his confusion, were falling away.

Something in the air here, something surrounding him, was so quiet, so comforting, so still, that it was as if the world itself had stopped breathing.

CHAPTER TWENTY-TWO

. .

THE NEXT MORNING, everything was in an uproar. Alex Johnson had been found. The details of how he had been found and in what shape he'd been found travelled as fast as lightning, and with the same effect.

Grown men took a step backwards on hearing the news; their mouths opened but made no sound. Women's faces shattered. Children were looked for and ushered back into their cottages, as if they'd suddenly become invalids and needed rest and quiet.

Some older children escaped and ran up and down the shore and between the cottages, shouting to each other, feeling almost hysterical, feeling a charge of electricity in their blood, bewildered and excited and full of wonder.

All at once the talk began, as if everyone had recovered the facility of speech at the same time—a torrent of words to try to give shape to something shapeless, to make sense of the nonsensical, to circumscribe, with detail and motive and speculation, the boundless.

And when that didn't work, the men became angry and gathered in swarms, and the women, their children safely with them, went into their rooms and curled up on their beds. And they all knew that, no matter what they did or didn't do, no matter what they said or didn't say, it wouldn't make any difference. Someone had come into Alex Johnson's life and ended it. And someone had come into their lives too.

Bobby's father hadn't said a word as Bobby followed him up from the river to the house. He hadn't needed to. His father had already said all he needed to say when he'd told the cop that he hadn't seen Alex Johnson, and when he hadn't corrected Bobby's statement that he hadn't either. They were together in this, father and son. The message was clear. His father would protect him, no matter what. He had no choice.

Bobby was clever in his way. He knew that his father wouldn't say anything because he was terrified, not for Bobby but for himself. The family name. The Plant. The disgrace. And deeper than that was his horror that he could have sired such a son, that from his glorious loins such a thing as Bobby could have sprung.

And Bobby, lying awake in the middle of the night, smiled to himself at this thought, and rolled around on his bed and tried to picture himself as a troll with a great hairy head and pointed ears and a hump of flesh growing out of his back. He would live under bridges and in hollow logs. He would sing to himself and people would mistake his voice for the voice of the wind. Winter would come and ice would encrust the marshes and the woods, and Bobby would move through the dark trees like a skulking shadow, impervious to the cold.

Then Bobby had another thought: that underneath it all, his father must love him. And the more he thought about this, the more he realized that, beneath everything, his father had always loved him. Even when he had seemed full of scorn, even when he had seemed to hate him the most.

Bobby stood in the middle of his bed and spread his arms out. He was not a troll, he was a god, because he dared to live in a high place, far above the common bleating masses with their little thoughts and desires, their little comforts and fears. His father had always thought of himself as special, and now Bobby was even more special than his father.

He imagined his father standing there in front of him in his dark bedroom. His father, amazed. This is my son!

Bobby began to cry. He didn't know why. Maybe because he was so glad that his father loved him. Maybe because he was so far above the world that he'd become frightened. Maybe because, finally, in the middle of the night, in his family's summer house, he knew he was absolutely alone.

Tears washed his face and he lay there pretending he was under the river. His father was looking for him. And finally he fell asleep.

The lightning arrived at Bobby's home at about ten that morning, when Alice Thorgood from the general store in Weirtown knocked on their door to tell Bobby's mother (in whispered tones, for fear Bobby and his sister might overhear the frightful details) what her husband and some other volunteer firemen had found just inside The Tract about an hour before.

His mother went over to the Johnsons' to see if she could be of any help. His sister was told to stay in the house, as was Bobby.

His father heard the news from Bobby's mother before she left. He was wearing his silk dressing gown over his pyjamas and had his leather slippers on. He was standing in the kitchen, looking as if he'd hardly slept. As she told him, his face lost some of its colour, he nodded a couple of times and, uncharacteristically, he suddenly held his wife to him as if to comfort her. He held her for a long time.

Bobby's father was packed and ready to go back to the city by the time the two OPP officers (neither one of them the fat cop of the night before) reached their summer house. Some business problem had suddenly occurred to him, and he had to drive back that afternoon rather than stay the next two days as he had originally planned. It was almost two in the afternoon.

Everyone sat in the front room. The two cops, his mother, his father, his sister and Bobby. The cops were apologetic that they had to bother people so soon because everybody was so upset, but it was best to ask questions when people's memories were as fresh as possible.

Bobby's father and mother nodded, so the cops asked their questions. And, as it turned out, no one in Bobby's family had seen Alex yesterday.

Bobby's mother thought she had seen him two days before, but of course that wouldn't be helpful. One cop, the smaller one, said it might be, and asked in what circumstances she had seen him. She said she thought she'd seen him returning empty pop bottles for deposit in Weirtown. She went on to say that Alex tended to show up in lots of places. Everyone knew him. He had been a very enterprising and inexhaustible little boy. With that, she began to cry. His sister wiped away a tear or two as well.

The cops apologized for the intrusion and got up to go. The larger one, a giant in his black, thick-soled and highly polished boots, looked down at Bobby and smiled. He asked him what he had been doing yesterday afternoon. Was he swimming? Fishing?

Bobby's father had been sitting slightly apart from everyone else, staring out the window, as motionless as a statue. Now he stood up but he didn't look at Bobby, he looked a foot or so over Bobby's head, as if something of extraordinary interest hovered there, as if it might just fall down.

Bobby said no, he hadn't been fishing or swimming. He'd helped his father fix his boat, and then he'd gone back to the house. He hadn't felt well. His mother had told him he should get into bed, and so he had.

The cop said, "Do you feel better now?"

"A little," he said.

After the two cops left, Bobby's sister went running up to her bedroom to have a good cry. His father followed Lennie upstairs, not to comfort her but to bring his suitcase down. He was getting ready to go. He didn't want to wait for supper.

Bobby was in the back hall, watching his father and mother in the kitchen, when his father said, "I want Bobby to come with me tonight."

His mother, who was standing at the kitchen sink and distract-edly washing potatoes for potato salad that evening, turned and stared at her husband as if he had just said the most amazing thing.

"Why?" she asked. Her voice sounded tight and small.

"He'll be sixteen soon. There's a few things he should start to do after school and on Saturdays. Office-boy stuff. Break him in now, while he's still on holidays. It doesn't hurt."

She turned back to her potatoes. Bobby thought, from where he was standing near the doorway, that her hands were trembling. But she didn't ask any more questions. He knew what she was thinking. She was thinking about that boy he'd hit on the head at Southam Military Academy. But so what? He was going back to the city with his father. His father had made his choice and his choice was Bobby.

"Get some things together. We're leaving now," his father said, somehow knowing that Bobby was standing there watching him though he had not once turned to look at him, had not looked at him all day.

Bobby's heart soared. He felt triumphant.

He climbed the stairs. It was true that he was not like other peo-ple. He had used Alex in such an extraordinary way that he had been transported into ecstasy. He loved Alex now. Alex had shown him the way. But the way to what, he hadn't exactly sorted out. The way to be different? The way to be a god? The gods were always killing off mor-tals. He had seen a picture once of some god squatting by a dead man, his hands cupped and running over as he drank the man's blood.

And a god has sprung from my father's loins, and he is amazed, he thought to himself. He had read something like that once—a man amazed, standing in front of a god. He loved to read about the Greek gods and the Roman gods and the ancient Nordic gods. The world was teeming with gods. People just couldn't see them.

Bobby stood in the upstairs hallway and decided that he was invisible too. *What mortal eyes cannot see and what mortal hearts cannot fathom.* That had been the line under a coloured picture of Jacob wrestling the Angel. Suspended above them in the starry night was the golden ladder leading into heaven. The picture had been in a book some relative had given him too long ago to remember. But he did remember the picture. He had stared at it for hours.

I am invisible, he said to himself.

He looked at his sister's door. She'd left it open a little. He pushed it open a bit further. She was curled up in her bed under her covers, facing away from him. She was probably still crying over Alex, he thought.

Don't cry, Bobby almost said out loud, Alex is in heaven. And he had a vision of Alex wading in a lake in heaven, making a perfect raft. All the pieces were the same length and they all fitted together.

He stepped inside her room, convinced that he was invisible now. He walked quietly across the floor to stand beside her bed. All he could see above the covers was her dark hair. Now he could do anything he wanted. He could slip under her covers, if he wanted. He could whisper in her ear and tell her that he was a god, and she would think she was dreaming. He could cover her and press her down like a deep sleep. He could suck out her breath. He could open up her legs and thrust himself inside her. She would groan and wrap her legs around him in her dream, they would cling together and fly up the ladder.

His sister raised her head and looked at him, as if she had known he was standing there all the time.

"What are you doing?" she asked.

"Nothing," he said. "I'm going away. Father's taking me with him."

"Oh," she said, and lay back down on her pillow. She wiped her hands against her eyes. They looked shiny in the half-light of the room.

Bobby sat down on the edge of the bed. He'd never sat on her bed before. She turned away and curled up under the covers again.

Only his father knew the whole truth. Only his father knew he was a god.

"Alex is in heaven," he said, out loud this time.

She didn't reply.

He reached out slowly, almost invisibly, to touch her hair.

CHAPTER TWENTY-THREE

· ·

THE PHONE RANG right beside Walker's ear. His eyes opened but his brain was still asleep. He stared dumbly at the wall. The room was dark; there was a glow from a lamp somewhere.

On the fourth ring, he picked up the phone.

"Hmmm," he said.

"Glad you're awake," Krista replied.

Walker propped himself up on an elbow.

"I let you sleep in. It's almost six o'clock."

"Hmmm."

"I'm coming over. I know about that number now."

"What number?" Walker said.

"That phone number!" she sounded slightly exasperated. She hung up.

Six o'clock, Walker thought. Jesus.

He threw off his cover and swung his legs over the side of his pullout bed. That was as far as he could go for the moment.

How long would it take her to get over to his place? Not long if she was driving, but she was still without wheels. She'd already pointed out that asking one of the guys to drive her over was not a good idea, unless she and Walker wanted to be teased forever. So how was she going to come? By streetcar? Call another cab company? Wheelchair?

Robert Nuremborski had been in a wheelchair the previous evening, sitting in a cold red light. Walker remembered what he had felt there, a deep peace descending, his exhaustion falling away. It had seemed like a sign that this man really was his father, like a matching of auras, like a melting of one into the other.

Except the stillness had become too still and too deep. As Walker had continued to stare, Robert's face had begun to look artificial, like a construct, a death mask. Walker had had to fight an impulse to reach out and lift it off, to see the real face underneath. He'd backed away, hurrying down the driveway to Alphonso's car.

While Joe Smart was going over every square inch of the Cadillac, looking hopefully for scuff marks, mud, cigarette burns, ashes, crumbs, mustard—anything—Walker had crossed over to Ruby's, bought two coffees and two honey-glazed donuts to go and, feeling exhausted once again, walked back to the cab company.

Krista was sitting at her dispatch desk. She looked relieved. "Glad you're in one piece," she said. She even looked as if she meant it.

Encouraged, he circled around the counter and put a coffee and donut down beside her. He hadn't forgotten that she had inexplicably turned her back on him, that she had become cool and remote. But his day had been too long, and what he'd learned too shattering.

He sat on the edge of a desk and, between her phone calls and radio calls, he told her that it had been Jake Nuremborski's secretary who had been trying to scare them off, and that Heather Duncan, his protector, his best and only friend when he was a child, had been feeding information to Jake Nuremborski for years.

When he got to the part about Lennie not being his mother—about him being Robert's son, at least according to the secretary—she didn't seem to know what to say.

When he got to the part about the cheque, she recovered her voice. "Bullshit," she gasped.

"Four hundred thousand, certified," Walker repeated.

"My God, let's see it."

He hesitated. "I didn't take it," he said.

She stared up at him.

"Because I don't believe what he was saying," he explained. "Because it's a cover-up, because something happened to my mother and they're trying to buy me off!"

Krista nodded carefully. The explanation the secretary had given Walker sounded persuasive enough to her, but this obviously wasn't the time to question him on how he knew that Robert Nuremborski wasn't his father. He'd been saying that the man in the wheelchair could be his father for days now. Better to let him go home and sleep, and talk about it later.

"I saw Robert Nuremborski again today," Walker added.

"And?"

"And...." Walker paused. His face, for a brief moment, looked anguished. "I don't know."

He got off the desk and, pulling out the torn piece of newspaper he'd found at the summer house, asked her if there was any way of finding out if the phone number was a Toronto number, or a number near the French River, or maybe one from somewhere else altogether.

She said she'd try her best.

Walker had been too tired to bend down to kiss her. He'd just said, "Thanks," and walked out of A.P. Cabs on legs that had felt hardly there at all.

And now it was the next morning, Krista's shift had ended an hour and a half ago, and she was bringing news about that number.

By the time she arrived, Walker had washed up and put on fresh clothes, and he was waiting by the outside door, his jacket collar turned up against the cold.

She had chosen Nick. He pulled up to the curb in his old Chrysler, with Krista sitting beside him. She struggled out of the car with her crutches as Walker helped Nick extract her wheelchair from the trunk.

"Hey, man," Nick said.

"Hey, Nick," Walker said. "Cold, eh?"

"Yeah," Nick said, with a grin as wide as all of Ethiopia spreading across his face. He slammed down the trunk lid. "Maybe it'll get warmer," he said.

Walker didn't reply.

Nick called out to Krista, wondering if she still wanted him to pick her up at her father's place that night, to drive her to work. He'd been driving her back and forth since her car melted.

She said, "Of course."

"Just wondering," he said. He got back in his car and drove away.

Krista was dressed in a brown suede half-length coat pulled over a thick blue sweater, and she had a matching blue woollen toque stuck on her head, her blonde hair tumbling out from beneath it. Walker thought she looked great. Much more than great.

He rested the wheelchair against the wall inside the street door and carried her up the stairs. He could hardly feel her body through her coat and her bulky sweater. He resisted an impulse to press his face against hers. He knew her skin would feel cold and warm all at the same time.

He put her down and unlocked his door, then hurried back down the stairs for the wheelchair.

By the time he'd returned, she was in the kitchen, putting the kettle on. He watched her for a moment, a little surprised at how pleased it made him feel—Krista in his kitchen, doing such an ordinary, everyday thing as putting a kettle on for coffee.

"Okay," he said.

"Okay what?" she reached up in the cupboard for two coffee mugs. They were just within her reach.

"You said you found out about that phone number."

She leaned her crutches against the counter and began to take off her coat.

"It wasn't that hard," she said. "I just dialled it. No such number within our area code. Then I dialled it using the area code for the French River district. Right away, somebody answered."

She pulled her toque off and shook her long, tangled hair. Walker took her coat, hung it on the back of one of his kitchen chairs, trying to be patient.

"Who answered?" he said.

"An ambulance service. They don't have 911 up there yet. You have to call the ambulance service yourself."

"Where was it?"

"Sudbury."

Walker sat down on the other chair.

"So it makes sense, doesn't it?" Krista went on. "Didn't that man tell you that Robert Nuremborski fell that night? The nearest hospital would be in Sudbury."

"That was his story," Walker said.

"Well, it makes sense, doesn't it?" She reached for the instant coffee.

Walker started to roll himself a smoke. He didn't reply for a moment. When he did, he said, "We don't know when that phone number was used. It doesn't have a date on it. Maybe Robert fell some other time, not the day I was abandoned. Maybe that number wasn't for Robert. Maybe it was for someone else."

"Like?" Krista asked.

"Like Lennie. Or Kyle. Like my mother and father." Walker said stubbornly.

Krista opened her mouth to say something, then changed her mind. She searched a drawer for spoons but Walker had only one, and it was in the sink, sticking out of an empty can of beans.

"Is this your only spoon?"

"Uh-huh."

She lifted it out of the empty can as if it might give her a rash, and scrubbed it with the dishcloth.

Walker finished rolling his smoke. "Nobody knew who I was, Krista. How could a woman have a kid up there, even a *useless Indian*"—his eyes blazed up at her—"and nobody know anything about it?"

"She went away, Walker. People would assume she took her kid with her, wouldn't they?"

"Yeah," he said, "except they ran my picture in all the papers around there. Someone would have recognized me. They made a poster up, too. I saw it, it was in my file. They sent it to every post office in the district, and to police departments all over the country, with a big photograph. 'Do You Know This Child?' it said. And nobody did."

The kettle started to squeal.

"He offers me four hundred thousand dollars to go away. Don't you think that's a little much? Don't you think someone is really terrified of something? Don't you think the real truth must be much more dangerous to somebody—to Jake Nuremborski, for instance—than what they're saying? Why the hell would he care whether he had another grandson? He can leave his estate to anyone he wants to, anyway. Can't he?"

Krista lifted the kettle off the burner.

"A healthy, clean, well-looked-after child." Walker was really going on now. "Dressed in new clothes and new shoes, with a mother who knelt down beside him and loved him and whispered in his ear for him to hold on tight, a mother who put a letter and a photograph in her child's pocket so that, if something happened to her, her child would be identified and saved. Forget that phony story about a letter being mailed somewhere, being returned, lying on a table for some Indian woman to have the presence of mind to steal and stuff in my pocket!"

Krista spooned coffee into the mugs, poured in the steaming water. She got a carton of milk out of the fridge. She didn't trust herself to look at him, didn't want to look at his face.

"How old is this milk?" she said and, before Walker could reply, held the carton up to her nose. She couldn't help herself.

"I think it's okay," he said, relaxing a little.

She risked a glance at him. He was lighting up his smoke. He looked all right. "Smells fine," she said, smiling at him.

"Do you think I should have taken the four hundred thousand? Do you think I'm an idiot?" he asked, his face obscured by smoke.

"Of course not," she replied, though she wasn't sure just what she thought.

"It's about my mother," he said. "Where would I live, where would I go, how could I look at myself? It's my *mother*."

"I know," Krista said. She reached out to balance herself on the edge of the table, then bent down and kissed him on his smoky mouth.

She pulled back a little and put a hand on each side of his face. Their lips were as close as they could possibly be without kissing. She closed her eyes so that all Walker could see in front of him was her long eyelashes. He felt her tongue touch his lips, part his lips.

Everything was awkward and everything was perfect. It was awkward to lift her in his arms, but it was perfect the way she held onto him and kissed him with a kiss that lasted all the way from the kitchen into the living room.

It was awkward to set her down on the floor and pull out the damn bed, thinking why the hell had he put it away in the first place (because he'd thought it looked too crude sitting out), but it was perfect the way she smoothed down the sheets that were all crumpled up inside, and patted out the pillow.

And it was perfect how she crawled onto the bed, her hair hiding her face, and lay on her tummy with her face buried in his pillow, so that he straddled her there, rested his face against her face, softly kissed her cheek, her forehead, her hair, her ear.

The phone rang.

Krista's eyes opened.

"Don't worry about it," Walker said.

It rang again.

"Oh God," she said. A long breath left her body.

"It's nobody," he said.

It rang again.

"Answer it, Walker."

He reached out and picked up the phone. "Yeah?"

"Is my daughter there?" George Papadopoulos asked.

"Who?"

"Krista Papadopoulos is who."

"Oh, yeah. Just a sec." Walker got off Krista and handed her the phone.

"Who is it?"

"Your dad," he whispered.

"What the hell's he doing?" she whispered back. Walker shrugged.

"What are you doing?" she repeated into the phone, not too kindly.

Walker got off the bed to give her a little privacy, and crossed over to one of his two windows. It was only six-thirty. Church Street was just beginning to stir.

"What?" Krista said, and once again, "What?" and finally, sounding a little frightened, "You're kidding!"

Oh no, Walker thought.

"Okay, okay!" she said, and put down the phone. She sat on the edge of the bed and looked across the room at him. "Something's wrong."

"Like what?"

"My mother and father had a fight. Which is no big deal. But it's always my dad who storms out of the house. Always. But this time, he thinks my mom's run away."

"Oh," Walker said, sitting down beside her.

"He's really upset. I've never heard him like that before."

"How'd he get my number?"

"I guess from Alphonso. When I was late getting home from work, Dad must have called him."

"How did Alphonso know you were here?"

"I don't know. He guessed. Walker, that's not the point. The point is my mother!"

"Right," Walker said. "I'm sorry."

She pressed her face against his cheek. "I should go home, Walker."

"Yeah."

They sat there, heads together for a long moment. Finally Walker picked up the phone and called her a cab. But not an A.P. Cab.

A few minutes later, he was lifting her wheelchair into the trunk of a Diamond Cab. He pushed down the lid. Krista was waiting for him by the car's open door.

He grinned and walked up to her.

"That was the worst," she said.

So she wouldn't feel so bad, he kissed her. She still felt warm. Hot, actually.

"I wish that call hadn't come," she said.

"So do I," Walker replied.

She put her lips close to his ear and whispered, "Hold onto that thought, okay?"

"I'm going to have to hold onto something."

After she was gone, Walker stretched out on his bed. He could still smell her perfume on his pillow. He could almost feel her underneath him. He closed his eyes. Never even got her shoes off. Or her sweater. Untying her shoes wouldn't have been a problem but that bulky sweater might have been trickier. Contemplating these things, he fell asleep.

When he woke up, it was almost eleven o'clock. The sun was slanting through his windows, pretending it was a warm day out, but Walker knew better.

He reached for his wallet and pulled out a business card he'd slipped inside the summer before. He sat up and dialled a number.

"Good morning. Sudbury Children's Aid, how can I help you?"

Walker asked to speak to Carolyn McEwan. He waited on hold for a moment, until a bright, cheery voice came on the line. "Good morning, Carolyn McEwan."

"Hi, Carolyn. It's Walker Devereaux. I don't know whether you'll remember me, but I came around last summer."

"Of course I remember you. Of course. How are you?" She sounded as if she cared. Walker was hoping she did.

"Okay. You know how I was looking for any information on my birth parents?"

"Yes," she said.

"I think I'm really close to finding something out."

"Really?" She sounded genuinely surprised, but then, why wouldn't she be surprised? She'd seen the meagre contents of his file. "That's wonderful," she said.

"I need a little help. I knew you'd help me if you could."

She hesitated for one heartbeat. "Of course, Walker. If it's something I can do."

"How many hospitals are there in Sudbury?" he asked.

"Two main ones. The General and the Catholic. Why?"

"Do you have much to do with them, when you're tracing birth parents and getting medical histories?"

"No, not for that kind of thing."

"Oh." His spirits sank a little.

"I do go over to the General every once in a while for adoptions. Usually it's some really young unmarried girl who's agreed to give her child up. I'm the go-between. She signs the child over to Children's Aid and I make the transfer to the adopting parents. That's all completed and registered at the hospital."

"You'd know people in the records department, then?"

"Sure. But you have to realize that any medical records would be confidential."

"I don't need to know about medical records," Walker said. "All I need is admission records for the emergency department, for the night of October 4, 1979, or maybe the morning after. Just the name of a person who was brought in by ambulance that night from the French River, from around a place called Weirtown."

Silence on the other end of the line. "It might have been one of my parents," he added.

"That's a long time ago," Carolyn finally said.

"The same day I was found beside the road."

"Really? What's the name I'm looking for?"

"I don't know. That's what I'm trying to find out. I just know that my mother and father were in some kind of accident that night. Something happened."

"Walker, I'll see what I can do."

"Great," he replied. He felt hugely grateful.

"I'll tell Heather you called."

"No," he said quickly, "I'd prefer you didn't. I'm so close to finding my parents now. And the thing is, I'd like to surprise her myself."

"Oh? Well, okay then," she said.

He gave her his phone number. Then he dialled Kim Miller-Best. It was just eleven in the morning. He hoped she'd still be coherent.

"Hello?" a child's voice answered.

"Hi. Is your mom there?" Walker asked.

"No," the little girl replied.

"Do you know when she'll be back?"

"She's gone on a holiday," she said, in a very serious tone of voice.

"Where?"

"To Grandma's."

"Is that your grandma in Toronto?"

"Yes."

"Do you have two grandmas in Toronto?" he asked, just to be sure.

"No."

Walker could see Kim through the window in the front door of her mother's house even before he rang the doorbell. She was sitting in the kitchen at the far end of the hallway, talking to someone. She was wearing a housecoat and looked thinner than Walker remembered her. When he pressed the bell, she jumped.

Kim got up and came down the hall towards him. He could see her mother standing in the kitchen now, dressed in tailored slacks and a shirt, made up to perfection, in sharp contrast to her daughter.

Kim opened the door.

"Sorry to bother you again," Walker said. "This will be the last time, I promise."

Kim had her hair pulled back and half caught up in some kind of bun. She didn't have any makeup on at all, and her skin had a yellow cast to it. She looked more pinched and strained than the first time he'd seen her.

"Did you find the place up on the river?" she asked, not backing up, not letting him in the door. Her mother, looking anxious, came halfway down the hall.

"Yes, I did. Thanks a lot."

"Was it helpful?"

"Yes, it was. In a way."

"Did you find anything out about Lennie?" she asked. She ran her tongue around her lips, as if her mouth was too dry. She started rubbing one hand on the back of the other, agitated, back and forth.

"No. Not really. That's why I wanted to ask you one more question," Walker said.

Mrs. Miller came up behind her daughter and put her hand on her shoulder. "It's Walker, isn't it?" she said pleasantly.

"Yes. Hello, Mrs. Miller. It's nice to see you again."

"He wants to ask me another question about Lennie," Kim said, in a distracted way.

"This isn't a good time, Walker," Mrs. Miller said. "Kim isn't feeling all that well today. Perhaps some other time."

"No, it's okay," Kim said, trying to force a smile. "It's better, actually. It gives me something to do. Come on in, Walker."

Kim backed up. Her mother gave ground a little, though she didn't look pleased.

"I guess Kim told you what my real story was, and that I wasn't exactly honest with you," he said to Mrs. Miller, now that he'd gained the front hall. "I'm sorry."

Kim closed the door behind him.

"Oh, that's neither here nor there," Mrs. Miller said, keeping an anxious eye on her daughter. "I can understand you wanting to know about your family. It's just, you have to appreciate that Kim can't really help you any further. And it's a bit upsetting, the circumstances as you describe them. About Lennie, I mean." Now Mrs. Miller was looking directly at Walker, her eyes wishing him back out the door.

"I was just wondering," Walker persisted, "about Lennie and Kyle. If you remember exactly where they stayed in Jamaica. Where I was born."

"God," Kim said, "it was so long ago."

"But you wrote her," he replied hopefully.

"All the time. But I threw all my stuff out. Everything. Just before my wedding. A kind of purge. Didn't I, Mom?"

"Yes," Mrs. Miller said, with a hint of a sigh.

"It was just somewhere in Jamaica. I can't remember where. Why?"

"Because someone might remember me down there." Walker thought he must be looking particularly lame to these two women, standing there in the hallway, grasping at straws.

"It was eons ago," Kim said. "Everything was a big secret, she wasn't supposed to communicate with anyone. Jake had threatened to disown her if she did. I trusted Mom not to snoop in my stuff but, just the same, I burned all her letters as soon as I'd read them. It seemed more romantic that way."

"Right," Walker said. He opened the front door a little. "Okay. I hope you'll be feeling—"

"Oh!" Kim said.

He stopped.

She turned quickly to her mother. "You still have my old study desk, don't you? Out in the sunroom?"

"There's nothing in that desk," Mrs. Miller replied firmly. "Just as you said, you threw everything out."

"But it's not in the desk, Mom." Kim padded down the hall in her slippers. Mrs. Miller sighed again, more audibly this time.

Kim stopped in the kitchen. "Come on," she said, her face animated now. She did seem grateful to have something to do.

Mrs. Miller started down the hall after her. Walker closed the door and followed. By the time they had traversed the kitchen and a den and reached the sunroom, Kim was down on her knees in front of a small Arborite desk. The desk had two drawers on its left side. She pulled out the bottom drawer, lifted out some loose newspaper clippings and put them on top of the desk.

"I just keep recipes in there," her mother said.

"Not *in* the drawer, Mom." Kim turned the drawer over.

Walker came up to her on one side, and her mother on the other. All three of them stared at the bottom of the drawer. In hard-pressed ballpoint pen, where no one would ever find it, fourteen-year-old Kim Miller had printed, in bold blue letters, "Robinson's Place, Three Mile Hill, Reef Island, Jamaica."

"That's where you were born," Kim said.

• •

THE RED LIGHT ON WALKER'S answering machine was flashing. It had been his mother's idea for him to get an answering machine, because he was never home when she called and she never knew whether he was dead or alive. She'd sent him a cheque to pay for it, plus a little bit extra for emergencies.

Walker, back from seeing Kim, crossed the room and pressed the play button.

"Hi Walker, it's Carolyn McEwan," the clear voice rang out. "A friend at the General just looked up their emerg intake records for me. It only took a few minutes, because you had the date. You were right. There was a person brought in from somewhere on the French River that night. At about four in the morning, actually. He had serious trauma to the head. He remained in Sudbury in intensive care for about a month, then was transferred to the Bayview Hospital in Toronto. His name's Robert Nuremborski. I hope this helps. Keep me posted. And Walker, don't tell anyone how you found this out. Bye."

Walker sat down on the edge of his rumpled bed.

Not Lennie. Not Kyle. Robert.

At four o'clock, Walker walked through the front door at A.P. Cabs. Krista was already there, though it had taken most of the day for her to get her mother and father straightened away. She'd only managed three hours' sleep. She had dark shadows under her eyes.

Walker took one look at her and knew that Nick and the rest of the drivers would happily misinterpret her bedraggled look for sexual exhaustion. It would be the topic for the evening.

"Hi," he said.

Donna, in a bulky old sweater coat, was still dispatching. Krista was sorting through a pile of bills, deciding which ones she could put off paying for another thirty days and which ones she'd have to persuade Alphonso to pay now to avoid court action. This was a monthly routine. Alphonso never paid anyone until the last possible moment. It was an important principle with him and he never deviated from it.

"Hi," she said.

Donna, reading a paperback and lighting a smoke off her previous one, turned around to look at Walker.

Krista said, "Let's go down the hall. Alphonso's taken the night off. Again." She swung her wheelchair around and wheeled past him.

Walker had never pushed her in her wheelchair. As far as he knew, no one ever had. He figured it would probably be worth your life to try, even in a foot of snow.

He followed as she pushed herself along the hall, bumped down the ramp and turned into Alphonso's office.

"Donna's nosy," she said. "We found my mother."

Walker sat down on the arm of Alphonso's battered leather chair. He had some news too, but he wasn't in any hurry to tell her. "Where?"

"She'd gone over to my aunt's. She only lives a couple of blocks away, but it really scared Dad."

"Did she come back?"

"Yeah. On condition that Dad and I stop fighting all the time."

"Is that possible?" Walker smiled at her.

"Just barely," she said, and smiled back a little. "That was kind of weird today, wasn't it?"

"What was?"

— 223 —

"You know what."

"Yeah," he said.

They stared at each other for a long moment. It was Walker who broke the silence. "I found out something about that ambulance."

"Oh?"

"Yeah. It was Robert Nuremborski who was admitted into hospital that night."

"What night?" Krista asked.

"The same night I was found beside the road. That night."

"Really?" she said. "That fits the story about Robert being your father, doesn't it?"

He studied his worn boots. "Yeah," he said.

Walker drove cab all that night, wrapped in a numbing depression. It didn't help that it was raining. He tried to think about Reef Island, he tried to think of someone there who would recognize his name. Walker, not the name the secretary had told him. Not Edward William Jenkins, who lived in England and was studying in Edinburgh. But Walker. Walker with no last name.

As the multitudinous lights of the city smeared against his windshield, he tried to think of beaches and waves, a turquoise expanse of water, an impossibly blue sky. And playing there, a boy called Walker. Or Little Kyle because his father was Big Kyle—that was what Kim had said.

At that exact moment—as if the rain had suddenly frozen in place, as if all the cars had screeched to a halt in the watery light— Walker saw the answer. It was right there. Not Edward William Jenkins. And not Little Kyle, either. Walker saw the truth.

• •

IT TOOK A LOT LONGER THAN USUAL to get rid of the rest of the breakfast club over at Ruby's that morning. They were in a particularly loquacious mood, smiling at Walker and Krista and commiserating with them about how tired the two of them must be. Working during the night and then working during the day too. Double-shifting and all that. Ha, ha.

Finally they left.

Walker began to play with a package of matches, flipping it between and along his fingers. Over and over again.

"What's the matter?" Krista said.

"Why?"

"It's finding out who was in that ambulance, isn't it?"

"Could be."

"Look, Walker," she said, "it's not the end of the world. At least you know who your father and mother are now. And that nothing terrible ever happened to your mother. She just went away. That's a good thing, isn't it?"

Walker looked up at her. There was real pain in his eyes. "I think I've figured out why I'm so stupid. It's really obvious, once you see it."

He's having some kind of breakdown, Krista thought to herself. "What is?" she said.

"Well, think about it! Why was Lennie banished to Jamaica? What would have made her father go that crazy? Is it just a coincidence that Lennie was flying back to Toronto with her child just before Robert's child, also three years old, was abandoned? Two children, two boys, both three years old, both part Indian? Don't you see?"

Krista put her head close to his so that her hair touched his face, and she held his arm tightly with both hands. "No, I don't see," she whispered.

"They're both lies!" Walker hissed.

He looked away as if it was difficult to say anything more. "There's only one baby, one three-year-old boy," he finally said. "I'm Lennie's son. I'm Robert's son too!"

Krista's grip on his arm tightened.

"Lennie was lying to Kim about a boyfriend. There was no boyfriend. It was her own brother. It was Robert!"

"Why wouldn't she have an abortion if she was pregnant with her brother's child?" Krista said.

"Because she was too afraid and too ashamed to say anything. She was only fourteen. And by the time she couldn't hide it any longer, she was too far gone. So she lied that some boy had gotten her pregnant. I don't think Jake Nuremborski knew the truth when he banished her to Jamaica to have her baby. He found out later. Maybe not until after I was born. But at some time she must have told him. Or maybe Robert did."

"How do you know?"

"Because when she wrote Kim to say she was coming home, bringing the incest baby, the monster, back to Toronto, Jake went crazy. He killed her. He almost killed Robert. He abandoned me."

Krista was so close to his cheek that he could feel her breath. "Is that why he offered you the money? Why he wants you to go away forever?"

"I'm the living, breathing evidence that Jake Nuremborski is a murderer," Walker said.

It all fit. It all made some kind of horrible sense. Even to Krista.

Heather Duncan, the informer. The secretary trying to frighten them off. The four hundred thousand dollars.

They sat there in silence for a long moment.

"I know where I spent the first three years of my life, I got the address from Kim earlier today," he said. "When they found me, I remembered my name as Walker. Maybe if I go to Jamaica, I can prove I was the child who was born there. I sure as hell can prove I was the child who was abandoned. If there are people there who remember a kid called Walker, or if there's a birth record somewhere and I'm listed as Walker, I can connect myself to Jamaica and to Lennie. Then I can go to the police. They'd talk to Jake. They'd order a blood test on Robert. They'd start looking for Lennie."

Krista had to ask him. She took a deep breath. "Are you sure you want to prove you're the child of a brother and sister?"

"I have to."

"Yes," Krista said. "Walker, I have a little money saved. I can give you some."

"I want you to come too."

She looked closely at him. He seemed reasonably rational now that he'd got his story out. And he seemed to mean what he was saying.

She thought about Mary's Point. She could feel her crutches slipping away from her in the sand, she could feel her breath short, her lungs burning. "You don't want me there. I'll just slow everything down."

"Yes I do," he said. "We can do this together. Besides, Jake Nuremborski isn't going to give up just because I refused his cheque. But he isn't in Jamaica. We'll be safe there."

Krista hesitated for a moment. "Okay," she said.

Once Krista was in action, things moved amazingly fast. She booked tickets that afternoon for three days later, with a five-day stopover. Walker wasn't sure five days would be enough time, but Krista said they could rearrange their flight home if they needed to.

The main obstacle was George Papadopoulos. Krista had known he would be. All she had to do with her mother was be honest, say she wanted to go with Walker. Her mother read the rest in her face, everything she needed to know. Finally, Krista was making herself vulnerable again. She loved this guy, she wanted him and she wanted a life.

George was another matter. At first he said it was out of the question, as if it were something he and he alone could decide. Krista told him that it didn't have anything to do with him, she was just letting him know. George thundered that it sure as hell did, because where the hell did she think the money was going to come from if not from the trust fund he'd established for her. Krista said she never used her trust fund, she hated her trust fund, she was using her own money, and if she didn't have enough she'd put it on her charge card. George said, how did she think she had money in her bank account in the first place, because he didn't charge her rent, that was how. Krista said she'd told him a hundred times that she'd pay rent, she wanted to pay rent, but he always refused because it was his way of holding something over her head. George asked her (speaking of heads) how he was supposed to hold up his head with his daughter running off with some jerk and sleeping with him without benefit of a goddamn engagement ring let alone a goddamn wedding ring. Krista said it wasn't any of his goddamn business, she'd do what she goddamn wanted to. George said she should think of her mother, what was her mother going to say, that her daughter had no morals, that she was out of control, that she was so desperate for attention she'd go anywhere and do anything with anybody.

George had crossed the line, as he often did. But this time—to George's amazement, and Krista's, too—it was her mother who called him on it, who told him that she, for one, was proud of Krista, and that Krista was twenty-six and could run her own life, and that if George was so sick he couldn't let a grown daughter be with another man, he should go see a doctor.

George Papadopoulos didn't say another word.

Walker and Krista landed at Norman Manley International Airport in Kingston, Jamaica, three days later, at seven-thirty in the morning.

CHAPTER TWENTY-FOUR

· ·

ETECTIVE SERGEANT KISS SLID DOWN the steep embankment under the west end of the Gerrard Street bridge, in a very foul mood.

For one thing, the pain had come back the previous night, and it was worse this time.

It always came when he was sleeping, as if it were sneaking up on him, and he always felt it first in his ass. It filled up his pelvis, pressed against his spine, radiating pain into his bum cheeks and down his legs.

He'd got out of bed and, doubled over, he'd shuffled down the hall to the bathroom. He'd chewed a fistful of pain pills and sat on the john for half an hour. Then he'd walked in circles around his dark apartment, finally lying on his back on his living-room rug, his feet up on the couch.

Cancer. What else could it be?

Every time it came, it scared the hell out of him. Every time it went away, he figured he wouldn't worry about it. He lived alone. His wife had left him twenty years before. His two daughters never called.

He could almost see the goddamn thing. Started out the size of a grape. Snuggled into the lining of his bowels, liked it so much there that it continued to grow. An apple. Then a grapefruit. Oh God.

About four-thirty in the morning, the pain had subsided,

flickered out, disappeared. Kiss had held a cold, damp washcloth to his face, stared at himself in the mirror. Maybe it wouldn't come back.

But it would. He was convinced he was dying.

And another thing, he was thinking to himself as he half ran, half skidded down the path, scuffing his shoes all to hell: he shouldn't be there in the first place. He was homicide. From the description called in by one of his detectives before he'd even had a chance to hang his coat up in his office, it didn't sound like murder to him. But who gave a flying shit? Staff Inspector Hicks was under pressure from upstairs to investigate every goddamn thing that died. Used to be the coroner's job. It still was. But some clown somewhere had decided that every death, outside of one in a hospital bed, should be treated like a crime until otherwise identified.

As if he had nothing better to do. As if he didn't have enough files he'd never have the time or manpower to look after. It was all politics, optics, cover your ass, it was all "community policing" or some such nonsense, it was all making sure you were visible, making sure you seemed to care, even if you didn't give a flying fuck.

Kiss reached the bottom of the incline. He was feeling better. Seething inside was his only exercise. He was five foot six, weighed exactly one hundred and thirty-nine pounds; seething kept him thin.

Detective Constable Amos Alberni came to greet him. "Sorry to bother you, Sergeant, but I thought you should take a look."

Alberni was not long out of university, about as street-smart as a bunny-rabbit, as far as Kiss could tell.

The inspector didn't bother to reply. Why should he? He was dying; this kid would live for another hundred years.

The two of them walked towards a circle of other men, including a couple of uniformed officers. Kiss knew everyone in suits, including the coroner.

He could hear the hum of morning traffic crossing the bridge directly above his head. A wooded ravine stretched north and south of him, laced in both directions by dusty paths. This was not quite the place for a woodsy stroll, though. It was in the very heart of the city. Public housing on one side and the old Don Jail on the other.

Do not go into the woods today, Kiss was thinking idly.

A man was hanging from a rope. He was a big man, so he had chosen a thick rope. A wooden crate was knocked over on its side below his still suspended feet. He had positioned the crate on end, stood on it, reached up over his head to a bridge support, tied a sturdy knot around an iron rod, fashioned a slip-knot on the other end, put the loop over his head and kicked the crate away. Case closed.

The man's hands were not tied together or in any way restrained. They were soft-looking and clean. There was no tape covering his mouth, no gag of any kind. His mouth was fixed in a grimace, as if he were trying to pull a particularly stubborn cork out of a wine bottle. No marks on his face of any struggle, no cuts, contusions, just bland and very grey except for his bulbous nose, which seemed to retain some living colour, some fleshy tone.

There was nothing to suggest death by misadventure, unless by misadventure you meant the private circumstances that had driven him to such a lonely and despairing end. There was nothing exceptional at all; it was just one more of the suicides that big cities and small towns, even country folk, had to deal with.

Except that the man was naked.

Like a large slab of white meat hanging there, curing in the fresh air, curing in the shadows and sunlight.

The white belly was huge and distended. The legs were surprisingly thin, the knees looked bony and for some reason elicited a rare shiver of pity from Kiss. They seemed like an old man's knees, like his; they seemed heartbreaking.

Kiss could smell urine. The man's crotch still looked damp. A little stream of shit had dribbled halfway down his left leg.

"They stripped him," Kiss said, not turning to anyone,

continuing to examine the cadaver hanging in front of him. "The derelicts who camp down in this ravine. He was probably wearing a suit, shirt, tie, good leather shoes. The bastards took everything. You'll find his shitty underwear within thirty feet. No one is that desperate."

"We've already found them," Detective Alberni replied, holding up a plastic bag.

"The man committed suicide, some wino degenerates found him and they stripped him. That's all," Kiss reiterated.

Alberni was standing closer to him now, still holding the plastic evidence bag.

"Get that thing away from me," Kiss said.

"No, Sergeant, it's not his underwear. Something else."

He handed Kiss the bag. Kiss held it up in the sunlight.

Through the plastic, he could see a pair of glasses. One of the lenses had been smashed and bits of glass had been gathered up too, and put inside the bag. The round wire frames were mangled and broken.

CHAPTER TWENTY-FIVE

. .

WALKER HAD BEEN TOLD, by a very young, very beautiful woman at the Jamaican Tourist Bureau in Toronto, that Reef Island (she hadn't heard of it; she had to look it up, first on her computer and then, when that didn't work, in a reference book) was only about fifty miles from Kingston, on the south coast. Three Mile Hill was apparently the name of both the most dominant physical characteristic of the island and its only town. There was no causeway to the island; it was reached by a privately owned ferry service whose schedule was not in the reference book.

At A.P. Cabs, Walker and Krista had pored over their map of Jamaica, studying the route from Kingston to Reef Island. It seemed straightforward enough. Allowing an hour to get out of Kingston and an hour or so to drive fifty miles, they estimated that they should be at Joy's Grove, the town opposite the island, no later than ten in the morning. Lots of time to find accommodation on Reef Island, if there was any.

What they were going to do to pass the time that first night, they hadn't discussed at all. The question had hung in the air between them, though, for the last three days.

Roger Dumont, their taxi driver, pulled up in front of the ferry dock at Joy's Grove, in a cloud of dust, at exactly twenty minutes past ten. Walker and Krista stepped out of the air-conditioned car into the searingly hot morning.

A crowd of boys, dressed alike in private-school uniforms, were milling around on the wharf. More boys were arriving, some in cars full of family, and two in chauffeur-driven cars. They were all shades and heights—from short to tall, from white to light to golden brown to ebony.

"You're in luck," Roger said. "They're crossing to the school. Ferry's been called."

Within ten minutes, a boy standing on top of a piling announced that the boat was on its way. Within another minute, Walker and Krista could see it, a black beetle on a shimmering stretch of blue.

Walker studied it from behind sunglasses and beneath a white straw hat, both purchased at a kiosk at the airport. Even at seven-thirty in the morning, he and Krista had nearly fried traversing the tarmac from the plane to the moderately cool interior of the main terminal building. Krista had bought a straw hat too, with a large brim and a lavender bow, and two bottles of suntan lotion with the highest sunscreen rating she could find.

Every once in a while Walker shifted his gaze from the ferry, as it metamorphosed into a small iron boat red with rust, to the high green spine of Reef Island beyond. Streamers of mist rose off the island like fairy wings, disappearing into the air.

The boat, slab-sided and rust-encrusted, finally sloshed backwards into a slot in the dock. In the din of its engine, Roger shoved a hand-printed card into Walker's pocket. "Call this number when you want to come back. I'll come here. No problem," he shouted.

Walker nodded, and with Roger's help they managed to get their luggage and Krista's wheelchair on board, despite two trucks laden with boxes of goods bumping and roaring up the ramp beside them.

The students streamed by, dock hands shouted and cursed, the ferry's whistle blew and the captain glared blackly down from the wheelhouse. Finally he gave the order to pull away and, with much groaning and thumping, a tired old engine somewhere below responded. The propeller began to churn. The ferry slowly retreated from the dock, swung its blunt face out to sea, shuddered and resigned itself to once again making its way to Reef Island.

Krista and Walker ducked quickly inside the cabin to escape the sun. While Krista settled herself on a wood bench, Walker bought a cold bottle of Red Stripe beer from a boy in a torn undershirt standing behind a tiny counter. Krista didn't want anything, cold or hot.

As Walker sipped his beer, he thought about having made this crossing before, probably on the very same ferry. He could almost see Lennie, fourteen or fifteen years old, sitting beside her mother, maybe where Krista was sitting now. Dark-haired Lennie, pregnant with her own brother's child.

He glanced at Krista. She'd split her spending money with him, giving him exactly half so he wouldn't feel like a boy toy, as she'd put it. He had some Jamaican dollar bills, but mostly he had a roll of U.S. tens and twenties.

As soon as they came down the wooden ramp and stepped onto Reef Island—Walker making two trips for Krista's two suitcases, her travel bag, his hockey bag and her wheelchair—three hard-looking men, two women and some kids hurried towards them.

The private-school students, making as much noise as possible, were clambering onto a waiting bus. The two trucks roared by. The men, women and small posse of kids surrounded Krista and Walker, all talking at once, making impassioned, hand-waving speeches as to where the best tourist houses could be found. All their suggestions were different. The general shouting turned into a more pointed argument, then a kind of scrum as they began to fight over the luggage.

Krista looked up a steep hill and saw a cream-coloured building with a cluster of small balconies clinging to its side, overlooking the harbour. It wasn't difficult to spot; at three storeys it dominated the village.

"What's that?" she asked. Everyone stopped to see where she was pointing.

"Sam's Inn, missus," a boy said. "I'll help you there." And faster than anyone else in the crowd, he picked up Krista's larger suitcase and started off with it. The other children scrambled for the remaining bags. Hurrying up the hill, they soon left the adults behind.

Krista studied the steep climb up to the main street for a moment, then started to unfold her wheelchair. The three men and two women watched her glumly.

She handed Walker her crutches. "You're going to have to push me," she said, and eased herself slowly into her chair.

He began to push her uphill, steering around the roughest places in the dirt road. It felt a little strange, as if he were her nurse. He could see now why she had always resisted this.

Sam's Inn was owned by a middle-aged German called Sam Weiss, who favoured lederhosen no matter how hot it got. In a loud, barking voice, he called a man he referred to as his porter, an old man with sinewy arms and a bent back, from the empty dining room. He introduced him as Tom Tait and asked him to retrieve Walker and Krista's luggage from the kids.

Walker handed out Jamaican dollars. The kids laughed to feel the money in their hands, and raced back into the bright sunlight and down the street.

The room Weiss picked out for them was on the third floor, but there was no elevator.

"Do you have a room available on this floor?" Krista asked.

He looked surprised. "There are no rooms on this floor, only the bar and the dining room. I can give you a room on the second floor, but it faces the street. I've got permanent guests residing here," he explained, leaning across the reservation desk and looking down at her. "It's part residence, part hotel."

Walker leaned down and picked her up in his arms. "Third floor's fine," he said. "Key, please."

Their room was small but clean, with one double bed and a dresser made of matching blond wood, and two bamboo chairs.

Krista stretched out on the bed, wincing as she drew up her legs. "You better help that old guy with our stuff before he kills himself," she said.

Walker met Tom on the stairs, carrying both suitcases, the duffel bag and Krista's travel bag around his neck, all without much effort. Walker ducked by and got Krista's wheelchair and crutches from the lobby.

By the time he'd climbed back up to the third floor, Tom was coming down the narrow hallway towards him.

"Have you been here long?" Walker asked, handing him twenty dollars in Jamaican bills and leaning up against the wall.

"Where?" Tom replied. His eyes were large and red-rimmed.

"Reef Island."

"All my life."

"Do you know a house called Robinson's Place?"

"Gone," the old man said.

"What do you mean?"

"No longer with us." He rubbed his nose thoughtfully. "Gone to the boys' school now."

"To the boys' school?"

"Yes sir. The boys' school. Used to be a house, not now. Now it's a boys' school. Three, four buildings besides old Robinson's Place."

"But you knew it when it was just a house, I guess. When people lived there."

"That would be correct. Two mile up the road."

"Did you know the people?"

"Know everybody, one time or another. Even the fancy people. And everybody else. Related to half of them."

"Did you know a family by the name of Nuremborski, who used to live at Robinson's Place?"

"Mmm." The old man thought about that for a while. "The name again?"

"Nuremborski. A woman. And her daughter, about fifteen. And a baby boy."

"Ah." Tom's face came awake. "Yes sir. I was digging a ditch one day, to lay pipe up there. Nuremborski." He was remembering something clearly now. "He said next time he'd hire a dog. A dog would dig faster." The old man chuckled.

"That's funny?"

"I handed him the shovel. I said, okay, start digging. You should have seen the man's face. I can see it yet." He grinned and started down the stairs. "Never did work there another day."

"Do you remember his wife and his daughter?" Walker called after him.

"There were folks around. People come, people go. I sure remember him, though." Tom chuckled once more as he disappeared around a turn in the stairs.

Krista had manoeuvred herself into the tiny bathroom by the time Walker got back to their room. She was getting out some pills.

Walker put her wheelchair and crutches down and stood in the doorway of the bathroom, watching her.

"Are you okay?"

"It's nothing," she said. "Just some pain I get in my hip sometimes. So what's the plan now?"

"Look for someone who remembers me. Maybe in town. Or maybe someone still living near Robinson's Place. It's only two miles up the road."

"You go find us a ride," she said. "Meanwhile, I'll rest for a little bit, okay?" She took her crutches from him and, swinging back to the bed, crawled up on it and gathered up a pillow.

"You're sure you're okay?"

"Yes."

Walker slipped out of the room, closing the door softly.

Tom was setting tables in the dining room. Walker could smell food cooking behind a double door at the end of the room. It was almost noon but there were no customers in sight.

He walked into the dining room and asked if there was any way of getting a ride up to the school. "People have to get around the island some way, don't they?"

"Oh, sure," Tom replied. "Sitting in the back of Simon's truck. And the fancy folk, they take Andy's minibus up to their places, most of the time."

"Where's Andy?"

"Could be anywhere. But most likely he's not."

"Which means?"

The old man circled another table, selecting a knife, then a fork, then a spoon from his fistful of cutlery, setting them down carefully one by one.

"This time of day, he'd be home."

"Where's home?"

"It'd be the place with the minibus." The old man lifted up his head to look at Walker. He was teasing. "Just up the road a ways, that way," he said.

By the time Walker returned to their room, Krista was asleep. He pushed open a glass door that led to their tiny balcony, stepped out and closed it quietly. He had only four and a half days to find someone who knew something. And Krista was asleep.

He looked around. There wasn't enough room for even one chair. Walker hitched a foot up on the low wrought-iron grille that fenced off the balcony, and started to roll himself a smoke. He figured he could stand the heat bouncing off the building for about five minutes. He stuck the smoke in his mouth, fished in his pockets for his matches, struck one. Already sweat was beginning to trickle down his forehead.

Krista opened the glass door. "I feel better," she announced.

As it turned out, Andy's minibus was broken but Andy, a skinny black guy in a muscle shirt and with a glass eye tinted blue (he must have got it cheap, Walker surmised), had an ancient Toyota truck he would rent by the day.

Walker made the deal and bumped back down the street in the tiny, mud-smeared truck. Krista was waiting for him, standing in front of the hotel.

"Nice," she said.

"Well, at least this way we're by ourselves," he pointed out, helping her up into the cab.

"Anything you say." While she'd slept, the pills had begun to work. The pain in her hip had retreated.

Walker turned at the wharf and headed along a soft dirt road up a gentle hill. After a climb of about half a mile, the road narrowed and levelled off, heading west up the island. Now and then, through the trees, they caught glimpses of the ocean far below.

Wooden shacks and colourfully painted cement-block houses clung to the hillside above them, and to the steep slopes below. Women worked in small gardens, a man was putting on a new roof, children waved.

They began to pass more substantial-looking driveways, built up and reinforced, leading down the steep slope to, presumably, the winter homes of the "fancy folk." Then the road sloped sharply down out of the trees. A large plateau opened up, like a broad shoulder on the side of Three Mile Hill.

Some boys dressed in whites were playing a game of cricket on a large, flat field. A laneway led off the road between two stone pillars supporting a painted wooden sign. The Christian Way School, the sign said.

Walker drove under the sign and down the laneway, past the boys and the cricket field (kept green by sprinklers throwing streams of water in sweeping loops even as the boys played amongst them), and headed for a cluster of buildings on the edge of the plateau.

The nearest buildings—low-slung and new-looking, built of board and white plaster—were surrounded by a grove of massive oak trees. Further away, near the edge of the plateau, was a kind of villa. It was finished in what looked like limestone, painted white, with a flower garden in front. That had to be Robinson's Place, though Robinson—the original owner or perhaps the builder—was long since gone. The house looked to be about seventy years old.

Walker pulled up in front of the house and stared at it for a moment. He had hoped he'd recognize it. "I might as well be seeing it for the first time," he said.

"Three-year-old kids don't remember things," Krista replied. She'd already told him that she couldn't remember anything from when she was three. But she could. She could remember her metal braces, shiny and cold on her skin. She could remember balancing on them, she could remember falling down.

A discreet sign in front of the house announced that it was the administrative offices and the residence of the headmaster of The Christian Way School.

Krista let Walker go into the house alone. She didn't want to watch him wander around, trying to remember what wasn't in his head to remember, and she was sure that no one at the school would have any knowledge of who had lived there sixteen years before. They'd be teachers and administrators. They'd all be new.

There was a wind coming off the ocean. It was presumably the hottest time of the day, but the heat didn't seem as humid or exhausting as in the village.

Krista's hip had weathered the short trip in the truck not too badly. The soreness was still there, but for the moment it was satisfied to send the occasional scouting mission up her right side. But she did need to stretch a little, so while Walker went up a walk of white crushed stones into Robinson's Place, she swung along another path, until she reached the very edge of the hill.

A series of well-worn trails led through the thick green vegetation towards the ocean below. Robinson's Place was relatively high up, but Krista could make out the lazy, rising shape of blue rollers as they swept in long lazy lines towards the shore.

This is beautiful, she thought.

When Walker came back out of the house, Krista was nowhere in sight. He hadn't had much luck. The headmaster couldn't talk to him until four o'clock. His secretary didn't know anything about the family that had previously owned Robinson's Place. She'd only been there for two years and, besides, she was from Philadelphia. She didn't hold out much hope that the headmaster would know anything either. Though he'd been at the school for over ten years, he'd been born and brought up in Montego Bay and educated in England.

Nothing in the interior of the house had looked familiar to Walker. Either he had never been there or he had been too young to remember, as Krista had suggested. His mind had closed down, his memories going no further back than that wire fence, the sound of the cars swooshing by, the red-faced man materializing out of the dusk.

He looked around. Krista wasn't back in the truck. She wasn't walking around the garden or standing at the edge of the hill. He felt a rising panic, and was about to run over to the steep hillside and look down when he saw her. She was almost halfway back to the cricket field, perched on a plank bench that encircled a huge oak tree, talking to a black man dressed in green work clothes.

"Walker," she announced, sounding triumphant, as he came up, "this is Jamie O'Riley. He knew your grandmother. He knew everybody."

Walker felt an electric shock run through his body. He sat down on the other side of the man. The man looked younger close up than he had at a distance.

"You knew my mother?"

The man shrugged. "A little."

He was about thirty, Walker guessed. Slim, almost skinny, a handsome, quick face.

"She was older than me," Jamie continued, and added, with a warm smile, "She was very much a source of fascination."

"Why's that?" Walker asked, tensing a little. How much did everyone around here know about her? About Robert?

"Because she was pregnant so young. For a white girl."

"And her husband?" Walker asked. He could see Krista looking at him now.

"No. Like I said to the young lady, I don't remember her husband. I do remember when the baby came, though. Miss Emile looked after it."

"Who's Miss Emile?"

At that, Jamie pulled out a store-bought cigarette from his shirt pocket, looked warily towards the villa and lit it up.

"My old granny," he said.

Walker ventured the big question. "What was the name of the baby?"

"Well," Jamie said, "it was a boy, I remember that much. You want to know if I remember his name, if it was you."

Walker glanced at Krista. How much had she told him? "That's right," he said.

"I didn't pay much attention. I was only eleven years old." He looked at Walker half apologetically.

"But your grandmother will know," Walker said.

"Miss Emile is ninety-three. She might. I've already said to the young lady, I'll take you to see her. But I wouldn't count on anything too much. Miss Emile's been sick."

"What about your mother, or someone else?" Walker asked.

"My mother died. My father lives somewhere in America. Miss Emile brought us up. Miss Emile, she is my mother."

Walker nodded. He understood; it was the old lady or nobody. "I'd be really grateful if you'd take me to see Miss Emile," he said.

Jamie studied him for a moment, looked back at the villa, smiled his warm smile again. "Sure I will," he said.

Walker and Krista returned to the hotel and ordered either a late lunch or an early supper. They were alone in the dining room.

When they went back up the stairs, they discovered that their room was several degrees hotter than hell. Even though some cool air was straggling out of a small vent over their door, it had been a mistake to switch off the two fans in the room when they'd left. Walker switched them back on. Krista lay down on the bed.

Walker turned on the tap in the bathroom and splashed cold water on his face. He soaked a towel and wrung it out for Krista to put on her forehead. By the time he stretched out on the bed beside her, she seemed to be asleep. "Do you want a cold towel? Got one," he whispered.

She murmured, "No thanks." She was definitely falling asleep.

Krista woke up at six-thirty. The room felt a little cooler. Walker was sleeping beside her, his face looking like a little kid's, his hair falling over his eyes.

She snuggled closer and watched him. She studied his face, the dark skin, the sharp bones under his eyes, the line of his jaw. She'd already decided that she'd let him go alone to see Miss Emile. She couldn't protect him from whatever he'd find out, anyway. Incest? She tried to put it out of her mind. It didn't make any difference. It didn't.

At about quarter to seven, she touched the end of his broken nose with the tip of her finger, and pushed. His eyes opened.

"Time to get ready for Jamie," she said.

∘ ∘

JAMIE ROARED UP TO THE FRONT of Sam's Inn on an old motorcycle, sliding to a dramatic stop.

"Where's the truck?" he asked, as Walker got up off the bench where he'd been waiting.

"I took it back to Andy. Krista said to say sorry, she's really tired, maybe she'll meet Miss Emile sometime before we leave." He swung up on the seat behind Jamie.

"I guess she would get tired," Jamie agreed.

He gunned the throttle a couple of times as a signal for Walker to hold on, spun out into the middle of the dirt road and tore through the village. He took the curve by the wharf at half speed, then gunned up the long gentle road that meandered up the side of Three Mile Hill.

Ahead of them, the sun was beginning to set; it was already half hidden and turning red behind the trees that topped Three Mile Hill. Long shadows flicked over them, the still-hot air streamed by, the motor hummed.

Jamie had discarded his work shirt for a clean white T-shirt, but he was still wearing his work pants and boots. His hair, slicked back close to his skull, was staying in place. Walker's hair was blowing all around. They leaned into the wind, balancing low.

Cutting the engine back, Jamie suddenly turned off the road just before the plateau and The Christian Way School. They dropped almost straight down a steep hill, following not much more than a path through the trees.

"Shortcut," Jamie hollered back at Walker.

Turning at a right angle and clinging to the side of the hill, he guided the bike up and down little bumps and hollows, heading deeper into the surrounding woods. The trees interlocked over their heads. A steamy greyness began to rise from the ground, and the air smelled damp and pungent. Within a few minutes, they roared out into a clearing.

Jamie slowed down as he approached a tiny shack. Pulling up in front, he spun the bike to a stop. Walker climbed off.

"Nice ride," he said.

Jamie grinned and balanced the machine carefully on its kick-stand. "This is Miss Emile's old place. Where she grew up. She has a nice house closer to the school. But she's come back here to die."

Walker nodded. His head felt as though he were still going up and down.

Jamie climbed up the rickety wooden steps and pushed the door open. A girl of about twelve appeared in the doorway. He gave her head a soft tousle and disappeared inside.

Walker came up to the steps.

"Hi," the girl said, not looking particularly surprised that this stranger should appear out of the woods.

"Hi." Walker looked past her into the dark room. A red glow from a fire in an old cast-iron stove flickered in the shadows. Bunches of what looked like grasses and herbs and cobs of corn hung from rafters overhead.

Jamie reappeared. "Come on in," he said. "Miss Emile is feeling up to visitors."

Walker stepped past the girl into the tiny shack.

Though the fire was crackling in the stove, for some reason it felt to Walker at least several degrees cooler inside than outside. The air was full of the tangy smell of the drying plants. He ducked under them and followed Jamie towards a kind of alcove.

Inside the alcove, Walker could see that a large iron bed with a voluminous hand-stitched comforter—startlingly bright with orange moons and purple skies, white stars and yellow suns—filled most of the space. As he came closer, he saw that underneath the comforter, making only the slightest rise in it, was a body, and above the comforter, supported by two pillows, was an old face. It looked more like an ancient mummy than a living human being. Except for the eyes. The eyes shone in the light of several candles clustered on a table nearby.

"Miss Emile," Jamie said, "this is Lennie's baby."

Her face didn't move, but the old lady's eyes stared up into Walker's. He felt cold.

"You remember Lennie," Jamie went on, coaxing recognition from her. "You remember her mother, Sarah? Remember how Sarah died before the baby was born? You looked after Lennie's baby until she left."

Walker wished one of her hands were lying on the outside of her comforter. He wanted to pick it up, hold it. He wanted to kneel by the bed and look into the old woman's face. Because she had bathed him and fed him and rocked him and kissed him and sung him to sleep. This was Nana. Over and over again, Walker had called out for Nana. It had been one of the earliest reports in his file.

But he didn't recognize anything in her wizened face. And by the look of her, she didn't recognize him, either.

"What was the name of Lennie's baby?" Jamie asked her gently. "What did you call the baby? What was its name?"

The old woman opened her sunken mouth but, instead of a name, some sound came out of the depth of her like a far-away plaintive note. She repeated it and Walker heard it this time, as plain as day. "Broken child," she said.

Jamie glanced at Walker and smiled, but he looked a little frightened. He turned back to the old woman. "What do you mean, Miss Emile?"

"Spawn of the Calf," she said. She drew out an arm as gnarled and hard as an old stick, and pointed her finger, not at Walker, but just to the side of him. "Rollin' Calf," she said.

"No it isn't, Miss Emile," Jamie said, a trickle of fear in his voice. "You hear it first. You hear its chains first."

She ignored him and reached up towards Walker's hand. Walker bent down to her. He felt something more than cold now, he felt as if he were slowly immersing himself in freezing water. His body began to shake.

He felt ridiculous, too, because they could see he was shaking. He felt helpless.

He gave her his hand and she closed her fingers around it, and her mouth opened like the mouth of a cave.

She whispered twice, so he couldn't miss hearing, "Run. *Run!*"

CHAPTER TWENTY-SIX

• •

1976

BOBBY SLIPPED INTO THE BEDROOM his father was staying in. It was in the opposite wing from the bedroom his mother was using, because she was dying.

His father could hardly bring himself to look at her gaunt face and burning eyes, let alone sleep in the same bed with her. All her hair had fallen out. Usually she wore a kind of white turban, but Bobby had caught a glimpse of her sitting at her dressing table in her bedroom, and her head was perfectly bald.

At first they'd stayed at a hotel near the hospital and visited her twice a day. His father had wanted her to fly back to Toronto, where he could get better care for her, but she'd refused. She didn't even want to stay in the hospital in Kingston any longer, she wanted to come back to the house on Reef Island, so they all had to come back here.

Bobby reached into one of his father's suitcases and pulled out a bottle of fine aged whisky. His father wasn't hiding it, it was just the bottle he kept handy in case he felt the need of a glass or two in the middle of the night. There were several other bottles of the same whisky scattered around the house. Bobby had had drinks from all of them.

He took off the cap and drank straight from the half-empty bottle, taking the time for five deep, burning gulps. Then he pulled a small bottle of tap water out of his pocket, used it to top up the whisky bottle, and placed it back in exactly the same position in the suitcase.

He was feeling a bit desperate. At home he'd had a deal with an older stock boy in his father's factory to buy him a bottle whenever he needed it, for a slight commission.

He was needing it more and more all the time. He loved to drink. When he drank, he didn't feel restless. He felt happy and he could sleep. His very best days were the ones where he could manage to be slightly drunk all day long.

But here, far from the accomplice stock boy, he was being forced to dilute his father's whisky too much. He'd have to steal a whole bottle soon, and if it was noticed—and it would be—he'd have to blame it on the help. "These people are all thieves, Father."

His father wouldn't believe him, but that wasn't the point. They had to play the game; Bobby had to pretend to be innocent so his father could pretend to believe him. They'd been playing this game for the last two years.

Bobby slipped out of the room, walked down the hall and pushed the French doors open, stepping into the front garden. It was twenty degrees hotter outside than inside where the air conditioners hummed, but he didn't really notice. The whisky had stopped burning in the pit of his stomach, but it was racing like little bonfires all through his blood. The outside temperature felt cooler than he did.

He walked aimlessly through the flowering garden. The air was full of perfumes of all kinds. His head felt pleasantly light and just a little dizzy. Contentment hummed through him.

He knew this feeling would last for less than an hour. By degrees he'd start feeling edgy again, restless, a stranger to everyone and everything.

Lennie was sitting in the shade under one of the oak trees, reading a book. She looked like Humpty Dumpty. She was due to have the baby any day. It was a race between life and death. Which one would arrive at the house first?

Death, Bobby thought.

He walked towards her. "We'll be leaving soon," he said.

"What do you mean?"

"You heard what I said," he replied, puffing himself up a little, trying to look important.

She turned away. She wouldn't look at him. He stood close to her, over her. She was afraid to look up, he figured. He reached out and touched her hair.

"Don't," she said.

Bobby walked back to the house. Sweat was trickling down his face, he needed to get into the air conditioning. He thought he'd go to his room and lie down, be perfectly still. The alcohol in his blood would last longer that way.

As he lay on his back on the bed, he thought about his mother. She was dying—what did that mean to him? Not much, as far as he could determine. She used to hug him and read him stories, buy him clothes and make a fuss over him, but that had been a long time ago. Anyway, her attention only frustrated him. She was a shadow on his face, she was the door that closed him off from his father.

In the last two years she had retreated from the field, giving him over to Jake. He'd taken Bobby out of his alternative school and put him in a small private school located in an office building, with instructions that Bobby was not to leave the classrooms from the time he arrived until the time someone picked him up. Sometimes his father would drive him there himself in the morning. Bobby liked that. Quite often, a toady from his father's office would pick him up in the afternoon, a large, ambitious mouse with steel-rimmed glasses and a superior expression fixed on his inferior face. Bobby liked that too, but in a different way.

This ass-licking mouse would deliver Bobby either to his father's office or to the sports club where his father worked out, furiously slamming a ball around a court. Bobby liked to peer through the large window and watch his enraged father dash this way and that.

His father took Bobby to meetings in restaurants. He took him on business trips, where at least one of his staff always kept Bobby company. People began to remark on how wonderful it was for a man as busy and powerful as Bobby's father to spend so much time with his son. They said this to Bobby.

Bobby knew what they really meant—that it was wonderful for a father to take his slow son, perhaps even his retarded son, along with him and not be ashamed. Because Bobby didn't fit in, didn't speak up, remained mostly silent, his mind miles and miles away. He knew he was a constant embarrassment to his father, but still, his father and he shared a secret. His father could see the light that Bobby had in him, and in fear and trembling his father kept him close.

He thought of Alex. Alex was spinning in the air. Alex was dancing in the clouds. Alex had great snowy wings sprouting out of his back. Bobby could see him where the ceiling of his bedroom used to be, suspended above him, peering down at him.

Bobby closed his eyes and tried to think of something else. He thought of his sister, her stomach huge, sitting under the oak tree. He could see her clearly, too. She was looking steadily up at him now, she wanted him. He moved closer to her and put his hand down her blouse. Her breasts felt soft and warm with milk.

He opened his eyes. Alex was gone. His sister was gone.

There was a muffled scraping sound, then a steady *chop chop* from somewhere outside. Bobby got up, walked over to his window and pulled open the curtain. A boy was hoeing in the vegetable garden. He was the son or grandson of the old woman who was supposedly helping his dying mother, though she never seemed to do anything.

Bobby watched the boy strike the dry ground with the hoe. He swung it down and dragged it towards himself, turning over red earth and weeds. He took one step backwards and swung down again, working his way along the row of pepper plants towards Bobby's window. The only clothing he had on was a pair of old khaki shorts. His skin was almost blue, it was so black. Bobby could see all the small bones in his spine. He could see his young muscles flex below his shoulders. His neck was slim and delicate.

Bobby was mesmerized, caught up in the pleasure of watching. He pressed his face against the cool window and closed his eyes.

CHAPTER TWENTY-SEVEN

• •

A N OLDER WOMAN, carrying a large cloth bag full of food, climbed the dusty path to Miss Emile's house. She nodded to Jamie and Walker sitting together on a rough bench on the porch, as if she'd expected to see them sitting there, and she went inside.

They continued to sit in silence and smoke. Finally Walker asked, "What did Miss Emile see?"

"Miss Emile is old, she's past ninety years old," Jamie said. He smiled and pointed to his head, as if Miss Emile was not all there, but he wasn't very convincing. "Don't pay any attention to Miss Emile," he said.

Walker wasn't going to be put off that easily. "What's the Rollin' Calf, Jamie?"

Jamie stared at his boots for a full minute. "There's two worlds on this island. The Christian world, like at the school where I work, and the spirit world. Miss Emile knows things, she sees things."

"Like what?"

"She sees what's there," Jamie replied. "If she saw the Rollin' Calf, he was there. Maybe he was standing still, because they say he carries chains, like slaves from the old days. That's why you can hear him."

Jamie glanced at Walker to see if he was looking incredulous or scornful, or amused. Or all three at once. But Walker was just staring.

"Why would he stand beside me?"

"He marks out souls," Jamie said. He smiled at Walker. "This is called superstition."

"Do you believe it?" Walker asked.

Jamie sat motionless for a moment. He flipped his cigarette out into the encroaching dark. It bounced on the hard-packed earth in front of the porch, rolled to a stop.

Walker took his silence to mean yes. "So he marks out people who are going to die?"

"No," Jamie said, looking uncomfortable. "Not die, exactly. He marks out people for the undead. The undead need living souls."

Walker felt poised on the edge of a very deep hole. "A broken child. Is that like a child born from incest, from a brother and sister, something like that?" His words sounded sharp in the air, like pieces of glass.

"Broken child, that's a new one to me." Jamie shrugged. "I don't know."

Walker pressed on. "Lennie's baby, was he born on this island?"

"Joy's Grove," Jamie said. "Dr. Joshua Green. Everybody around here loved old Dr. Joshua Green, even Miss Emile. She did say, though, that she could have born Lennie's baby right here just as well. She's born thousands."

"Was the baby all right?"

Jamie smiled. "You weren't broken, if that's what you mean. If it was you."

"Yeah. If it was me."

Jamie brightened. "Maybe they still have the birth records over there at the clinic. Maybe the name Walker is written on them."

"Good idea. I'll check when we go back," Walker said. Dark had arrived in a hurry. He could hardly make out the individual shapes of the trees that surrounded the clearing. "When you were talking to Miss Emile, did you say that Lennie's mother died?" he asked.

"About a week before the baby came. She was supposed to go back to Kingston, back to the hospital there, but one night before they could move her, she just died. Miss Emile said it was for the best, because she loved it here. She was buried here."

"Where?"

"St. Thomas Church. That's where she always went to pray." Jamie got up now. He wanted to go.

Walker sat on the bench for a moment longer. There was one more question he had to ask. "You were saying about the Rollin' Calf marking people out. How does a person lose his soul?"

Jamie walked down off the porch as if he hadn't heard the question. He looped a leg over his motorcycle and started fooling with the gears.

Walker got up and followed him.

Jamie looked reluctant to say anything more, but whether this was from fear of the spirit world or because Walker might think he was a backward fool, Walker couldn't tell. He kept his face turned away. But when he did speak, it sounded like a warning.

"The Rollin' Calf marks you out and somebody rises up from their grave. They tie you up and cut you open. They reach in and steal your soul," Jamie said. There was no mistaking the conviction in his voice now.

•   •

KRISTA WAS SITTING OUT FRONT of Sam's Inn in the dark, waiting for Walker, when Jamie drove up and dropped him off.

"How did you get down here?" Walker asked.

"I wasn't going to sit in my room all night. Tom Tait."

"Tom Tait?" He sat down beside her.

"The old man who carried our bags. I called down to the desk and he came up, and I asked him to help me."

"Did he pick you up, did he carry you?"

"Uh-huh."

"Did you feel safe?"

"Uh-huh. Are you jealous?" She picked up his hand and dragged it firmly into her lap, capturing it in both her hands. They felt incredibly warm and soft to Walker. So did her lap.

"What did Miss Emile say?" she finally asked him.

"She said she didn't know me."

"But you didn't expect her to know you after all this time."

"No."

"Did she remember the baby's name?"

"No. She's over ninety. She's senile. Let's go have a drink," Walker said quickly. "Let's have ten. Tom Tait can carry us both up the stairs."

The bar was filling up with permanent residents of the inn, who for whatever reason had run aground on Reef Island, and inhabitants of the village itself.

Sam Weiss made a big show of sitting down at the piano and playing semiclassical pieces. As the evening progressed, they all began to sound like "The Blue Danube."

Drinks in hand, people began to join Walker and Krista at their table, until they were ten in all, everyone friendly and everyone curious to find out as much as possible.

Where were they from? How long were they staying? How in the world had they found Reef Island? What were they planning to do while they were here?

An Italian lady of indeterminate age, with a dark, tragic face, bright red lipstick and a surprisingly rich, sonorous voice, asked if they were honeymooning. Everyone leaned forward a little in anticipation of the response.

Surely they had seen young lovers before, Walker thought to himself, whether honeymooning or otherwise. He felt the source of their interest lay more with Krista, the cruel twist to her hips, the aluminum crutches. And the little group at the table couldn't even be sure they were lovers. Perhaps they were just friends. Or a devoted brother and sister. It was a bold question put by the Italian lady. Walker was sure everyone appreciated her daring.

"I asked Walker's mother but she said he was too young to get married," Krista declared. "We're just practising right now." She smiled pleasantly at the Italian lady, as if to say that, since her question had been straightforward and without guile, so was the answer.

Everyone laughed, even Walker, though he winced a little at being made to sound so young. He leaned back in his chair, caught old Tom Tait's eye (he evidently waited on tables as well as doing everything else) and ordered a round for everyone.

"Walker's independently wealthy," Krista said.

At midnight he carried her up the stairs to their room. Since he'd had only four rum-and-Cokes, he managed reasonably well, bumping her head on the wall no more than once—and that was more a brush than a bump.

This was the moment they hadn't spoken about. And this time there was no chance that George Papadopoulos would interrupt them.

Krista looked at herself in the bathroom mirror, three drinks the worse for wear. She rubbed at the bags under her eyes. They looked enormous. She hated her nose. Her chin was too wide. She ran the water so Walker would think she was actually doing something, but she just stood there and stared at herself.

When she came out, Walker was sitting cross-legged on the bed with just his jeans on, rolling yet another smoke.

"You're going to get tobacco over everything," she said, then immediately wished she hadn't. It didn't sound very romantic.

He stopped and smiled at her. He looked tired. No, she thought, he looks exhausted.

"I'm trying to get used to my body. It doesn't feel the same now," he said. He started rolling his smoke again. "Robert and Lennie, you know?"

Krista leaned her crutches against the wall and sat on the edge of the bed. She reached out and rubbed his knee with her hand. "You should see my parents, they're no prizes either."

Walker laughed. He put his smoke down on the bedside table unfinished, and the tobacco spilled out of it. He touched her face. "I'm glad you're with me," he said.

"Me too," she said. Walker's eyes seemed teary to her. It upset her. She put both her hands on his face.

Walker got up on his knees and drew her to him. He kissed her. She kissed him back.

It had always been an act of extreme bravery, or the premeditated result of getting really drunk, for Krista to be with a man in whatever circumstances, but it was not that way with Walker. Though she'd been worrying about it, about getting undressed in front of him—her one hip concave where it should be rounded, her right leg slightly withered, scar tissue cutting across her bum and tracing rivers of sutures down her legs like the coming-of-age markings of some obscure tribe—she needn't have been.

He was just there, with his dark eyes, his long sinewy body. He swept over her, he was everywhere at once, he was like a sudden storm. They were falling into darkness, they were blind, in sweet urgency his hands danced all over her and he entered her and she was truly the queen of love, the queen of passion.

And afterwards, Walker didn't trace the outline of her scars, and he didn't kiss them, either, to prove what a humanitarian he was, like another lover she'd had. He just encompassed her whole being with his arms and legs, the warm skin of his belly, his chest. And his hand, his wandering hand, went wherever it wanted. He bit the end of her nose. His tongue began to search for her tongue again. And once again he was everywhere.

• •

ANDY, THE FRIENDLY BUS MAN, was in his front yard the next morning, working on his out-of-commission minibus.

As Walker came up to him, he was holding a carburetor in his greasy hands and glaring at it, as though it had personally betrayed him and he might just throw it over his neighbour's fence.

"Like to rent your truck again," Walker said. Over breakfast, he and Krista had decided to visit St. Thomas Church. Tom Tait had given them directions. "I just need it for the morning. What's the half-day rate?"

"There's no half-day rates," Andy said.

"But I'm only going to use it for an hour or so. We're just driving up to St. Thomas Church," Walker said.

"There's no half-day rates," Andy repeated stolidly, fixing Walker with his one good eye.

"There should be," Walker said stubbornly.

"Okay," Andy replied, "you win. I'll give you a half-day rate."

"Great," Walker said. "How much?"

"Same as full-day."

Walker stared at him for a moment. "All right," he said.

He helped Krista into the truck. He thought she looked more beautiful than ever. They'd been smiling at each other all morning, feeling a little foolish and even, for some reason, a little shy.

St. Thomas Church was the opposite way out of the village from Robinson's Place. The dirt road swung down low to the harbour, past some fishing boats already back safe from their morning work, past weathered storage sheds and what looked like huge wooden paddle-wheels covered with drying nets and tackle. Soon it narrowed to one track and began to climb the edge of a cliff more and more steeply, until the old truck was almost standing on its tail. Walker had to shift down to first gear. All they could see out the windshield was an expanse of blue sky and a scud of high white clouds. It seemed that, if the road became any steeper, they would either slide back down or tumble backwards, end over end.

Krista clung to the door handle on one side and to Walker's leg on the other. The truck's dusty nose slowly settled as they cleared the top and reached level ground. The ocean spread out far below, speckled white with flying seagulls. A line of cliffs guarded the island as far west as they could see. The road made a wide circle on top of the cliff and then, as if giving up, headed back down the hill.

Walker drove around the circle. At the furthest spot from the edge of the cliff, he pulled up in front of a small wooden church.

It was bright white, freshly painted and sparkling in the sun, with one narrow stained-glass window beside the blue front door.

Walker climbed out of the truck and helped Krista down.

The little church felt welcoming, perhaps because of the contrast to the starkness of its surroundings, the massive thrust of the underlying rock, the short tough grass clinging precariously to life in the constant wind, the vast ocean below and the profoundly vaster sky above. In the centre of it all, sat this minuscule dot, this frail refuge.

They opened the gate and walked up the path to the well-worn wooden steps. It was a Thursday morning, and no one was around. Skirting the building, they followed a footpath towards the back. They were looking for the church graveyard that Jamie had said was there.

Walker wanted to pay some kind of homage to this lost grandmother of his. He didn't know exactly why. Perhaps because he felt it was as close as he was ever going to come to his family.

They walked along together, Walker going slowly, Krista swinging on her crutches. They could feel the warmth of the sun bouncing off the side of the building; they could smell the fragrance of the wildflowers, delicate as any northern flowers, that grew in sparse clumps here and there.

The breeze felt almost cool to Walker, but when he glanced at Krista he could see beads of perspiration forming on the bridge of her nose.

"I don't see any graveyard," she said.

They were standing at the back of the church. The land fell slowly away towards a mass of trees in a deep valley below.

"They'd have to use dynamite to make holes in this rock," she said. "Are you sure this is the right place?"

"I'm sure," Walker replied. "Let's keep going."

The path angled away from the church through knee-high grass, down towards the trees. Krista examined the steep hill for a moment. "Okay," she said.

Walker followed along behind her. Her blonde hair danced before him. The back of her neck was growing red from the sun or from her exertion. The long grass wound around her crutches on either side, pulling at them. Going downhill was as tough as going uphill on crutches; each step was too long, the crutches too short. Walker thought that at any moment she might pitch over on her face.

"There it is," he said.

She raised her head from her fierce concentration on the path. "Where?"

He didn't have to answer. The graveyard was in clear view below them. Surprisingly large, it was surrounded by a newly painted picket fence. Just beyond, the forest stood in silent watchfulness, the closest trees bending over the white fence with long, weighty boughs.

They walked down the rest of the hill and through the open gate. There was a mix of wooden grave markers and pebbled stone markers, and a few of shiny pink and black granite.

Walker knew enough about Jake Nuremborski to know what he was looking for. The biggest stone, the most impressive one in the graveyard.

Off to one side, near the fence and shaded by the branches of a tall ceiba tree, a coral-coloured granite pylon rose fifteen feet into the air.

Walker went over to it. It looked lonely off by itself. He wasn't surprised when he knelt down and read on the base, In Loving Memory of Sarah Clair Nuremborski, née Harper, beloved wife of Jacob Ivan, born April 1936, died March 1976.

Krista came up beside him and read the writing out loud. A sadness descended on Walker, pervasive and heavy.

"Hello," a voice said, somewhere above his head. It was so rumbling and cavernous that Walker thought he might be hearing things. But at the sound of it, Krista swung around.

A very tall, skinny man was standing behind them, dressed in a black suit, a black felt hat and a snow-white clerical collar. His face was as dark as his clothes, and as long and thin as the side of a hand. He stood amid the grave markers, still and resolute as any of them. He could have been a statue standing against the green of the hill and the blue of the sky.

"Hello, Father," Walker said, an automatic response, realizing a heartbeat too late that he was at an Anglican church and kneeling in an Anglican graveyard.

"Hello," Krista said. "We're just looking."

As opposed to what, Walker thought, buying?

"A relative?" the minister finally said, nodding towards the coral gravestone, his bass voice rumbling again, without one hint of ministerial pomposity but as deep as the ocean floor.

Walker wasn't sure how to respond. He took his time, straightening up to his full height. The minister still towered over him, even standing two rows of gravestones away.

"We're not sure," Krista said. She moved closer to the minister. He glanced at her crutches, her flexed hip—just a quick flicker of his eyes. He looked at her face again.

"Maybe you could help us. We're more or less lost."

"Lost?"

"Not lost here. We know where we are. But just lost. Aren't we, Walker?"

Krista had sensed something in this austere figure that had escaped Walker. It wasn't Holiness or Grace or any of those big capitalized words, it was just kindliness. This man standing in front of her could do nothing, be nothing, that wasn't decent, considerate and kind.

"Walker is searching for his parents," she said. "He thinks Sarah Nuremborski might have been his grandmother, but he doesn't know for sure."

The minister shifted his gaze back to Walker, looking at him more closely now, as if he half expected to recognize him. "Mrs. Nuremborski was a wonderful woman," he said—almost defensively, Walker thought. "I knew her for many years."

He looked around for an appropriate tombstone to sit on, found one, eased his seven-foot frame stiffly down on top of it. "She came here, I suppose, about thirty years ago now. She loved it here. Said she felt at home right from the first time she laid eyes on our little island. Not so her husband. As I recall, he was one of those gentlemen who buy something with great enthusiasm and, when it doesn't quite answer whatever they hunger for, become impatient and move on. We are blessed with a number of that kind of folk from faraway places on our little island. But Mrs. Nuremborski kept coming back, once in a great while with her husband, most often with her children. Christmas. Easter. Sometimes for a month or so. She felt at home. She felt at home in our church, too. And I'm sure she feels at home right here." He tipped his hat up a little on his brow, perhaps to cool off, or perhaps as a secret signal to Mrs. Nuremborski, lying under her pink stone.

"You'd know her daughter, then? Lenore?" Krista asked.

The man looked at her as if he'd been expecting that question. Now he seemed a little sad. "Yes," he said, "a beautiful little girl.

They would come to church together, mother and daughter. Sometimes Mrs. Nuremborski would come simply to pray. The door was always unlocked in those days. I would come up to do some business or other, and she would be sitting alone in the church, deep in prayer. She prayed alone and made no public fuss about it."

"Did you know Lenore's brother, Robert?" Walker asked, watching the minister's face closely.

"Not so well, no. Not so well," the minister replied, as inscrutable as the gravestones behind him.

"Did you know Lenore when she was older?" Krista asked pleasantly. "She had a child here, didn't she?"

The minister reached up and took his hat off. The grey hair on his temples had receded, leaving a shiny black pate on top. He rolled the brim of his hat in his hands, traced the ribbon with his finger. He looked at Walker as if he knew where this line of questioning was going. "I married them," he said.

Walker stared at him for a moment. So did Krista.

"You what?" Walker said.

"That's not possible," Krista said.

"Oh yes. In secret. Shortly after they arrived." He looked at Sarah Nuremborski's grave again, this time betraying some uncertainty. "I'm sure it's not a secret any more."

Krista moved closer to the man, but Walker stayed where he was. He scarcely wanted to breathe, in case this tall black apparition might somehow be disturbed and disappear.

"Why in secret?" Krista asked.

"Because of Mrs. Nuremborski's husband. Apparently he hadn't taken a liking to the young man." He took his eyes off Walker and looked at Krista. "But Lenore was having a child and Mrs. Nuremborski knew that they were in love and they would stay in love, and so, in the sight of God and Mrs. Nuremborski but in the sight of no one else, early one morning I married them."

"Married who?" Walker said, his voice trembling. "Who did she marry?"

"Why, her young man, of course," the minister replied, a shadow of concern passing over his face, as if Walker might need to be ministered to in some way. "Here, I'll show you."

With that, he pushed himself off the tombstone, walked across the graveyard and out the gate. He headed purposefully up the slope towards the church.

Krista and Walker followed him. They didn't say a word to each other. They hardly dared look at each other.

Krista tried to hurry, but it was hard work going uphill. Walker followed slowly behind her. He knew that, if he got ahead, he wouldn't be able to stop himself from running after the fast-disappearing minister. He didn't run ahead. And he didn't pick her up and run with her. He just watched as she struggled up the hill. It nearly killed him.

They finally came up over the rise. Krista's face and hair were as wet as if she'd just gone swimming. The minister was nowhere in sight but the back door of the church was open.

They hurried to the open door and stepped inside. It was dark and cool in the interior of the church, but they couldn't see a thing. They heard a shuffling noise somewhere in front of them, a door slammed, an overhead light flashed on.

They were standing in a slightly musty-smelling storeroom. The minister—almost as tall as the ceiling, wearing glasses now—stopped the swinging light bulb with his long, bony hand. Without a word he began to examine the contents of a wooden shelf, pulling off several large, leather-covered books.

With a solemn air he placed them on a table and selected one that had "1970–1979" written in neat blue ink across a yellowing white label. He blew off the dust and began to leaf carefully through the pages.

Walker and Krista stood a little way off, wary, as if they were about to witness a terrible accident.

The minister's lips pursed in concentration as he turned each page. Finally he arrived at a page that pleased him. He turned slightly towards them and, pressing a remarkably long finger against the paper, said, "The Nuremborski nuptials."

Walker approached the table and looked down at the open page. He saw, forming a kind of wreath, drawings of several pink, winged cupids, their delicate parts strategically covered with blue flowing banners; they were all blowing trumpets. In the middle were some lines in black Gothic print and, below these lines, several signatures in the same blue ink as on the front cover.

Krista came up to him. He could feel her beside him. They read silently together.

"On this twenty-first day of October, in the year of Our Lord nineteen hundred and seventy-five, Lenore Janet Nuremborski was United in Holy Matrimony with Kyle Walker Tennu."

Krista gasped and held her hand to her mouth. Walker just stared at the page. His eyes began to burn.

"You were named after your father," Krista said. "See? Kyle Walker Tennu." As if Walker couldn't see for himself, as if his eyes weren't burning a hole in the paper, as if his heart weren't bursting through his chest.

"You see?" she went on. "Lennie told Kim the truth. All of it. You are Lennie's son. And you're Kyle's son, too."

Walker pointed to a lower line, where Lenore and Kyle had entered their nationality. Beside her name, Lenore had written, "Canadian." Beside Kyle's name was, "Cree Nation."

The minister saw where Walker was pointing. "Yes," he said, "I didn't notice that until later. I never mentioned it, I didn't feel it mattered."

"He was making a political statement. My dad was," Walker said, and he thought, my dad, my dad.

"That was part of the problem, you see. At least for Mr.

Nuremborski," the minister replied. "That your father was part Red Indian. He couldn't abide the shame of it."

"Uh-huh," Walker said. He rubbed his hand against his eyes. His cheeks were wet. He felt like yelling as loud as he could. Something. He didn't know just what. Yes! Yes! Yes!

"Walker," Krista said softly, almost to herself, "you're a Jamaican Indian."

Walker walked back to the truck in a daze. He forgot to help Krista back in, he just slammed the door and sat behind the wheel. She had to manage by herself, so she did.

She sat there for a moment beside him.

"Hello," she said.

Walker was staring out across the barren, windswept grass, towards the edge of the cliff and the sky beyond.

"Walker Tennu," she said.

Walker nodded. He said, "Jake Nuremborski killed my father too."

CHAPTER TWENTY-EIGHT

. .

1980

WHEN BOBBY OPENED HIS EYES, he saw seaweed and bits of coral and a convoy of little fantailed fish in a multitude of colours. And everything else was blue.

Maybe he had drowned. He could feel his body light as a leaf all around him, but he couldn't see it.

There had been some kind of accident. Water bubbled somewhere, and the murmur of his blood, too. He couldn't see it but he could feel it, a faint spongy song.

A face filled up all the blue. A round face of a young man, eyebrowless, almost featureless, his small eyes devoid of colour, his tiny mouth held tight in concentration. Was this God?

Bobby looked up at him through the fixed crystal lenses of his own eyes. And the man's face came down on him, and he could feel the man's lips pressing gently against his lips, and his eyes, just above Bobby's, were now half closed. He was humming, droning into Bobby's throat like a thousand bees. And then he went away.

Bobby rolled his head ever so slightly, cautiously, to the side. He could feel his head now. He could feel that it was resting on something flat and hard.

The man was dressed all in white—white T-shirt, pants, running shoes. He was standing before a rack of medicine. He was filling up a syringe.

There had been an accident, Bobby thought once again, some kind of accident. A faint memory moved on the edge of his mind, but he couldn't see it. He couldn't make it out.

Who am I?

He pondered this question as the man prepared the syringe, sat down on a chair and tied his own arm with a rubber thong. With an audible sigh he slipped the needle into a vein.

I am Robert Nuremborski, Bobby thought, and I have been saved from drowning because I am a god. I am one of them.

The man groaned. He closed his eyes and slumped back in the chair.

Bobby watched him with eyes that never moved and never closed, blind eyes that his nurse had become all too familiar with over the last many months. Except that now they could see.

The nurse got to his feet and put the empty syringe down on a white porcelain table. He turned back to look at Bobby. A slight question mark passed over his face; Bobby's head seemed to have turned slightly from where it had been before. It didn't trouble the nurse for long. He continued to stare at his patient, but now with a blissed-out slackness. His tiny mouth tightened again. He pulled his T-shirt slowly up over his head.

Bobby could see a white swelling belly.

He was falling away again—so tired now, so ready to fall back under his crystal eyes, so willing to sink down and down.

CHAPTER TWENTY-NINE

· ·

T HE SAND CAME UP TO MEET WALKER'S FACE with a soft whump. It still felt warm, though the sun had already set and the sky on the horizon was changing from rose to deep purple.

Jamie reached down and helped Walker to his feet. Jamie was half drunk. Walker was blotto.

He led Walker down to the edge of the water, where the rollers were crashing in. They knelt together in the surf. Walker could feel the water pulling the sand out from under his knees, and he teetered dangerously. Jamie scooped up some water and threw it on Walker's face. It felt hot, like from a hot spring. Walker threw some on Jamie's face and then fell over on his shoulder. The next surge of surf covered his head. Jamie picked him up again and, laughing, got him on his feet.

"Feeling better?" he asked.

"Yes," Walker said.

They walked up on the beach, arms over each other's shoulders. Walker looked towards a cabana some distance away, where some of Jamie's friends, from a small settlement along the beach below Robinson's Place, had marinated and cooked fish and chicken to perfection over open coals. Everyone had drunk rum punch and Red Stripe beer, and smoked a prodigious amount of ganja. Someone was playing a guitar. People were singing.

Walker could see Krista's blonde hair shining in the light of the fire. She was sitting on a picnic table, singing too. She was having a good time, Walker could tell. He was glad she was having a good time.

He sat down carefully on the sand beside a large log, leaned back against it. Jamie dropped down on the sand beside him.

"It's beautiful here," Walker intoned. His tongue felt paralyzed.

"It's home," Jamie said.

"Thanks for all this."

"You're welcome."

"Krista and I still want to pay half," Walker said.

"You brought a bottle, and a box of Red Stripe. You're cool," Jamie said. "Everybody's glad you finally came home. Walker Kyle Tennu."

That same morning, they'd looked up Jamie and told him the good news. By that evening, Jamie had organized the party.

"I want to see Miss Emile again," Walker said.

"Sure. You can do that," Jamie replied.

"Because I was born here." Walker turned to look at Jamie. "Do you think that makes Miss Emile's words more true?"

"Miss Emile's words are always true," Jamie said, "in one way or another."

"So when do they usually come get your soul?" Walker said.

A frown clouded Jamie's face.

"After midnight? While you're asleep? Or does it matter?"

"You don't believe it?" Jamie said.

"Well, I was hoping she was speaking metaphorically," Walker replied. He thought to himself, that's pretty good, stoned. How many syllables is that?

"Sometimes things happen. Sometimes they don't," Jamie said. "Depends on the Circle. Who's calling up who. Who's dancing and who's praying and who's casting spells. On sacrifice and blood and everything being right for the right time." He struggled back up on his feet, stood there a little unsteadily, looking down at Walker. "But it's real, all right. I'll show you." He reached his hand down. Walker took it and Jamie hauled him up, then struck off down the beach, angling towards the dark hill that loomed above them.

Walker looked again at Krista. Somebody had turned on a transistor and reggae music was in the air. The young boy with the guitar was playing along. People were up on their feet, weaving and shuffling, dancing in the firelight. Krista was sitting with two other women, doing backup singing, looking happy as anything, high as a kite.

Walker trotted after Jamie, caught up to him. He was coming down gently now from booze and smoke. He could almost feel his legs underneath him, muscle and bone. That was a good sign.

"Where are we going?" he asked, stumbling through the sand.

"You should take Miss Emile very seriously," Jamie said.

They came to a wall of trees that shut off the hill above them. Walker could see a well-worn path that led through the underbrush into the woods.

One last sliver of light streaked the sky crimson from the horizon to above their heads. The wind was starting to come up, off the ocean. Walker thought he could see, far off to the south, some darker mass in the sky, something tumbling.

Jamie had disappeared into the trees so Walker followed him. They walked through the sombre woods and began to climb.

"The school is above us," Jamie said. "But it was before the school was here. It was when it was just Robinson's Place."

"What was? Where are we going?"

Instead of answering, Jamie took a few more steps up the path, until they walked into an open space. There was more light there. Walker could see Jamie clearly as he stopped and turned to look at him.

"They'd had a Circle," Jamie said, "the night before. They'd called up Jeffrey Cole, who'd been killed in a fall and was two months in the ground. I didn't know. Miss Emile didn't know either or she would have warned me. I was coming home, coming down this hill. I was about here." He pointed to the far edge of the clearing. "It was the middle of the night, and all the way down the hill I could hear him coming. He made a kind of whining sound. Then somehow he got ahead of me."

Walker could see that Jamie was starting to sweat, his face gleaming in the fast-fading light. Gusts of wind were swirling down and blowing over them. Jamie looked around as if he expected to see Jeffrey Cole coming out from under the trees, flesh peeling, white bones showing.

"I tried to see him," Jamie said. "The moon was in the clouds but every once in a while it would break out and shine a light over everything. He came up behind me."

Jamie turned around. Sweat was showing through his shirt, and he was shaking. The wind felt cold. The air smelled full of salt.

"With the power of the undead, he struck me!" Jamie said.

He unbuttoned his shirt and came close to Walker. He held his shirt open.

Walker looked from Jamie's face to his chest. He could see all his ribs clearly, pushing out from under his skin. He looked down at his stomach and saw what it was that Jamie wanted him to see.

A scar, raised and ragged, faintly pink against his black skin, began below Jamie's breastbone, ran downwards and stopped just short of his belt.

"He tied me up," Jamie said. "When my eyes opened, I was hanging from a tree. Blood was running down my face from where he'd hit me. And I could see something, I could see this dark shape in front of me. I could hear it breathe. Whimper. And pain was coming from somewhere. I looked down and a loop of my gut was hanging out, like a snake coming out of me. I started to scream."

He stopped and looked around quickly, as if he'd heard

something besides the rush of the wind, now rising to a roar, sweeping through the tops of the trees.

"Frank Shine was coming up the path with a girl. They heard me and they came running. The thing disappeared."

Jamie looked up in the trees. They were thrashing in the wind. "Jeffrey Cole was trying to claim my soul for his own, you see?" he said. He reached up and took Walker's face in his hand, holding it so firmly that, no matter how stoned he was, Walker would hear him and get it straight. "When Miss Emile tells a soul to run, believe her," he said.

Walker nodded. Jamie let his face go. He had shown him and he had warned him; that was all he could do.

Jamie turned to go back down the path, but Walker reached out and caught him by the shoulder. He had to yell against the noise of the wind to be heard.

"You said it was still Robinson's Place. Who was living there?"

Jamie looked a little surprised. Why did it matter? "It was just after Mrs. Nuremborski died," he yelled back.

"Who was in the house that night?"

"The old man. He was still there. Miss Emile was sitting with the daughter, because it was about her time."

"And my dad?" Walker said.

"No. I still don't remember him. He must have been away. I was there to go fetch the water taxi if the baby came. That's why I was up so late. But it wasn't her time, so Miss Emile sent me home."

"So the old man was there, my mother and Miss Emile and you."

"And the brother, your uncle," Jamie shouted. "He was there too."

Walker let go of Jamie and stood there in the roaring dark, as if trying to sort something out.

The rain hit, drenching them both, stinging their faces.

"Come on," Jamie yelled. Walker followed him. He felt as if he were running under water. The last of the light was gone and there was nothing but inky blackness and torrents of rain and branches blowing by and leaves beating against his face and the sound of trees crashing to the ground.

Walker slipped, fell in the mud, struggled back up and ran into a tree newly sprawled across the path. He fell again, tangled in vines and branches. Rainwater flooded down the hill above him, pushing him along in its rush.

Walker tried to crawl around the fallen tree but began slipping down the side of the hill instead. Everything was being swept downhill. He bumped into a massive cottonwood tree and, crawling to the protected side, wedged himself between its roots. Pressing his face into the ground, he lay there to wait out the storm, or be washed away or be crushed by a falling limb. He could feel the cottonwood vibrating above him.

Almost as quickly as it had come, the storm began to abate, settling into a long, unsteady dirge in the trees, dissipating into a groan, finally just a murmur. On all sides Walker could hear the sound of water cascading down the hill.

He knew one thing: he wasn't stoned any more. Every sense was alert, every nerve end jumping and raw. He tried to calm his breathing, slow his heartbeat. He wondered, with sudden alarm, what had happened to Krista. But they would have seen the storm coming from the beach, they would have had time to help her. She'd be in one of their houses, dry, he thought. She'd be okay.

He twisted around on his back, leaned up against the tree and waited for Jamie to come and find him. And he thought about the Nuremborski summer house on the French River, and the story of the little boy strung up in a tree somewhere near the house, his stomach cut open, his guts sliding out.

Then Walker heard a sound. It was very close; it seemed to come from the other side of the tree. A scraping sound. Whatever it was, Walker knew it wasn't Jamie. It was too close, and trying too hard to be silent.

Walker eased away, sliding on his side down the hill. He'd moved only a few feet when he saw a mass, darker than the surrounding darkness, pass in front of him.

Walker dug in his boots and slowly got to his feet. Now he could see a kind of face, ghostly, round as the moon. It looked both otherworldly and familiar. And then it disappeared.

Walker cut across the hill, stopped to listen. At first there was nothing to hear except the rushing water. He heard a thrashing in the bushes somewhere above him. And then he remembered where he had seen that face.

He began to half run, half trip up the muddy hill, over roots and vines. He saw a dark shape in front of him, someone clawing uphill on his hands and knees.

Walker crashed into him. The man twisted, kicking at Walker and falling on his back. Walker slipped too.

The man grabbed a fistful of Walker's hair, and his face, flat and bland as a dead planet, came up hard to meet Walker's, smashing into his already crooked nose. Pain shot through him, but Walker held stubbornly onto the man's shirt.

Tumbling over each other, they began to slide headfirst down the hill with the rest of the floating debris. Suddenly the man lurched and threw Walker, who was lying half on top of him, further down the hill.

Walker rolled up on his knees, hands in front of his face, ready, but the man didn't come leaping down after him. Walker waited. Nothing. Nothing but the sound of the water beginning to recede, some last gusts of rain and thick darkness.

Walker was gulping for breath. He touched his nose, felt something wet, tasted it. It tasted like blood. His shoulder hurt. He'd wrenched it somehow. He waited a while longer. Still nothing.

He began to slide down the steep embankment, then made his way down the rest of the hill.

He could hear the sea before he could see it, huge breakers rolling in, crashing high up on the beach, sliding back down again with a constant, hissing roar. He pushed through the last trees and stumbled out on the sand. His shoulder felt on fire. The flow of blood from his nose had decreased to a trickle, though, and as sore as it was, it didn't seem broken. He sat down carefully on the wet sand and looked around.

He could see a white line of surf some distance away, like a snow squall suspended in the dark. A light was bobbing along by the edge of the trees. Someone was calling his name.

He called back, "Over here! I'm here!" The light swung closer, accompanied by a chorus of voices, then found him kneeling on the sand as if he'd been tossed up by the sea.

"Jesus Christ, where'd you go?" Jamie said, running up. "Are you all right?"

"Uh-huh," Walker said, but he grimaced when Jamie and the others hauled him up on his feet. "I hurt my shoulder, whacked my nose."

"I thought you were behind me, I tried to find you but I couldn't see a goddamn thing, there was a fallen tree in my way," Jamie said, feeling terrible, feeling he had somehow let Walker down. "I went back for help."

"I can see that," Walker said.

Krista was safe and dry and even partly sober, waiting in one of the houses by the dirt track. When she saw Walker come in, his clothes torn, his face scratched and bloody, mud caked all over him, she got up from a bench near the fire and kissed him all over his face.

Everyone went, "Ahhh."

Then she retreated, looked him up and down and said, "Throw him back."

• •

ONE OF THE MEN, who happened to be going that way anyway, drove Krista and Walker home in their rented truck. Despite two hot rum-and-butters, Walker's shoulder and neck had stiffened up and he was carrying his head at a forty-five-degree angle. He didn't want to drive.

Tom Tait was sitting in the empty lobby, reading a newspaper, when they came in. He looked up at Krista coming unsteadily through the door on her crutches, still a little buzzed, and at her boyfriend following her, mud-splattered and blood-splattered (though he had washed the blood off his face, it was still all over his shirt) and holding his head on his shoulder as if he'd just been slapped.

"Hi, Tom," Krista said with a blurry smile.

Tom nodded.

"Tom," Walker murmured.

"Mmm," Tom said.

Despite considerable pain, Walker managed to carry Krista up the stairs. There was no way he was going to let Tom Tait do it. When they got inside their room, Krista insisted on taking off his clothes. It was almost sexy her pulling off his boots, his jeans. He even let her strip off his wet underwear, while he leaned back in the bed and grinned at her.

And it would have been sexy, too, if his damn shoulder hadn't hurt so much. It was evident to both of them that Walker's body could think of only one thing at a time.

Krista ran a hot bath and insisted he go soak in the tub. He stumbled into the bathroom and eased himself into the steaming water. She came in and sat on the toilet seat and said he should get his shoulder X-rayed.

"Where?"

"Joy's Grove, when we look for your birth certificate."

"It's fine, I can tell. It's okay," he said.

"I was scared," she told him.

"Were you? I'm okay."

Krista nodded. The steam from the bathtub had dampened her hair. Curls were sticking to her forehead and cheeks. Her face still looked a little smudged from booze and the potent Jamaican smoke. She eased herself to the floor and sat beside the tub, reached into the water and splashed Walker on his chest.

"I'd kiss you, if I could move my head," he said.

She got up on her knees, slowly and awkwardly, and leaned over the edge of the tub, and they kissed.

"I had a fight with someone." Walker had decided to tell her about it. She had to know everything. It wouldn't be fair to her otherwise.

Her face went still. "What do you mean?"

When he got to the part where Jamie showed him his scar, she retreated to the toilet seat and started pulling toilet paper off the roll.

When he described the man he had had the fight with—the same man he'd seen at the top of the stairs in the Nuremborski summer house, the man Walker had wanted to believe was a wandering derelict, but who was obviously in the employ of Jake Nuremborski, just as the secretary was—perhaps Jake's second line of defence, perhaps his ultimate lethal line of defence—she closed her eyes as if hoping for an out-of-body experience.

When he told her about the murdered boy hanging in the tree close to the Nuremborski summer home, she braced herself against the sink and stood up, letting the toilet paper fall to the floor. She opened the bathroom door and left the room.

"It wasn't just my mother and father," Walker shouted after her, "Jake Nuremborski is a serial killer!"

CHAPTER THIRTY

. .

1985

BOBBY SAT IN THE BACK of the silver limousine and looked
out the tinted glass.

Across the dark street, there was a series of plate-glass windows
all lit up. Behind the glass, inside a large room, he could see about
a dozen men and women in multicoloured shorts and leotards, towels
around their necks, running shoes on, working out on stationary bicy-
cles, treadmills and various weight machines.

Some of them were listening to Walkmans and seemed to be in a
trance. Others, gleaming with sweat, were deadly serious about their
workout. Yet others were chatting, carrying on casual and not so
casual flirtations.

Bobby pulled the plaid wool blanket tighter around himself, and
as he did so, his pale hand trembled as if with palsy.

How pleased they all seemed as they gazed at their reflections in
the long rows of mirrors against the walls. A little pout here, a toss of
a manly head there—how precious they all were, how special.

Bobby's thin blood began to stir a little. The ambitious and
charming, the accomplished, the movers and doers, he thought. He
was entranced by them. It had become his habit to sit there at least an
hour almost every night and watch.

Bobby was sitting alone in the back seat. His nurse was sitting in
the driver's seat, with the blue chauffeur's cap that Bobby insisted he

wear perched on top of his head. Occasionally he'd start the car and run the heater. Perhaps he was feeling bored. It was difficult to tell because he was a junkie. Either his eyes were hungry for his drugs or they were dead, and his mind was always somewhere else.

The nurse was Bobby's creature, his companion, his servant. He had been for some time. Tonight Bobby's creature had taken him out for a little drive again. At first it had been once a week, then two or three times, but now it was almost their nightly routine.

They'd drive and drive. Past clusters of hookers, transvestites, rent boys, all on their own special corners, all on their segregated strolls, like competing tribes. Bobby would order the nurse to slow down so he could look at them. Sometimes their painted or ghostly faces lit up, hopeful that the car would stop, that they could turn one more trick. But it never did. Bobby didn't pick anyone up. Ever. No one stirred his imagination sufficiently, let alone his blood, except for the perfect young men and the splendid young women strutting their stuff behind these glass windows, with tight little buttocks, bulging crotches, perky breasts. They were like mice in a shiny glass cage. They were all eager to get ahead.

Bobby's father had become exasperated some months before, standing by the car, huffing and puffing with his tubes up his nose, berating the nurse for wasting gas on a man who could not hear and could not see and, in fact, didn't know where the hell he was.

But luckily, Dr. Stanton had said that the rides would do no harm, and that in some obscure, possibly inexplicable way they might do good. They were stimulation, after all, which was always a good thing.

The nurse had quoted the doctor back to his father.

His father had called the doctor an incompetent, money-grubbing, pathetic excuse for a physician, who only dropped by for five minutes every other day so he could maximize his charges to the government medical plan. Though he was a physical and mental wreck by then, Bobby's father still had the shrewdness of an old carnivore. And it was true, Dr. Stanton was a money-grubber.

The doctor liked to write prescriptions for morphine, too. Bobby was becoming more and more uncomfortable, according to his nurse, so Dr. Stanton continually increased his dosage. The fact was that Bobby had never received morphine while under the care of his nurse, not even at the very beginning, when his father had the addition built on the back of the house and hired this strange, bland-faced young man from some agency.

If Bobby had gone through withdrawal because he'd previously been receiving morphine in the hospital, he didn't remember it. Perhaps he had had withdrawal, perhaps he had spasmed, groaned and foamed at the mouth. If so, his nurse hadn't done anything about it. For months Bobby had been mindless, stable enough to be taken off his respirator within three weeks of the accident, but with a tube up his penis and a colostomy bag pinned to his side.

And then he had woken up. It had been five years ago, and in all that time it had been the nurse who needed the morphine, and the nurse who gobbled up the various other drugs Dr. Stanton prescribed. Bobby had allowed him to do this. It was part of their bargain. Bobby didn't need any drugs because he had been called back by the gods. He had been raised up out of his blue grave.

In those first months, as he slipped in and out of consciousness, flickering like an uncertain light, Bobby would wake up to the nurse holding his head and stroking his hair, gentle as any mother. Or the nurse snoring in the next room. Or the nurse bringing home new fish for the fish tanks, cooing over each one as if they were his children. The nurse was evidently very happy in Bobby's home.

And when the nurse was away, Bobby would practise moving his head. Moving his fingers. Trying to find a voice, pushing any noise up out of his throat, some little sound, some feeble mewing.

Late one night, Bobby had flickered awake to the feeling of

warm water splashing over his chest, running down his sides. It had filled his heart with hope. He could feel the water. In joy he almost blinked, focused his eyes, before he caught himself. The nurse didn't notice anything. He started tugging at Bobby's waist. Bobby could feel something slipping slowly out of his insides.

The nurse went away. Bobby continued to stare blindly up at the overhead light. He heard a loud splashing noise from across the room, heard the toilet flush.

Bobby was tired. He was sinking below the crystal lenses of his eyes again.

He could feel the nurse's hands once more, all soapy and warm, running over his body, calling him back. It was pleasurable.

He could feel the nurse sliding one arm under him, turning him gently over on his belly, so that his face was soaked with water and he could smell the rubber mat underneath him.

He could feel the nurse sponge his back and his legs and his feet and between his toes. Water was running everywhere, and the nurse was humming loudly, like some demented washerwoman happy in her work.

Bobby slid down the wet table like some hapless fish in a fish plant. He could feel the nurse soaping the slack, wasted cheeks of his bum. He could feel his legs being opened up like scissors, and held by the nurse, and now he could feel something warmer than the water, sliding around, nudging, pressing and then suddenly, painfully, penetrating.

Bobby's spine spasmed. He lifted his head up and hissed so loudly that it sounded like a scream. And then he was falling, slipping off the table, sliding to the floor. His head wedged up against the leg support. His legs and arms flopped out like soft rubber, lifeless as a corpse.

The nurse had backed up, his mouth open in horror. His tiny eyes looked terrified. His blind, wet cock stuck out from his pants, erect and amazed, swinging dumbly.

"No, oh no," he groaned, and frantically stuffed his cock back inside his fly.

Oh no what? Oh no, don't come alive? Bobby wasn't sure what his nurse meant. But the nurse just kept mumbling, "No, oh no."

Sprawled helplessly, naked and wet as the day he was born, Bobby knew he would make his nurse pay. He had all the power. He had come from the gods. He was darkness and he was light. He was immortal.

Bobby opened up his mouth. "Hello," he said.

CHAPTER THIRTY-ONE

· ·

After Walker got out of the tub, Krista made him wedge a chair up against the door that led to the hall, and lock the glass door to the balcony. Then, wrapped in a towel and holding a hot washcloth against his sore shoulder, he sat down on the remaining chair and pondered how the man in the woods had known they were flying to Jamaica.

"Because he was following you and you were stupid enough to go to the Jamaican Tourist Bureau, that's how," she said, sitting in the middle of the bed.

As Walker remembered it, the Jamaican Tourist Bureau had been her idea, but he didn't think it was a good time to argue the point.

"Jake Nuremborski would have told him exactly where we were going," Walker said. "He didn't have to get on the same plane and follow us around. He'd just go straight to Reef Island, stay somewhere in the village and wait for us to arrive."

"Shut up." Krista lay down and pulled a pillow over her face. "They're going to kill us," she said, in muffled tones.

Walker crawled on the bed, stretching out beside her.

"I want to go home," she added.

He got back up and turned the light off, and lay down beside her again and carefully, because his shoulder still hurt like hell, put his arm around her.

She came out from under her pillow and rested her head on his chest. She didn't say anything more. She just listened to every noise in the hallway, and every sound beyond the dark windows. It was two in the morning before she fell asleep.

Walker was still awake. He looked down at her face. He felt fiercely protective. If anyone tried to hurt her, he thought, and he didn't have to complete the thought. He felt a charge of adrenalin flooding his bloodstream.

He tried to fall asleep too. He thought of Kyle Walker Tennu, who went to sea in storms. He thought of Lennie Nuremborski, who was too young and was dark-haired and was always looking away. They're dead, Walker said to himself. There was no other explanation he could think of. They were dead.

●　　●

BY THE NEXT AFTERNOON, Krista and Walker were back at Norman Manley International Airport in Kingston, trying to get on that evening's flight to Toronto.

There was no room, they were informed, but if they wished they could take a flight out the next morning.

The moon-faced man was nowhere in sight.

"Yes," they both said.

They took turns sleeping on a plastic bench in the waiting room and watching the glass doors. The moon-faced man stayed away.

By two the next afternoon, they were back in Toronto. Despite the sweaters and coats they'd wrestled out of their luggage, the cold outside the terminal went right through them. They struggled onto a bus heading into the city. They were going straight to the police. There was nowhere else to go.

They'd been over everything again and again, holding their heads close together, whispering, rehearsing in the waiting room in

Jamaica and on the plane. But whether they had enough evidence, whether the police would even listen to them, they didn't know.

Walker had kept pointing out, as if he'd suddenly become a lawyer, that they lacked documentation. "The letter from Kim to Lennie, and the photograph. And Jake Nuremborski's contract, his attempt to buy me off. They're all gone."

"But you've got Kim herself," Krista had said. "She'll tell the cops that Lennie and Kyle were planning to come back to Toronto, and obviously they did come back, because you are who you say you are. We can prove that now."

Before starting for the Kingston airport, they'd asked Roger Dumont, their taxi driver, to stop off at the Joshua Green Memorial Hospital in Joy's Grove. Walker had gone up to the desk and identified himself as the son of Kyle and Lennie Tennu, saying that the hospital could call the Reverend Charles Bryant at the Church of St. Thomas if they needed confirmation. He had asked if he could purchase copies of his birth records, which he needed for emigration purposes.

The hospital clerk, an older woman in an immaculately white uniform, had looked up and said, "Reverend Chuck is a cousin of mine, on my mother's side. He's no better than the rest of us."

Somehow satisfied by the veracity of her own statement rather than his, she had gone looking for Walker's records. He'd walked out with two photocopies each of two documents, one recording the birth of a six-pound, twelve-ounce boy on March 13, 1976, referred to as Baby Tennu, and another, a release form, indicating that Lennie had left the clinic with her baby, Walker Abel Tennu, three days later.

Krista had secured one set of copies in a small zippered pocket in her shoulderbag, while Walker stubbornly carried the other set folded up in his shirt pocket, beside his tobacco and cigarette papers, despite her mentioning several times that that was the stupidest place she could think of.

Walker didn't care. He liked to feel them there in his shirt, because that way he knew where they were, and besides, though he didn't tell her this, just the feel of them, their slight weight against his chest, pleased him immensely. He existed in the world now in a way he never had before.

Riding the bus into the city, he recited over and over, in his head, the list of disjointed but—at least to him—persuasive evidence he hoped would excite the police into some kind of action. Sometimes the information seemed electrifying, sometimes of no substance whatsoever. One moment he could see a group of police officers huddled around him, listening in rapt attention to every word he said. The next, he could see them kicking him out the door. Or taking him to a psych ward.

They got off the bus at the Royal York Hotel and, with all their luggage in tow, hailed a cab (not an A.P. Cab; that was all they needed, Alphonso Piattelli helping them with the cops) and rode some blocks north to police headquarters.

They pushed through the heavy glass doors into a large foyer. A honey-blonde cop sat behind a wide reception desk. Walker, still wearing his white straw hat, went up to her while Krista stayed behind and watched their luggage. They had agreed that he should open with what they both thought would get them the most immediate attention.

"I know who killed a young boy up near a place called Weirtown on the French River twenty years ago," he said.

She fixed him with a pair of very beautiful, but expressionless, brown eyes.

"The French River is not in our jurisdiction," she said. "That would be a matter for the Ontario Provincial Police."

"What if the murderer lives in Toronto?" he said.

"That's beside the point, sir. The investigating force would still be the OPP. I can give you their phone number, if you like."

"But what if I'm under some kind of threat? What if this guy is likely to kill me and my girlfriend, who happens to be sitting over there"—he pointed to Krista in her wheelchair—"and who happens to be a citizen of Toronto, as I am, as this guy is, and what if he's threatening to murder us right now, right here in your city, right this minute?" Walker didn't want to sound hysterical, but he didn't seem to be getting through.

The woman looked at him hard. Her brown eyes, no matter how pretty, were definitely cop's eyes, assessing his credibility or lack thereof, and his mental state.

"Why don't you take a seat?" she finally said. "Someone will be down to talk to you shortly."

"Good," he said. He walked back to Krista. "They're going to talk to us."

Krista nodded. She looked small sitting there, and helpless. Walker wondered where all her toughness had gone, all her fire. She looked frightened and tired. She looked as though she wanted to go home to her father.

Detective Thomas Lee came down to meet them, and they rode an elevator up to the fourth floor with him. He was immaculately dressed in a deep blue suit, fluorescent tie, shiny dress shoes and a light blue shirt. His jet-black hair was combed straight back. He was about thirty-five, reasonably tall and handsome, soft-spoken and courteous. He looked bored.

Walker had been hoping for some hardbitten, grizzled old detective who would listen closely and get passionate. Maybe even get pissed off. Detective Lee looked as though he should be selling mutual funds or giving a seminar on real-estate opportunities in the Far East. Walker could feel whatever confidence he had mustered drain right out of him. He tried to remember his list, his sales pitch, so to speak, but it was all a jumble in his head. All he could think of was the graveyard behind the church, the rows of markers and the great ceiba tree with its limbs sweeping down over the white picket fence. Everything else was a blank.

Detective Lee ushered them into a pleasant interview room with a sofa and a coffee table and upholstered chairs. Krista decided to stay in her wheelchair; her hip was throbbing, and whatever energy she had left, whatever powers of concentration and persuasion, she wanted to conserve.

She glanced up at Walker. He looked exhausted too, and he was moving oddly because of his stiff shoulder. And why was he still wearing that stupid hat? Who would take anything he said seriously? Why hadn't she thought of that?

"Why don't you take off your hat?" she said.

"Why?"

"Because."

"Sit down, please," Detective Lee said. Then, realizing his gaffe, he flushed a little and pulled out one of the chairs so that Krista could swing her wheelchair closer to the coffee table. Walker took his hat off and sat down beside her.

There was a file on the coffee table, and a notepad and pens. Walker read the label on the file. It said, "Standard Forms."

"So," Detective Lee said, closing the door and sitting down across from them. "I understand you have some information you'd like to give us."

Krista was already unzipping the pocket in her shoulder bag where she'd hidden the copies of Walker's hospital records.

"That's right," Walker said.

It was surrealistic; at least that was what Walker thought. He and Krista began to explain everything from the beginning, starting with Walker, three years old, abandoned alongside a road. Detective Lee nodded and seemed attentive, but he didn't ask any questions and he didn't tape them or write anything down.

It was as if Walker and Krista were in one world, of panic and murder, and Detective Lee was in another. It was as if, once they'd run out of things to say, he might look up and respond, "Pardon? I was thinking of something else." As if he only cared about how they said things, not what they said, as if the information they were trying to convey was of secondary interest, if any.

As Walker stuttered on, with Krista jumping in now and then, the detective remained perfectly still, until Walker mentioned Jake Nuremborski by name. Then Detective Lee wrinkled his brow. But that was all.

When Walker talked about Jake's secretary, Lee asked his very first question. Did Walker know the name of the secretary?

"No," Walker said, "I can't remember."

"Just wondered." The detective began to settle back into his semi-comatose state again.

Walker stumbled on, finally getting to the part about the boy hanging in the tree and Jamie hanging in a tree too, both with their guts hanging out.

"Pardon?" Detective Lee said.

Walker repeated himself.

"Excuse me for a moment." Lee got up quickly and left the room.

Walker turned to Krista. "I think we're getting somewhere."

"I don't. I think we should be put in protective custody."

Walker was dying for a smoke. He took out his tobacco pouch and started to roll one.

"You can't smoke in here." Krista looked as if she was getting a headache.

When Detective Lee returned, he was accompanied by a small, compact man in a wrinkled grey suit. He had a tough, weather-beaten face that made him look like an ex-boxer or a retired jockey.

"This is Detective Sergeant Wilfred Kiss," Lee said. "Krista Papadopoulos, Walker Devereaux."

Introductions accomplished, Lee sat in the chair a bit removed from the table, and Sergeant Kiss sat in the chair across from Krista and Walker.

"Do you mind going through your story one more time," Kiss said, without a hint of a question or a smile on his leathery face.

Walker had seen faces like that all his life, on men who made their living outdoors. Gerard Devereaux was getting a face like that. But Walker wasn't sure how a cop in a big city could be windburned and sunburned, skin worn smooth as driftwood.

Detective Lee put a small tape recorder on the coffee table and pressed the play button.

"For the record," Sergeant Kiss said. Then he did smile. His black eyes lit up, but his face didn't go anywhere.

Walker and Krista went over it all one more time. There was no question that Kiss was listening. There was a powerful centrifugal force about him; he was like a black hole.

After they were done, he said, "Has it ever occurred to you that your parents just went away somewhere? People do strange and peculiar things, sometimes they do the opposite of what you'd think they'd do."

"No, it hasn't occurred to me," Walker said. He'd been over his story twice. He could feel his blood getting up, but he knew he had to control his temper.

"And of course you don't have any idea what your parents were like. Maybe they were a couple of space cadets."

He's trying to piss me off, Walker thought, he's testing me, but why? What does he want to hear?

"Maybe your grandfather wrote them off a long time ago and all he was trying to do was get you out of his hair. Maybe you were mistaken about the man in the summer house and the man in Jamaica being the same man. Maybe the guy in Jamaica was just a local fruitcake."

Walker glanced at Krista. She was staring at Kiss, her eyes blazing. Kiss leaned back in the chair as if their story was all too much, and closed his eyes.

Walker and Krista and Detective Lee sat there. They waited for a long time, until Krista couldn't stand it any longer. "Look, we're in danger," she said. "So what are you going to do?" Her chin was set but it was quivering.

Kiss opened his eyes again. They weren't lit now, they looked smudged and smoky, they looked dead. "I'm sure that's not true," he said to her, his tone betraying an edge of scorn. He turned to Walker. "What do you think happened to your parents?"

"They were murdered," Walker replied. "I think you'll find their bodies somewhere under or around the Nuremborski summer house. He closed it down soon after they found me, and he's never sold it."

"So you think your grandfather killed your parents."

"Yes."

"Motive?"

"My father was a Cree. Half Cree, anyway. He hated him. And my mother married him against my grandfather's wishes. And they were coming back to Toronto to humiliate him."

"So he killed them both?"

"Yes."

"This is what you think?"

"Yes!"

Kiss looked at Walker for a moment longer. Then he said, "Anything's possible, I suppose."

He got up with an almost disgusted air and headed for the door. Just before he went out, though, he stopped and turned back to them. "Thanks," he said, and he left the room.

"What about protective custody?" Krista asked, in a voice that sounded very small to Walker.

Detective Lee shook his head. He accompanied them back down to the foyer. They retrieved their luggage from behind the reception desk, where the honey-blonde cop was keeping an eye on it.

"Here's my card," Lee said, giving it to Krista, for some reason—perhaps to make up for asking her to sit down, or perhaps because Kiss had been so abrupt with her. "If there's anything more, you can call that number. If I'm not there, leave a message."

Krista looked up at him. It was not a friendly look.

They left the building and started along College Street, Walker carrying her suitcases and his duffel bag and Krista pushing herself in her wheelchair, her aluminum crutches secured on the back, her shoulderbag and travel bag on her lap. When he stopped to light a smoke, he watched her manoeuvre around a delivery truck pulled halfway up on the sidewalk, and bump over a steel grate.

I wonder what happens when it snows? he thought to himself. He had an image of her spinning her wheels, mired in one spot, and the snow coming down, covering her, turning her all white.

Walker felt sick, sick about everything. The cops hadn't taken them seriously. Nothing had changed.

Just before Yonge Street, they passed a restaurant. Krista wanted to go in. She wanted to talk.

Most of the tables had fixed benches, but there were a couple at the back with chairs that could be moved to accommodate a wheelchair. While Krista wheeled herself to the back, Walker followed with the luggage.

She drank a coffee slowly. Walker ate his way through a plateful of french fries with gravy, and drank a beer. She watched him as he picked up the ketchup bottle and shook ketchup on top of the gravy, and then mixed it all together.

"Jesus, you're making me sick," she said.

"Want some?" He grinned at her. He was wearing his stupid straw hat again.

"What are we going to do?" she said. "They'll know we've gone to the cops." She looked around warily.

"Maybe they'll figure it's too late now, since we've already gone to the cops," he said.

"Maybe since we were just in there for an hour or so," she countered. "They'll figure nobody listened to us this time but they might next time. Maybe they'll figure it's time for us to have some kind of accident!"

Krista's eyes were filling with tears. "Do you want to live together?" she said.

Walker stared at her.

"They know where you live," she continued. "They probably know where I live too, and they know where we work, but we could find some new place to live. And we could find new work. My father can get me a job in about a thousand places. He could find you work too, Walker. We could just disappear."

Walker nodded. He reached carefully for his tobacco pouch and started to roll a smoke. He could feel Krista's eyes on him.

"It was just a thought," she said.

"I want to live together," Walker said, which was the truth. "I was going to ask you," he added, which was a lie. He hadn't really thought about it in any serious way. "I just don't like the disappearing part."

"That's the whole point."

"I'm not running away from anybody."

Jesus Christ, Krista thought.

"I have to get Jake Nuremborski. You know I do. For my parents. I won't let go."

She put her head down on the table—whether in despair or from fatigue, he couldn't tell. He reached over and stroked her hair for a while. He was beginning to wonder how long she was going to stay like that when she looked up at him.

"Let's look for a place to live," she said. "That's the first thing, anyway. The rest is negotiable."

"No it isn't," he said.

She looked away. There was no arguing with him. Besides, he was right. How could it be any other way? Lennie and Kyle—they were non-negotiable.

"Besides," he said, "hiding's no good. If they know where you live, then they know where your parents live. You couldn't go back there to visit, in case they were watching the house. And maybe they'd threaten to hurt them, to flush us out. It wouldn't work."

"Oh," Krista said.

When they'd finished eating and Krista had paid the bill, they decided to call A.P. Cabs after all. They needed to save money, since they were still in agreement that they'd look for a new apartment first thing in the morning. Krista's spirits seemed to be reviving a little, Walker noticed. At least she had something to do now.

First off, she had to go home and pretend she'd had a good time, and get some sleep. Then she had to talk to her mother about moving out, which would be easy, and to her father, which would be absolutely crazy-making. And then she'd get the morning papers and start looking for an apartment for her and Walker. For Walker and her. She said that several times in her head. It sounded kind of good.

She watched him standing by the curb, surrounded by luggage, waiting for Nick to come and pick them up for free. To Krista, he looked vulnerable standing there, looking down the street. It was a shock.

She made him promise that he wouldn't go out that night, and that he'd make sure his door was double-locked. Next morning, she wanted him to come over to the cab company. She'd meet him there with a list of apartments that were immediately available, and they would begin their search right away. They might as well be as safe as they could be, until they figured out what to do about Jake Nuremborski.

When they got to Walker's place, Krista made Nick wait while

Walker went up and checked his apartment. He came back down and told her that everything looked just the same as when he'd left. Then he kissed her, said goodbye to Nick and walked through the old wooden door beside the pawnshop.

Watching him go, Krista tried to set aside her worries. She had so much to do. And she had somebody in her life who really needed her, somebody to care for and care about. Everything would be all right. She willed herself to believe that. Everything was going to be all right.

•   •

DETECTIVE SERGEANT KISS was feeling good. In fact, he was feeling delighted and excited, even ecstatic, though none of this showed on the outside. He looked the same as always on the outside.

He sat at his desk in the dark, because that was how he liked it— the blind pulled down over his window, only his desk light on—and looked at a large, glossy black-and-white photo. He turned it over and picked up another one. There was a pile of them, all OPP photos, some in black and white, some in garish colour, taken twenty-one years ago. August 12, 1974.

A ten-year-old boy named Alex Johnson was strung up in a tree. Intestines protruded from a slit in his belly, trailing almost to the ground. Even in black and white they looked bluish. Kiss could almost smell them, that unmistakable, sickly sweet visceral smell.

There were pictures of the little boy lying on a rubber sheet on the ground. There were pictures of him lying on a stainless steel table in a coroner's lab. And always the camera seemed drawn to the same thing, the gaping wound and the sad, small, ropy viscera.

This was Kiss's most cherished cold file. This was the one he wanted to solve above all others.

It hadn't even been his case, originally, but when the crime was still unsolved after a couple of years Kiss had asked the OPP for a copy of their files. They'd sent him everything, as if they'd wanted to get rid of it, as if they'd looked at those pictures long enough.

Johnny Johnson, the boy's father, had been a Toronto cop too. He and Kiss had been the best of friends. The murder had destroyed Johnny's life. His son butchered. His wife dying by her own hand—a handful of sleeping pills, to be exact—four years later. Johnny had tried to be strong, tried to keep working, until one afternoon alone in his office he'd started to shake. Once he'd started, he couldn't stop.

It was Kiss who'd driven him to his doctor's office. And it was Kiss who'd taken him, that same day, to a hospital.

Johnny Johnson didn't come back out for six months, and he never worked again.

That had been fifteen years ago and, summer and winter, Kiss still visited him, sitting on that back porch, nursing a few beers, because it didn't seem as empty as the house. And then, God Almighty hallelujah, a kid called Walker Devereaux walks in off the street bringing tidings of great joy. Kiss could hardly believe it.

Jake Nuremborski. According to the kid, he'd be about seventy by now. The name had tugged at Lee's memory because of the suicide under the bridge; it was all in a file the detective had just dropped off. Kiss turned away from the photos to look through it.

A woman had identified the body as her husband's. He'd been missing for three days when she'd received a letter from him:

Dear Ellen,

For thirty years I've done whatever Nuremborski asked of me. Today I have no self-respect left, and no job. I am tired and I am ashamed. Mostly I am ashamed. Forgive me. I love you.

Chester.

According to the notes in the file, Lee and Amos Alberni had visited the man's employer, one Jacob Nuremborski. They had found him very ill, suffering through the final stages of emphysema. He wasn't able to say much, but he did confirm that he had seen his secretary just a few days before his death. He denied that he had fired him.

Alberni, thorough little shit that he was, had noted that the old man was being looked after by a male nurse, and that there was an invalid son in the house as well.

The conclusion the detectives had come to, pending the final pathology report, was that one Chester Simmons, age fifty-two, private secretary, had committed suicide by hanging himself and had subsequently been stripped of his clothes by a person or persons unknown. No foul play suspected. Case closed.

Case fucking open, Kiss said to himself. He couldn't have been happier.

Twenty-one years ago, Jake Nuremborski had been living a few hundred feet from where Alex Johnson was killed. Two years later, he'd been living just up the hill from a Jamaican kid of about the same age as Alex, who was attacked in exactly the same way. Three years later, his son-in-law, whom he hated, and his daughter, who had betrayed him, had gone missing. And finally, he'd offered this Walker Devereaux a whole shitload of money to forget whatever he knew and get lost.

Kiss leaned back in his chair. His thoughts turned to Devereaux and his little crippled girlfriend. Were they really in danger?

While Walker had been talking, Kiss had been making a calculation. The private secretary—who had even killed the kid's cat, for chrissake—was dead. Walker didn't know that, but Kiss did. No more danger from that quarter.

The man in the summer house who the kid said had also been trailing him in Jamaica was more troubling. It was quite possible Jake Nuremborski had hired someone else. But the way Walker told it, he was the one who'd started the struggle in the woods, he was the one who'd jumped the guy and wrestled him down the hill, not the other way around.

And besides, Walker and his girlfriend had been digging into Nuremborski's affairs for months. If it was somebody's job to make them dead, they'd be dead.

The old man doesn't know what to do with them, Kiss mused. He's tried intimidation, he's tried bribery, what does he do next?

After Walker and Krista had left, Thomas Lee had expressed the opinion that it might be a good idea to put someone on those kids. At least until surveillance was set up around the house in Forest Hill.

Yes, Kiss thought, cover the kid and the girl. I don't want them getting in the way. He didn't know where they lived, or whether they lived separately or together. He hoped Lee had all that.

Kiss picked up the phone and asked Lee about the surveillance.

"In place by midnight."

"So when's Alberni coming in?"

"He's on his way."

"I want him assigned to that kid and his girlfriend. Got their address?"

"Yes Sergeant. Two addresses."

"Okay, so watch both of them. Double-shift Tony Capri. He can go with Alberni tonight. They can decide which of them watches who, starting at ten tonight, till ten in the morning. Then report back to me."

"Where will you be, Sergeant?"

"Where I always am. Right here."

Kiss hung up the phone. Things were moving. The chase was on. It felt good.

Almost in response, as if he shouldn't feel too good, something stirred deep inside. He got up and walked carefully across his dark office and sat down on his couch. He stared across the room at his desk, at the glowing light over the photos of Alex Johnson.

He felt it again—between his hips, curled up under his pelvis, nudging against nerve ends. This was new. Usually it came in the middle of the night, when he was asleep.

He tried to concentrate on Johnny Johnson. He had lost a son, a wife, lost everything in the most horrific way. To some kind of monster. To some unspeakable, uncomprehensible thing.

He felt the pain again. "Go away," he said to the grapefruit inside him. "Go away."

CHAPTER THIRTY-TWO

1 9 9 5

F IFTEEN YEARS BEFORE, shortly after Bobby had wakened to
the nurse bathing him in a most unusual manner, they had come
to an understanding.

Jake Nuremborski would surely die sometime. That would be
sad, but Bobby didn't think it would be too sad. Not any more.
Circumstances had changed. He had escaped the grave and now it was
his father's turn to go down, falling forever. Besides, his father had
betrayed him, hadn't he?

Bobby had thought about that a lot. There was always a story of
treachery, always someone close to the hero who was too weak to
stand the light, who betrayed him.

Bobby had felt anger, but he'd cried, too, bereft of any anchor in
the world.

But now he had the nurse to compensate. Addicted to his drugs,
abuser of his patient, caught now with his cock out, ruined, destroyed
if Bobby ever chose to destroy him, quivering mass of degenerate
bum-fucking perversion that he was.

How Bobby loathed him, this creature. How Bobby loved to
torment him with threats and promises, with silences and compli-
ments, with plans for their future together, with threats of his imminent arrest.

The nurse would bathe Bobby and whimper to kiss him on his

lips, and Bobby would stare up at him, his head lolling on the nurse's arm, and dare him to try. He never did. He was too afraid. But sometimes, stoned and euphoric, he'd confess that he loved Bobby. He'd gather Bobby's hands up and kiss them. He'd kiss his feet too, but that was as far as he'd dare go. And they struck a deal.

Jake Nuremborski, with his oxygen cylinders and his atrophying lungs, would surely die soon. And when he did, the nurse would call in Dr. Stanton and perhaps one or two others to witness what could only be described as a God-inspired miracle: Bobby's recovery.

Jake would die and Bobby would recover. It was as simple as that.

Bobby would petition the court and prove that he was of sound mind now, competent to look after his inheritance, the Nuremborski estate, which he confidently estimated to the nurse to be worth at least ten million dollars.

At that number the nurse's little eyes lit up behind their druggy haze. He and Bobby could travel all over the world together. He could continue to bathe Bobby and kiss his hands and his feet whenever Bobby let him. They'd have enough money to buy him all the drugs in the world. He'd be safe with Bobby, and Bobby would be safe with him.

So the nurse helped Bobby exercise in secret, and he had access to all Bobby's drugs, just as before. He kept tabs on the old man, reporting everything, and the old man remained blissfully unaware that Bobby had come awake. Fifteen years, dreamlike, isolated and druggy, slipped by.

And then Walker Devereaux showed up at the door.

Bobby had seen Walker twice, in the dark beside the gazebo and in the last rays of light on another day. Bobby had watched him. Measured him. Smelled his sweet, smoky scent.

His father was beside himself, berating his secretary, sending him out on skirmishes, sending him on a failed bid to bribe Walker.

Through his spy, Bobby knew everything. The nurse followed the secretary, and the secretary followed Walker, and all the time Jake railed that something had to be done about this Walker Devereaux, this lost and found grandson, something had to be done!

Bobby thought something had to be done too.

How long had his body been dead? For a very long time. Even driving through the dark streets past men and women for sale, even watching the boys and girls exercising in their City of Mice, his body had remained dead.

Until one magical day Walker Devereaux, his one and only nephew, had arrived.

The smell of Walker holding his face so close to Bobby's, crouched so near in the red light of that dying day, had made him shiver. Sparks had been flying off all his fingers and toes, if only Walker had seen them. Alex had been dancing in the air. The taste of Jamie's blood had been on his lips. Walker's smell had been full of wonder and delight.

The secretary had hanged himself from a bridge. Too bad. Walker had jumped the nurse in Jamaica. That was almost funny. Everything was changing and everything was the same as it had always been, as it always would be.

Bobby looked around his room, his blue watery cavern, only the nurse's fish there to keep him company.

His father was breathing laboriously somewhere upstairs. The fish were blowing bubbles. Bobby was deep down where nobody could find him.

Besides Jake and Bobby and the fish, the house was empty.

CHAPTER THIRTY-THREE

• •

ALKER UNLOCKED THE DOOR of his apartment for the second time, having just run downstairs to assure Krista that everything was all right. He double-locked it behind him, and looked around, more leisurely this time, at his couch, the chest of drawers, his lamp.

Krista wanted to live together. Krista would fill their new place with furniture, put curtains up in the windows, pictures on the walls, colourful mats down on the floors. She would fill the closets with her clothes and the bathroom with her cosmetics and the kitchen with shiny pots and pans and there'd be the smell of coffee brewing and supper being made.

And Krista would tumble over him in the dark, and afterwards they would fall asleep together, her warm body curled up against his.

He circled the room slowly. Some storm was coming, looming at the very edge of his mind.

He decided that he should sit on his pullout couch and think happy thoughts.

Living together. What did that actually mean? It sounded good, like the thought of warm, freshly baked bread. It sounded complicated too.

It was a commitment. That was the word, the word his mother would use. But to what? To happiness? Who wouldn't commit to happiness?

The storm was gathering.

Maybe if he went up to the house with a concealed tape recorder and got Jake Nuremborski to say something. But he didn't have a tape recorder and he didn't have any money to buy one. Besides, that was stupid, Jake wouldn't say anything.

He got to his feet again and paced around the apartment, in and out of the kitchen, the bathroom, the living room. His heart was beginning to race and he was having difficulty catching his breath. Kyle and Lennie, Lennie and Kyle. He had let them down. The storm was as close as a breath now.

He was in the bathroom. He looked in the mirror.

What had happened to that certified cheque?

The question was just there, like a gift. It stunned him.

What had happened to the cheque for four hundred thousand dollars, with his name on it, and Jake Nuremborski's signature? The piece of paper that linked them together and proved that at least part of his story was true?

What do you do with a certified cheque when the person it's payable to doesn't want it? he asked his reflection.

They would have destroyed the contract he'd been asked to sign, that would have been easy. But the certified cheque? They had to recover their money from the bank, didn't they? How would they handle that? He didn't know, he was no banker. But in the question was a small glimmer of hope.

Walker risked a smile, at least in his own mind. The cheque had been Jake Nuremborski's big mistake. He'd never thought, even for a moment, that Walker would turn his back on all that money. He had no agreement with Walker. Walker might do anything, be capable of anything, including going to the cops.

If he destroyed that cheque after Walker refused it, the money would be gone. If he deposited it back into his own account, the evidence of the transaction would still be floating around in the banking system.

And Walker thought, Jake is too smart. The stakes are way too high. He wouldn't risk depositing that cheque.

He ran some cold water over his hands, rubbed his face. He was feeling better.

"He's holding onto it," he assured his reflection. "At least until I get lost, one way or another. That's what he's doing with it. He's hidden it in the house."

• •

Number nineteen was sitting all alone, parked in the dark shadows at the side of the garage. Nobody else had taken the cab out that night because no one else wanted to.

Walker walked through the open bay door in the garage and took the cab keys from the board. Without talking to anyone, he got into the cab and drove uptown.

He parked one street from Jake Nuremborski's house, and glanced at his watch. It was only half past seven. It was dark enough, as dark as it would get in Forest Hill, but it was much too early to break in. He'd have to wait until after midnight, until everyone was asleep.

Now's the perfect time to scout, though, he thought.

He was hoping there'd be at least two or three lighted windows he could look into. He needed to figure out where Jake Nuremborski's bedroom was. The old man was sick, he probably spent most of the time in his room. That would be the logical place to hide the cheque.

The secretary would surely have his own home, but the moon-faced man might be staying with Jake. The secretary had told Walker that Robert had a nurse, so possibly four people in all. He'd have to locate every one of them, watch their bedroom lights go off, one by one. And he'd need to find a vulnerable door or window he could break in through later.

I could drive to a convenience store and buy a flashlight, Walker thought. They might even have a screwdriver kit. And I could use the tire iron in the trunk of the cab.

He took a deep breath. It would all work out.

He got out of the cab and walked up the street and around the corner. As he approached the house, he could see that all the front windows were dark.

Walker stood beside the leaning board fence at the side of the yard. He couldn't see anyone. He hoped no one could see him.

Ducking down, he moved swiftly along the fence until he reached an overgrown cedar hedge that blocked his way. It crossed the yard to the side of the house where the old brick left off and the yellow brick of the addition began.

He pushed himself into its branches, knelt down and rested for a moment.

The ground felt cold against his knees, and he could see his breath in the air. The cedars still held their pungent, sharp smell; he moved his face against the flat leaves and inhaled. The smell of cedars had meant trout fishing in the spring and rabbit-hunting in the winter. It had meant a cool, shadowed place to build a fort in summer. And when he was older, it had meant a place to read, a place to dream.

Walker felt homesick all of a sudden, for Big River and for the great woods beyond. For his mother and father, who had been so good to him. For his six sisters, whom he had grown up teasing, and who had teased him.

Staying tight to the cedars, he brushed through the branches and crept towards the house. The windows were still the old original ones, as far as he could make out; they hadn't been replaced by double panes, and no storm windows had been put on yet, either. He checked the nearest window as quickly as he could.

They'll be latched from the inside, he thought.

He'd have to find something to stand on, but then all he'd need to do was break one pane of glass and, reaching his hand through, turn the latch. The only problem would be the noise he'd make.

Walker had read somewhere that the best way to break glass and not make a noise was to cover it completely with tape first. He decided to buy tape, when he bought the flashlight.

And he knew right then that he was ready to crawl through a window and sneak up the stairs and, with the murderer, Jake Nuremborski, wheezing in his bed, search all through his room for that cheque, even under his mattress. He had been on a long journey and now was the time to act. He was prepared to do almost anything.

A car went by. Walker stayed still, watching its lights disappear past the fence. Then he crawled under the cedar hedge into the backyard.

When he stood up, the first thing he saw was the faint domed shape of the gazebo where Robert Nuremborski had once been sitting. Walker moved across the yard to make sure the gazebo was empty this time. He sat down on the wheelchair ramp and stared at the back of the house.

A faint light glowed in a hallway, through the small window in the back door.

Lights were on in the same windows as the last time: the small one just under the eaves on the third floor, and the two larger ground-level windows in the new addition, which were full of soft blue light.

He got up and crossed the long grass towards them.

They were higher than he was tall. He stood on his toes and, reaching up to one of the metal windowsills, pulled himself up the brick wall.

Fish tanks and rows of blue fluorescent lights were all around him. The whole room looked as though it were under water, awash in trembling light.

Robert Nuremborski was sitting in his wheelchair, staring at nothing in particular, locked forever in his own watery world. His thin arm lay weakly over the side of the chair, his head lolled a little to one side, his eyes were open but looked blind.

Walker wondered what it would be like to be Robert. Just to drift. To experience no memory, no regret, no pain, no guilt. You wouldn't have to say anything, do anything, feel anything.

Robert's phone rang. Walker could hear it plainly through the window. It rang again.

Walker expected to see a nurse come from somewhere to answer it, but no nurse appeared.

The phone rang again. Robert slowly straightened. His arm came up on the armrest of his wheelchair. With some effort, he got up and walking unsteadily across the room, as precarious of balance as a windup doll, he picked up the phone. He listened for a moment, then he turned slowly and looked straight up at Walker.

Robert smiled.

Walker ducked backwards and dropped to the ground. He didn't know whether to run or stay where he was. And then it didn't matter.

Something flicked down past his eyes so fast he couldn't see what it was, clamped around his throat, and tightened. He fell to the ground. A face hung in the dark just above him, a face as bland and white as the cold November moon. And everything went black.

Almost immediately, or so it seemed to Walker, a faint light appeared out of a vast darkness. But not a light, a reflection, he thought. On chrome. On milky glass.

He strained to open his eyes. It was a dome light, that was what it was. It wasn't on but it was reflecting lights from somewhere. Moving lights.

He stared up at the light for a long time, trying to figure something out, only he couldn't remember what he was trying to figure out. He could hear the low hum of a car engine, he could smell the heavy odour of plush leather.

He began to realize that his legs were under him somehow, his arms behind his back. He couldn't feel his hands. Everything began to hurt. He tried to swallow but the pain was almost unbearable, it burned through his chest.

He turned his head a little.

He was in a car, on the floor. That much was clear. A big car. Lots of room. He could see the edge of a yellow plaid blanket as street lights and car headlights flickered by, and the shape of someone sitting there in deeper shadows.

A voice came out of the dark, like a whisper or a long sigh. "Welcome home," it said. The shape moved and Robert Nuremborski's pale face came into the flickering light. He looked at Walker with shiny eyes.

"Welcome to your home," he whispered again.

Walker, lying on his back, his head against the door, arms and legs folded underneath him, didn't reply. His muscles were on fire.

He closed his eyes. What could he say? What do you want? What are you going to do? An interesting question, except that he was already figuring out the answer.

"You surprised me," Robert said, "with your tenacity."

Walker opened his eyes again.

Robert leaned closer. He reached out a thin, shaking arm and his hand touched Walker's face. The hand felt like ice. It trembled against Walker's nose, against his cheek, his lips. Walker stayed perfectly still.

"Have you ever wanted to be a girl?" Robert asked.

CHAPTER THIRTY-FOUR

• •

BOBBY SAT BESIDE WALKER, watched the passing lights go by, and remembered.

He would always remember the scream. It hadn't been his sister's husband's scream, because he couldn't scream, his mouth was full of rags. His arms had been pulled up over his head. He was dying.

No. It had been his sister's scream.

She had been standing on the path in the woods behind the shed. She wasn't supposed to be there. She was supposed to be in the summer house, waiting for Father.

Bobby had lied about Father, lied when he'd met them at the airport and told them that Father had received their telegram giving the date of their flight home from Jamaica. Father had never seen that telegram, because Bobby had been watching for it and had picked it up first. And he'd lied when he'd told them that Father was waiting at the summer house and wanted Bobby to drive them right up there. (Not that he had a driver's licence, but his father had given up watching him every second of the day; perhaps he'd even convinced himself that he had been wrong about Alex Johnson and Bobby five years before.) And he'd lied when they'd arrived at the house and Father was nowhere to be seen, telling them that he was probably in Weirtown, buying groceries for their supper.

Bobby had looked at his sister in a way he hoped would seem innocent. And then he'd looked at Kyle.

Kyle wore his hair down past his shoulders, fanning out Indian-style. He was slim, his voice soft and lilting, his face dark and sensitive. Bobby hadn't seen him in over three years, he hadn't seen any of them in over three years, but before, when Bobby had been in Jamaica, it had been the young husband, coming home from working the charter boats, who had always haunted Bobby.

And everything had gone as planned.

He'd asked Kyle if he wanted to go for a walk, while his sister tried to put the boy down for a nap.

They'd walked together behind the house, strolling under the tall, sweeping trees. Bobby had hung back for a moment, picking up a hammer he'd hidden there. Blood had pounded joyfully in his heart as he'd brought the hammer down on the back of Kyle's head.

And he and Kyle had flown up the ladder together, high above the French River, high above the forest, tangled in ropes, a herky-jerky dance high above the world.

And then Bobby had fallen away.

And then his sister had screamed.

She was holding the boy by the hand, not twenty feet away, and she was screaming.

In that moment, everything had gone from perfection to confusion. Bobby had realized that, though he had planned so well up to that point, he hadn't really thought about what to do next. He had only thought about Kyle. Beautiful Kyle.

He'd just assumed that his sister would have to keep quiet about it, because his father wouldn't allow anything bad to happen to him, he would protect him once again. But she wasn't keeping quiet, and the boy was looking up at her, clinging to her, terrified because his mother was terrified although he didn't know why, and he was beginning to scream too. It was all wrong.

Bobby ran towards her and, holding his knife against her neck, told her to shut up, shut up, shut up.

He pushed her back down the path, dragging the boy along too. He made her sit in the front seat of the car and he put the boy in the back. The kid had gone all silent, his eyes unblinking, his body rigid. He was causing no commotion at all now, but Lennie was still sobbing, she was having trouble breathing. She began to bang her head against the dash, as if she wanted to knock herself out. She kept doing it, again and again.

Bobby managed to get the car pointed down the road towards Toronto and his father. He drove as fast as he could, trying to ignore the sound of his sister's head thudding, thudding. Father would figure everything out, he always did.

Bobby glanced around at the boy. He hadn't moved. He was just staring fixedly at his shiny new shoes.

Finally Lennie stopped crying and sat looking out the window, blood trickling in little streams down her face. But Bobby wasn't reassured by her silence. He knew now that she would go to the police, no matter what his father said to her or told her to do. Bobby could just tell that she would.

By the time he reached Highway 69 and turned the car back south, he was beginning to relax a little. He looked over at his sister. Her head was down on her knees, her long black hair falling all around. He couldn't see her face.

"You killed Alex Johnson," she said, from somewhere between her knees.

Bobby didn't respond, but it didn't sound like a question anyway.

She straightened up and looked at him. "What are you going to do?"

He didn't answer, he didn't have to. He just took another look at her as he drove along. He imagined that she could see the answer in his face. He'd have to cut her throat. That would be the easiest. Let her bleed to death. That was how people slaughtered animals. Bobby had seen the old woman in Jamaica kill chickens that way. Except she'd cut off the whole head.

His sister's face looked dead already. Her husband was dead so maybe she didn't mind, maybe that was what she wanted him to do.

"Let him go," Lennie said.

At first, Bobby didn't know who she was referring to.

"He's only three. He doesn't know what happened. No one knows who he is, they won't be able to trace him. Please, please, let him live!"

She was crying again, but almost silently this time. Bobby appreciated that. He glanced around once more at Walker, her papoose. He was still just sitting there, eyes fixed, staring at his shoes.

Bobby turned down a side road and drove on for a little while. Finally he stopped.

Lennie got out and, picking Walker up, carried him up a long, grassy slope. Bobby followed right behind her with his knife. She walked until they came to a fence, and then she put her boy down.

He watched as she knelt and put her face close to her son's ear, and whispered something. Then she got up and left him.

Walker didn't cry. He didn't even turn around. He just stood there holding onto the fence.

They drove back to the highway. Lennie was silent now, and perfectly still. At first her silence and stillness were comforting, and then they began to make Bobby uneasy. After a while he turned off the highway again.

This time he drove along a narrow gravel road until they came to some trees. Without a word, Bobby got out of the car. Lennie got out too.

They walked together towards the trees. She was walking faster than Bobby, and he had to hurry to keep up.

As soon as they entered the grove, she knelt on the ground. Bobby didn't have to say anything to her. She put her hands together. She was praying. Yellow birch leaves chattered in the wind.

He knew there would be no pleasure this time. It was merely something he had to do.

And then there would just be him. And Father. No brother-in-law his father seemed to be warming up to. No sister to tell on him. No grandson to take his place.

Bobby held her head up by her hair and sliced her throat. Blood pumped out for a long time. She never made a sound.

And all the leaves over his head became still, and the clouds high above the trees froze in the sky.

He squatted beside her and rummaged through her pockets, removing anything that would identify her. Then he buried her under some leaves. While he was doing this, he realized that he'd have to go back to the summer house and cut her husband down before somebody saw him, and hide him somewhere. He'd have to hide the hammer and the ropes too.

Bobby sighed. It was going to be a long day.

· ·

RAIN HAD STARTED TO TAP against the windows in the house in Forest Hill by the time Bobby returned that day. He walked down the long hall and into his father's study and told him all that he had done.

Bobby began to sob, his whole body shaking. He asked his father to forgive him.

And all the while Jake was listening, he kept saying *no*, like a kind of prayer, as though, if he just kept repeating *no* long enough, Bobby might stop saying these things and admit that it was all a story. But Bobby didn't stop. He explained everything—how he had only been doing his father a favour, because they were going to disgrace him by coming back to Toronto, and how it had all got very confused, and how he had never meant to hurt Lennie or her little boy.

His father called the house in Jamaica. There was no answer. He grabbed Bobby by his shirt and, dragging him down the hall and out of the house, threw him into one of his cars.

Jake drove north, racing through the dark and the rain, but they ended up going in circles because Bobby couldn't find the right gravel road, he couldn't remember the stand of trees where his sister was lying hidden, where she might not be dead, where she might still be breathing.

His father drove around and around, screaming at Bobby, pushing his head and punching at him. Then he just clung to the steering wheel, driving blind through the rain, sobbing great wrenching sobs.

"You're making this up," Jake said finally. "It's all in your head. It never happened. You've gone mad." He almost sounded happy.

"I know where the Indian is," Bobby said.

"No you don't," his father replied. And then, more tremulously, "Show me."

They drove up to the summer house and Jake got out the flashlight he'd brought. He followed Bobby around to the back. The rain had almost stopped, but it was still running in thin, noisy streams off the roof. The sandy ground felt soft under their feet.

Bobby lifted up a trap door on the boardwalk that covered an old cistern. He slid off the heavy wooden top and wrestled it up on its side.

His father approached the hole and shone the flashlight down into the dark.

Kyle was staring up at him, intestines swarming like a nest of snakes.

Jake stood there for a long moment, and then handed Bobby the flashlight. Bobby peered down into the hole too, and shone the light on the body. It wasn't the same now, but he didn't expect it would be. Only the faintest pleasure, like a dim memory, stirred in his blood.

And that was the moment Bobby most remembered, remembered as clearly as if it were happening now. Glancing around and seeing his father approach him through the mist and rain. His father's eyes red, his face death. His hands holding a shovel, swinging it so that it came flying out of the dark like a judgment....

Bobby looked away from the limousine window, back towards Walker. He could see him still huddled on the floor, vagrant lights flickering across his body every once in a while.

Bobby almost felt like crying. Why would his father do that to him? He could almost feel, once again, the steel edge of the shovel crashing into his skull and the world reverberating and falling away.

CHAPTER THIRTY-FIVE

• •

IGHTS FROM PASSING CARS and street lights were no longer streaming through the tinted windows, but Walker could tell that the car was still moving. It was going more slowly though, making tight turns, descending, tipping down and down.

His arms and legs were past the point of pain. They were numb, hardly there at all. Walker was only a head and a torso, breathing. And Robert was somewhere close in the dark.

Walker knew there were only two things he could do, scream or talk. Screaming was not going to be of much use. It would only provoke a swift response, if not from Robert, then from whoever was driving the car.

It had been Robert all along. Robert up at the summer house the day Alex Johnson was killed, Robert in the Jamaican house the night Jamie was attacked, Robert in Toronto the day Walker and his parents had flown to Canada. Robert, not Jake. Not the old man at all.

Walker closed his eyes. It was too late to feel like a fool. Besides, all he felt was a leaping panic.

"Mental telepathy?" Robert said.

Walker opened his eyes again. He still couldn't see a thing.

"Or cellphone? How do you suppose I knew you were at my window? Of course, you saw me on the telephone. Cheater."

"I don't know," Walker said. His throat convulsed with sudden pain from where the rope had nearly throttled the life out of him.

"Mole had been following you all day. Mole saw you peeking in my window like some mischievous little boy. He placed a call," Robert went on, sounding pleased with himself, "to ask me what he should do. Poor Mole. Not a bright mole. And do you know what I replied?"

"No," Walker forced out of his mouth.

"I said, catch him. Mole will do anything I tell him. Do you know why?"

"No."

"Because he has no choice," came the hissing answer.

Okay, Walker thought, now's the time, maybe my only chance. "Did he follow me to the police?" he asked. His throat felt as if something were chewing on it.

There was no reply, but Walker could sense that he'd caught Robert's attention. Some hyper-alertness in the air, watchfulness, like a wary animal.

"The first thing I did when I got off the plane," Walker went on, despite the pain, "was tell them about the dead boy up on the French River, the Jamaican boy, my parents, everything. If I show up dead, you and your friend are first on their list."

Walker could see two shifting specks of light looking at him out of the dark. The car pulled up and stopped. The driver's door opened and the interior light over the driver's seat went on.

Robert was suddenly there, sitting a little away, wrapped in his yellow plaid blanket and looking down at Walker with a perplexed expression, as if he were trying to work out some relatively benign but nevertheless vexing problem. The driver's door slammed shut and the light went out again.

"You've upset Mole," Robert said.

The back door opened and this time the dome light over Walker's face flared, and everything in the back seat turned startlingly bright. The moon-faced man appeared, wearing a small blue chauffeur's hat perched ludicrously on top of his round head, and copious tears were running down his face.

"You see?" Robert said.

"They came straight from the airport," the frightened-looking man cried out. "They had luggage, I saw him get out of a cab at his place."

"And you've been watching our little friend ever since. Yes, yes," Robert replied, looking up at the man's quivering face. "But how do we know that they didn't go to the police first?"

Robert motioned for Mole to come closer. When he did, Robert reached up and gave him a kiss on the mouth. "Do exactly what I told you," he whispered.

Mole flushed a little, looked surprised. Robert had never kissed him on his lips before.

"I'll go away," Walker promised. "You'll never see me again."

"Tape his mouth first," Robert said.

The crying man closed the door and the light went off. It was even blacker than before, blacker than anywhere Walker had ever been.

"Please," he croaked. "Please!" He could hear the creak of the trunk as the lid was lifted. The car rocked ever so slightly.

"Mole's getting out the tools of the trade," Robert said.

The door Walker's head was resting on opened. His head dropped and hung outside the car. Scream, he thought, scream, but he was too late. A broad width of tape was slapped over his mouth. He could feel it being wrapped around his head, and wrapped again.

The man groped underneath him, searching for the rope that hog-tied Walker's feet to his hands. He found it, and hauled Walker steadily backwards until Walker fell out of the car.

The man shifted his grip and, groaning and straining, began to drag Walker behind the car, across a narrow road and down a path through some trees.

Walker bumped along on his back until Mole stopped and let

him go. Then he rolled over onto his side. He could smell leaves and pungent mould and the sweet, sweet earth.

Mole was beginning to cry again. Walker looked up and saw him wiping his flat nose and tiny eyes with the sleeve of his jacket. He disappeared back towards the car, his whimpering fading away.

Walker looked up in the sky. Where were the stars? Where was the Milky Way? Where was God?

Mole was back, and he wasn't crying any more. He moved with a quick, desperate determination now, as if he'd decided that he would get through this. Whatever this was. He'd get through it and never think about this night again.

He put down what looked to Walker like a battery-operated camp light, and turned it on.

He threw a rope over a limb of a tree.

Walker watched him work in the pool of light. He knew what the rope was for, he had known all along.

Mole pushed him over on his face and cut the ropes from his wrists. Walker could move his shoulders now. He drew his arms to the front of his body. Blood surged and a searing pain rushed down to the ends of his fingers.

Mole began to drag him towards the tree. The rope he had tossed over the limb dangled by Walker's face. Walker tried to flex his arms but they wouldn't move, they didn't seem attached to his body.

Mole squatted in front of him. Walker could smell his sweat.

He retied Walker's hands, using one end of the dangling rope. He started to hum, bubbles formed on his lips. Humming, humming. Walker could tell that the man was out of his mind with fear.

Mole stood up and, with a struggle, lifted Walker to his feet and started to haul on the rope. It was all he could do to lift Walker off the ground, to get him up on the toes of his boots, spinning a little; then more hauling, more groaning, until Walker was finally swinging off the ground.

With his arms stretched over his head and his mouth taped, Walker was having trouble breathing through his nose. A terrible weight pressed down on his chest. His head was being forced up. He knew he had to keep his chin down to breathe.

He tried to picture the kitchen in Big River. He could see Gerard Devereaux sitting at the table. Mary Louise was there, too. And his three little sisters.

And he could feel the man cutting the ropes that tied his feet together, feel other ropes being looped around his ankles, his legs pulled apart.

Despair overwhelmed him. He had let everyone down. Especially Lennie. He had let his own mother down, his young mother who had somehow managed to save him. For what? For this?

Walker could see Mole hurry away. He fought to breathe, fought the blackness descending over him. His despair turned to fury. He would not die like this, would not die.

He hauled on his hands with all his strength. His body started to rise. He could see his hands for a moment, tied at the wrist, but his weight was too much to hold up. His arms straightened and he dropped down again.

He looked around as best he could. He was still alone in the pool of light. He tried to kick one leg, the one tied to the trunk of the tree, but the rope held. He swung his other leg as violently as he could. This leg was tied to something less rigid, perhaps a sapling. It gave way a little, bending, and the knot slipped up until it caught on something. Walker could feel a bit of play now; his right leg swung more loosely beneath him.

He looked down, straining to see what the rope was tied to, but instead, he saw someone standing at the edge of the light.

Robert was standing there, perfectly still, looking at Walker with rapt attention, as if he himself were just a member of an audience, and Walker were on stage. In the spotlight. And such a performance!

Robert started to teeter towards him, managing to cross the small clearing one short, halting step at a time. As he came closer, Walker could see that his face was full of expectation and rapture. And he could see that this was the end of the world. The knife that Mole had had a moment ago was now in Robert's hand.

Robert came up close. Walker could feel him begin to open his leather jacket, pull his shirt open with faltering fingers. He could feel Robert's cold lips press against his skin.

The muscles in Walker's stomach tightened like a shield. He could hear Robert mewing against his stomach, could feel the knife go in—no more than a dentist's needle, just a sudden sharp pain, slick as a scalpel. He could feel his skin opening.

"Oh God," he cried, somewhere deep inside.

Robert backed up and looked up at him, his eyes rolling back, perfectly white. His lips were bright with Walker's blood.

Walker bucked his body, ripping his right leg back, and felt the rope give some more. Lifting his knee, he drove his boot heel straight into Robert's blissed-out, blood-smeared mouth.

Robert's head snapped back. He fell. He didn't move. He lay on the ground, as if he'd been shot.

Walker pulled down on his hands again, slowly raising his body. When his mouth was even with his hands, he scraped the tape away with his fingers. He bit into the knot but he couldn't pull it loose.

Walker could feel blood running down his belly, under his belt, like warm water bathing his loins. He sank back down. His right leg was swinging almost loose now, the rope bellying to the ground. He swung himself the other way, towards the trunk of the tree. The rope that was tied to a sapling pulled free.

He swung towards the trunk again, and managed to hook his right leg over a low branch. He scissored the branch between both legs and hauled himself up over it. Now he inched his face upwards towards his tied hands again, with his weight supported by the branch. The rope went slack.

Walker had one chance, the slightest of chances. He began to work at the knot with his teeth. He knew that he couldn't let himself panic; he needed to keep his head clear. Everything he did had to take him one step closer to freedom. Every second had to bring progress. Time was ticking. The moon-faced man, Mole, wherever he was, would soon get worried and come back. Or Robert would wake up and call for his help.

The knot shifted, came loose. Walker wriggled his hands free, untied the rope around his left ankle, and dropped to the ground.

Walker dared to look at the slit in his skin now. It looked like pouting red lips, like a perpendicular extra mouth. His jeans were soaked with blood.

His head started to swirl. He looked up. Mole was standing right in front of him. His fist smashed into Walker's face.

Walker lurched back, stumbling. The man, surprisingly fast and desperate now, was on him, his hands around Walker's neck, squeezing with all his might. They staggered, lost their footing, fell.

As they hit the ground, Mole's grasp loosened and Walker's street-fighting reflexes took over. He jammed his thumb deep into the man's eye.

Mole rolled away, screaming. Walker rained punches down on him until the man went limp and Walker was too tired to go on. He got up, and untying the ropes still trailing after him from his right leg, tied Mole up.

Robert was still lying on his back. As Walker approached, he opened his eyes.

Walker knelt beside him, and picked up the knife. He pressed his other hand down on Robert's face, covering his watchful eyes. He pressed Robert's head into the ground as hard as he could.

Robert didn't make a sound.

Walker took the knife and cut Robert across the throat, gently, lightly, just enough for a thin line of blood to bead out.

Then he got up and walked away.

His knees felt ready to buckle, blood roared in his head. He staggered back down the path, found the car and got in.

He felt in the dark for the keys in the ignition, and they were there—miracles still happen, he thought, just don't die and miracles can happen.

He started the car and pulled away, following the narrow, twisting road through the park, around and around and finally up out of the steep, wooded ravine.

Walker was drifting now. The blood roaring in his head had faded away. He was half asleep. Everything felt warm, everything was comfortable. Lennie's face came out of the shadows and he could see her in front of him. She had a beautiful face. It was so soft. And her eyes were so dark, and they held his face in their reflection, and her voice was like music and her words were like a kiss. "Hold on," she whispered, "hold on tight."

The wheels of the car bumped up over something, and then the car stopped with a thud, throwing him against the steering wheel. Somewhere far away, a car horn began to scream. It was disturbing his rest. It was a nuisance. Walker thought somebody should do something about it. It was almost enough to keep him awake.

CHAPTER THIRTY-SIX

• •

THE FIRST THING HE SAW was Krista's face. She was staring at him, her nose almost touching his, her blue eyes concerned and expectant, as if she were waiting for him to do something remarkable but wasn't entirely convinced that he was up to it, as if she were watching television and he were behind the screen. He didn't know what she was hoping for. A song? A speech? He reached out and tapped the glass. She went away.

A moment later (Krista would insist it was three days later) he saw her again, but now she was looking bored, her chin propped up on her hand, her elbows resting on the side of his bed. Walker knew where he was. He was in some room painted light green. There was a window right behind Krista, with long plastic strips hanging down to keep out the light.

"Wake up," he said.

She jumped.

"Christ, does my throat hurt," he said.

Walker heard Gerard Devereaux's whisky voice saying, "He's awake," and his mother loomed up behind Krista and she had her hand over her mouth and her eyes were shiny with tears, and his sisters, big and small, were suddenly all over the bed, and Stewey was standing over by the door, grinning like a fool. Even his brothers-in-law were there.

At first it was all confusion and tumult, all teary and glorious. Slowly, things began to sort themselves out.

Krista had been at the centre of everything. She'd told the Devereauxs what had happened to him and why. She'd gone over every little detail with Detective Sergeant Kiss and his team, again and again, starting with the lost letter and the photograph of the two little girls.

And she had sat in his room for two weeks while his body fought a rampaging infection caused not by the six-inch slash in his flesh, but by a small puncture in his intestines. Fortunately, Robert had hardly begun his work.

After the Devereaux family and Stewey finally dispersed to their hotel that evening, Krista turned the lights in his room down to half. She sat beside him and told him everything she knew about Robert and the moon-faced man and Jake Nuremborski.

She had called the police when Walker didn't answer his phone that night, after Nick dropped him off. Sergeant Kiss had been angry. He was organizing surveillance of the Nuremborski home and he didn't want Walker going there and screwing everything up. But it was too late.

"You'd already done it," she said darkly. Another promise broken.

Kiss was so concerned that he went up to the house personally. When a detective showed him cab number nineteen sitting empty around the corner, and Kiss saw Walker's picture ID on its dashboard, he was not amused.

The surveillance team searched all around the house. No Walker. Kiss had a tough call to make. He could assume that Walker was inside and in some kind of imminent danger, which would give him legal grounds for barging in and searching the place without a warrant, or he could guess that Walker had seen his men snooping and had decided to slip away. But if he banged on Nuremborski's door, there would be no sense in going ahead with the surveillance.

What to do? Jake Nuremborski could be happily slitting the kid up that very moment, he could be garlanding the house with the kid's intestines, for all Kiss knew. He had to proceed with utmost caution—had to dot all his "i"s and cross all his "t"s—or he'd never get the case past a Crown attorney, let alone into a courtroom, let alone win the case. This Walker kid was for sure and truly fucking him up.

Kiss fumed in the dark outside the Nuremborski home for about twenty seconds. "We're going in," he said.

They rang at the front door. No one came. They pounded on all the doors. No one came. They broke in through the back door. A very frightened Jake Nuremborski was hiding in a third-floor bedroom. Robert, his invalid son, was nowhere to be found. And neither was his nurse.

Kiss put out a city-wide alert for Robert Nuremborski and Walker Devereaux. Within an hour, he had been notified of Walker's exact location. He was in a hospital emergency ward.

Walker had been brought in by ambulance after a home-owner called 911 to report that someone had driven up onto his lawn in a limousine and crashed into the corner of his house. Not long after, two cops patrolling a nearby ravine park saw a light shining through the trees.

They walked down a path towards the light and found a man lying on the ground, tied up with rope. He had been badly beaten and one eye seemed in terrible shape. He was still alive, though, and conscious. He was crying.

Another man was sitting under a tree. From a distance, he looked as if he had lipstick smeared on his mouth and around his neck. He seemed to be smiling at them.

When they got closer, they could see that his mouth was full of blood, and his neck was ringed with blood, too. They knelt beside him and asked him what he was doing there.

The man's eyes were alert and bright. He seemed in a good mood. "Waiting for my father," he replied.

Krista put her face close to Walker's. "Robert Nuremborski's being held on an attempt-murder charge," she said. "That man that was with him is being held for attempted murder too. Your grandfather collapsed. He's under police guard in a hospital."

"This one?" Walker asked.

"No," she said, touching her forehead against his.

"Good."

He was tired. His throat still hurt like hell, and some indistinct pain throbbed in his abdomen.

"You lied to me about going out that night. You lie all the time," Krista said.

"I'm sorry," he replied.

But he wasn't sorry. He was deeply satisfied. He had come through a storm, and the world was different now. Everything was different. Walker Abel Tennu felt more than satisfied, he felt reborn.

He asked how she was making out with his mother. A long silence ensued, and then she assured him that they were getting along fine.

"Uh-huh," Walker said. "And Stewey?"

"I love Stewey." Krista smiled.

"Don't tell him that," Walker said. Krista pressed her face against him again.

"And your dad? About you moving out and everything? How are you getting along with him?" he asked.

Krista left her face where it was, against his cheek, but she hesitated for a heartbeat or two.

"I haven't actually talked to him about that yet," she said. "I did tell him everything else. He said I had to come to the hospital and I couldn't leave. He's been going up and down the Danforth boasting about you. He thinks you're Hercules or something. He thinks you're a hero."

She kissed him. He kissed her back. Their faces were as close as a breath apart.

"I've been thinking, Walker," she whispered. "I mean, about getting an apartment. Maybe I'll get one on my own. You can visit any time you want. But there's no danger any more, and maybe you'd like to stay in your own place. And we can just see how things go, okay?"

"What things?"

"I don't know. Maybe you'll want to travel somewhere. Do something different now."

Walker tried to look at her but she wouldn't show him her face. What was she really thinking?

"My place is crappy," Walker said.

"No, it isn't," Krista said.

●　●

HEATHER DUNCAN CAME TO VISIT WALKER one day. It was the middle of the afternoon. A late November sun was shining through his hospital window, and he'd dozed off.

When he opened his eyes, she was sitting in a chair against the wall, looking at him. She was wearing a winter coat and a large pair of fuzzy earmuffs, and staring at him intently through her glasses.

He stared back at her. They remained like that for some time.

"You know, don't you?" she finally said.

Walker hadn't greeted her, and now he didn't answer her. That seemed to be all the proof she needed. She answered herself: "Of course you do."

"I thought you were a friend," he said.

"It was my understanding," and here she faltered, but only for a moment, "that if anything came of my information, it would only benefit you. You had a secret protector, so if you ever needed some help or some money, I would just have to ask. That was what I was told. I didn't know who your protector was or any of the circumstances, I only knew the go-between."

"How much money did you make?" Walker could see her lips trembling, but he refused to feel sorry for her. He knew he'd only be able to hold out for a few moments, though. She'd hugged him, given him chocolate bars.

"Have you told anyone?" she asked.

So that was it, the reason for the visit. Not for him, for her own preservation. "My girlfriend," Walker said. "And the police," he added. "Expect a call."

She nodded, as if she'd known her fate all along, as if she'd come just to hear him confirm it.

She lifted her stout body awkwardly out of the chair. She used to bounce and spin, despite her size, with a kind of enthusiastic delicacy. Now she seemed stiff and old. She stood in the middle of the room, looking marooned, then turned and walked out.

Walker didn't feel triumphant at all.

Detective Sergeant Kiss never visited Walker while he was in the hospital, and he was there for over three weeks. But as soon as he was released, Kiss sent word that he wanted to see him.

Walker went alone. Krista was too busy dispatching cabs at night and, during the day, decorating her new apartment. It was a large one-bedroom with a bigger than usual bathroom and a wide hall, just off the Danforth, on the first floor of an older building. She could get in and out of the place easily. She was very happy, and Walker was happy for her. Sort of.

"We found your father," Kiss said, as soon as Walker, still moving gingerly, entered his office and sat down.

"Where?" Walker said.

"Where Jake Nuremborski said we would. In an old cistern behind the house."

Walker nodded. He would not cry.

"Part aboriginal," and here Kiss looked up from a sheet of paper in front of him. "Or First Nations, if you prefer. Approximately twenty years of age. Approximately five foot ten."

"His name was Kyle Walker Tennu, you know who he was," Walker said.

"Yes," Kiss said, "but we're going to try to corroborate the identification with dental records, that kind of thing."

Kiss's weathered face creased a little around the eyes, perhaps an attempt at a comforting smile. "As for your mother, I had her in a drawer all the time," he said.

"Pardon?"

"Unidentified female remains, found by hunters in the spring of 1983. Near the place Jake Nuremborski says his son told him he hid her body. So we had her in a warehouse the whole time."

Walker hadn't really believed that, somewhere, somehow, Lennie would be found alive. Wasn't he the one who had been saying all along that she was dead, they were both dead? He would not cry.

"Her friend said my mother broke her leg when she was a kid." Walker was clutching at a straw.

Kiss looked a little surprised at this information. He studied another sheet of paper for a moment and nodded. "Yeah," he said.

"Can I have them?" Walker said. "Can I have my mother and father?" His face was breaking.

Kiss had to look away.

●   ●

IT STARTED TO SNOW THE DAY Walker buried his parents. It was January but there had been a thaw. Frank Ellen, who worked at the cemetery in Big River, got out the front-end loader and broke through the ground.

Walker not only wanted to bury his parents in Big River, he

wanted to put their bones in the same casket. He said they'd been separated long enough. The Devereaux family—daughters and sons-in-law, uncles and aunts—blanched a little at that but, as they almost always did, quickly closed ranks. With Father Perrot's permission, everything was arranged. Walker would get his way.

The night before the funeral, after the rest of the family had gone back to their homes and his three little sisters were asleep, and while Krista was getting ready for bed in the guest room, his mother, looking as if she had something on her mind, sat down at the kitchen table with Walker and Gerard. After making idle conversation for a while, she said, "So I guess you have a new name now."

Walker was just finishing his last beer of the night, keeping Gerard company. His father was the night owl of the family. In bed by two, up by six, was the way Gerard Devereaux ran his life. His wife had been telling him almost every day from the day they'd been married that if he didn't get more sleep he'd die, but he was still stubbornly hanging on.

His mother's question caught Walker by surprise. "What do you mean?"

She pushed back her thick brown hair and fixed him with her grey eyes. "You're Walker Tennu now," she said.

He nodded. He looked down at his hands. They were dark, darker than either his mother's or his father's, despite Gerard's years of hard labour, summer and winter, in the bush.

"I don't remember Kyle Tennu," he said. "I remember Lennie now, barely." He glanced up at his mother. She hadn't taken her eyes off him. "I'm proud to be their kid, from their blood. But I know who my family is. Who my mom is. And my dad. So I'd like to stay Walker Devereaux."

• •

A LITTLE LATER, Walker went in to visit Krista in the guest room. His mother had taken Krista's bag straight into this little first floor room, as soon as they'd arrived. Krista was dressed in her pink flannel nightie and she had thick wool socks on.

"Your mother's floor's...freezing," she said, as she pulled back the covers on the guest bed and snuggled under the wool blanket and comforter.

Walker snuggled in with her.

"You're supposed to go upstairs."

"I will," he said.

They lay there together for a moment or two, and then Krista reached up and turned off the bedside lamp.

He felt her hand under the covers, tugging his shirt out of his belt. He could smell her perfume and whatever it was she put on her hair.

She stroked his belly with the back of her hand, along the ridge of his scar. Even though the sutures were out, the scar was still itchy. Her hand felt good.

"Someday we'll have to go back to Jamaica," he said.

"For a holiday this time."

"We could see Jamie, compare scars," he said.

"Great."

"I wonder if Miss Emile is still alive."

"Why wouldn't she be?"

"Because she was on her deathbed." Walker tried to remember the tiny shack in the woods, and the old woman, black skin stretched tight against the bones of her face, lying under her purple blanket of suns and moons and stars.

A broken child, Miss Emile had said.

Walker looked at Krista's face caught in the faint light coming through the window. Her hand was still moving softly against his belly. He kissed her.

"What's that for?"

"I don't know."

"We're not going to make love, Walker. We can make love at my place, when we get home."

"I know," he said.

• •

THE NEXT AFTERNOON, the church was full of the sympathetic and the merely curious. Various versions of Walker's story had been sweeping through Big River for weeks. He had become something of a local hero, as much as anyone can be a hero in a small town. All eyes were on him and his crippled but cute-as-a-button girlfriend. The adopted son of Mary Louise and Gerard. Part Indian, you know.

Father Perrot, who had worked hard to get special dispensation for the funeral and the burial of Walker's parents in consecrated ground, on the basis of exceptional circumstances—a scandal, some of his parishioners felt—gave them a simple ceremony, but Walker thought he spoke with great warmth and conducted things with dignity.

After the interment, people straggled back to their cars. Father Perrot and Walker's family also moved away from the graveside, away from the mahogany casket that held both his parents. Only Walker and Stewey and Krista remained.

"Walker?" Krista said. "Do you want to stay a little longer?"

Walker nodded.

Krista turned on her crutches and made her way carefully through the slush towards the gate. Stewey got the message and walked alongside her.

Walker stood close to the casket for a long time.

That's when it began to snow. Great, soft, wet snowflakes. They clung to everything.

Acknowledgments

* •

MIDNIGHT CAB FIRST CAME TO LIFE as a CBC radio drama series. It found its final expression through the collaboration of many talented artists, both in front of and behind the mic. In particular, I want to thank my long-time radio producer and friend, Bill Howell. When I started thinking about writing a novel based on these same characters, I had the good fortune to show literary agent Beverley Slopen an early outline. Her enthusiasm for this story fueled my own, and her encouragement and advice were invaluable. My editor, Diane Martin, was crucial in helping me find the story's natural shape and voice, and I am extremely grateful to her. And in particular I want to thank my family, for just about everything.